THE QUEEN'S GENERAL

By Lliam West

First published in the UK in 2007
by TAMARISK

Trewynn, Lodge Hill, Liskeard, Cornwall, PL14 4EL

ISBN 97809541911-2-2

Printed in Cornwall.

Tredethy Manor

Those sampling this third effort I trust to have responded positively to my first two stories, and maybe shared my fascination with the interestingly chronicled lives and legacies of such as Shute, Waugh, and Britten. So where to now for a comparable excursion? Can the library shelves yield another life to stir in my imagination an intrigue such as I developed around those piles at Trelissick and Ince, with their respective occupants, Ida and Alan L.B?

Maybe, for here's a promising tome. An *official* biography boasts the cover, and while the adjective might too often be a synonym for *fawning* there's always much to be divined between the lines, and also, in this case, from a batch of wonderful, wonderful photos...... few more fascinating than that taken of the subject, in early 1946, as he sits at a garden party in Bangkok with his host, the young 'King of Siam'.

January 1946

Mountbatten with King Ananda

4

BOOK ONE

Bira (l) RAF, Chula (r) Home Guard
during the war.

Lausanne 1935; Bira with
Ananda and Mama, and a shy
younger brother.

White Mouse, pre-war.

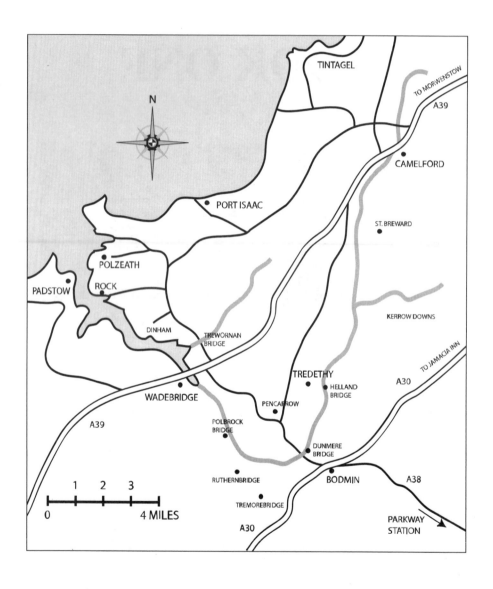

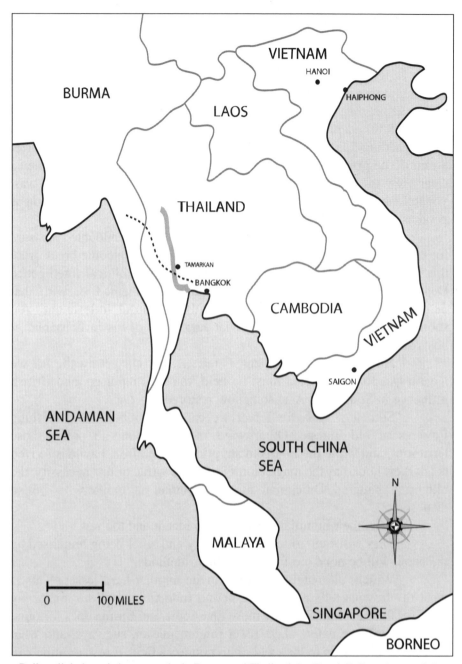

Built to link the existing networks in Burma and Thailand the 'Death Railway' crossed the Kwae Maekhlong River near Tamarkan.

March 1944….. Delhi, India.

"Very good Peter, very good indeed. This, unmistakably, is the young King……. and this, obviously yourself. Our friend is once again to be congratulated on the quality of his camera work. If his pedigree is questionable, then certainly not his talent. Further Royal commissions can be his, tell him, and I have friends too in Hollywood. If he can just find a way of adding a little *gentility* to that name of his then a glittering carrer awaits." The prints had been spread across the desk, allowing both men a clear view of all four. "Yes, exquisite…….. drugged the Monarch was, you tell me, but see how he looks to be enjoying every moment. Giving as good as he gets, it could be said."

"Well let's just say that the assignment was an undoubted pleasure for my self also," minced the Irish born lackey. "A welcome break from this heat, away from all these stuffed shirts of the Political Intelligence Department. And such an attractive young age the lad is, with that delicious feel for the clarinet…… a truly delightful little talent. You should come with me next time. That Jazz Club of his in Lausanne, it hosts such a game clientele."

"How enticingly decadent, Peter…… but not yet awhile for we have a war to win. Burma must be held, the Japs repulsed, and British influence in South East Asia somehow restored."

"Somehow, yes, for I fear we can never rebuild the far flung Empires of old Europe. Other ways must be found to police those territories, and while the Englishman, pride flushed from having survived his darkest hour, has the magnanimity to make virtue of this necessity, the blitzkrieg battered Dutchman and Frenchman is unlikely to be so disposed……."

"…….their humiliations being too recent and too raw."

"*They* will want to re-assert mastery and, after being brutalised by the Nazi, will be none too fussy as to their methods."

"Which, ultimately, can only invite another hard lesson. This is what my Edwina tells me. Indonesia and Indo China will no longer lay open for their exploitation, any more than India and Burma does for ours. No more will the native slave for a foreign master, she says, and what access we might gain to the yield of his country's field, forest, or mine will depend on our willingness to share the benefit. Like the dodo of Madagascar the old Colonial Governor has had his day. Instead we must try to ensure that the new indigenous breed of top man can be as friendly and forgiving to the former master as he will be revered by his populace."

"So our challenge must be to find and install the right *top men*," concluded the pictured Peter, nodding down at the prints with a lascivious smirk, "and to squeeze out the wrong."

"Where we can, where we can," sighed Mountbatten. "Oh that the shape of a new east might be determined solely by we of tired old Europe........ but of course we both know differently." He gathered the prints to pass them back. "These, my friend, are for the moment to be kept firmly under lock and key. Within the next two months we will be taking this HQ further south. For serving me so well you are to be rewarded with a larger office and more staff. Material such as this, though, must remain strictly confidential between you and I. Four special trains are being laid on for the bulk of our business, but you will go by air, and this will be part of your hand luggage."

*

August 1945...... London

"Good evening........ I would like to speak to a Mr Ulius Amoss please. I've been told that he's staying at your hotel."

"Just a moment while I check for the room number......then I'll put you through. Can I give him your name?"

"I'll do that myself, if it's all the same. Tell him that I've *agency* matters to discuss."

The receptionist complied, and within twenty seconds.....

"Amoss speaking."

"Mr Ulius Amoss?"

"That's me, and I'm afraid I don't recognise your voice."

"Good...... I can introduce myself properly when we meet. How long are you in London?"

"Only tonight. Tomorrow I'm due in Paris. The Newhaven train leaves at ten in the morning."

"From Victoria?

"So my ticket says........ but with your freshly elected Government having promised to change so much!"

"I can be at the News Kiosk closest to your platform at nine fifteen. That should give me long enough."

" 'Agency matters', I was told......"

"....... Which are far too sensitive for this line Mr Amoss....... or for any line, come to that."

"None being secure in Mr Attlee's *New Jerusalem*, is this your meaning?"

"What prompts this call is the interest that I'm quietly told you take in the *Old* Jerusalem, a city which for a while yet must remain under British rule....... whether we like that or not. Bear it in mind please that, unlike you, I have to continue living and working in this country. Be on the lookout for any followers. You will see me reading a copy of *The Financial Times*. I will listen for you to ask for a Daily Telegraph and also this month's *Punch* magazine. Make your way then to the station buffet, take an empty table and I'll join you."

"*The Financial Times*........ does this mean you like to play the markets? It's good to hear that capitalism hasn't gone entirely out of fashion in this Country."

"Sounds like you might have a tip, Mr Amoss."

"If you can keep it under your hat."

"Naturally I can."

"Get out of sterling. Mr Attlee and Mr Dalton won't know this yet, but by this time next week Mr Truman will have cancelled the wartime lend-lease provision. In case you hadn't noticed the Japs have surrendered. The good ship UK must henceforward bale itself out."

"So, no more war, no more handouts .... but it is to be remembered that as day follows night a resolved conflict must beget new tensions. Some, such as that which now exercises you and I, Mr Amoss, will be relatively localised, others more global, and if in its response the good ship US of A should wish to add further to its string of overseas military bases then, by the same token, it must find other ways of appropriating for itself the necessary real estate."

*

October 1945....... Laos

"We have been impressed, Colonel Tsuji, by the resourcefulness shown in your efforts to evade capture by the victorious allies." A cigarette was offered, but refused.

"Resourcefulness, Captain, has throughout been a key feature of the Imperial Japanese Army."

"Resourcefulness *and* cruelty, and for the latter there are many who wish that you should pay."

Tsuji eyed his three lantern lit interrogators with haughty disdain.

"And is that supposed to frighten me...... the threat of the gallows?"

"Out here in the wild, Colonel, we have a measure of discretion."

"Meaning.......?"

".......we are not necessarily bound to hand you over to the formal process. The law of the jungle will sometimes decree a less humane remedy, something you might care to bear in mind as I enquire further on how you've lain low in Thailand over these past weeks. This disguise you've taken as a Buddhist monk, to get you to the border and over......do you think it might work again?"

Tsuji considered....... sipping at his captor's coffee. While less preferable to his ascetic's palate than tea, this was better than nothing.

"In reverse?........ Yes, I'm fairly certain."

"Good, for we're thinking we might have a little task for you in Bangkok, an opportunity for you to save your own skin......"

"........by proving myself useful."

"Are you ready, Colonel Tsuji, to hear more?"

"Speak on, do."

Tsuji.

*

11

December 1945……. Cornwall

"Do I intend to make Tredethy my permanent family home?" Chula gazed eastwards across the Camel valley to the frost burnt bracken of Bodmin Moor. "Over these past six years I've come to love Cornwall, Bira, and I've come to love its people too. I would have liked for us to have stayed at Rock, but in many ways this place has the greater potential."

"So 'yes' would be your answer," smiled the younger cousin.

"It would, Bira, were things more settled back in Bangkok. It is whispered from Lausanne that the young King is seriously considering abdication."

"Surely not in favour of that even younger brother."

"If Ananda went then they would all go. The younger brother, the elder sister, their mother, plus the Regent who rules in their absence. They were installed by Marshal Pibul's people, remember, and he currently languishes in jail."

"Hardly fair…….when accepting the throne, ten years ago now, the Mahidols couldn't have anticipated his collaboration with the Japanese."

"Even so, Bira, it can be said that Pibul's humiliation must taint the prestige of his preferred Monarch, and therefore, should Ananda remain, the prestige of the Monarchy for all time. I sense that we might be drawing near to that situation we spoke of in hypothetical terms back in July."

"When you were warned by Lord Louis to hold yourself in readiness lest you yourself be invited to take a Crown thus relinquished. Have you heard from him recently?"

"He sent me a Christmas telegram from his new HQ in Singapore. It tells me that he'll be visiting Bangkok next month, Ananda being over from Switzerland for a few weeks."

"Obviously an occasion for finding out more…….and this will be passed on I'm sure."

"He said also that if Marina was coming to Cornwall again for Easter then his other nephew, young Philip, he might appreciate an invitation also. The person to contact, he said, was Genereal Frederick Browning….."

"……..who I've got to know quite well since finding a mooring for ny boat over at Fowey."

*

12

June 12th 1946
BBC Radio News (Home Service)

'It is reported from Siam that as thousands of his former subjects converge on Bangkok to mark the preliminary funeral rites of King Ananda the authorities there appear no closer to offering a conclusive explanation for his sudden and violent death. As speculation swings from probable accident to possible suicide, foreign observers of a volatile political situation anticipate that a number of dissident factions will seek to make capital under a climate of mistrust. This uncertainty is likely to encourage rumour of murder and conspiracy.

It is known that the young King was found in his private chamber with a single fatal gunshot wound to the head; also that he was the owner of a pistol which he usually kept in that same room.

We have been told, though, that the King's distraught mother ordered a cosmetic reconstruction of facial and head damage in readiness for an open display of the corpse, and that the promptness with which the appointed morticians went about their task might have compromised any thorough forensic investigation.'

*

27ᵗʰ September 1946

The News Chronicle

ARMY COLONEL KILLED IN HONG KONG PLANE CRASH `

It has been confirmed that the crash of the military transport plane reported briefly in yesterday's edition claimed the life of Colonel Cyril Wild. Colonel Wild, a former prisoner of the Japanese who spoke their language fluently had, for much of the past year, been heading the United Kingdom War Crimes Liaison Mission to Tokyo. His task had been to build files on those Japanese officers yet to be brought to justice for a catalogue of cruelties dating back more than a decade to the infamous 'incident' at Nanking, an atrocity against Chinese civilians which prefigured similar, later excesses in Shanghai and Singapore.

Colonel Wild is reported to have been returning to his Singapore headquarters with much note-form material, his intention being to prepare this for formal presentation to The International Military Tribunal for the Far East (IMTFE). It is feared that the work has perished with the man, and that both might be irreplaceable. Colonel Wild leaves a wife who is said to be expecting a first child early in the New Year.

Singapore 1942.... Britain's most shameful defeat, Japan's Greatest victory. General Percival shoulders the Union flag, Cyril Wild (then a Major) the white flag of surrender

14

20th November 1946

.........saw fighting break out between the Vietminh and French troops in the port of Haiphong over who had the right to collect customs duty.

On the morning of that day a French patrol boat had seized some Chinese smugglers. The Vietminh then intercepted the French boat and arrested its crew. This sparked an incident, and by the afternoon there were barricades in the street. When these were flattened by French tanks, the Vietminh opened up with mortars, while a troop of Vietnamese actors in the Opera House held off the French with antique muskets.

A ceasefire was agreed, but the French decided to use the incident as an excuse to drive the Vietminh out of the city. This resulted in hand-to-hand fighting with Vietminh positions being bombed and strafed by the French airforce and shelled by the French navy. When it was all over the Vietminh claimed there were 20,000 dead. The French say it was no more than 6,000. No one denies there were several thousand civilian casualties.

Nigel Cawthorne   'Vietnam; a war lost and won.' p21 (Capella)

Ho Chi Minh.

*

15

June 21st 1948

A cargo ship, formerly a US Naval vessel now renamed the *Altalena*, bobs heavily in the waters off the nascent state of Israel. Purchased in Brooklyn (New York) for $75,000 by sceenwriter Ben Hecht and novelist Louis Bromfield it waits to unload soldiers and munitions intended now for Menachem Begin's *Irgun*, one of two Jewish armies vying for control of a new nation.

The next morning reveals that more than one third of the cargo has been moved from the ship's hold onto the beach at Kfar Vitkin...... and then comes the first hint of trouble. On the cliffs and on the beach two of Ben Gurion's *Haganah* regiments, complete with tanks and artuillery, surround the *Irgun*, while at sea three of his corvettes stand waiting for orders. The *Haganah* officer in charge, Moshe Dayan, gives Begin ten minutes to surrender.

Though given more time Begin and Ben Gurion are unable to reach an accord.

By evening the former has returned to the beach and the latter is ordering his forces to attack. Immediately Begin flees in a rowboat to the *Altalena*, under fire from the warships on the horizon. On the beach two *Haganah* men are killed and six wounded before the *Irgun* are forced to surrender.

The *Altalena* courses southward towards Tel Aviv where, no more than 100 metres from the shore and within sight of journalists and UN ceasefire officials on the terrace of the Keta Dan Hotel, the ship runs aground. *Irgun* sympathizers swarm the beach amongst rumours that what remained of the cargo was to be offloaded to Begin's zealots with a view to their setting up an independent state and directly challenging Ben Gurion's authority.

To thwart them Ben Gurion calls an emergency meeting of his government and wrings from them permission to take over the ship using whatever force was necessary. The order is issued;

"Arrest *Begin*....... and sink the ship!"

Menachem Begin fails (conspicuously) to keep his powder dry!

Ben Gurion

Begin

St James Park (i)
........August 1956

"As First Sea Lord, yes, I certainly have a strong voice on the Admiralty Committee. It's the sailor's voice, Philip, and such technical and professional advice that I bring to its affairs will command considerable respect.......this you know."

"But in the end, the Navy that you endeavour to keep honed is merely a tool, one of the many placed at the disposal of our politicians......"

".......to be wielded at their discretion. Whatever we might advise, they have the ultimate say-so, as voiced by the First Lord, the civilian departmental head who, through democratic process, is answerable to the people."

"Fair enough, Uncle Dickie, but when one is the figurehead of the ship of state it can be comforting to have some appreciation of the shoals that lay ahead. The First Lord of the Admiralty might have her confidence, and yours, but, to be blunt, the conduct of her First Lord *of the Treasury* begins to attract our concern. My wife believes strongly in the Commonwealth. She also believes strongly in the United Nations. Neither is without blemish, we know, but in this far from perfect world we hold each to be a well meaning force for good. In support of both projects she and I have gladly travelled many a difficult mile and worked many a long hour........"

"........ and naturally there would be dismay should this superb effort be undermined," nodded Mountbatten. "Well at least I can say now that Anthony's initial rush of blood seems to have subsided. MUSKETEER, the go-it-alone military operation against Nasser, has been shelved, and you can tell your good wife that nothing similar is now likely to be launched before October."

"Giving our legions of diplomats a chance, one hopes. So how might this affect my trip to Melbourne in November? You know I'm expected there to open the Olympic Games. I suppose this finishes such hopes I had of Elizabeth flying out to join me."

"The country will need Lilibet here, Philip, just as she and the Commonwealth will need you to be there. In your absence I will ensure our Queen can be appropriately advised."

"And my travel arrangements, Uncle Dickie......? Originally I was to use the Royal Yacht, Melbourne being but one port of call in what was to amount almost to a world tour. Then I'm informed that *Britannia* is likely to be required as a hospital ship, presumably as part of the OPERATION MUSKETEER."

"*Britannia* will no longer be required in the Mediterranean, Philip. She's yours to take to the southern oceans. And Commander Mike Parker is joining you as a travelling companion, I understand."

"Something to lift his spirits during a distressing divorce. He has been a good friend over the years......"

"........and is now a friend in need, and likewise our esteemed Baron? I'm told that he's likely to be needing help in getting back to his feet, booked in as he is for a minor hip operation."

"It's that arthiritic hip, Uncle, legacy of a car crash back in '22. He'll be able to convalesce at sea."

"And for all the fun and games out in Melbourne he'll be just the man I'm sure. Good for them and good for you!"

*

Summer 1963
Buckingham Palace ..... and an interview

"..... and you must be told, Your Majesty, that the Secretary of State for War has tendered his resignation." Macmillan paused, wanting his Monarch to be aware that his next words had been carefully weighed. "And it is with particular regret that I inform you that this has been accepted, for I know that his role in this unsavoury episode, denied initially but now finally admitted, must come as a personal disappointment to yourself, and to other close family members. It is hoped, though, that we can now move towards drawing a line under the matter."

"Thank you Prime Minister...... and am I to understand that doing so will entail the commissioning a Judicial Enquiry?"

"I fear so, Your Majesty....... but I intend to put this with the Master of the Rolls, Lord Denning, one who has always quite deservedly enjoyed a good press......"

"...... as well as the confidence of your own Party of Government, and also those in Opposition. I suppose he can be expected to want to re-affirm this reputation for impartiality."

"Naturally Your Majesty...... whilst at the same time, of course, wishing to demonstrate again that he has a safe pair of hands. He'll be wanting to hear all the evidence there is to hear, of that we can be sure...... we can trust, though, that in his eventually published report he'll not be minded to stretch his narrowly drawn terms of reference....."

"......and minded also to honour what guarantees of anonymity might be required, Prime Minister."

"Strictly so, Your Majesty....... and particularly, of course, where they might protect the prestige of the Monarchy, a prestige that you and your parents have worked so diligently to raise to previously unparalleled heights." Macmillan's hand went to a jacket pocket. "This paper, passed to me by our Secret Service, lists all in your immediate and wider family who our Master of the Rolls might wish to informally interview. It could help greatly if you were to privately pass on to these individuals my assurances." The Queen stood to take the list, and, as a significantly aged First Minister rose too, it was read, folded, and returned..... the regal nod signalling that enough had been said and seen. The advice would be accepted. The audience was at an end, and now, the document re-pocketed, Macmillan allowed himself to be guided door-wards...... a brief pause, there, for the formality of the parting bow before passing through and away.

A resignation matter.

*

Autumn 1963
.......Westminster.

Having ushered his secretary from his private office and firmly re-closed the door, Lord Denning turned warmly to his older brother.

"Do sit down, Reginald. How kind of you to come up to London so promptly!"

"And how rare it is, I must say, that in *any* aspect of your work you should be seeking my assistance. I only hope, Tom, that I won't disappoint. Something very much out of the ordinary, I must presume. Is this to do with......"

"It is," confirmed Denning, "to do with what's filled the newspapers over these past few months."

"Won't it die a death, now that Profumo has resigned?"

"The embers need a proper raking Reg, lest they should at any time flare anew."

"And if they be found to be still dangerously hot?"

"Then a damping down might be required."

"Such as might carry full judicial authority, you mean."

"Yes, and while I have some discretion, Reg, as to what I decide to publish......"

"...... it is important that you should at least know all there is to know. It sounds like this could be taking you into the world of the Secret Services. I can only wish you the best of luck. Not my domain I'm afraid. But then I was never anything more than a regular soldier."

"But a very accomplished regular soldier, one who rose to be a confidante to the very top brass...... and this is why I'm wanting to pick your brains. Putting aside the intelligence sphere, I'm also anticipating that my enquiries might take me into the exalted world of Royalty."

"Another *Secret Garden*......

"..... to which the self-appointed gatekeeper is your former Commander in Chief, Lord Mountbatten of Burma, to whom, whenever there's been mention of the man between us, you've always been staunchly loyal."

"This being the way of things in the army, Tom."

"Of course Reg, of course...... but do I not remember a reservation or two from you concerning the kind of civilian company that our great hero grew a little over fond of?"

21

"From amongst his old student friends, at Cambridge in the '20s....."

".......and one in particular, his close friend Peter who, sadly, has been reported to be less than well of recent. But why these reservations, I ask."

"I think, Tom," faltered the brother warily, "I think perhaps you need to be talking with someone a little more closely connected with the very top wartime ranks than I then was,"

"But you've risen since, Reginald, and perhaps now by casual enquiry you can learn far more than one of my official standing might." A hand moved across to the corner of the desk to a shallow pile of hitherto disregarded documents. Lifting the top two, the third he slid out and passed to his brother.

Reginald read.

The dangerous manner in which the Alfa Romeo car was being steered towards Truro was recalled in a statement given by the driver of a following car. After frequently veering to the wrong side of the road the accused then proceeded to pull out and pass a long line of standing traffic. After narrowly missing the leading vehicle, a van, he actually struck the truck immediately behind. A tyre was heard to burst, but instead of stopping he continued, the flat tyre losing him further control. A second (approaching) line of traffic was caused to stop suddenly resulting in a collision between two vans and a motorcycle, the motorcyclist being thrown from his machine to sustain head injuries and a fractured wrist. The accused drove on at speed, even after being signalled to slow down by other drivers. It took a police motorcycle patrolman to eventually bring him to a halt by which time the punctured tyre had completely shredded down to the wheel rim. The accused was unaware of both accident and resultant puncture. On arrest, a subsequent blood test revealed a content commensurate to the consumption of eleven whiskies. The accused admitted to having been drinking from the half- emptied bottle that lay on the back seat of his car.

"The Truro road, Reginald?" prompted the eminent Judge, wondering as to whether his brother might have already heard something of the case.

"And a very serious matter," commented the other, looking still at the report. "Should I know the accused? Is this why I'm here, and have this now in front of me?"

"It is. For I think it likely that you would indeed know the man very well, he also having soldiered in Burma. Like you, too, he has enjoyed a distinguished post war career, until recent retirement to Cornwall......."

"...... where, sadly, it now looks to be on the brink of major blemish. I've known people to be imprisoned for less..... oh dear. With those clues, yes, I can make a good guess as to who this is. An honourable man, I would say, one guaranteed to be appropriately contrite."

"That's good, for I want him to know that were he to plead guilty then we are well placed to dissuade a local bench of magistrates from being over harsh in their sentencing."

"But you'll be expecting something in return, Tom. I think I see where this is headed. You want me to conduct a subtle interrogation. We're back to that enquiry. You're hoping he might be persuaded to whistle."

"*Interrogation*, this is too strong a word...... but I do have some questions that I feel that you might be able to put to him in the course of an informal chat. Discretion assured, of course. Have yourself a few days in Cornwall. The house I often take down at Helford is available and has been booked. Train, taxi, we can meet all expenses. Look the man up. Sounds like he might appreciate an old comrade at his side."

"So these questions, Tom, that you want putting......."

Lord 'Tom' Denning and
General Reginald Denning.

*

23

December 1963
.... and a phone call from the same office.

"Good afternoon....... Royal Marsden."

"Good afternoon, this is Lord Denning, speaking from Westminster."

"In an official capacity, am I to understand?"

"Correct."

"And your enquiry......?"

"...... concerns a wish of mine to visit one of your patients." Denning opened his desk diary.

"Name?"

"His Royal Highness Prince Chula Chakabrongse."

"Prince Chula, yes, he's still with us. Over the past eight months we've got to know him very well....... a sweet man, and so brave. He has a private ward of course, and the best I can do is to put you up to the relevant floor. If you could just hold the line......"

"Thank you." The Master of the Rolls lifted a pen in readiness, and waited. A good minute passed. What was being said, he wondered, before the eventual response....... from another female voice, this of more authoritive tone.

"Lord Denning?"

"Denning here, yes.........Prince Chula is being treated on your floor I understand."

"In a palliative sense, he is. You must understand that he is a very sick man."

"Throat cancer, I've been told."

"That's right, a terminal case."

"Is he taking visitors?"

"Wife, children, his Buddhist priest..... they watch and they wait."

"But for a nosey lawyer......?"

".......there would be no point. We are at the stage where he must be kept under constant sedation. The family have said farewell. Now, at their wish, and also his own written instruction, Prince Chula will not be allowed to regain consciousness. He has fought hard against a cruel illness. He sleeps peacefully now, Your Lordship, and cannot be disturbed."

*

June 1964; Peter receives a visitor.

"Walter, how good of you to call. With word coming to me that you've not been so well too, I wasn't over hopeful. Do excuse my not standing. Take this chair by mine."

"Thank you Peter. I was surprised to hear of this wish of yours to see me, it's been quite some time. I'd heard, of course, that you were beset by health problems. Are you any better?"

"Up and down, as is the way with multiple sclerosis. The downs steadily out weighing the ups"

"So......?"

"So with the right kind of care I might last another two years. You're getting stronger now, I trust, and can boast a more optinistic prognosis."

"I wish that were so, Peter," replied Monckton, "but it's arteriosclerosis with me. The arteries harden, and as circulation fails so, one by one, will the main organs......"

".....giving you....."

"....perhaps six months."

"And the expected decline will be mainly physical."

"I remain sound of mind," asserted the lawyer. "And I must warn you that my memory is as sharp as ever."

"That's good to hear, Walter, good to hear....... for as my own stays in hospital become more frequent and more prolonged I'm anxious to be receiving there the best possible treatment. I was raised a Catholic, and as such it's not death that worries me so much as the prospect of being taken without warning. *Unprepared* you might say."

"We would all of us hope to stand before our maker fully absolved, " nodded Monckton, " but I fail to see how *I* might guarantee for you *the best possible treatment*, particularly as Lord Louis is ensuring that you want for nothing in the way of nursing care. My understanding is that your devotion to him over the years has not been forgotten."

"This is true. He continues to give financial support. I cannot complain there, but on the medical side it's a risk that I might be the recipient of *the worst possible treatment* that I wish to minimise."

"So when can you imagine yourself being subjected to such, and why?"

"I think back to September '56, Walter. You were a Cabinet

Minister then, I well remember, under Anthony."

"Defence Minister, I was, working quite closely with Lord Louis once more. Ten years before he'd been Viceroy of India, when I was acting for the Nizam. This time he was high in the Admiralty."

"First Sea Lord," nodded Murphy, "and with all that was going on down Suez way it was proving a difficult time for those concerned ...... for Anthony, for the Queen, for Mountbatten, and for yourself, a born mediator."

"A very difficult time," agreed Monckton.

"During which Anthony was himself plagued by medical problems."

"He was, and while in the end they might have offered a pretext for his resignation, I certainly wouldn't want you to imagine that a fit and well Eden would have been less bellicose. He enjoyed the best of attention. Don't allow yourself to think otherwise."

"Worry not on that score, Walter. I wasn't thinking of Anthony.......for he survived, of course, and now looks better than ever. Not everyone did though."

"Did what?"

"Survive."

"Is this about a lesser politician? Refresh my memory, do."

"Not a politician, but certainly a dabbler in issues political."

"A dangerous time to be dabbling."

"Exactly, so all in all, for one given to such, a dangerous time to be entering hospital, even for no more than a minor hip operation......"

"......which was not survived," guessed a grim faced Monckton. "I take your point."

"Good," continued Murphy, "for it's with a view to reducing the risk of medical mishap to myself that I want you to relieve me of these." A large envelope was passed, unsealed so as to invite Monckton to inspect the contents. He did.

"So they actually exist," he gasped, "those rumoured Lausanne photos, commissioned by Mountbatten."

"You sound surpised, Walter."

"Because such mention of them made within my hearing has tended towards the apocryphal rather than the substantive....... a result, perhaps, of their never having been used as intended."

"The King being mysteriously killed before any deployment"

added Murphy, "this, perversely, adding to their potential for triggering diplomatic mayhem now."

"You allude to the current situation in South East Asia, I take it."

"A theatre in which the west is needing all the friends it can muster....... and this is why, for me, those snaps have become too hot to handle. I want rid, Walter."

A brief glance having been sufficient, Monckton slid the three large monochrome prints back into the envelope.

"And Lord Louis, does he have a view?"

"Dickie ordered me to destroy them, not long after the King was killed."

"And he assumes that order to have been carried out."

"This is what I've told him," confessed Murphy.

"And what you instead retained, thinking it might prove a personal asset......"

"......now becomes a burden. But my hope is that through your myriad of contacts, those most deeply anxious as to existence and possible where-abouts of these prints can be asured for definite that they *won't* be found in *my* possession. You can pass them over, Walter. You can destroy them yourself, or, judging me over-fearful, decide to keep them and just *say* they've been destroyed. Whatever, you're the one who has the trust of what, for me, looms as a worryingly vexed beast. Morsel you can proffer, or more. Please yourself. If it can be your fingers that so feed then no one else is going to sustain a bitten hand........that's my thinking."

Peter Murphy.

*

June '79; at a workshop in Derry

"And I agree with you, Mr Kellegher, like I agreed with you last year, the year before, and goodness knows how many years before that. As dignitaries go Mountbatten does indeed repeatedly offer himself as an easy enough target, and I can find no fault at all with your planning, but once again I am saying that *not* harming any member of the British Royal family remains a policy of the Revolutionary Council."

"With respect, Mr McBeamish, I would say this to be a policy due for immediate review."

"The High Command appreciates that respect, Mr Kellegher, and along with your enthusiasm also notes your opinion."

"As yet another August slips by," muttered the rebuffed zealot.

"Not this August," corrected McBeamish, "for it is our long eastablished policy to, where and when possible, wreak vengeance upon the British Para, and it is our decision that Bank Holiday Monday will be a good day for moving against the regiment currently based down in Ballykinler."

*

August '79
ITV News at Ten

NEWSCASTER

"Two bomb attacks in Ireland, this morning just off the coast of the Republic and this afternoon just inside Ulster, have made today one of the bloodiest in the history of 'the troubles'.

The first in County Sligo claimed the life of Lord Louis Mountbatten, as well as those of his fourteen-year-old grandson, his daughter's mother in law, and a fifteen-year-old local boat boy. Lord Mountbatten is said to have died instantly as, detonated by radio signal, at least fifty pounds of explosives reduced his thirty-foot pleasure craft to matchwood.

In the second, at Narrow Water on the Ballykinler to Newry Road, the combination of a ruthlessly timed double explosion plus sniper fire left eighteen soldiers of the British Parachute Regiment dead and as many again seriously injured.We must warn you that some of the pictures that follow in this report might be considerd to be of an upsetting nature.

*

September '85

"Greetings gentlemen, I trust that the long flight from Tokyo was not too uncomfortable."

Blindfolded and shackled as they were, the two still carried menace, less though than that positively radiated by the man welcoming them, who while aged and wheel-chaired was without assistance, manoeuvring for himself a commanding presence."

"When it's been prison furniture for the last three years, then even a seat in a plane will offer relief," replied the stouter and slightly shorter of the pair.

"Relief yes, but not release, so perhaps now you will be pleased to hear from me that there will be no going back to that jail."

"We understood we were in for life," responded the second, his manner more confrontational.

"I remember the feeling," snapped the invalid, "from all of forty years ago and, what's more, I was in the queue for the gallows. But then, just as you're about to be, I was offered the opportunity to earn a reprieve."

"An opportunity you obviously took," said the shorter.

"And the alternative for us, now, is death," realised the other. "If this is an offer to us then we are to know that refusal will be suicide..... the gangster ultimatum."

"Because on the evidence of your files, gangsters you most definitely are. Ruthless killers, they tell me. Efficient killers who will accept prison rather than inform against the master."

"And you wish now to be our new master, in an entirely separate matter......."

".......because with age comes physical frailty. And because, with time, the stitching around one of my more important jobs threatens to undo....."

".... you seek suitably qualified assistance," concluded the taller, daring to hope that he might after all be in a sellers market. At the very least, he ought to know this person's name. "So who is it that we have the pleasure of dealing," he asked, emboldened, "and where might we be?"

An icy silence ensued, to be broken by an almost placatory reply to the second enquiry;

"You can be told that you have been brought to the United Kingdom......," and this should be the least of your concerns, the voice implied. *Just wait until you hear the rest*.....and they did wait, through three further seconds of increasingly intimidating silence, "....... where you stand in the sole presence of *The Butcher of Singapore*."

And wholly intimidated these hardest of men indeed were, this title in itself sufficient.

"Master strategist of the Japanese Imperial Army," responded the shorter.

"The *Devil of Shanghai*," added the other, no less awed, "and afterwards the conqueror of all Malaya. In Japan we are told that you were finally killed back in the late '60s."

"Devoured by a tiger in '68, whilst on the run in Laos," nodded the warlord. "This was but the last of a number of feints that have helped ensure my survival....... even in a country such as this, the nation whose military reputation, built over a thousand years, I was able to destroy in less than a month. From Buddhist monk to tiger's breakfast, my repertoire of disguise has known few bounds. My expertise was in demand in Laos, much as it is here, now. If you're a little too young to properly remember, be reminded that by '68 the war in neighbouring Vietnam was at its height."

"And you were encouraged to field a militia of your own....."

".... which, again, is what the pair of you can amount to here. Sign up today and training for deployment can begin."

"How can we refuse?"

"How indeed, when already you know too much."

*

"So now, Your Highness, you've come to this opinion that there might be something rotten in the House of Mountbatten- Windsor."

"Firmly so, Bira." responded the Princess into a collar raised against chill of the winter's night.

"There's always been the odd bad apple, as in any barrel."

"But sometimes, Bira, mere death and decomposition will be insufficient to protect a younger crop, so vulnerable it can be to dangerous myth. The truth must out, however unpleasant. Now the last time we met you spoke of a cloud that had been for too long allowed to gather and hover over the posthumous reputation of your cousin. I heard of your wish that it might be dispersed, and there was a suggestion that between us we might find common ground. Mention was made of a particular gathering, and of a photograph. Now to my friends in the popular press a picture, however old, that tells a story ..... "

"....... can be trusted to attract a feeding frenzy."

"So did you locate this thing?"

"Down in Cornwall, Your Highness, at Tredethy, the very place that it was taken. There it was, up on the wall."

"At your cousin's old place."

"Which is now an old people's home. It was taken there by one of their residents, a certain Foy Quiller Couch, who was subsequently taken into the asylum in Bodmin where she has since died. The proprietors of the home were keen to keep it."

"Naturally.......so they made an offer to the woman's representatives?"

"They did, and found out from them that ownership lies with a friend who still lives....... and that person is happy to let them keep this on the wall at Tredethy."

"But by now you will have sought this owner out and made a more than generous offer."

Bira shifted uneasily on the bench, casting an over-the-shoulder glance towards the trees behind.

"I might have done, Your Highness......"

"......but no?"

Bira went lower again. "No..... because what remains is less than we might have hoped."

"In what respect?"

"The photo has been altered. I don't know when, or by whom......"

"....... but the effect has been to remove some of the entourage."

"Exactly, and at this stage, rather than attract attention to myself or to the picture I decided that it was best left where it was."

"So you envisage a next stage?"

"There would have been negatives, and I'm sure they wouldn't have been destroyed."

"Having been made all the more powerful by the doctoring of that print."

"Yes, so I've made a few discreet enquiries......"

"......in Cornwall still?"

"In Cornwall, and specifically in the Fowey area."

"Any luck?"

"A lead or two, yes."

"And should these come to anything then you'll let me know."

"I will Your Highness, of course I will. In the meantime, did I read it somewhere in the newspapers that you have developed a friendship with a grand daughter of Sir Walter Monckton, he that played a significant role in the abdication of the Queen's Uncle David?"

"Quite probably you did, Bira. Rosa and I get on well."

"That's good, for this might prove a valuable contact. It's a friendship to be strengthened at every opportunity.

Bira circa 1980

*

32

2 days later (Xmas Eve)

CAPITAL RADIO

PRESENTER;

"And it is with sadness that as a final item in this morning's sports bulletin I must report the sudden death yesterday here in London of Prince Bira Birabongse. He will be remembered with affection by older motor racing enthusiasts who followed the sport just before and just after the last war. While outwardly an active and fit 71 year old, he is said to have collapsed and died at Barons Court underground station. Heart failure is suspected.

Prince Bira was the driving talent in the privately financed two-man racing partnership managed by his older cousin Prince Chula who, until his death almost exactly 22 years ago, was well known in Cornwall where he'd made his home.

Whilst during the war Bira himself rented his own house in the county, he has in recent years preferred to move between a yacht on the Mediterranean and a home in his native Thailand where many still hold him to have been the country's greatest ever international sportsman. Often found in the company of the rich and the famous, Prince Bira was certainly a lively character. While we mourn his passing, it can always be said of him that he knew how to enjoy life to the full."

*

Scilly; Spring '86

With the late morning tide now at mid flow the pale crescent of sand that is Porthcressa Beach finds its westernmost tip screened by a pier of naturally piled granite, fractured and smoothed by wave and weather so as almost to appear purposely heaped. If the whole strand is sheltered from all but a normally kind southerly wind, this corner gains from the natural partition an additional degree of seclusion, notwithstanding the petering edge of Hugh Town behind......... a scattering of modest dormer roofed bungalows at sea wall level and older, more traditional terraces raised on the sloping ground behind. Indeed, as the bay fills, their occupants can fancy themselves the beneficiaries of a private foreshore.

Amongst those terraced properties the more immaculately maintained are Duchy of Cornwall owned, and for one particular temporary resident this sense of proprietorship might perhaps be justified. In beachwear perhaps tailored more for the intrusive lens than for comfort or anonymity she sits alone on a blanket, watching her two sons play at the water's edge. The younger, not yet two, splashes in the water as each successive wave washes at the castle of sand still being energetically replenished by a brother who has just turned four. Two small paper Union flags fly close to its summit, but topmost place is given to the single, green and white backed Red Dragon. *Yes*, mused the mother, *definitely the father's son!*

A man then emerges from a cottage neighbouring her own. She turns and beckons him to her side. He complies, and as he approaches the blanket she makes room. He sits. The eldest son glances up, and then plays on. A casual intimacy between the couple would suggest the arrival to be of a father, but this he most definitely is not. While the boys and their mother might be here on holiday, it is his work that has brought this man to the young woman's side and, to her chagrin, this same work will soon be taking him away and out of their lives, eventually for ever.

Eventually……..but not quite yet, for she is asking him now to remain in discreet contact, and quietly he'll pledge continued assistance.

High hopes!

*

34

Book Two

Mama Mahidol with the Ramas 8 and 9 and their older sister.

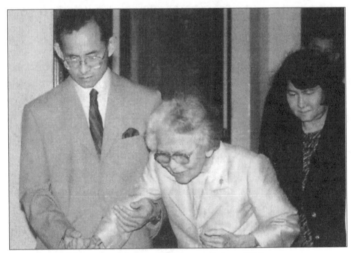

Mama in old age with the surviving children.

October 1987, Paddington Station

.......where, due to a temporary signalling problem at Reading, there is a sluggish thirty minute move through the cab rank for Eamon Carroll. Finally, though, he can edge to pole position and with a glance to his wing mirror confirm his fare to be the solitary man, bearded, with hat and glasses, but no luggage. Briskly the fellow climbs in, and with the clunk of the closing door driver and passenger are away, all seeming routine until......

"Stanstead please, Mr Carroll, for my evening flight back to Belfast."

Eamon recognises the voice.........too well. That beard and those glasses are fake.

"Mr McBeamish..... a coincidence, this, I trust"

"No coincidence, Mr Carroll. A few short months ago you proved yourself a valuable asset to our movement. My purpose today is hopefully to ensure you can remain loyal to the leadership whose hand you considerably strengthened."

"In terms of your negotiating position with Westminster, you mean."

"I do," confirms the passenger. "The efforts of you and your friends brought about a significant softening of their stance. Despite the Thatcher rhetoric we can look forward to certainly an eventual share of power in Ulster, the end of the RUC, plus a phased release of our jailed comrades."

"All this, and you would yet doubt my loyalty?"

"Because, to some in our movement, *all this* amounts to less than enough. There emerges amongst us a strand of opinion that holds strongly that the valuable insights won by yourself and your associates were squandered. I re-emphasise that my concern this evening is with your loyalty to *my* leadership. I know, for instance, that within this capital there are nationalist cells well informed enough to know at least vaguely what HIGHLAND CLEARANCE has been about, and who would be eager to demonstrate how much more exacting they could be should they happen across something of comparable moment."

"So you're thinking that word could have seeped to them of my unique resources, and an attempt could be made to recruit me to such an endeavour."

"Exactly Mr Carroll, and from what I've heard you might be approached quite soon."

"How soon?"

"Possibly before the end of the week......in which event I'll want, indeed I'll expect, you to contact me, personally, using this phone number and the names SLIGO for you and CAVAN for me." The number, ink-written on a half a postcard drops over the driver's shoulder.

"And would you want me to then steer clear, or play along."

"That would depend........"

"...... on the dangers I might face?"

"More on who they might be," growls McBeamish from the back. "And on what they might have."

*

North London...... two days later

"Frankly, Mr Carroll, while having been greatly impressed by your contribution to a considerable strengthening of the movement's position we have, by the same token, been somewhat disappointed at the rather feeble bargain struck by our High Command."

"You think more might have been made of what I took to McBeamish...... that we were letting the Brits off lightly."

"This is what I argued from what is, true, a rather minor position on the executive .... only to be firmly slapped down." Kellegher's face creased to a scowl. "Now my father died for the cause, as did many a friend. Those who paid with their lives deserve better. Would you not agree?"

Eamon, who'd arrived alone, was in no position to disagree.

"A rare opportunity wasted," he nodded uncomfortably, "perhaps unique."

"Or perhaps not," joined Conlon, Kellegher's henchman, the clock behind the bar thinly chiming a quarter past midnight as just the one bulb shines dimly from a cobwebbed, tobacco-stained wall to accentuate the cracks that craze and spread from the bulged scars of botched repair to the surrounding plaster. These were two violent men. They were killers. With his back to that wall Eamon was cornered, but he had to keep his nerve.

"So do I sense that the pair of you are looking to break away from the IRA?"

"Maybe we are," said Kellegher, "but it can't be done on the dubious strength of a stash of guns and dynamite. To prosper we would need the kind of bombshell you brought back from Cornwall, something that might rock the establishment if revealed, or severely compromise Government prestige amongst NATO, Commonwealth, or EU partners."

"And you have the potential revelation, the particular insight?"

"Not quite, Mr Carroll, but we do have a lead. Making something of this, though, requires a particular kind of talent, a talent we recognise in you."

"Credit belongs to my contacts."

"Who you found."

"It was more a matter of them finding me."

"Either way, we deem them a valuable resource … one available, we hope, for further use."

"And all that we found out, that I took to McBeamish, and which he, you say, sold too cheaply, does not that remain to you as a lever?"

"Too dangerous, Mr Carroll. McBeamish will consider himself to have sole use of that, and should word get back to him of an attempt by *any* Nationalist to assert otherwise, then punishment will be swift and severe. No, what we need at the moment is to be quietly shaping a fresh lever of our own."

"And you're trusting me to lend discreet assistance."

"Because until we're equipped to break away from the main Movement we shall retain a position of authority therein……. from which we might arrange your execution."

"At any time, no questions asked," added Conlon. "For while your recent adventures in the far south west did realise for McBeamish a handsome dividend, there does persist still amongst his councils, a lingering query as to what might have prompted your initial arrival at the Boyd's place, so conveniently on the eve of that planned visit from Prime Minister Thatcher and her husband."

"The episode remains an affront to the man's sense of control," summed Kellegher.

Eamon slumped forward in his chair, elbow on table now to support head in hand. This was a dangerous game, and threatening to become ever more so. He'd contacted CAVAN earlier, and been told to make helpful noises, but this, of course, was likely to embolden them while at the same time rendering himself less and less useful and, accordingly, more and more a risk to be eliminated. He had to take that chance, though, for from where he now sat it might at least buy time....... another week, another month. This was how he'd learned to survive, by subsisting on flows of information, not so much as a purveyor than as a mere conduit.

"So your strategy," nodded Eamon, "is to assemble something with which you might more than match the pressure that has been exerted on Westminster by McBeamish, and, with this, impress the less contented amongst his rank and file."

"Men given to wayward conduct, such as yourself but, for the moment, persuaded that it's only him that the British are ready to listen to. But I say this can be changed."

"And to effect such a change you've identified an insight no less marketable than that which has bought my reprieve," angled Eamon. He gulped at his glass which was topped immediately by Conlon from the three quarters empty bottle of Irish Whiskey. "A secret, similarly dark and of comparable political moment...... and this is what?"

"We hope such a lever might be shaped," answered Kellegher, "from this." He produced a tape cassette from his pocket. "Something to play to those clever friends of yours."

"It's a tenuous lead," added Conlon, "and one we've happened across by total chance......"

"...... all lending towards adequate cover, one hopes," said Carroll. "You have an indiscretion there, I take it. Of the sort usually gleaned by a hidden microphone."

"Not this time, Mr Carroll, in fact far from it. What's on this tape could hardly have been broadcast more widely. At least twice it went out, on national radio."

Eamon leant forward, angling his head to read aloud what he could of what was on the card within the case.

"*Desert Island Discs*, and 'Denning'....... would that be the judge?"

"Lord Denning, Lord Thompson Denning," confirmed Kellegher. "Still very much alive as Master of the Rolls, and deigning on this to give the public a selection of favourite music, the choice perhaps reflecting a series of chapters in the illustrious life briefly chronicled while interviewed between the pieces."

The tunes were listed. Eamon started with the topmost.

"So *Greensleeves*......"

".......can be taken as a personal response to the Arcadian sanctuary which is pastoral England," said Conlon.

"While *Land of Hope and Glory*......."

".......evokes the expansive, more messianic concept that is Britain, dispensing its gold standard justice to the furthest corners of the globe in imperial measure."

"And the next," continued Eamon, "is *Colonel Bogey*. I guess this reminds us that, for Denning's generation, these things were not secured without cost."

"Indeed, a tune playing as he and his friends entrained on their journey to the Western Front. A one way ticket for so many. *Roses are Blooming in Picardy* follows to express remembrance, and the gratitude of a survivor."

"Then," continued Conlon, "we have *To be a Pilgrim* and *Mine eyes have seen the glory of the coming of the Lord*, reminding us that here we have a staunch Protestant...... and we know what that kind thinks of the likes of us."

"With the second of these two he is remembering the companionship of his equally high achieving brothers," said Kellegher, "Norman in particular, for whom it was sung, apparently, at a memorial service. Then, in celebration of his own career, we have the *Judge's Song*, a nice little touch of Gilbert and Sullivan."

"So that's seven," calculated Eamon. "And they are allowed eight so......."

"......so this is where the mischievous octogenarian forgoes his earlier transparency to leave what we take to be a riddle, the riddle that we were hoping you could help solve."

"His final selection, then, is......"

"....... *I whistle a happy tune*, a Rodgers and Hammerstein number, from the show *The King and I*."

"And this also relates to an episode in the Judge's life?"

"Consistency requires so."

"To which episode, then, and how?"

"We can only speculate, Mr Carroll," sighed Conlon, "and, for the moment, far, far too loosely."

"Hence our eagerness to secure some input from yourself," Kellegher added. "But our view is that if there is any one episode that wanted for transparency then this has to be the enquiry he was asked to make into the Profumo scandal back in the early '60s. To believe that plenty of evidence was gathered is to accept also there to have been a decision made to keep much of it out of the public domain."

"There was a whitewash, you're saying," Carroll looked again at the tape, "with a number of misdeeds escaping exposure, the miscreants escaping censure."

"And with that last selection, in this programme made a good sixteen or so years on, Denning could be reminding any survivors that while at the time they might have evaded public disgrace they would do best, still, to consider themselves lucky rather than in any sort of way clever."

"So this broadcast, it was made....."

"...... in 1980," said Conlon.

"So what inference could possibly be drawn from *The King and I?*" shrugged Eamon.

"We think that there might be a Royal dimension to this," ventured Kellegher. "Back in '63 the Profumo business was brought to a head with the trial of that Dr Stephen Ward, the society osteopath-come-artist-come-provider of good time girls. It is known that at least one of those services could be styled *by Royal Appointment*."

"But *The King and I*," scoffed Carroll, "what can that mean here where there's been no King for more than thirty five years. And that's some leap of the imagination, from a prettified account of old Bangkok to a supposed seediness in the Buckingham Palace of now........ could we not be reading too much into what many would say was very little?"

"I too would be sceptical," conceded Kellegher, "were it not for the circumstances under which that tape came into our hands, a chance combination of events which almost implores us to make that leap, and to indeed think the well nigh unthinkable."

"So tell on, do. Convince me."

"This begins with my colleague here, and a motorcycle."

"I drive an *Evening Standard* delivery van," joined Conlon. "I'm on my usual North London round when I pass a motorcycle, and even beneath a helmet I recognise the pillion passenger from a photo we've long had of him on file. He was a member of the Home Office's special VIP protection squad. Not so long ago he'd been assigned to a possible target, and we'd had a good look at his details then."

"And you say he *was* a member of the squad," prompted Carroll.

"I do, because as the motocycle moves ahead of me there is a chance accident. A learner driven car emerges unexpectedly off a side road to cause a collision. The pillion passenger is thrown, and he dies almost instantly from head and neck injuries. I see this happen. I stop. I do what I can. Later I even give a witness statement. Amongst the debris though is this cassette. It looks to have escaped from the deceased's torn jacket pocket."

"So you find space for it in one of your own."

"I do, being curious as to its content....... which didn't, at first, appear to carry too much significance."

"We assumed, initially, that the dead sergeant had recently been attached to Denning," continued Kellegher, "but learned that if this were so then his duties had been occasional and sporadic, rather than of the more constant sort."

"You obviously made enquiries," said Eamon.

"The most telling of which being a visit made to the widow. Spotting the obit and funeral notices we locate a family home south of the river. We give it a month or so and then call, under the pretext of returning the tape......"

"...... of which you would have made a copy, or two, or three."

"We had," confirmed Kellegher, "but, in the event, unnecessarily. She acknowledged that tape to have been her husband's, but adamantly refused to take it. This had been part of the work he'd done at the Palace, she explained..... from when he'd been assigned to a Royal figure."

"Which one?"

"She wasn't saying..... and maybe couldn't. There was a sense of her having been cut out of this part of his life, possibly as a security precaution, possibly for reasons otherwise. Either way, there was certainly a note of resentment. Her blunt advice to us was to take this to the Palace, for that, she said, had probably been where it was heading."

"To Buckingham Palace?" Carroll's eyes widened.

"Our words again, to which the response was a somewhat despairing shake of the head. '*I can't say that for certain,*' she said, before going on to explain that to be attached to 'The Palace', in Protection Squad terms, was to be available for duties at a variety of Royal households."

"So in London that would also include Kensington Palace, the Palace of St James, and Clarence House."

"And the officer would be expected to travel with whichever resident, to wherever their duties or holidays might take them. And the picture is further blurred when one remembers that while Buckingham Palace might be a single household, laid on exclusively for the Queen Bee and her chosen Consort to use as a main residence, some of the others are broken down into apartments, these to accommodate second and third tier royalty.......be they workers, or drones, or nurses. Take, for instance, Kensington Palace. Those fond of the London life might make the place their main home, yes, but that won't suit all. Others of more rural inclination will only visit sporadically, as their Court diary might dictate."

"And bodyguard work can be correspondingly irregular," followed Eamon.

"Exactly. Bear in mind, though, that to a seasoned Royal watcher, the likes of Kensington Palace will be by far the more interesting place," continued Kellegher, "not least because of the rivalries and jealousies that simmer away beneath all that staged decorum. As with any close knit colony tensions will develop, some long standing, some too thinly concealed. Take for instance that spot of bother that hit the Kents a couple of years ago."

"Concerning Prince Michael......"

"......younger brother to Edward, Duke of Kent, and the sister, Alexandra, and for almost ten years, now, married to his Marie-Christine, herself an Austrian Catholic......"

".......of somewhat dubious parentage," remembered Carroll, "for did it not emerge in the press that her father had been a serving Nazi, in the SS even. Hardly the fault of the 'Princess Michael' though."

"Quite, and an immediate closing of the Windsor ranks might have been expected," said Conlon. "Instead, though, there was a telling hesitancy, some observers even going as far as to say she was hung out to dry."

"Adding that some within 'the firm' were not displeased to have the Kents hauled down a peg or two," said Kellegher, "particularly amongst those old enough to have been stung by the haughtiness of the late Marina of Kent, she who, in her long widowhood, took every opportunity to impress upon those three children her own impeccable

Royal pedigree...... a pedigree second to none, certainly in comparison to her sisters-in-law."

"So you're hinting, Mr Kellegher, at manipulation by the Queen Mother," said Eamon, "who in fact lives at Clarence House."

"But she has another, younger daughter, remember."

"Margaret, who does live in Kensington Palace..... and who can, perhaps, be linked to Stephen Ward, fall guy in the Profumo business." Eamon looked down again at the tape. "So hazard a possible scenario that might include that programme."

"We're talking Palace intrigue," began Kellegher, "and we know that Princess Michael was new to the game, and vulnerable. If she's to survive then she needs to be better armed, she decides, and it comes down to the old maxim...... knowledge is power."

"If she can get the low-down on some of her neighbours then she'll be a little better equipped for the future."

"Quite, Mr Carroll, and it is to this purpose that she quietly grooms one of the Royal protection personnel."

"And he could have been on to something, you think....... but what?"

"If we already knew that then you wouldn't be here," said Conlon.

"The tale we want will concern the Windsors," said Kellegher, "we're fairly sure of that, but it's as if it lies in a secure safe.......the stout door locked against us. Acting upon guesswork can be noisy and, beyond a certain point, counter-productive. We are at that point. A key we need, such as can only be fashioned from facts......"

"..... facts that we are trusting you to marshal," Conlon added.

"From where, though...... from Cornwall?"

"As you've said, Mr Carroll, it's *who* you know," continued Kellegher. "You have contacts down there...... knowledgeable contacts, obviously. See what they make of this signpost that Denning offers, with its pointer to Royal Bangkok. There could well be a Cornish dimension to this."

"You think so," muttered Eamon in open disbelief.
"And all in some way linked to Profumo!"

*

Plymouth (Elvira's) ….. 4.30pm the next day

"But the reason I wanted to see you so soon, Sally, is that Dad had a surprise visit yesterday that Declan from across at St Erney."

"Known, in another lifetime, as Vincent...... one of the few people around to have personally encountered your grandfather."

"The very same, and he's in contact again with 'Peg' Willis," continued Chas Cross, "the old friend of his who moved so suddenly and mysteriously to Scotland."

"Neighbour and tenant," added Sally Shaw, "as well as friend."

"Yes, and you might remember it having been mentioned that during those lost years McDaid had taken it upon himself to keep Peg's boat in serviceable repair..... having had it lifted into the boatyard, just upriver from where the railway crosses the Lynher. Now with Peg wanting to stay on in Scotland the pair have got to talking about this boat."

"What's to be done with it, you mean."

"I do, and it was agreed that as well looked after as it has been, the thing needs a bit of use also. Too much drying out and a degree of seaworthiness will be lost, irreparably...... and this is where we, that's my father and I, and yourself should you be interested, might wish to help."

"In what way?"

"It is proposed that if we were to assist with the necessary preparation then it might be the Diving School's to use during the summer months."

"And does that appeal to your father?"

"It does, partly because he's thinking that such a project might have a newsworthy aspect."

"Oh yes?" smiled Sally. She'd heard something like this before.

"Apparently, before taking the job at Port Eliot and coming to live at St Erney, Peg helped maintain the grounds down at Menabilly House, near Fowey. He'd been taken on there by his old commanding officer, a General Browning. All was well with this until the General died leaving the widow, the famous author known more popularly as Daphne du Maurier, with the limited benefit of an almost expired lease. Reluctantly she found herself obliged to relinquish her loved family home for a smaller place nearby."

"And she had to let Peg go."

"Yes and he was invited to take with him that cabin cruiser, which had been the last of a whole series of mainly sailing craft that the General had owned and enjoyed since way, way back in the '30s. Lady Browning wasn't quite so keen herself, but boats had always been part of the old boy's life. Accepting it as part of his pay off, Peg had brought it in to St Germans. He'd motored it along the coast from Polkerris. With his then taking Declan's cottage on the Lynher it became his means of getting to and from work."

"And the 'newsworthy' aspect, Chas......this presumably concerns the General and his widow."

"She's alive still, but old and frail. She could go at any moment and, when this comes, the death is likely to trigger an upsurge of interest in her life and times. If we could get it back on the water then we might cruise that boat back down to Fowey, for regatta week or some such similar event. Sound your father out."

"Well let's just see how long the old girl lasts." Sally was ready to at least acknowledge the diver's sense of enterprise, if not taste. "Dad'll remember doing that D Day stuff with Peg for sure, and yes, I suppose that this might hold postscript potential. But all that aside, just doing it up sounds a fun project..... something we could get stuck into over the winter. It would be a chance to use some of those shipwright skills they're giving you in the 'yard'."

*

Cornwall….. a morning stroll.

"An unexpected pleasure, Eamon, hearing from you again so soon...... and as I said on the phone, you're welcome to stay with me at the cottage for as long as you wish."

"Jim, believe me, that was as good a night's sleep I've enjoyed since I don't know when. It's a long drive down......"

"….. which I hope we can make worthwhile. An interesting enquiry you bring," continued the curious man, "and all the more so for perhaps giving me an opportunity to learn a little " It had been a gentle stroll down from Tremorebridge and they could pause here at Boscarn, where their by-way bridged the Camel just below Nanstallon.

Yes, and pause they well might, thought Eamon, seeing now how steeply the lane climbed northwards out of this valley.

"Worry not," smiled his host, sensing the apprehension. "A branch of the old Southern Railway once crossed here, running with the valley of course, and with the track now lifted we're left a path along which we can follow the river almost to where we're going."

"Upriver or down?" It was almost a demand.

"Up...... we re-cross at what once was Boscarn Junction and then, after perhaps tanking up with a little liquid at the *The Borough Arms*, we stay with the Camel. Leaving the old passenger spur to fork up to Bodmin North we follow the way of the old Wenfordbridge clay line ... pretty at any time of year, but now, in autumn, spectacular."

Briskly over to where the crossing gate had once swung, Eamon was off that lane in a trice, revitalised more, in truth, by the prospect of a beer than any promise of scenic beauty. Twenty minutes and they were settled in the quiet pub.

"So you're telling me Jim that this great grandson of the illustrious King Mongkut actually lived for a while around these parts."

"He did, and for quite a long while at that. We're now at Dunmere Bridge. Here the main Bodmin to Wadebridge road crosses the Camel as it emerges from the southernmost end of Dunmere Wood, one of the true glories of inland Cornwall. As you'll see, a boulder-strewn river drops gently through a mile or two's worth of oak canopied trout pools. At its northernmost end we'll come to Hellandbridge, the next vehicle crossing. Like that at Nanstallon, it carries a mere country lane. Climb this for perhaps half a mile or so westward and we'll reach an isolated manor house called Tredethy. Here it was that this Prince Chula and his wife lived out their love of England and its ways."

"So, having come to live so near, did you ever meet the fellow."

"He died back in the '60s. That was well before I arrived here, and if the name 'Chula' cropped up then it meant little to me beyond a distant boyhood memory of pre war motor racing, of the era when what was to become the Grand Prix circuit was in its infancy."

"So he was a driver?"

"No...... he financed and managed a team, his star driver being a younger cousin known to all who followed the sport as Prince Bira. For what was essentially a rich man's indulgence they were quite successful. Then the war closed down all competition, and afterwards there was a whole new technology to catch up on. Despite Bira's undoubted skill at the wheel their small team was soon rendered uncompetitive by the corporate outfits. You'll appreciate that most of this was before Richard Rodgers and Oscar Hammerstein elevated the Thai royal family to curio status."

Eamon had managed, just about, to avoid the *King and I* connection, anticipating that it would before soon be broached by his companion. Here now was the opening. He could probe without disclosing how central the musical was to his own agenda. Refreshed, they entered Dunmere Wood.

"So apart from seeing his old house, Jim, this stroll won't be telling me too much about Prince Chula."

"You're getting the lie of the land, Eamon, and maybe for me there'll be a clue from you as to what's prompted this enquiry."

This wasn't unexpected. Carroll smiled weakly….. almost as if to invite a measure of mild speculation. Busbridge duly obliged.

"Your nationalist friends attempting to further strengthen their hand……yes?"

"Having come to appreciate the value of the right kind of information," conceded Eamon cagily, resolved as he was to mention neither Royal bodyguards nor Denning. But then, anything was possible with a man like this, one who could be trusted to alight on something like the Profumo affair as if by instinct.

Conversation lapsed now, to give way to gentle birdsong and the soothing babble of the river. They strode on, Jim's pensive demeanour suggesting that he could indeed be about to drop onto '63 intuitively.

But not this time, the curious man could also surprise.

"In these parts, as the years go by, casual mention of Chula becomes less and less frequent. Of the little that is remembered the merest fraction will be of any consequence….."

"……such as might be of any interest to yourself, you mean."

"I suppose so, but not so long ago he did, intriguingly, crop up in the course of a conversation I was having with my cousin Peter."

"Peter Bright, he of *Molehunter* fame."

"The very same, who, when with MI5 would be occasionally be entrusted with the interrogation of some of the more minor Russian agents found to be working in this country. More often than not the task was about collecting and assessing information being volunteered in return for immunity, and there was one character he had before him, a woman named Tania, who told of instructions she'd been given to seek out the company of Chula and Bira."

"And she was successful in this?"

"Particularly with the latter, a renowned ladies man by all accounts, who during the war years would invite her to Cornwall as a house guest."

"So what were her masters wanting to know about a play boy racing driver?"

"Bira was close to Chula, remember, whose mother had been a Russian aristocrat."

"So he was of White Russian blood."

"From his mother, and this is what had disqualified what by the late '30s, could otherwise have stood as a strong claim to the Thai throne."

"But running a small motor racing team falls a long, long way short of mounting a counter revolution against Stalin's Russia," snorted Carroll.

"Granted, and that was my reaction towards Peter, but on reflection maybe that was only a part of this woman's brief. We can't assume she was owning up to *everything*."

"And neither can we assume, Jim, that in a conversation with you, Bright would pass on *all* that he'd been told by this woman. Some things could have slipped from his memory, other things he might have deemed too insignificant."

"True enough," conceded Busbridge, "and anyway, the someone somewhere who has sorted you out as their bloodhound wouldn't be going to the trouble of sending send you so far merely for something so stale. That kind of stuff has been in the public domain for years, thanks largely to those journalists who specialise in Soviet infiltration. They will have listened to cousin Peter for far longer than I. My guess is that there are hopes that your proven nose for the as yet uncovered can sniff out something that lies a-festering a good deal deeper. I can ask Peter for more on the Reds' interest in Chula's Russian connections, but in the meantime it could be worth looking again at Bira's guest list."

"For more spies?"

"Chula did study at Cambridge, this is true, and probably did encounter the likes of Philby and Blunt and friends, but I was thinking more in terms of British Royalty and those amongst them who were given to a measure of political activity which could even now be regarded as controversial..... or scandalous even. One could take Prince George the Duke of Kent, for instance."

"Killed during the war, his plane hitting a Scottish mountain....."

"...... leaving Marina and the three young children, who continued to come down to stay with Bira and Chula."

"And this holds political significance?"

"Maybe, for one hears it whispered that for a brief while the Kents came under serious consideration for a role as constitutional monarchs, this out of an almost desperate political expediency."

"Really,"

"But we'll perhaps come to that later," dodged Busbridge. "For the moment we're best keeping an open mind."

Maybe, shrugged Eamon, but what a fascinating morsel from this curious man. To where might he be alluding? Probably some Balkan principality, at the Greek end of what was to become Tito controlled communist Yugoslavia, part of the Kingdom reigned over by Marina's sister Olga and brother in law King Paul before they'd incurred a lasting exile for their want of anti Nazi backbone in '41. Any suggestion that George of Kent, a wayward child of the English protestant establishment, might have been considered for the throne of Buddhist Bangkok would be just too preposterous. But then there had been that selection by Denning from *The King and I,* and back in '63 the Judge might well have interviewed Marina. Was something to be made of this?

Carroll shook an increasingly perplexed head......but having come so far what was there to be lost from tapping his companion's memory further?

"Tell me about Marina, after her husband died," he continued. They'd left the woods, and were joining the lane now to cross Helland bridge. "She never re-married, I know that..... but any notable escorts?"

Busbridge took his time. Retail of gossip he considered beneath him, but notable could only mean notable, so......

"The ever debonair Mr David Niven for one, and the all-singing all-dancing Mr Danny Kaye for another, and before them, in his bachelor days there was the still youngish Jack Profumo."

"Profumo," echoed Carroll, softening the eagerness of his response to barely a murmur. But he had no intention of letting this pass. "So the would be queen took for herself a knave. And you say *still*

50

youngish, so that's what?"

"Mid '30s for Profumo, and attractive early '40s for Marina."

"Now was there not a judicial enquiry into the Profumo scandal?"

"Conducted by Lord Denning, the Master of the Rolls."

"And how thorough was this enquiry?"

"More thorough than his published report," answered Busbridge.

"You mean there was plenty that he kept under his wig."

"And that's where it stays to this day, Eamon. The old boy is still alive, remember."

"So that report of his, is there any area in that which to you seems particularly thin?"

"You might recall that Profumo initially denied any improper involvement with the Keeler woman, and that the Prime Minister claimed that in accepting this denial from his Secretary for War he had been no less deceived than the rest of Parliament."

"Absolving himself of any complicity."

"Macmillan's astute line was, to admit mere complacency, and while Denning was ready to go along with this in his report it has emerged since that he might have secretly concluded that crafty old Harold had been told enough from a variety of sources, domestic and foreign, to be more than a little suspicious of his War Minister's conduct. It is known now that Keeler's handler, the Dr Ward who'd put her within Profumo's too loose orbit, had been approached by MI5 with a view to laying the same woman as bait before the Russian involved...... the idea having been to blackmail secrets from him."

"And that this ploy had been rendered useless by Profumo's parallel involvement would have been perfectly well known in Number Ten......."

"........ while the Minister was brazenly telling the Commons something very different."

"Macmillan might have been hoping that Profumo would get away with his lie," ventured Busbridge. "A possibility that Denning would appear to have deliberately suppressed."

This was Eamon's moment.

"So if Denning was ready to protect a Prime Minister, why not also Royalty?"

"Maybe," conceded Busbridge, "but bear it in mind that by this time Marina was approaching 60, and acquiring dowager status...... even if, as an official title, this was far from her liking. And also, of course, Profumo himself had been almost ten years married. The fact that the pair had been seen out together a dozen or more years before was hardly sensational in itself."

"But leaving aside Marina, was it not said that there were links between that Dr Ward and some of the then younger members of the Royal Family? Did not some consult him as an osteopath...... Margaret, the Queen's sister, maybe, or Alexandra, Marina's daughter?"

"I think there might have been some question as to his effectiveness as an osteopath ...... but not as to his flair in sketching portraits, something much valued amongst the wealthy and the vain. He could have published an illustrated *Who's Who*. I think when the scandal broke he was actually staging an exhibition, much to the embarrassment of more than few of those customers."

"Because every picture might have told a story," chuckled Carroll. They were over the river now and climbing. "So this house, it's currently what?"

"For the moment, an old peoples' home...... but I've heard it to be on the market, offering a potential for a small but select hotel. There's a swimming pool ready installed, unused since Chula's time. It just wants for that little bit of money and imagination."

"A good location," observed Eamon. "Quiet, not far off the main road......why don't we pretend to be prospective customers? We can invent an elderly aunt " The curious man had to be game, naturally, and after a short winding climb from the bridge they found the driveway opening invitingly to their right.

And the house, in all its gleaming granite symmetry, did indeed look fit for a Prince. A gravelled apron before the main entrance was wide and level enough to have made a parade ground, the lawn beyond sweeping down and away to open a commanding view of the wooded valley below.

A young tunic-clad care assistant answered the door. Little more than a girl, she politely bade them into the hallway and across to a visitors' book to enter names and a purpose. They were led through, then, to a spacious high-ceilinged day room where perhaps a third of the armchairs contained a comfortably ruminating resident. Most dozed, only a few eyes following their selection of a dining chair apiece from the scattering purposely provided for visitors. The proprietor would be with them shortly, they were assured, before being left to admire the well maintained fabric of the room....... the wood beading set into the ceiling and the precise panelling and plastering of the walls, the understated hang of the elegantly drawn window curtains, all combining to enhance further the autumnal spectacular beyond the glass.

But winter would come soon enough thought James Busbridge, to the muffled chime of a hallway clock, and some here would have accepted they had already seen their last spring, and be hoping now to wither and fall as gently those leaves that decorated the valley.

"Good morning Mr Busbridge..... and Mr Carroll." Correctly named, the visitors were impressed, but had the proprietor merely guessed right, or did she already know something of the curious man, perhaps from his more than modest local press profile? If so, thought Eamon, then maybe she would suspect an ulterior purpose to this inspection. This had been his own idea, yes, but the talking, he decided, would be best left to his companion.

A quick tour was offered, and accepted, an obviously busy woman being brisk almost to the point of severity. Bedrooms were presented, and bathrooms, the kitchen, and laundry room. Nothing, they were assured, would be too much trouble. Finally they were brought back to her office, to sit before the ordered desk which neatly accentuated the clinical ethos of the whole. Sitting herself, and reaching for a pair of glasses, the proprietor was clearly ready now to address the matter of *coin*...... except that suddenly she was aware of a distraction. The attention of these potential customers was being drawn to the wall behaind her, to the framed black and white photograph hanging thereon, and the group assembled therein. A quick glance over her shoulder was enough to acknowledge this competition....... and prompt James Busbridge.

"Of those three men standing behind the bench I take it that the shorter and less caucasian must be Chula."

"That's he, to the left. Half Thai, half Russian, and you might recognise the youngest guest, over on the right as we look at them."

"Would that have been Prince Philip, in his bachelor days."

"Correct, Mr Busbridge...... I think you note the affectionate hand that he places on the shoulder of the lady who sits before him at his end of the bench."

"Yes, a bit older she, but attractive nonetheless. I feel I ought to know her, but a a name eludes me totally."

"And I couldn't say either," conceded the proprietor, "but what about the other woman at the other end of that bench, older again yet very elegant still."

"That looks like the late Duchess of Kent, Marina, mother to Edward, the current Duke, Michael and Alexandra.....and a cousin, I guess, to young Philip."

"Princess Marina, it is...... as confirmed over the years by a number of my residents."

"But they haven't been able to help you with that lady at the other end," joined Eamon, "nor she that sits so demurely between them.

"Not yet, Mr Carroll."

"So what about the other guy," persisted Eamon, "who stands between the two Princes?"

The proprietor turned again in her chair and looked up.

"For him," she shrugged, "there's not even an initial."

"Like there are for the others?" queried Busbridge, rising from his chair and stepping towards the picture. The woman stood, too, with a sigh of regret. She would have to take the frame down now and unclip its backing card...... it was all so bothersome. Off it came, and with the back of the photo revealed both men could scrutinise the faded line up;

Pr C.   Pr P.
Pr M.   T.   A.

"So we can assume that neither lady *A* nor lady *T* carried a Royal title," said Busbridge.

"And as for this other guy," added Carroll, "he without even so much as a single letter, it's anyone's guess."

"And yours would be as good," said their host, re- assembling and remounting picture.

"I can see that it was taken outside there, on the lawn, " continued the curious man, "but when would you say?"

"Not long after Chula came here." The proprietor adjusted the hang. "I have it on good authority that this gathering were enjoying Tredethy over the Eastertime of 1946."

"On whose good authority" pressed Eamon.

"I was told as much by Prince Bira himself." She returned to her chair. "Less than two years ago this was. To our surprise and delight he just strolled in and introduced himself, much as you have today. He looked deceptively well."

"Deceptively?"queried Eamon.

"Because within just no more than three weeks we were shocked to hear of his sudden death. Heart failure, it was said. Such was his fascination with this photo that I was prompted to tell him that it wasn't actually my property. I was convinced, you see, that he would want to buy it and offer cash."

"But no such offer was made," checked Busbridge. "You would have forestalled this."

"That's how it seemed."

"But those mystery identities........ did he help, or was he not disposed to?"

"He was vague, and asked if we knew of any surviving visitors' book from those times. I said no, and this led him to mutter something about a Mrs Crocker who could have been staying overnight, and a Mrs Allen."

"So A for Allen perhaps," posed Eamon.

"And T for tenuous,"quipped Busbridge, sensing the pretence that had won them acceess to this office to be wearing a little thin. "Sounds like the fellow at the back may have been just a day visitor. Did Bira mention being there, with this group, and perhaps even being behind the camera, pressing the shutter button?"

"He didn't say, but he could well have taken it I suppose. Some one had to," she added wearily, "so yes, why not him?"

"A final question," said the curious man. "If the picture wasn't yours to sell, am I to take it that it didn't come with the house?"

"It came with the belongings of a person who we hoped might be moving in with us, one Foy Quiller Couch. In the event her condition deteriorated before she could follow her things here. Sadly she had to be admitted to St Lawrence......"

"......, and that's where she died. I remember."

"On sounding out her representatives we were to find that the ownership hadn't been hers either. A friend had let her have it, just to look after and keep safe, this friend being the writer Daphne du Maurier, Mrs Browning to us. For the while her people are content for us to hold on to it here, where it's felt to belong." The proprietor stood once again. The picture was ready to be re- hung, and she'd given time and information enough. If these 'prospective customers' wanted to return then they had to be out now.

So they rose too, each sensing themselves to be seconds from being shown the door. Eamon, though, was moving within reach of the photograph she held and in passing braved a last enquiry."

"How old would we put the Duchess of Kent in '46?" He pointed casually to Marina. "She held a certain glamour for sure."

"Fortyish?" ventured the woman curtly.

"Bang on," Busbridge almost bragged. "I can tell you that she was born in 1906, making her fifteen years older than her cousin Philip whose wedding she was shortly to grace, the encore coming a few years later for his bride's Coronation."

"And thus in an elegant prime, we endeavour to preserve her," said the proprietor, carefully returning the group to the wall before stepping back to check a final adjustment. "We know that Marina died almost twenty years ago now, out of which it's just for the last ten that I've actually been here. In that time there's been just that one call by that one person with any connection to that group."

"Bira," nodded Busbridge, "who was to die shortly afterwards, despite seeming to be in robust health."

"As I've said, Mr Busbridge." The tale of the aged aunt was no longer believed, this was clear. They were ushered doorwards. "Now if you'll excuse me I've plenty to do."

Within ten minutes, replete with brochures, the two men had re-crossed Helland Bridge, Eamon having learned on their way down that, while neither Foy nor Bira had lived to see '86, now, almost two years later, Daphne was still alive. But only just, he'd been told, and with a greatly diminished capacity of mind. She too had had a spell in St Lawrence and while the pharmacy there had facilitated her return to a reasonably stable home life it had to be accepted that the once formidable memory was shot, to the extent that she was struggling to name even her grown children and grandchildren. As for Bira, and Anna, and even the regal Marina, these names must long ago have passed irretrievably beyond recall.

"So where else for more on that photograph," posed Carroll. "A nice letter to Marina's family perhaps. They might have their own print and be better placed to name our unidentified three?"

"A bit conspicuous, Eamon. I can imagine *that* having been Bira's planned next stop, but whether down to ill health or otherwise he didn't survive. Accordingly I'm loath to follow too closely in his footsteps. Seeing what we saw just now, and hearing what was said, I'm pretty sure that there's more to that print than met the eye."

"You mean apart from that trio?"

"I do. I suspect it might have been altered."

"And your grounds, Jim?"

"The woman spoke of Bira giving it close scrutiny. Perhaps he'd retained a mental image, and had felt there to be discrepancies."

"Touched up, you mean?"

"Or perhaps a little trimming. I noticed that the side edges had no white margin, unlike the top and the bottom, and also that width-wise the frame was a distinctly over large. It might be that a wider original included a couple more characters, one to the left of Philip ...."

"....... and one to the right of Chula."

"This would have corresponded with the two paler blobs that I noticed on the reverse......"

"......flanking the scant information given. So two corresponding initials brushed over, you reckon, and these of people more famous."

"Unless one could account for the un-named figure," said Busbridge.

"But in that case, why trim the print down both sides?"

"Yes, and either way Bira finds less than he sought."

"So where does he then go? I guess he looks to sound out dear Daphne who could have been significantly less ga-ga at that time than you say she is now. Or, taking the bolder line, perhaps, as you said, he went straight to the Kents, or even to Prince Philip, the top man."

"Bold to the point of foolishness that, Eamon, for the very purpose of the concealment could have been to spare the Palace embarrassment. Of those pictured you're going to be safer with the untitled, and out of those, the two who looked to be younger than Marina........"

".......meaning *not* the bloke, who looked as if he could be ten years older than the Princess who, were she to have lived on, would now be eighty."

"And, say, between 5 and 10 years older than the other female companions, A and T. While we needn't yet discount the gent, our best chance has to be that either or both of those might have survived."

" 'A'......," pondered Eamon, "that could stand for 'Anna'."

"Merely because of an initial letter?" scoffed Jim. "It could equally stand for Abigail, Alexandra, or even Anastasia!"

But Denning could have been hinting at the former, thought Carol, remembering that the character who sang *I Whistle a Happy Tune* was an Anna, even while never having seen the show.

Busbridge remained sceptical.

"So the T, maybe that's for 'tenuous'," he mocked. "Any way, wasn't the woman told that a Mrs Allen was the likely candidate there, and told this by Bira himself?"

"Yes, but to go with that reasoning makes the 'T' for the other woman problematic……. For how might this fit with the name Crocker?"

"OK," relented Busbridge, "so if, for a minute, we call A 'Anna', what name are we to pin on 'T' ?"

"Why not Tania?" pounced Eamon gleefully, "the name you raised earlier."

"Why not," the other conceded. "We have to start somewhere, I suppose, and yes, why not with an Anna and a Tania……..an Anna Allen maybe, and a Tania Crocker, as long as we don't close our minds to other probabilities."

"Like Anna Crocker and Tania Allen," said Eamon, joking off a mild resentment at the other's patronising tone.

"I'll check with my cousin Peter," placated Busbridge. "If theTania he mentioned ever took the name Crocker or the name Allen then he'll know, I'm sure, and be able to say if she's alive still, and perhaps even where she lives. Find her and she might have something to say on her companions."

One of the thousands of down fluttering leaves glanced against Carroll's nose. He swatted it away. "Like *who* might have been excised from that picture," he rambled, "and *when*, and *why*…….."

"…….and the *by whom*," added Busbridge. "Things which at the moment we can only guess at."

"But it's educated guesswork from you, Jim. Speculate on. You've said that a restored print might even now embarrass the Palace. Just how, tell me.

"OK, the snap was taken just after the war, early '46 we've been told. Now I can imagine it staying intact, as a proud possession, adorning some one's wall until around '63, and then someone looks at the line-up and the kind of location."

"The country house party," nodded Eamon, remembering what had emerged from Cliveden, "with two prominent members of the Royal Family consorting with goodness knows who."

"And again recalling cousin Peter's story, there could well have been an active Soviet agent lurking there amongst them."

"That Tania has captured your imagination, I can see."

"Just one colourful possibility amongst several, Eamon......... perhaps Jack Profumo himself was stood next to Marina, or to each side we might have found any one of a dozen or more members of the Thursday Club, Philip there having been inducted into this ribald coterie by his uncle, 'Dickie' Mountbatten, and his cousins, the Milford Havens. Chula might have been the more staid, but Bira, he certainly would have been familiar with their revels."

"So does this come down purely to a need to sanitise Prince Philip's past?"

"One shouldn't discount political skulduggery, not if Philip's Uncle Dickie Mountbatten happened to be in the frame. He had his own brand which sometimes, when it suited their purposes, the Reds could be ready to encourage."

"So Chula and Bira," ventured Eamon. "Were we to say that Mountbatten saw in one or the other a political potential....."

".......as a pawn, you mean?"

"I suppose I do."

"Go on."

"Well then we should be mindful of a probable awareness of this in Moscow......"

"That's right, Eamon, even while the Thais themselves might have been blind to any manipulation. It is known now that more than one of Mountbatten's closest confidantes had communist sympathies."

"For instance?"

"One could start with his wife Edwina, an heiress for whom the term *champagne socialist* might have been invented, so utterly shameless was her appetite for both men and women of dubious political persuasion. Some will argue that her Lord's single minded careerism stemmed from his marital humiliations."

"So she was bi-sexual?"

"As, by many an account, was Lord Louis...... although perhaps not so flagrantly, or indeed fragrantly, as the Duke of Kent had been

before marriage to Marina. But staying with poor cuckolded Dickie.......
of all the reds under his too often empty bed, none gathered more
suspicion than one James Jeremiah Murphy, like yourself, a man of Gaelic
descent. Here was a Marxist in the grand manner, a fully blown
homosexual Cambridge leftie. Ever assured of his patron's confidence, he
was taken by Mountbatten to the South East Asia Command HQ and, as
you might imagine, the subordinated Generals were none too pleased."

"Because they were the professionals operating in the field," said
Carroll, "and having to endure the meddling of Dickie was quite bad
enough....."

"..... without having to contend with this one man blend of Guy
Burgess and Roger Casement," chuckled Busbridge, the mention of the
second, *Casement*, drawing from Carroll a seriously quizzical glance.

"So are you suggesting we could be in the market for something
akin to *A Black Diary*?"

"Now, so many years on, and in a world that is a lot less easily
scandalised, I would suggest that to carry lasting political moment it
would have to be something a deal worse than that."

"But one would imagine that aside from their interest in Chula's
White Russian ancestry, the Reds could also have been assessing the
Prince's value to any outside power looking to reshape the new post
Hiroshima Jap-free Thailand."

"Indeed, Eamon, for Moscow had long had ambitions in South
East Asia where French Vietnam, the Dutch East Indies, and British
Malaya and Borneo offered easy pickings. Those IJA battalions might
have got there first, but after they'd been driven back it was game on once
more. From way back in the '20s nationalist leaders had been armed and
encouraged, and it was from a firmly established covert cell in Bangkok
that so much of this kind of mischief was co-ordinated. Stability there was
important to Moscow, more so than revolution."

"And few things can be more stabilizing that a well respected
monarchy," nodded Eamon. This scene setting was useful, but with names
such as Profumo and Denning having been brought up earlier he was loath
to have them slide from the conversation.

"So going back to that print at Tredethy," he resumed bravely.
"You mentioned Profumo as a companion of Marina."

"I did."

"So were we to say that he'd been snipped away, do you think knowledge of this might have reached Denning?"

"What if, what if," mocked Busbridge. "I suppose it's not inconceivable that Denning himself might have suggested, or even insisted upon, such a trimming! Don't underestimate Denning, Eamon. The one certain thing about him is that he knew a lot more than he let on."

"So people tell me."

"Knowledge, as ever, being power......"

"........ but would it not have had a limited shelf life, so many of the principals now being dead? "

"And beyond embarrassment, eh? We're back to the issue of political clout, and any diminution thereof." Busbridge looked suspiciously at his companion. "Is this why you're here? You've been sent, in the hope thaty you might return with another HIGHLAND CLEARANCE." Carroll was silent. He couldn't contradict "Someone in your movement has panned himself a nugget, and it's hoped you might open the kind of seam that was so profitably mined back in the summer."

"Something like that," conceded Carroll, reflecting on a predicament less simple, and also what little the day had so far yielded. That photo had merely matched the tape...... the speculative for the speculative. Might each, separately, hold a link to Profumo, and a deliberately concealed link at that? Who could say while any fancied alteration remained unconfirmed. What he needed was a link between picture and tape, then he might have something for those fact-hungry handlers of his. As yet, though, he could offer them next to nothing and, as they re-took the old track back into Dunmere Wood, brown leaves drifting across and down to the river now on their right, he was left to reflect that fuelling a renegade initiative was doubly dangerous.

No reminder of this was needed and none, in truth, expected......... but with each step one steadily approached, and now was just a bend away. The track began to straighten, and they were seen. A voice called, a familiar voice.

"Mr James Busbridge, and Mr Eamon Carroll!" Jeremy Barnes sounded as delighted as he was surprised.

"Jeremy.......Kate!" responded Busbridge, halting with Eamon as the couple hastened towards them.

"Now Jim," laughed the lecturer, "you're part of the scenery here, but yourself Eamon, never. We thought you to be back amongst the smoke and the noise of the capital."

"Just visiting a friend," countered the cabby, "as you would also appear to be."

Jeremy ignored the riposte. The pleasantries done, his tone became grimmer. "In fact, on hearing the radio news this morning, Kate and I wondered if you'd even become a small and fleeting part of it all."

"Noise and smoke?" Eamon was puzzled.

"There was a report of a bombing in a north London pub," explained Kate. "The device went off after closing last night. Two men killed....... the sole occupants of the bar at that time, said to have been active Republicans. So it's good to see you before us, as large as life."

"District?"

"Cricklewood."

"*The Duke of Connaught?*"

"You obviously know the place," said Jeremy. "They could have blown themselves up by mistake, I guess, but there have been suggestions that the victims were leading figures in a breakaway group." An inquisitorial tone hinted strongly at murder of Fenian by Fenian...... an analysis that Carroll couldn't be comfortable with. But as qualified as he might have been to express a measure of doubt, for the moment it could stay unvoiced. Instead he would quietly heed this as a warning.

He'd changed his car before leaving, but otherwise there'd been nothing furtive about his drive down, or indeed the phone call to Tremorebridge by which he announced this intention. Had he been tailed, or might the line have been bugged? Unlikely, he thought, but that wasn't to say he couldn't be tracked. It would be wise to move on promptly from Jasmine Cottage, he felt...... but to where?

"So what brings you pair this far into the woods," asked the curious man.

"The valley," teased Kate.

"Nothing more," said Jeremy, more defensively.

"And nothing less," added the nurse, acknowledging the glory of the season. "And you?"

Busbridge looked to Carroll. It was for his companion to say. Eamon shrugged, and obliged.

"The Thai Royal Family."

"Then you've been up to Tredethy," said Jeremy.

"We have," said Busbridge, "and can I assume that your interest too has, at some time, been drawn to the former occupant?"

"A passing interest, being a historian....... like yourself," added the lecturer cautiously.

"But I'm a relative amateur, Jeremy. You're the real deal, and far better equipped, I'm sure, to give an overview of Chula's place in Thailand's history........ or should we be calling it Siam?"

"Siam officially became Thailand in '39," said Jeremy. "Then, in '45, with the defeat of the Japanese, a reversion to Siam was decreed...... but four years later the figure who'd been so keen on 'Thailand' was back in power."

"And Thailand it became again," smiled Eamon.

"Remaining so unto this day," said Busbridge, "so we are best to stay with Thailand."

"That's a shame," said Kate, "for there can't be a songstress who has never dreamt of serenading the King of Siam......*Shall weeee dance dada da daa*," she trilled and twirled.

"And, for the historian, the least said about *that* portrait of old Bangkok the better," chided Jeremy. "There was a Monarch, a King Mongkut, a progressive and enlightened King, and he did have many wives and, therefore, many children. And he did entrust them to an English governess...... for a while, until quite sensibly moving her on..... but her accounts of her time in the job, written for a late Victorian western audience, were fanciful. They still cause great offence there, as does that musical. Believe me, if Hollywood are looking to do Bangkok again, there's a far better story than that waiting for them...... a true rags-to-riches tale, of Zhivago-like dimension."

"Excellent," enthused a gleeful Busbridge. "And if we can work in our Tania then we could indeed put together something special."

"Tania?" Queried Jeremy.

"Your tale first," said Busbridge. "If you've come far enough, why not accompany us back to the *Borough Arms*?"

A glance at Kate, met with a nod, and Jeremy was accepting.

"Good idea...... back to the *Borough Arms*, where we left my car. When refreshed we can run you back up to Jasmine Cottage."

The couple turned, so that with James Busbridge to his left and Eamon and Kate on his right Jeremy was set to treat all to what what he knew of the Thai monarchy.

"The forward looking King Mongkut established a tradition of benevolent innovation that was followed fairly successfully by subsequent

Kings until the early '30s, the time of the world economic slump. Foreign investment dried, the confidence of the middle classes wilted, and the pace of reform failed to match growing discontent at unfair and inefficient land rights and tax rules. In response, a reform movement grew that drew support from the top ranks of the armed forces and civil service."

"A powerful lobby," agreed Busbridge.

"Calling themselves 'The Promoters of Political Change'...... which *didn't* mean towards a western style democracy. Instead, the absolute power that was previously the monarch's was wrested into the hands of an elite. Less fettered by Buddhist holy writ, law making became even more arbitrary..... and where once regulated by an altruistic priesthood, order came to be imposed by the police and the military. As in Italy, Germany and Spain, anxiety about Communism fostered a home grown species of National Socialism."

"Replete, I suppose with, matching charismatic leader."

"In fact there were two. There was Pibul, who'd emerged from the military strand, and there was Pridi....... he a civilian technocrat with more of a feel for the centrally planned economy."

"So pinkish in tendency," said Busbridge.

"Relatively speaking, yes, and with each wary of the other, a rivalry developed...... the tension that has uniquely shaped the modern day monarchy."

"The product then of a particular stir of personalities," offered Kate, "Pibul and Pridi......."

"....... and we must blend in with that pair one Mama Mahidol, a half Chinese slum girl born in 1900 during the reign of King Chulalongkorn, he the progressive son of Mongkut, and grandfather to the Prince Chula who was to settle at Tredethy."

"And she is our Cinderella," smiled Kate.

"Determined to become a nurse she won for herself a place in a government school and then a training scholarship at one of the King's large new hospitals, this at the tender age of thirteen. Within five years the training had taken her to America where she met the future husband with whom she was to father three children, a daughter, followed by two sons. While unimaginable at the time of their conception and birth, both the boys, Nan and Lek, were to become Kings of Siam."

"But they must have had Royal blood," insisted Busbridge.

"Yes, inherited from the father, a Prince Mahidol whose

remoteness in the Royal lineage gave him licence to study to be a doctor, as I've said, in America."

"Where he played the Prince Charming role......"

"......except that he was happy enough to be just plain Doctor Mahidol, and felt far from exalted when by biological quirk he found himself heir presumptive to a childless half brother, the previous king having had just the one child, a daughter. An elevation to the throne, though, was not to happen for Dr Mahidol. He fell ill and he died before his eldest son, Nan, was even five."

"So mama was widowed....."

"......at the age of twenty nine," confirmed Jeremy.

"So no *happy ever after* for poor Cinders," remarked Eamon.

"Far from it," continued the lecturer. "And the next twist comes with the 1932 Promoters' revolution which abolished the absolute prerogatives of the Crown, this prompting Mama to take her three children to Switzerland. As Pridi and Pibul fell into argument over a the division of the spoils Chula's uncle, King Prajadhipok, could have rallied popular support and perhaps reasserted something of his former authority, but this he decided against, preferring to abdicate and choose a life of exile in this country, in Surrey. In '35, within days of the abdication, a telegram arrived in Switzerland. Ignoring the fact that that the half Russian Chula might have a better claim to the throne The Promoters were wanting the half Chinese Nan as their King."

"At the age of ten," Kate calculated, "a boy King....."

"......as their puppet, knowing that a vacant Kingship could be exploited by any faction, be it domestic or foreign, looking to enthrone its own candidate. For the best part of a year Mama and Nan hesitated, but then accepted, acknowledging that continued uncertainty would only jeopardise stability. Part of the deal, though, was that the boy should be allowed to continue with his Swiss schooling. A visit to his kingdom was organised in 1938, by which time Pibul had staged a military take-over, declared himself Prime Minister, and adopted the title of *National Hero Number One*."

"More than a hint there of hollow pomposity," smiled Busbridge.

"Which was quickly seen through, and a nation began to look again to its monarchy for a measure of guidance."

"From this child?"

"Supported as he was by Mama, who took the title of Her Royal

Highness the Princess Mother, and an uncle who was appointed Regent. On the king's return to Switzerland early in '39 Pibul launched a purge against the Royal Palace. The Regent himself was amongst those imprisoned on a charge of treason. But this merely compounded Pibul's sense of insecurity......"

".......by putting the hearts and the minds of the populace even more firmly with the King and his Mama," suggested Kate.

"That's so," confirmed Jeremy, "and while a few less lucky Royalists were executed she, just by wielding the threat of abdication from distant Europe, was able to secure a reprieve for the Regent."

"Then war breaks out," prompted Jim.

"And as Paris falls to the Nazis, Pibul heroically sends troops into French Laos and Cambodia. He now adds *Extensive Warrior* to that already overblown title, the new boundaries approximating to those of the legendary 'Greater Siam'."

"But the following year these are opened to the Japanese Army as it drives southward to Singapore and eastward against Burma," continued Busbridge. "And for Pibul's gains to last the bold Japanese gamble must succeed."

"And had it, then this expanded Thailand's future could only have been that of a Quisling province," said Jeremy.

"But it didn't succeed," said Eamon.

"It didn't" repeated Jeremy. "The atom bombs drop. Hirohito throws in his hand, the Cold War looms and this, dear friends, is where things get truly interesting....... for even today the long east-west stand-off is still not at an end, and much of the truth about forty years ago Thailand remains hidden."

"Concerning the Monarchy, you mean," said Kate.

"Concerning the Monarchy and how it figured in the plans of rival power brokers, both at home and abroad."

"So abroad," followed Busbridge, "you have the victors, Washington, London, and Moscow....... each with its own agenda."

"While in Thailand the main figures are still Pibul and Pridi," continued Jeremy, "and of course, with the defeat of the Japanese, their Quisling......"

".......Pibul, National Hero Number One......"

"...... is obliged to slink away from centre stage. This is left to Pridi who during the war had been active with the Free Thai movement, to the extent of being recruited by British Army Intelligence. Now he can enjoy his moment in the sun. Pibul is actually jailed for war crimes...... but do not yet write him of.."

"Not when new threats are perceived by those in the west who hoped to re assemble Sout East Asia according to their own needs and interests," nodded Busbridge. "Throughout the whole theatre, nationalist movements were moving to ensure that *former* colonies remained just that, finding ready encouragement from Moscow......and with the Free Thai, like the *so called* Free French, perhaps prone to communist infiltration it was wondered if Pridi was the man for the task of holding down Bangkok."

"Or might Pibul still be the better bet," posed Jeremy, "despite the taint of collaboration with the defeated Japs? A Thai Darlan, you could say, spared the assassin's bullet on account of Pridi falling critically short of being his country's de Gaulle."

"Cut a deal with the man and the guns are in place," agreed Busbridge, "plus you gain access to his intelligence files."

"And as further bonus," continued Jeremy, "you might take home a covert stake in the lucrative poppy yield of those remote northern provinces. With this in mind we can start to understand how Pibul's former standing amongst the occupying Japanese troops came, perversely, to aid a rapid rehabilitation. We are led to believe that, with surrender, all were stripped of their weapons and sent home to assemble cheap trannies and motorcycles. In fact, many were kept in uniform and, placed under allied command, continued to police vast tracts of Indo China, the territory they'd officially relinquished. Alive to the general drift of things Pridi decided to free Pibul, in the hope that his own position might be strengthened were they to find a way of working together."

"And the Monarchy, Jeremy, it did survive all this?" Kate was wondering how.

"*Barely* is the answer to that. A suggestion that Mama and the boys, the King still just twenty, should make a short visit to Bangkok late in '45 was taken up, and while it had been their understanding that they would be able to return to the safety of Swiss home before the end of the next month......"

".........this was to prove mistaken," guessed Eamon.

"Because they were drawn into the rival political intrigues. Fears that Pridi was pro Red gained currency, and what trust remained in him at the Palace suffered with his insistence that he might appoint a new Regent on Anand's departure."

"So the three of them stayed," said Jim.

"And how did it sort?" asked Kate.

"For the family...... disastrously. On an early June morning in 1946 the young King was found dead, on his Palace bed, shot once through the head. His pistol lay nearby."

"So suicide," offered Kate, "or an accident."

"If by his own hand, then maybe. There have been suggestions, though that others might have been involved...... a range of suggestions, a range of others."

"Murder theories," said Busbridge, "wonderful stuff."

"With some more plausible than others," cautioned Jeremy, "the least so being offered by Louis Mountbatten. In a letter to George VI, he is supposed to have named Mama and younger brother Lek as the perpetrators."

"Because Lek inherited the Crown?" said Eamon.

"He did, beneath which he survives to this day as King Bhumibol...... but rarely in modern times can so seemingly poisonous a chalice have been passed. Pibul's supporters took the opportunity accuse Pridi and the Communists, and as the champion of the Free Thais wilted beneath the whispers, others saw in all this a conspiracy to advance a return for National Hero Number One."

"For this is what happens," said Jim.

"It does," confirmed Jeremy. "Lek, then a teenager, takes the Crown, albeit back to Switzerland. Pibul makes a comeback. And Pridi is finished."

"And Mama," wondered Kate, "she went back to Europe too, with her surviving son?"

"She did, and another abdication announcement was widely predicted."

"But we know this didn't happen," said Eamon.

"It didn't, and the story is that in the face of his mother's grief and despair this disaster endowed young Lek with a determination to rise to the task left to him. He studied on for four years, listening to advice, surviving a car crash, and finding himself a suitable future Queen..... she a daughter of his Ambassador in Paris."

"Then returned for good," said Kate.

"Or ill," added Eamon.

"Yes, for the world had moved on," said Busbridge. "Burma and India were now independent nations. Mao had become the main man in China, and his troops were about to square up to the Yanks and the Brits in Korea. And close by, of course, at an astonishing expense of blood and treasure the French were clinging desperately to Vietnam."

"And if anything was certain it was that the Thai people would still respond to majesty," continued Jeremy. "So it was with due spectacular ceremony that in 1950 Lek brought his betrothed to Bangkok for the rites that would confirm his intent..... the cremation of what remained of his brother, a Coronation, and a Royal wedding. His subjects were enthralled, and sensing this the King was sufficiently emboldened to actually resist Pibul's demands for even greater power."

"The people were looking to be protected," said Busbridge. "Their totalitarian tin-pot was going too far."

"Imagine for yourselves a Central American Republic," concluded Jeremy as they approached the *Borough Arms*, "with the Church as a balance to the military. For Thailand you take away the Catholic Primate, and insert instead a Buddhist King. Now what about this Tania..... before we run out of time."

"Might be a little too public in here," cautioned Eamon, disquieted as he'd been by Jeremy's news of that bombing in London. But the others were not to know why, of course, and his edginess at merely having to leave the cover the woods and cross a busy highway went unnoticed. James Busbridge, though was hanging on his reaction.

"Well why not all come up to my place now? I can get the kettle on, and there's some cheese in the fridge."

"And I'll get some crisps from in here," said Kate. And this she did as Jeremy, having eased his car from its space, tidied the spread of documents on the rear seats.

To Jasmine Cottage in the vehicle was but barely five minutes, and soon the four were settled around their host's kitchen table, sipping and nibbling, and hearing his account of the intriguing Tania. And in many ways it was a tale to match and even complement that of Mama Mahidol......the doomed Tsardom, and the business of survival in the face of relentless political change.

Tania, they were told, had been a foundling, rescued as an infant from a pile of dead and dying cholera victims by one Elizabeth Gaubert.

At the time serving in the Tsarina's corps of nurses, she was a member of a long established business family whose fortune was ultimately forfeit to the victorious Bolsheviks. Then, with a significant British strain in the Gaubert ancestry opening the possibility of Elizabeth bringing Tania to this country it seemed to suit all that a rumour be fostered that Tania was an Anastasia style survivor of the purged Russian aristocracy. When they arrived in Britain in the '30s the claim offered a useful entrée into circles peopled by such as Chula, this making her a valuable asset to the KGB for whom it is now known she had been persuaded to work.

"On such pragmatism does the survivor survive," remarked Jeremy. "So you think she would have been tracking Prince Chula during the turbulent '40s, on behalf of Moscow."

"Through a friendship fostered mainly with Bira, his cousin," explained Jim.

"The racing driver."

"Who came to Cornwall at the start of the war, the cousins renting a house at Rock. Lynam House it's called, a subtantial property that must be worth hundreds of thousands at today's prices. Tredethy was purchased by Chula shortly after VJ Day. The gathering on its lawn captured by camera for our benefit today...... that would have had to wait until the following year."

"By camera," repeated Kate. "You've seen a photograph?"

As their host readily divulged what he could remember of the picture's history and composition, Kate suggested they make a sketch. Busbridge fetched paper and, finding a pencil, outlined thereon the garden bench.

"Three on the bench, all female," continued the nurse, "and three males standing behind." Jim had passed the pencil. She inserted and labelled matchstick figures. "Prince Chula to our left, a tallish guy in the middle, and a young Prince Philip here, over to the right ....."

".....with a hand that rests on the shoulder of the lady in front of him," pointed Eamon, "she an A, possibly an Anna."

"And with her on the seat, you say, is the Princess Marina," said Kate.

"Yes, at the other end, between them being a third woman, T, maybe a Tania," added Busbridge. And there they were;

Pr Chula   ?   Pr Philip
Pr Marina T(ania) A(nna)

"So it was just the six, Jim" checked Jeremy.

"Stiil pictured, yes."

"Still pictured," repeated Kate. "What's that meant to mean?"

"We think the photo might have been altered," explained Busbridge.

"To what extent?"

"Two names eradicated on the back, suggesting two clipped away, one from each edge."

"A concealment then," said Jeremy, and the man was hooked. "Any guesses?"

"The group was thought to have been snapped early in '46," offered Busbridge. "The alterations, though, they might have been made in the '60s."

"And your grounds?"

"Country house, maybe even a Russian agent."

"Aha," Jeremy snapped his fingers, "63, Profumo….. I like it."

"But I wouldn't say we can enter his name just on the strength of that," chided Kate. "For the moment I'll just add an extra double question mark to each flank, any original presence being doubly questionable."

?? Pr Chula   ?   Pr Philip ??
Pr Marina   T(ania)   A(nna)

"So where to now?" she asked. To Edward Trembath, thought Jeremy, preferring for the moment to hear what the others might suggest.

"The question marked tall fella," obliged Eamon. "Perhaps he originally owned the picture, hence the lack of an initial or anything else. He wouldn't have needed to remind himself of his own presence."

"Good point," acknowledged Kate. "How did you say it had been acquired, Jim?"

"With the belongings of one Foy Quiller Couch. She was to take a bed there, but, in the event, never turned up, so dire had been her deterioration. What wasn't passed across to St Lawrence went back to her people, save for that picture. It had found its proper home, it was felt, and with the permission of the owner, at Tredethy it stayed."

"The owner of the House or of the photo?" asked Kate, having already jotted 'Q Couch'.

"Of the photo, I meant," said James. "It was the property of a friend of hers, the writer Daphne du Maurier."

'Daphne DM' pencilled Kate. "And she is still alive?"

"Old and also frail of mind," said their host...... while Jeremy rose from his chair, his eyes, though, staying with the sketch.

"Take me to your bookshelves, Jim," said the historian. "Sometimes it has to be the tedious process of elimination. The sooner we start......"

Busbridge stood. Could it really be that Daphne's work might hold the kind of key provided before by Waugh and by Shute? He did have a copy of *Vanishing Cornwall*, he remembered, but his paperback edition of *The House on the Strand* had been donated to the hospital's League of Friends library. He'd hung on, though, to a collection of short stories titled *The Breaking Point*, sensibly judging this a little too rich in the macabre and indelicate for the likely readership. He ushered Jeremy through to the living room shelves, only to be called back almost immediately by Eamon.

Drawing up outside was a car...... to the cabby, a familiar one. Out the two occupants climbed, and yes, they had to be calling here. Through the gate they came and, with the knock, Jim was there at the door to greet his visitors.

"Tony, and young Chas, what a pleasant surprise. Do come in and join our party." Crosses senior and junior followed into the kitchen. "No introductions needed with these two, and Jeremy is just scanning my bookshelves." Eamon and Kate bounced to their feet. A round of handshakes and kisses ensued. "You should have phoned," added the host. "To have come so far just on the chance....."

"In normal circumstances yes, certainly," the professional diver was grave, "but suddenly Im once again having to be wary of listeners."

"Something's happened?" Eamon wondered if it was he that had prompted a renewed surveillance, a result maybe of a bomb squad investigation into Kellegher's activities. His own departure from London could have been noted, and an arrival somewhere at this end of the country perhaps guessed at. But only guessed at....... paranoia was to be resisted.

"It might be nothing of consequence." Chas was almost apologetic.

"But you can't yet dismiss it as such," Eamon said. The boy nodded. He would explain.

"Following all that business in the summer to do with the gold and the *Surcouf* and the rest, we sense this to be a kind of after-tremor. You might recall Peg Willis's boat....."

"......kept in that yard on the Lynher," remembered Busbridge, "just down from McDaid's cottage."

"Well it had been offered to us, Sally and me that is, to work on, and be made seaworthy again so that it could be put to use."

"Not that it was a wreck," joined the father, "for Declan had checked any serious rot."

"But the offer was accepted, and we'd actually started," continued Chas, "giving it the odd afternoon of the occasional weekend. I suppose we hadn't done a lot, not yet......."

"Hadn't?" queried Kate. "A second use of that tense hints at a change of plan."

"A forced change," acknowledged Tony Cross.

"Because last night the thing went up in flames," explained Chas. "McDaid phoned us early today. We drove across, only to be shown a few charred ribs smouldering amongst a pile of ash. We left Declan with the task of informing Peg by phone......"

"...... and came on here," said Jeremy, who'd re-entered the kitchen, a book in hand. "Good to see the pair of you. That's sad news you bring, be it just misfortune or whatever else."

"Foul play, you mean?" wondered Eamon.

"What do we know about Peg's cabin cruiser?" asked the lecturer.

"That he actually arrived in it," said Chas, "having found work with the Earl of St Germans, at Port Eliot."

"Arriving from a previous position where?"

"He'd worked at Menabilly, near Fowey," remembered Tony Cross. "As a former Para he'd been taken on by his old Commander, the General who'd been married to the writer woman, that Daphne du Maurier. That had been where they lived, but the General died and with her lease expiring the widow had to move out."

"Not far though," said Kate, "only to Kilmarth, a dower house on the edge of the estate."

"But Peg had to go," continued Cross senior, "and this small cabin cruiser, previously the General's, was made part of the pay-off."

"And that photo we've seen today," said Eamon, with obvious unease, "at one time it probably hung in the big house, and maybe afterwards at......at where was it?"

"......at Kilmarth," said Kate.

"And no one's heard of that burning down?" Chas half joked.

"That was *Manderley*," replied the nurse lightly.

"Jim, Eamon, let me show you this." Jeremy entered, opening a book pulled from the host's shelves. A hard back with dust jacket still, this was no novel.

"*A Bridge too Far*," confirmed Busbridge. "Cornelius Ryan's examination of the Arnhem fiasco...... and I think I know where we're heading. He'll be in the first batch of photos."

Jeremy duly turned to the plates, and found his man. The book was placed on the table, opened. James Busbridge merely nodded, it was Eamon who spoke.

"That is him, yes, the tall guy. Not bad Jeremy.....not bad at all. Kate, the name Lieutenant General Frederick Browning can be added to your sketch there, the man in the middle at the back. This said, he'd probably been promoted a rank or two by the time he came to be snapped at Tredethy with Prince Chula and friends. So what do we learn of him in there Jim?"

Busbridge lifted the book, holding it open so all could see the dust jacket picture, in fact a painting which showed an approach ramp to a large girder bridge, the road thereon being littered shell smashed vehicles.

"This is Arnhem in Holland, September 1944, and the bridge there over the Lower Rhine, the capture of which was the ambitious aim of the 1st British Airborne Corps...... in the event, too ambitious. The bid failed, ending any chance of forcing a way to Berlin before the end of that year."

"The bridge too far," said Tony Cross.

"And, according to Ryan, it had been assessed as such by Browning during the planning stage, using those very words. That was how he expressed his misgivings to Montgomery, whose brainchild the operation had been."

"But they were ignored," said Jeremy, "so Browning might have resigned, not wanting to be part of the adventure."

"He didn't, though," continued Busbridge. "For *Tommy* Browning as he was popularly known simply wasn't that sort of bloke. He wanted to stay with the guys he'd trained and previously, in Normandy, led to considerable success."

"An honourable man," said Jeremy.

"Neither weak nor reckless, although somehow he has come to be portrayed as such in the recently made film, an epic style adaptation of this book...... and why?" James Busbridge shrugged.

"To sell tickets," said Chas, remembering from the summer Nolwen's resentment at film makers' licence. "An audience wants heroes. Heroes need villains, plus the odd fool or scapegoat."

"And, understandably, Daphne was outraged," said Busbridge, "to the extent of going public with her indignation. Her Tommy had been almost twenty years dead. How could he answer back, she railed."

"But she will have done well enough out of the movie business over the years," said Cross senior. "Anyone seen *'Don't Look Now'*? Julie Christie, phworrr ...... bloody good, I can tell you that."

"So back when he was pictured at Tredethy," tutted Kate, "what would Browning have been doing by then?"

The host's finger dropped on to Kate's sketch.

"There is a Royal connection," he said, "and by no means a loose one. In the late '40s, around when Princess Elizabeth, heir to the throne, married her Philip, Browning was appointed Comptroller of their household, tasked, I guess with making sure their proper expenses were met, and that their staff were of sufficient number, and ability...... "

".......and discretion," added Eamon.

"I think the couple started at Clarence House, later moving, on accession, to Buckingham Palace...... with them, of course, the two young children, Charles and Anne. A swop was thus effected with the Queen Mother. Browning's office going to the Palace also."

Having already labelled her tall figure Tom B, Kate added 'Palace' to the name.

"So could it be that Daphne herself air brushed that picture?" she asked.

"Unlikely," said Jeremy. "I mean for what reason?"

"I agree," joined Busbridge. "She tended to keep well clear of the Court scene, and when busy writing in Cornwall she made plain to her husband that she found his presence intrusive."

"And isn't there that story of her developing a crush on Gertrude Lawrence?" asked Kate. "That would have been around 1950."

"More than once she crossed the Atlantic to be with Gertie," confirmed Busbridge, "allowing Tommy to bring girlfriends of his own down to Troy Town. It's a small place is Fowey. Rumour abounds to this day."

"So maybe those blobs obscure the identity of a brace from that little coterie," ventured Eamon.

"Except that this would make a group of two men with five women," said Chas. "I suppose the photographer might have been male, but that still leaves an imbalance."

"And we might ask why a widow should have entrusted anything so embarrassing to a friend," said Jeremy. "For her it would have made better sense to bin the thing......"

"........ unless what we have here is a hidden tale that is something more than merely a trifle saucy," concluded Eamon. Was this his moment to come clean, about Kellegher and Conlon at least? Something in his tone had caused the others to turn, and with this response the decision was made. He drew a deep breath........ and began. "Two pieces of news I've heard this morning, of a double murder in a London pub, from Jeremy, and of an arson attack on the boat by the Lynher River, this from you Tony and you Chas. Random events, you will be thinking, the targets so different and so far apart, even while occurring over the same night."

"But you suspect otherwise?" prompted Chas.

"I fear otherwise," said Eamon. "I fear there is a link, and I fear that link to be myself. Jeremy, the Cricklewood pub, *The Duke of Connaught* .... the night before last I was in that very place and taking instructions from what I'm sure we'll find to be the same pair that's just been blown to the hereafter. Known to me as Kellegher and Conlon, they'd come by this."

From a jacket pocket Eamon produced their cassette, placing it beside Kate's sketch.

"So a recording," said Chas.

"Of a radio programme, that's all," explained Eamon, "an edition of *Desert Island Discs*, the eight pieces here having been selected by crafty old Lord Justice Denning, each selection reflecting an aspect of his life, or even an episode in his career. Most are self explanatory, and where not he'll expand appropriately, save that is in the final choice...... and it has been put to me that this was directed at those who might have been complicit in the Profumo scandal and yet escaped public censure, largely as a result of the Judge's economy with ink when writing up his official report into the business."

"And that final tune?" Kate sat ready to write.

"Is from *The King and I*, " revealed Eamon.

"And from this," joined Busbridge, "there is divined a Royal dimension along which one is invited to scrutinise both the London and Bangkok based monarchies......"

"....... for post war shenanigans," added the Irishman.

"Let's just say 'irregularities'," said Jim.

"And we dosed well on these back there on the Wenford line," said Jeremy.

"Where it sounded as if any note on Thailand would probably be best left to you," said Kate, offering the pencil.

"Later," waved the lecturer. "So what does this other news from St Erney tell you, Eamon?"

"That those who did for Kellegher and Conlon are perhaps nervous about what our 'Tommy', the late General Frederick Browning, could have been sitting on. What looks to have been eradicated on the print at Tredethy might yet remain in a set of concealed negatives....."

"...... as an insurance policy?" wondered Tony Cross.

"Possibly, and if they're yet to be located......"

"...... then the next best thing might be to destroy any possible hiding places," said Chas, "though I can't recall seeing any document folder or wallet the vessel's cabin."

"But you hadn't yet delved behind the panelling, or beneath the deck planking," said his father.

"Peg might have, though."

"Yes, and we can be assured that his property will have been well sifted over these past couple of years," said Jeremy.

"Might he not be asked?" wondered Kate.

"Not from this distance," said Eamon.

"So this wariness of the post and the phones," probed Jeremy, "would it not indicate wariness of a Government security agency, rather than any outlawed nationalist outfit?"

"As well as," corrected Carroll. "At this stage, I'm ruling nothing out."

"Wise enough," conceded the lecturer tactfully, at the same time sensing an evasiveness in the cabby "I guess those assumptions fed out on the radio news were too easy to swallow."

"But what we can conclude, Eamon, is that you have an adversary," said Busbridge, "and that of whatever colour, and however well informed and dangerously active, it too could have erred with an initial assumption. Rather than that trek of ours up to Tredethy, a different course would appear to have been anticipated. It seems we were expected, somehow, to have been more quickly on to Browning....."

" .... and that rather than the Camel valley northward you would have chosen to follow the seaward flow of the River Fowey," said Jeremy, "with your enquiries then leading you on to the Lynher."

"So what on that tape might instead have sign posted you southward?" asked Tony Cross. "From *The King and I* to the Brownings looks an improbable leap."

"But there might be a connection," ventured Kate, "and it would go back to around the time of that photo, when the musical first came out as a stage show, on Broadway. We were speaking just now of Gertrude Lawrence who I think starred as Anna and ...."

The pencilled *A(nna?)* was there in front of them. Kate tapped at it, looking hopefully towards Busbridge....... only to draw a shake of his head.

"A good stab though Kate," he said, "for Gertrude Lawrence certainly mixed with the sort entertained by the Thais at Rock and Tredethy, the likes of Noel Coward for instance, and she might well have been caught by camera, but not alas for this particular photo. I would have recognised Gertie straight away. But I won't yet dismiss her as an irrelevance, for prior to wowing Broadway in *The King and I* she took the lead role in West End production of one of Daphne's plays."

"So that would have been when?" asked Jeremy.

"Late 1940s, not far off when that photo was taken."

"But *The King and I*," persisted Kate. "After the New York triumph it would have been brought to London, where Gertie was set, surely, to be received with even greater fervour, she being English after all."

"The posters were being designed and programmes printed on this assumption," explained Busbridge, "but then Gertrude, always so vivacious, was to suddenly sicken, and within a month of a collapse in her Broadway dressing room she was dead."

"So another Anna then had to be found for the London stage," said

Jeremy.

"Yes, and I forget, now, who that was," shrugged Jim.

'*But NOT Gert*' wrote Kate beneath her matchstick Anna, as if to sign off that topic and invite another.

"They were expecting me to be sharper than I actually was," obliged a pre occupied Eamon who hadn't so much as quarter listened to those inconclusive runinations of the others. "That's why they torched the boat, but in doing so they've alerted us to their pursuit......."

"...... and drawn our attention to Tommy Browning's presence in the frame," said Busbridge. "Not too clever, unless a deliberate scare tactic. But we're made of sterner stuff, aren't we Eamon?"

"I suppose we are," agreed Carroll, wondering where he might have left to run.

"So I guess, now, that there'll be little point in us sniffing around Kilmarth or Menabilly," sighed Tony Cross.

Although I do know that Browning owned a succession of yachts," ventured Busbridge. "Perhaps one or two could still be afloat on the estuary."

"And we find the one containing a pack of monochrome negatives, hitherto unnoticed," scoffed Jeremy. "Come on....... the thing now has to be to move quickly."

"But in which direction?" Carroll was anxious. It would be his neck.

"For you, Eamon, *not* back to London," Kate assured him. "Is that caravan of yours still over at Rame?"

"It is, but having just yesterday changed my car I'm without a hitch. Monday, Tuesday....yes I can get one fitted....but."

"There's a guy I know at work. He'll fetch it with his Land Rover, tomorrow with any luck."

"And there's a site near here?"

"There is, but you want to be a decent distance from this place and mine. We can take you out towards St Minver. Plenty of sites that way. For tonight, a B&B in Bodmin should do."

"That's comforting, but when you say move quickly Jeremy... "

"I say we try Carwinion. We might find Sir Edward at home."

"And he will tell us what?" asked Kate.

"I'd like his take on Profumo. We all know what the man was up to in the 1960s, Trembath would have known him long before then."

"So we go now," checked Tony Cross, "and we just turn up on his doorstep?"

"Three will be enough. Kate and Eamon have accommodation to sort out, and Jim......"

"I have a letter to compose, for cousin Peter."

"So you, me and Chas," said Jeremy, "and yes, we'll just turn up. Why squander the value of surprise?"

*

London

"Ah......yes, our Mr Grigson. Do come in."

"Captain Daniels, you wanted a private chat."

"Do call me Colin. Are you happy still to be Alan?"

"If a task so requires then Alan I must remain. I guess there is one, for why else the summons?" A careful but firm closure of the door affords Grigson opportunity to glance around. "They've given you a larger office," he observes.

"And wider responsibilities," smiles the officer, "without any elevation in rank, or indeed any rise in pay."

"A timely vote of confidence nonetheless...... with our collaboration not having enjoyed the best of starts."

"But that Ince business did work out well in the end. Sir Clive Faulds was most impressed by your input. Do sit."

"I have talented friends."

"Talents, Alan, that were effectively marshalled." Daniels at last settles behind his desk.

"So tell me about these wider responsibilities," prompts Alan, with a professional's indifference to flattery.

"VIP protection still, again ultimately under the Home Office, but stretching now to Royalty."

"So a more permanent kind of personage than your average Cabinet Minister."

"Hopefully so, yes, but less predictable."

"This doesn't sound like our Monarch and Prince Consort."

"You're right Alan, but that's Buckingham Palace. I've been allocated Kensington."

"Kensington Palace...... now would that be the Princess Margaret?"

"In one apartment, yes, with Prince Michael of Kent as a neighbour, and the Waleses occupying another wing."

"Three tenants for whom media scrutiny tends to the less reverential."

"Exactly," confirms the officer, taking a graver tone. "And it is from my concern that media interest will sometimes be *courted* by these lesser lights that I feel that you and your friends might be of further use."

"In a trouble shooting capacity, you mean."

"Damage limitation," nods Daniels.

"Starting when, and continuing for how long?"

"Starting now, Alan, to hopefully have things suitably tidied within three weeks."

"How do you mean, 'tidied'?"

"We're after a fuller understanding of certain risks being run," says Daniels, "so as to be better equipped to confront and dissuade those whose conduct could well draw calamity upon themselves, as well as their targeted others."

"So you want a more exact assessment of the potential mischief......"

"......and a more positive identification of those involved in the making thereof."

"But you do have your suspicions."

"Strong suspicions, and hence this three week window of possible opportunity. Only Margaret will be at home."

"The others......?"

"Out *in* the country, out *of* the country......"

"...... as prescribed by the court diary. So on their return you'll be looking to confront them with whatever follies you might have uncovered."

"As well as the projected consequences thereof," Daniels adds "Should strong advice be warranted then those offering such will need to be appropriately armed."

"And you think I'm the man for the job. The armourer, as it were."

"Largely because we're hearing that one of your pals might be enjoying a head start on us."

"One of my pals? Enlighten me, do."

"I speak of that Mr Carroll."

"Eamon......mixing with Royalty!"

"Not exactly, Alan. As you know, we have informants in the IRA command structure and......."

"...yes, I can imagine the ripples spreading still through the movement, that HIGHLAND CLEARANCE matter having caused a fair splash."

"But amongst some these are ripples of discontent. The insights won were squandered, some claim, and looking to prove their point they've seized on what they reckon as an opportunity to show how things might have been done better."

"And this was where contact was made with Eamon....."

"...... with a view to finding a way of recruiting those earlier mentioned talents."

"So they're on to another can of worms, one being prised open over there in Kensington Palace, and they hope it can be fashioned into a political lever."

"*Were* hoping, Alan, for at least two of the ringleaders have met a rather sticky end, we think at the hands of the main movement."

"But Eamon, being a survivor......."

"......either by luck or by judgement, yes, he survives. And he goes to ground. We could root him out, I suppose, but for the moment we feel that if watched he could, in desperation, do for us what those now shredded renegades had been hoping he might do for them."

"Mobilise our westcountry sleuths, is this what you mean Captain Daniels? You don't think, then, that he had a hand in liquidating those looking to co-opt him into their initiative."

"One wouldn't, at this stage, discount anything. But this said, I simply don't see in our Mr Carroll the cold cutting edge that Commander in Chief McBeamish would normally seek in his pruning shears. I'll venture that on hearing of those executions, Eamon will have felt almost as forsaken as he did when thrown into that tunnel down at Ince......"

".......and just see what that led to."

"Exactly, Alan, but bear in mind that rather than a world order, this time it's only the House of Windsor that we're wanting to save."

"In just three weeks, eh? Thanks."

*

Carwinion House

"I must say, Mr Barnes, that I wasn't expecting to see you again quite so soon." Sir Edward led his three unexpected guests through to his main reception room. "You find me alone at the moment. My son Hugh is just fetching his daughter back from Truro. I don't think you've yet met our Helen."

"So we're doubly lucky, it seems," said Jeremy. "Remind me again what she does."

"She's been taken on as a production assistant by a small but flourishing film company. Shepperton based, they specialise in the made-for-television documentary."

"So she lives where?"

"She uses my old flat in Belgravia, travelling out through the suburbs only when she needs to. Much of her work she'll do in the central libraries and museums. There's room up there for me when I need to be in London, but this is getting less often now."

"Quieter for you here, of course," joined Tony Cross, as his son glanced swiftly around the room, hoping for a recent photo that might prepare him for the coming encounter. There was none though.

"And the XR3 out there," ventured Chas, "that would be hers?"

"It is," confirmed the grandfather, as if a shiny red soft- top was sufficient in itself to command deference. *You needn't bother lad, she's way too good for you.......* that was the implication. "And you live in Plymouth eh?" Further disparagement was felt, and the grandson of an Admiral might have reacted sharply, save for a confident intervention from Jeremy, the old acquaintance who would always have the measure of the former MP.

"Tony and Chas have been fully briefed on your long association with the City of Plymouth, Sir Edward. In fact Mr Cross grew up amongst the rubble that you did so much to help clear."

"Yes, Mr Barnes, so must I take it that you bring another enquiry? Is this more on Lennox Boyd that you're wanting to know, or on Alan Clark perhaps?"

"Not for the moment. You primed us very well on that one and things were largely resolved. Now our attention shifts to another personality, one whose contribution to post-war Conservatism proved rather more colourful."

"The more colourful, the more inconsequential....... that's been the general rule, but do go on."

"What we would like to know, Sir Edward, is a little more than just the usual on Jack Profumo."

"He is still alive, of course, so you're best taking a little extra care on that score alone...... and he could last a while yet. He and Valerie, his wife, have a place in Belgravia, not far from mine, though far grander of course. But then, going back, he came in to Parliament at a relatively young age."

"And one could say much the same about his departure," added Tony Cross.

"But again, to the beginning," insisted Jeremy. "In some books we will read of his first being elected to Parliament in 1950......"

"....... as the member for Stratford upon Avon," agreed Trembath, "and this might be true enough, even though he'd represented the electors of Kettering between 1940 and '45, they having lost their Conservative Member early in the war. We must remember that by elections didn't happen for most of the duration so it's not unlikely that Profumo was in fact co-opted on the recommendation of Central Office...... and this could make it all the more remarkable that within just weeks, following the Norway debate, he sided with the clique which voted against Prime Minister Chamberlain."

"In the long term, an astute decision," said Jeremy.

"As it turned out," allowed Trembath. "But there was much bitterness at the time. The whips were apoplectic."

"But such bravado was obviously appreciated by the champions of Churchill....... the coming men, Eden and Macmillan, under whom his career later did prosper."

"And he had a good war, did our Jack. He soldiered with distinction in North Africa, rising steadily through the ranks and establishing himself as a key member of a winning team."

"And did he stand in the '45 election?"

"I'm not sure," answered Trembath. "He certainly wasn't elected, but whether this was through a defeat or on simply standing down, I can't say. What's certain is what you said, that he was elected in 1950."

"And during the interim?" asked Tony Cross.

"The mix of army and politics continued......"

"....... without the constituency responsibilities," Jeremy added.

"He had a role at Central Office, I remember...... Director of Verbal Propaganda, or some such grandiose title. This was as they were starting to seriously consider me as a prospective candidate."

"Sounds almost Orwellian," said Chas. "And there was army work, you said. Where did this take him..... abroad, to Palestine maybe, or to India?"

A Land Rover swung across the gravelled turning area outside their window, taking the attention of all.

"Ah....... here's Hugh now," said Sir Edward, leaving the boy's question to dangle. The lad had stopped listening anyway, for his eyes were on the passenger who was out of the vehicle now and breezing towards the entrance, her rich chestnut hair gleaming under the autumn sun. The woollen jumper, the corduroy slacks, the light yet sturdy lace-up leather shoes, all combined to declare a county quality, a style carried comfortably by a neat and active figure.

Chas approved. OK, their shabby Volvo might have drawn the briefest glance of distaste, but as she entered the room the face was again attractively bright and eager. If it was her grandfather's pleasure to entertain these strangers then it could be hers also.

With the father, though, the naturally sauntered entrance had faltered. He'd recognised Jeremy, and was now ruffled.

"Mr Barnes....... again. We thought you'd had done with this quiet corner of Cornwall. Someone said you'd moved to Bath."

"I will still visit occasionally, and of course I'm ever mindful what a fund of information your father can be."

"So you were taking a chance on him being here....."

"...... and yes, we've struck lucky."

"So am I to take it that coin is not an issue, and your companions have not been brought for enforcement purposes."

"For my protection, perhaps, should that have been necessary," countered Jeremy, "but I'm pleased to say that I feel safer here today than I've ever done. Meet Tony and Chas Cross, father and son, both expert divers, Plymouth based. Chas also works in the Naval Dockyard."

"Hugh Trembath, and my daughter Helen." Tepid handshakes ensued, eye contact tellingly sporadic......save between Chas and Helen, neither seeking to endorse the coolness that prevailed amongst the more adult.

"Nice motor you have out there," smiled the boy. "No messin' at the lights eh?"

"I'll show you. Follow me."

"Twenty minutes," said Hugh uncomfortaly as they slipped past him and through the door.

"Now," resumed Jeremy, "we were discussing Jack Profumo."

"Were you indeed!" said Hugh. "I think I can say with confidence that my father's hands are clean on that one."

"His early career," added the lecturer, tactfully. "It has been put to us that before he married he was an occasional escort of the widowed Duchess of Kent, and we were wondering if this could be discounted as idle gossip......."

"....... or, alternatively, confirmed to have more substance," said Hugh, "knowing how closely my father worked with old Walter Monckton, he who knew the Windsors like the back of his hand. So father...... what's the memory like on Court gossip?"

"During the late '40s and early '50s she was seen out with several, a number of them stars of stage and screen. And yes, for a while I'm pretty sure that Jack was in there with them too. That said, he married sometime around the Coronation, so we must suppose that with Marina at least his availability for such duties suffered severe restriction. Move on a further ten years and one can of course associate Profumo with Stephen Ward, a fellow who'd cultivated his own connections with Royalty, in his capacity as a portrait artist and osteopath......"

"........ and also as a long time member of that jolly band of *bon viveurs* known as the Thursday Club," added Jeremy. "Prominent among them the Milford Havens, their cousin Lord Louis, and young nephew Philip. We can imagine Lord Justice Denning having a few questions for that crew........ not that too much was going to be allowed to come out in the wash. What kind of opinion did Walter have of Mountbatten?"

"Walter was very careful with his opinions, seeking always to stay on the best terms with all....... but having been an adviser to David Windsor and to the Nizam of Hyderabad, and later a Minister of Defence, the man was well placed to come to a private judgement."

"Which you suspect to have been far from complimentary."

"In the navy he was remembered as being a dangerous man to serve under," offered Hugh. "He was said to have been as reckless with the lives and the reputations of others as he was careful in the preening of his own."

"And yet he rose and he rose," said Tony Cross. "When the IRA blew him up it was State Funeral, the lot."

"So was there anyone else you think we might perhaps help you with?" If Hugh sounded impatient Jeremy had the counter.

"Well while we're waiting for your daughter to return Tony's son we could perhaps bring an enquiry that's little closer to this wonderful home of yours. Tell us what you know of Chula Chakabrongse, the half-Thai, half-Russian Prince who, I believe, settled in Cornwall after the war."

"He did," confirmed Sir Edward, "up at Tredethy Manor, on the Camel, just past Pencarrow."

"He and his cousin, Prince Bira, made names for themselves in motor sport," joined Hugh. "Bira was the driver, and quite a talent too. Chula managed the team. *White Mouse* they called it."

"Interesting name," remarked Tony, "for wasn't it said of an ancient King of Siam that to those of his subjects that he wished to ruin he would make the gift of a White Elephant?"

"Which according to custom wasn't to be put to work," said Sir Edward. "The Princes came to Cornwall at the start of the war, taking a house over at Rock. Each contributed to the war effort, Bira initially as a radio technician on one of the airfields, and then a gliding instructor. Chula bought Tredethy after the war and stayed. He was to die at a relatively young age. Throat cancer, too many fags I suppose. He enjoyed Tredethy though, inviting many a friend down to stay."

And well might he have enjoyed Tredethy, thought Jeremy, who could not but reflect on the tragic events that engulfed Mama Mahidol and her two sons in far away Bangkok. But this, he sensed, was not the moment to broach those dark oriental machinations, and it was left to Tony Cross to advance the conversation with the very probe required.

"And what about that Walter character, would he also have had an opinion on this Prince Chula?" A natural question, and innocently posed….. so why now was Trembath so hesitant? The answer he *could* give wanted for a touch of editing; that was why. Sir Edward, the prey, glanced warily at Jeremy……. he, the predator, returning the scrutiny eye to eye.

An opinion had been passed from Sir Walter to Edward Trembath, Jeremy was sure, but it wasn't one to be shared today……or ever if it could be helped. But he needn't press. There was a little homework to be done on this one, and he could always return. He made a mental note; *Monckton/Mountbatten/Chula*....... enough, for the moment, to take away and consider at leisure.

The conversation stalled slightly, and Hugh, sensing his father's discomfort, took the opportunity to move on to matters maritime...... and for this, Tony Cross was a gift. The diver was more than happy to be quizzed on his adventures around the British coast and beyond, and with the mention of the *Edinburgh* the pair were looking set to fill the rest of the weekend.

And perhaps they might have, had it not been for Chas's father remembering that his boy had asked to be back in St John for six. There was a promised call to make on Sally who, on being told they were off to Tremorebridge had insisted she should be briefed immediately and fully on any outcome. Had Chas forgotten this, he wondered, in all the excitement of his spin with glamorous Helen? Just where might she have taken him in that car of hers? Cross senior checked his watch. They ought to be back, so they should at least be on their way.

In fact they were back, though not at Carwinion. They were parked just minutes away on the car park that served Trelissick Gardens....... a good place, Helen had thought, for a quiet chat. And naturally Chas was flattered, and of course he wouldn't mind meeting up again. She could have his number, he said, and he was more than happy to take hers.

"And that Jeremy, the lecturer," she continued. "How long have you and your father known him?"

"Only since the summer, since just after he went to your grandfather in London to ask after the late Lord Boyd."

"And he was helpful?"

"He certainly was. Sir Edward put him on to Alan Clark, a current Plymouth MP and also a Minister."

"And *he* had time for Jeremy?"

"He had time for me, Helen, as a constituent of course."

"With a genuine enquiry?"

"It was quite clever, but Jeremy can be like that."

"So I've heard. I think it was a couple of years ago that he first came to Carwinion. That was when he was lecturing in Camborne. Works up-country now, I'm told."

"Bath," confirmed Chas.

"So quite clever with Clark, you say....... how?"

"I had to make out I was a history student. I was looking at the way films can mould and even distort our perception of the past, the film *White Mischief* being a case in point. Clark put us on to his stepmother who in turn had this axe to grind over the portrayal her mother who'd been involved in the actual events the picture purported to record. It's a long story...... too long for now."

"Then perhaps we should get together again," smiled Helen, leaning provocatively across to open the glove pocket. "A card for you..... and a pen, so that in this you can write your number for me." A filofax organiser was slapped into his lap, and as Chas duly obliged she restarted the motor. "Interesting this," she continued, "being in the film business for real. *White Mischief* was wartime, I understand."

"And your work can touch on that?"

"Quite often...... feeding a steady market for the wartime documentary. There's plenty alive still who can give a first hand account. Did you ever see *The Bridge over The River Kwai?*"

"A difficult one not to see, so often is it put on the telly....... one of the first big budget war films."

"It has been proposed that we might do an hour long television piece on the story of how the real bridge was built and destroyed. The decision is yet to be made. I'm currently involved in assessing possibilities...... using models or locations, interviewing Brits who were there or even Japs."

"Then there's archive material, I suppose, and also clips you might want to use from that bloody film. Was there a book before the film?"

"There was, written by a Frenchman, himself a veteran of the Burma campaign."

"You say Burma..... but didn't the railway run through Thailand also?"

"Most of the railway did, and this is where the real river with the real bridge actually was..... in Thailand."

They were back at Carwinion now, where, politely escorted by their hosts, Jeremy and Tony Cross were already set to leave. Promising to be in touch, Chas thanked Helen, and was out and across to the Volvo before she was even properly parked. A cordial nod was exchanged with the father and the grandfather...... and that was enough. For while not, at least yet, wanting them to know, he fully expected to be back. And neither were *his* father and Jeremy needing to know. OK, she might have an angle on Thailand but, unless at her own express wish, it wasn't yet for him to open this to any wider discussion.

But as they journeyed back to Tremorebridge this wasn't to preclude his enquiring of them what they had gleaned within Carwinion House. Indeed, for the purpose of deflecting their curiosity this had to be the tactic, so easily and naturally could it be deployed.

"No," said Jeremy, "while Sir Edward was helpful enough on Profumo's antecedents, he was far from forthcoming on anything to do with the Thais. But this in itself was intriguing, for I was left with the impression that he knew far more than he was letting on. What did you think Tony?"

Cross considered. They'd cleared Truro, but driver's care was still needed as an approaching cortege turned across them into Penmount. As the road straightened and widened his answer came.

"A definite hesitancy. While ready enough to talk in general about that Walter and Mountbatten he suddenly clammed, and this on mention of Chula."

"As if there had been an issue between the three of them, Mountbatten, Chula, and Walter," nodded Jeremy, "which he was particularly reluctant to broach. An issue that probably flowed from Lord Louis' responsibilities in the far east."

"And events there that might have involved this Chula character?" ventured Chas.

"A possibility." Jeremy was cautious. Speculation was to be curbed. "What we do know, though, is that while the western allies stood firmly together to defeat Japan, success did bring tensions."

"Governments being at odds as to how best to police the liberated territories," joined Tony Cross, "many, of course, being former colonies......."

"......of the French and the Dutch, as well as the British, and throughout there beavered the agents of Moscow."

"....... scattering seeds of conflict to come in Malaya, Vietnam, and Indonesia."

"You have the picture," said the lecturer.

"And all this has relevance now?" queried Chas.

"HIGHLAND CLEARANCE did," Jeremy reminded him.

"Eamon is fairly sure of a link between the fate of his London associates and that boat of Peg's," said Tony Cross.

"But we're best looking for something more solid than Irish intuition," warned Jeremy. "Corrupted by fear, it can too readily sour to paranoia."

"So what about taking Mr Alan Grigson on board?" wondered Chas.

"You make a good team, Jeremy," his father added.

"Easier said than done," smirked Jeremy. "If he turns up then well and good, but don't ask me, or Kate, or Jim, or Eamon to just go out and find him. *Alan* he might be to us, but who's to say that's his real name? I bet he didn't leave either of you a contact number. He was in a jam, remember. That's how our last collaboration came about."

Philip with his 'Uncle Dickie'.

*

In London

And, contrived or not, Alan was well enough aware of the jam that had been. For the period of his suspension he'd felt, in professional terms, an absolute outcast, an experience he was reluctant to relive. Of course Eamon gave concern, but anything to be done for the guy now would have to be achieved strictly within the remit prescribed from above. It was a different sort of ask, requiring a different sort of response. This wasn't a matter to be unravelled at open-ended leisure. Instead, after due scrutiny, any volatile issue was to be neutralised as quickly and neatly as practicably possible so that the whole thing might be wrapped up, all within three weeks.

Those talents in Cornwall to which Eamon would naturally be turning to for succour, they might be there for his own use too, to be nurtured and channelled, and even exploited.......but this time from that arms length necessitated by a defined end and strict schedule. In this light, just for the moment, the cabby was probably best left to use them in his own way and thereby perhaps come to a truer personal understanding of his predicament. Busbridge he'll be contacting, for sure, who in turn would still be in touch with Kate and Cross & Son...... meaning plenty of assistance if required. So why, then, be in any hurry to follow, particularly as questions remained here in London?

Two rival theories were emerging within the intelligence agencies, together being so strongly touted as to exclude all else. While each held that the *Duke of Connaught* had been bombed by the IRA so as to cure the dissent gathering around Kellegher and Conlon they differed as to the role ascribed to Carroll. In one he is loyal to McBeamish and actually plants the bomb on behalf of the main movement; while in the other he is being persuaded to join the rebels, he knows nothing of the attack and only by good fortune does not share in their fate.

But the Eamon he knew would not have been playing it either way, Alan was convinced. As might be said for himself, the vindication sought and secured back in the summer at such risk was not to be so carelessly squandered. The routine scenarios built around this fresh incident were flawed, he felt, based as they'd been on the routine assumptions made about a character whose recent adventures had been far, far from ordinary.

Carroll had survived those adventures, yes, but that wasn't to say that he'd completely escaped the long shadow of HIGHLAND CLEARANCE, or indeed that he ever would. The thing had been so massive with so many a far-reaching consequence that even the most minor detail emerging now from the *Duke of Connaught* deserved the closest scrutiny.

Take this word from the Met's traffic division that one of the deceased, Conlon, had provided a witness statement on a motorcycle accident which claimed the life of a member of the VIP Protection Squad, an officer who not so long before had been attached to the Royal Family. There'd been a Royal dimension to HIGHLAND CLEARANCE, of course, so perhaps there was something to be gleaned in this direction. If, as he'd heard, that officer's Royal posting had been at Kensington Palace then there was a particular contact who could well prove useful, both in building a fund of information *and* in filtering measured quantities of the same down to the likes of Kate and her re-found *amour*, Mr Jeremy Barnes.

It was time to arrange a meeting with Gareth, the patched veteran of Bluff Cove first befriended on the banks of the Fal more than two years ago now. They'd kept contact since, occasional rather than frequent, and having not spoken since Easter there was now plenty that might be discussed.

*

Later, near Torpoint

"And who should be there with Jim Busbridge, Sally, but Kate and Jeremy."

"Together?"

"Together, yes, and also Eamon Carroll."

"From London?"

"He'd driven down late yesterday evening and stayed with Jim overnight. They'd gone out walking in the morning and met the other pair by chance....... Jeremy being at Kate's for the weekend I suppose."

Enough had remained of the day to light a short stroll from

St John down to the head of the shallow creek separating Torpoint from Millbrook. Known locally as the 'lake', it was for most of the day a wedge of mud....... but at high water, as now, on a still autumnal evening such as this, then for few brief hours a tranquil lake it could certainly resemble.

"So you had a wide audience......and surely some sort of response. Tell me, what was made of the destruction of Peg's boat."

"Eamon was the most affected by our tale. Slightly edgy on our arrival, by the time we left he was positively jumpy."

"Why slightly edgy?"

"There'd been this snippet casually passed on by Jeremy just a little earlier, something that came up on the radio news, you might have picked it up yourself and probably thought *well, just another of those.*"

"And this concerned?"

"An IRA pub bombing in North London...... but after closing, and seemingly targetting just a couple of specific individuals who might have been wanting to break away from the main movement......"

"......that pub being their nascent H.Q."

"And, apparently, Eamon had been a visitor to that very place just a few hours earlier. They were the reason for his travelling again to Cornwall, probably under a degree of duress. They'd given him this audio tape, hoping I think that it might re activate the undoubted talent of the likes of Jim and Jeremy."

"So what was on it?"

"A radio programme...... an edition of *Desert Island Discs*, would you believe, one put out in 1980 featuring the top judge Lord Denning as the guest."

"And he talks."

"He does, between the pieces of music which are chosen to celebrate, or at least signify, various aspects of the man's life."

"The more important things."

"I guess so, and most are self explanatory...... all in fact, save the last."

"Making this all the more of a riddle," nodded Sally. "And the tune is what?" She was expecting something complex, scored by Britten perhaps, with a lyric by some Bohemian poet.

"*I Whistle a Happy Tune.*"

"No," chuckled the girl in disbelief. "That ridiculously simple little ditty from *The King and I*?"

"The very same, written by Rodgers and Hammerstein for the governess hired by the ruler of Siam, supposedly to educate his many children; *Deee dumdiddy dumdiddy dum....Deee dumdiddy dumdiddy dum.*"

"*Dee dee dum dum,*" joined Kate. "*Dee dee dum dum.*"

"*Dee dumdiddy dumdiddy dum,*" returned Chas.

"So what profound sentiment underlies this?"

"It was suggested to Eamon that there could be a message in this from Denning to those who escaped public censure in his report on the Profumo scandal....."

".....back in the '60s."

"That's the one. The general feeling is that he found out a lot more than was prudent to publish."

"So the message, it's along the lines of '*OK I've let you get away with it, but don't for a second think that I wasn't aware of what you were up to.*' "

"This is the theory Sal, and with Eamon having brought that HIGHLAND CLEARANCE stuff to the IRA high command, he was deemed the man to snoop out that which Denning has been reluctant to tell......"

"....... but is ready to hint. So Carroll, I presume, thinks there to be a Cornwall connection."

"He does, and on hearing of it from me and dad he feels that this might even touch upon the destruction, last night, of Peg's boat."

"Stretching it a bit, I would have thought."

"Maybe, Sally, but if one follows the premise that there is a Royal flavour to all this then there might well be overlap."

"Royalty," smiled the girl. "And going back to the '60s and no doubt beyond....... sounds to be Jeremy's cup of tea. Excited was he?"

"Excited and informative, for soon we are feasting on the Princely intrigues surrounding two Royal families......."

".......and all for the price of one. So they centre on who, exactly?"

"On the late Lord Louis Mountbatten, grandson to Queen Victoria, distant uncle to our present Queen and, more closely, to her husband; and on the Prince Chula of Thailand, also deceased, and himself a contemporary of the Windsors' Uncle Dickie. At the end of the last war Chula came down here to live at a place called Tredethy, an old manor house in the Camel valley."

"So not far from where Jim and Kate live. And the overlap with the boat?"

"Concerns the owner previous to Peg, his former employer and one time General of the parachute army which came to grief at Arnhem. Following the disaster on the Rhine he was sent out to help Mountbatten with the Burma campaign, and after the war Uncle Dickie recommended him to his nephew Philip as a kind of financial secretary to what was to become the highest of all the Royal Households. Apparently there's this group photo hanging in the office at Tredethy which shows Prince Chula entertaining a party which includes both Browning and Philip."

"And Jeremy was on to this in a shot."

"He was, and in the blink of an eye he'd got Dad and me taking him down past Truro to see Edward Trembath, the retired MP who'd put him on to Alan Clark."

"On the off chance that he would be at Carwinion House, where his son lives."

"And we were lucky. He was there. You obviously know of Carwinion House and Trembath the younger."

"From my father mainly........Sir Edward had been a Plymouth MP until quite recently, remember. And you can add to this the mentions that Hugh Trembath will get in *The Morning News* for his local council work."

"I suppose he does," acknowledged Chas, his voice faltering momentarily. The Shaw's had these media contacts, of course they did...... but how far did they extend, he wondered, and was there a way to pre-empt the kind of enquiry he feared might come? Probably, but a prompt articulation of such required a far more slippery tongue than that tied behind his own teeth. The sideways glance from the girl made plain enough that he would need to fend.

"Did you see anything of the grand-daughter? Word is that she's forging a career in film production"

"Briefly," answered Chas, affecting a painfully forced nonchalance. "Seemed to enjoy showing off her car."

"And you weren't impressed?" Sally wasn't fooled, the edge in her voice sharpening that of the card in his jeans' pocket.

"Well I can't imagine that she thought too much of this rough old yardie down from Devonport. Hardly her type, eh?"

With a sigh half smiled Sally tugged Chas closer. "So long as she's not told you're the grandson of a French Admiral."

*

Mobile homes

With Kate's guidance the choice of site for Eamon's caravan was made in less than an hour. Dinham Field was considered ideal; small, secluded, tucked into the northern bank of the Camel estuary about three miles seaward of Wadebridge. From there, without having to tangle with town traffic, it would be a mere ten minutes moorwards to Tredethy; even less, seawards, to Rock, and no more than a quarter of an hour over the Camel to Kate's at Ruthern and Jim's at Tremorebridge. If he could be settled in before the end of the very next day, a Sunday, then all the better, said the owner. He could charge then at the off-season weekly rate and Eamon would get full value.

The friend with the Land Rover duly turned up, with Kate aboard, to collect him from his B&B accommodation before nine the following morning. By eleven his home was hitched and they were leaving Whitsand Bay site for a steady seventy minute wend back through Bodmin and Wadebridge and on to Dinham, their route lifting them over the dualled A30 a mile to the east of the first of these towns, at Carminow Cross.

The bridge itself, let alone the road beneath, is barely noticed, driver and passenger attention normally being drawn ahead to the roundabout that immediately follows. It was understandable, therefore, that even from his exalted passenger seat position Eamon noticed not the hefty Japanese marque motor-home cruising smoothly westwards below them, nor the vaguely filtered silhouette in the tinted glass of side and rear window.

Stock-still sat this wraith, strapped as it was into a firmly anchored wheelchair around which was arrayed an extravagant range of ergonomically positioned tools and comforts. The outward view from therein, though, was excellent and, as they picked out the beacon and then glanced at the satellite map on the screen before him, a pair of sharp oriental eyes could confirm to their wizened owner that his journey was all but complete.

As, shortly, would be Eamon's. By 2pm his caravan was in position at Dinham and, having been returned to his own vehicle waiting in Bodmin, he could take Kate back to Ruthernbridge from where she and Jeremy were then to follow him up to Jasmine Cottage. There, with all that had been achieved in the morning with the help of these friends, he could begin to feel comfortable, and certainly appear more relaxed than he had the previous day.

"Jim," he suggested, "let Jeremy hear more about Marina. You were saying yesterday how she and George were, for a while, candidates for an enthronement...... would this have been in place of the sister and brother in law who'd been obliged to leave Yugoslavia?"

"Olga and the Regent Prince Paul," joined Jeremy, "who for their want of anti Nazi vigour were to be deposed in the promptly crushed Belgrade coup that nevertheless famously helped to delay *Barbarossa*. If, after the German occupation, a monarchy was to be revived there then surely the grown now King Peter stood ready."

"You're right," nodded Busbridge, "but with the coming of Tito, of course, the wait was in vain. No, this idea of using George and Marina was hatched in London amongst a group of exiled Poles after it became clear that *Barbarossa* wasn't going to be the immediate success hoped by Berlin. Stalin would regroup, it was anticipated, and strike back so strongly as to take the whole of Poland as a client state."

"Which is effectively what happened," said Jeremy.

"But maybe it needn't have. This is the point. Not if the Germans had staged an orderly retreat and erected a Wehrmacht stiffened Poland as *their own* client state. Perhaps also, after dispensing with Hitler, negotiating a peace with Britain....."

"...... where we, as a seal of approval, could offer this spare Windsor as a figurehead," continued Jeremy, "but as did Icarus, the poor fellow fell out of the sky. So could this stuff have crossed STANLEY'S desk, we ask, and might that plane have been sabotaged? Wonderful story!"

"Maybe," said Eamon, "but what relevance can this have for now? All we're hearing is that in '42 George's politics were no less wayward than had been his morals ten years earlier. *The Polish King and I*, perhaps....... but by '46, the time of the Tredethy gathering, Stalin's people were in Poland to stay. If you're looking for somewhere that remained in the balance then it has to be Thailand."

"Fair enough Eamon," conceded Busbridge, "but bear in mind that, just like Mama Mahidol, Marina had two young sons and a daughter. And Stalin wasn't going to live forever. Few in the west predicted the emergence of Kruschev, and the firmness with which he was to keep his satelite states in place."

"So we're to think of Edward, our now Duke of Kent, as a young pretender?" smirked Kate. "But no Bonny Prince Charlie he! Perhaps Eamon's right, we needn't be getting too excited about Marina, not while there are others still to consider....... Tommy Browning for instance." She tapped at her sketch. "Dead, yes, but don't we know someone who served under the guy, and later worked for him?"

Princess Marina.
Duchess of Kent.

*

The next morning (Monday); London (and a day trip)

The pathologist drew back the plastic sheeting with the solicitous pride one might expect from an undertaker presenting a particularly successful example of the embalmer's art to an appreciative widow. Grigson glanced down. Flash fried flesh, protruding bone, and what remained of scorched skin lay positioned so as to account for two victims.

"And you've managed to positively identify two men..... from this?"

"Fingerprints, dental treatment...... we had records on file with which to match."

"And they must have been right on top of that device, poor sods. So for cause of death we've got multiple trauma, consistent with having been blown up. I guess they wouldn't have known too much."

The pathologist hesitated, as if to say he couldn't be so sure.

"And you are acquainted, it is said with a prime suspect."

"He was seen near the premises, shortly before this."

"Would you term him a strong man......one handy with a knife?"

"Is there something to suggest that?" This wasn't sounding like Eamon.

"See this neck vertebrae," pointed the pathologist, "and the single striation...... just there. His companion has similar, suggesting that they might have been killed before the explosion reduced them to........ to this."

"They had their throats cut, you mean."

"Requiring them to have been overpowered by more than one person."

"Unless the one person was strong......"

"..... and handy with a knife."

"And there could be more. From two men, even so shredded and cooked, I would have expected to recover more in the way of liver tissue."

"Meaning what?"

"That as well as the slit throat, a degree of abdominal mutilation might have been inflicted prior to the explosion...... and as to the order, Mr Grigson, I cannot be sure. Your friend, he didn't keep a pet cat?"

It was a grim joke, to which Alan grimly refused to respond.

"Sounds like we're talking about more than one assailant," he said, quietly certain now that neither would have been Eamon Carroll. But who, he wondered as the remnants were covered again, who in the world would do such a thing, and why? And just what implications might this obscenity carry for the cabby's further safety?"

Troubling questions, which were to follow him across to Paddington and out on the mid morning service to Bath where he was to meet Gareth, as arranged, on the Abbey side bank of the Avon, just below Pulteney Bridge. Only with the meeting and the greeting did their nag begin to subside.

It was a first get-together for the pair in more than a year, and there was plenty to catch up on...... not least, the three operation's worth of further face reconstruction undergone on the horrifically wounded-out Falklands veteran.

"Graft upon graft," said Gareth, without hint of complaint, "most taking well....."

"....... and some not so well." Finding the guardsman's eyes, the briefest of nods from Alan conveyed a mountain of respect. "But I'm not here to discuss advances in cosmetic surgery."

"So it'll be about your job."

"Yes, which back in the summer took me down to Cornwall again......quite a little adventure. Met some old friends, made some new."

"But no job will ever be fully done, eh? Always a few loose ends...... which is what this must be about." *So come on,* Gareth was saying, *time to make yourself clear.*

Alan was ready now to oblige.

"A key figure this time was this Londonised Irish guy. Runs a taxi..... Paddington, West London, Heathrow sort of area. He'd long done small-time bits for the IRA, but since having been seen to truly make a difference back in August it appears he's being scouted for the bigger league stuff. There was a pub bombing at the end of last week, in Cricklewood. You might have heard."

"Two men killed," confirmed Gareth. "Said to have been a renegade faction."

"Well Eamon, this friend of ours, he was reported to have been in the area just before the thing went off. Then, suddenly, he's nowhere to be found...... not at home, not at work."

"And you've not heard from him?"

"Nothing."

"So either as perpetrator or survivor of the attack he's on the run."

"Everything tells me it's as the latter, and that he's wanting to keep well down lest the former should be looking to tidy matters. My guess is that he'll have gone to ground in Cornwall."

"Seeking out who......Kate?"

"Kate, yes, and there's this friend she's found called James Busbridge. He's older, but certainly sharp enough still. He lives just outside Bodmin......"

"....... to where Kate has moved, after taking a job in the big psychiatric place there. I know that much."

"They sing together in a local choir, and Busbridge does voluntary work at the hospital."

"And you'll be looking to get down there, Alan, to catch up with this guy."

"Not immediately. I'm wary for the moment, lest others from the security services might follow."

"And you wouldn't want them bringing him in....."

"........because I can't assume that custody would give him sufficient protection, not knowing for sure who might want him silenced, and why. For the moment I think it best that I merely be kept informed...... discretely informed."

"I get it. You want me down there."

"That would help."

"But only if this Mr Carroll can take me into his confidence. To him I'm a stranger. He'll also be wary, surely."

"But he trusts Kate, and I know Kate trusts you."

"Is that enough, though, just being a friend of a friend?"

"I'm thinking, also, that you might be a resource to them...... as I'm hoping you can be a resource to me."

"In the manner of a lode that can be mined from different ends....."

".......according to the talents and techniques there available," added Alan. "How recently is it you've heard from Kate?"

"Not since June."

"It'll be news to you, then, that she and Jeremy are once again an item."

"A reconciliation having been negotiated in the course of this *little adventure*." Gareth's tone was almost resentful. The relationship......

that was fine, but how come he'd missed out on the general fun? Alan took encouragement.

"It's a long story, the telling of which is best left to its true principals. For now, though, it can suffice to say that Jeremy did well."

"If you're talking talents and techniques, then that I can well believe. The man's a one-off. It's just how these things are applied."

"Well this time, I confess, he helped pull me from what was looking quite a tricky hole."

"So I find this Eamon guy, on your behalf. I attempt to size up the difficulties that surround him, and I also keep watch for you on how Kate and friends might be attempting to assist. Plenty there to do, Alan, but I fail to see how this makes me a resource for both yourself *and* them."

"Fair point, Gareth...... and this is where, admittedly, I'm riding on little more than a hunch. It's what we do, though, and my hope is that on listening to Eamon our Jeremy might be moved to mount that same steed."

"And who's to say that he won't prove the better jockey."

"Certainly not me, Gareth, but for the moment, rather than joining them, I'm just wanting to know of their progress....."

"...... along what you envisage as a sort of parallel enquiry to your own." Gareth hesitated. "And there's something that I can offer to each of you.......the same something?"

"I'm hoping so, Gareth. From back when we first met I remember this casual mention you made of a fellow Guardsman. You counted him a good friend. Also a Falklands casualty, his wounds were psychological...... a case for Kate's place rather than a burns unit. The army career was over, but he was on his feet, you said, and sufficiently dosed to be given a measure of employment by the Prince of Wales no less, in his London household."

"David Evans, that was. Corporal David Evans."

"Is he still there, do you know?"

"As far as I'm aware, yes, even if he is becoming less and less enamoured with his employers. I guess familiarity with the exalted can breed double the contempt."

"No doubt." Alan's terseness belied the quiet encouragement to be taken from this talk of disenchantment. "So what sort of contact have you maintained?"

"I'll see him twice, perhaps three times a year....... the last occasion having been in May. It'll usually be a re-union gathering arranged through the Regimental Association."

"And he has live-in accommodation at this residence, which must be a part of Kensington Palace."

"He does," confirmed Gareth.

"Good, now this is a contact I'm hoping you might develop."

"You mean I don't wait until the next re-union."

"You don't, and should this prove the resource I hope it can be for me......"

"......then I'm to make the same available for Jeremy & Co."

"Bearing in mind, throughout, that time may be of the essence."

"For you're fearing that whoever might be after this Eamon won't be too interested in taking him prisoner."

"A real possibility."

"Then it's to Jeremy and Kate," resolved Gareth.

"And to Kate first, even if Barnes does live in this town. It suits me better that you and he should become re-acquainted through her."

"And if I have progress to report?"

"Then you wait until you are back in Wales, and likewise when instigating any communication with Mr Evans. I've got your home number. Should you feel it important that I should be in touch then say as much, and no more, on the tape you can talk to by dialling this." Alan passed a card. Gareth glanced briefly at the bare number thereon, pocketing it then without comment.

*

Plymouth

"And did you say something about a phone call, dad........ how long ago was that?" Chas was at the sink, tipping away the last murky dregs of coffee from his near empty flask. Once rinsed he would invert it to drain and dry, ready for the morning and his next shift at the yard.

"Half an hour ago, no more....... she gave a number. I've written it down, she'll be expecting you to call back." The pad plopped onto the worktop next to the drainer. "Here."

This wasn't Sally. Chas didn't need to look, any more than she would have needed to leave *her* number.

"Thanks dad."

"Did I recognise the voice?"

"I don't know," answered Chas evasively. "Perhaps when I've heard it......"

"*Rich birds*," rasped Tony Cross scornfully between a pushed out jaw and a wrinkled nose. Cautionary words, of course, for anyone familiar with wit and wisdom of Steptoe senior...... but not so for a slightly too young Chas. Mere envy, he mistakenly thought, while moving into the office area to settle behind his father's desk.

Phone now in hand, he purposefully dialled. Was she still there?

"Hello....... Helen Trembath." She was.

"Chas Cross, Helen, returning your call of earlier...... thirty minutes ago perhaps"

"Chas, yes, thanks for getting back."

"I'm surprised to be hearing from you so soon."

"Well yesterday, after seeing you, your father and Jeremy off, I was told that while we'd been joy riding the conversation back at Carwinion had also touched on Thailand."

Chas thought better of mentioning the photograph.

"They were intending to ask about Jack Profumo, I knew that. He of the political career famously ruined in the '60s."

"A contemporary of my grandfather."

"Who they hoped might remember something of his exploits back in the '40s. Court gossip is what they were after, skeletons that might have been set a-rattling when the Keeler stuff came up all those years later. As a young man he was supposed to have been a friend of the war-widowed Duchess of Kent, the late Princess Marina, an aunt to our Queen whilst at the same time being a cousin to Prince Philip. Any mention of him would appear to bring Lord Louis Mountbatten into play."

"Who during the war had been given overall command of our troops in South East Asia......"

"...... where Thailand became a key consideration, and all the more so with the building of your railway up into Burma. And should one think this to be all rather distant, it might be remembered that during the zenith of Mountbatten's influence amongst the Captains and the Kings there lived in a quiet corner of your wonderful county one Prince

Chula….. himself quite a prominent figure within the Thai Royal Family as it sought to survive exceedingly difficult times. Apparently, having been friends of the Duke of Kent from way before the war, he and his cousin Prince Bira, did as much as anyone to support the Duchess and her young children through their loss."

"So when was it that the Duchess died?"

"Princess Marina went in '68, and Chula perhaps five years before that. Bira, who was a fair bit younger, survived until quite recently. They were into motor sport, were Chula and Bira. Had their own team. Bira, the driver, was quite an all round talent…..something off a Biggles it seems. Get down to the archives. Between them they'd make an excellent half-hour documentary."

"Perhaps, Chas, as a later project." Helen didn't sound enthused "For the moment I've enough to do with this Kwai stuff…… which is why I'm phoning."

"Where from?"

"From London, I'm at the flat, having driven back here yesterday evening."

"So today you've been where?"

"Only across the river, to the Imperial War Museum for a few slow hours this morning…… but on getting back here things have quickened considerably."

"With the Kwai thing, you say."

"Yes…… before leaving Cornwall my father gave me a phone number, saying that it had been passed to him by one of his fellow district councillors down there who he'd known to be a member of the Burma Star veterans association."

"So this was an ex POW?"

"No…. he'd never been captured. He was part of Slim's force that as good as cleared Burma of Japs before the VJ surrender. They then moved southward into Thailand to liberate the Death Railway labour camps, earning the deep gratitude of the survivors. Lasting friendships were made, and one such, apparently, between our one-time-soldier-now-councillor and a Scottish captive named Alec Young who, despite his cruel ordeal, returned to his native Scotland where he was to live for further thirty years. He'd kept a diary whilst in captivity, and on his death his family offered this together with other related papers to the War Museum."

"And obviously it was an offer accepted."

"Only partly so," continued Helen. "Yes, they were more than happy to take the diary, but not an accompanying bundle of letters which had been received in the 1960s from Pierre Boulle, the French war veteran and writer of *Le Pont de la Riviere Kwai*, the novel from which the film was adapted. Such correspondence, prompted by the picture and maintained until the Scot eventually died, was felt then to be outside the scope of an institution that preferred to concern itself with factual records rather than recently made feature films."

"A pity, for stuff like that could have been so, so useful to your project now."

"And useful it might be yet, for what was passed to my father was a contact number for the Young family."

"And he's suggested that you might have nothing to lose by using it."

"And this, Chas, I've done already, explaining myself and my purpose to Young's people, and how I came by their number."

"And the reaction from them......?"

".......was more positive than I could have dared hope. They would make copies, I was told, but it was preferred that I should travel to collect these in person."

"They'll want to know a bit more about you, I suppose."

"And, I guess, about the project."

"So how far into Scotland will this be taking you?"

"I've been given an address in Perth."

"A good bit on from Glasgow, then," ventured Chas, uncertain as to what this might amount to in miles or hours. "Will you be taking a train?"

"I suppose so."

Chas sensed an *if I must* reluctance.

"You would prefer to drive?"

"Were I able to find myself a co-driver then yes, very much so. I was wondering if you had a licence."

"To get behind the wheel of that thing...... am I hearing this right?"

"With me in the car you would be insured. A couple of days and we could be there and back."

So simple did this sound to Chas, there just had to be a catch.

"So how soon?"

"As soon as you like."

"By juggling shifts and maybe missing my day at college I could, I suppose, give you from tomorrow, a Tuesday evening, through to Thursday midnight...... call it forty eight hours."

"Allow ten hours to get there, ten hours to get back, ten to do the business, and there's time left to take in some scenery......perhaps get to know each other a little better."

In truth, for Chas, the proposition was as irresistible as it was unexpected. He would, though, just for a few seconds, hold back on a response, for he wasn't so dizzied by these wiles of Helen's as to overlook the bonus that might be stealthily garnered were he to press for just a few extra miles. What was Inverness from Perth? Two hours at the most, double this and add an hour to find 'Peg' Willis and a further hour's worth of chat was then still do-able. Yes, this was an opportunity to get something more on Browning whilst avoiding the post and the phone. What concern need this be of a companion who would be more than busied by those enquiries of her own?

"I have this friend who's not long ago moved to Inverness. If we could take him in then I'd pay for the extra petrol."

Helen could hardly refuse. "I'll drive down to Plymouth this evening, I've a friend there who can give me a bed. If I pick you up from work tomorrow we can go straight off. Where will you be?"

"I can get a bus up to the Theatre Royal for five thirty. Pull in by the cinema next door."

*

Tuesday pm Ruthern

"And this, you say Gareth, is no more than a fleeting visit to Cornwall."

"Which makes calling upon yourself all the more important, Kate. Were you to learn I'd been this way and not bothered......"

".......then yes, that would certainly offend. So tell me, why rush away? You can stay here, you know that. I'll fill you in on Jeremy."

108

"So he figures again in your life."

"He does, and you can hear how this came about. I'll get my friend Jim down for supper."

"Jim?"

"Mr James Busbridge, who can help me explain the intrigue that was HIGHLAND CLEARANCE."

*

Later: M5 Northbound

"This friend of yours, Chas, for whom you're happy to travel to Inverness...... male? female? young? or......"

"It's a *he*, of good age. In his sixties at least is Peg Willis. Like your Mr Young, he served in the last war, but as a Para. While never captured he did take a wound to the leg, a severe wound, recovery from which was only partial."

Chas had been driving for fifty miles, having taken the wheel from a weary Helen at the Taunton Services. Comfortable with his handling of her car she'd then slipped into a good thirty minutes worth of much needed sleep. Now she was refreshed, and clearly inquisitive.

"So what took him from Cornwall to a place like Inverness? Family I suppose."

"An offer of work actually."

"And this would be something in your line..... to do with the oil rigs out in the North Sea?"

"Far from it. He did have a boat, though, a cabin cruiser which he had to leave behind. He liked to think it would be looked after, also that it would be used. I could do both, I thought, and he was OK with that."

"So remains there a problem? The voice I hear sounds far from *OK with that*."

"Because he'll not be so OK with what happened last Friday."

"Which was...."

"The boat was totally destroyed by fire."

"Deliberately, do you think?"

"I've no evidence...."

"....but...."

"....grounds for suspicion have emerged."

"At the scene, you mean, or....?."

"There's a chance that this was an attempt to destroy more than an old wooden boat, and this goes back to a previous owner."

"A previous owner who would have featured in the enquiry you brought to Carwinion over the weekend, the enquiry concerning Thailand and the Prince who lived at Tredethy."

"The Prince Chula, yes," confirmed Chas who was unsure as to whether his companion might have been better briefed than he on the scope of the conversation missed whilst sampling the delights of this XR3. "That previous owner was one of Peg's wartime commanders, going back to the Paras. After the war Peg worked for him, when he lived over Fowey way. He was the husband of the writer, Daphne du......."

".......Browning, you're talking about, General Frederick or 'Tommy' or 'Boy' Browning...... as you say, he was married to Daphne du Maurier. Go on."

And Chas did, lulled perhaps by the girl's obvious familiarity with the topic. He couldn't possibly be telling her anything she wouldn't already know.

"Well go to Tredethy and there's this old photo that hangs on the wall, taken there just after the war. It belongs to Daphne, and in it stands her Tommy...... alongside Chula, together with Marina of Kent and her young cousin, our current Prince Philip. I suppose then he would have been a Prince Philip of Greece....."

"...... a nephew, through his mother, of Lord Louis Mountbatten. Yes, I was told that his name cropped up at Carwinion."

"Well it is suspected that there was once more to this photo than now meets the eye, Helen, and that for some reason, at some time, a couple of characters were snipped away."

"But negatives might have stayed intact."

"Or those snipped away pieces might have been saved....."

"...... and put with the charts and things that were on that boat....."

"......from which my friend in Scotland could have subsequently shifted them elsewhere. He could even have taken them with him."

"A long shot," smiled Helen.

"But what a superb vehicle, nevertheless," chuckled Chas, "and what pleasant company."

"So after leaving the Brownings," persisted the girl.

"He moved from the Fowey estuary to that of the Lynher, bringing the boat as a pay off and taking estate work with the Earl of St Germans."

"So from Menabilly to Port Eliot," name-dropped Helen, the *arriviste* hoping to demonstrate a 'county' pedigree.

"Then, much more recently, to Scotland to do similar for the Lord Lovat...... another distinguished wartime commander."

"And would either of these top brass characters have been involved out in the east?" Helen asked.

"I think both figured in the Normandy landings, Lovat being badly wounded. Browning fought on and later was heavily involved in the Arnhem fiasco, which just about did for his cherished Paras."

"And was he then sent to help see off the Japs?"

Chas briefly raised a palm from the wheel. "This is the kind of thing that Peg would know of course."

"And could there be a link between the fate of Peg's boat and the liberation of Alec Young, I ask."

"Well having read his diaries you'll be better acquainted with Alec Young than I. I doubt, though, if you encountered any mention of ' *Boy*' Browning."

"Right enough there," acknowledged Helen.

"So tell me more about this later reaction of your Scot to the film, *The Bridge on the River Kwai*."

"Hopefully I'll be better able to do that when travelling back. I suspect, though, that he joined a general debate about the characterisation of the captured British Colonel who takes charge in the prison camp and sets about erecting the bridge with a single minded determination....."

"......which in the end becomes an obsession, so much so that he attempts to thwart the sabotage operation."

"There were complaints from survivors that this denigrates the real Colonel who did much to make conditions more endurable in the real camps. A Colonel Toosey, this was...... dead now, sadly."

"But clearly remembered with fondness."

"Great fondness."

"But I guess that notion of the egomaniac who wants to keep his bridge intact must have come from somewhere. Perhaps we're on the way to finding out."

*

A little later again.   Rock, Cornwall

Where a solitary figure pauses in his un-rushed progress along the moon paled strand, eyes briefly drawn to the glimmer of the far shore lights of Padstow prior to settling again on the reflected speckle thrown across the dark tide filled estuary between.

A fitful breeze following from the autumnal sea to the north stiffens with each gust, rustling through the dune grass to his left. It is time now for Eamon Carroll to be returning to the Golf Club and his waiting car. It would be just ten minutes, then, back to the caravan and a mug of whisky laced cocoa ...... just reward, he felt, for an afternoon and evening of not unsuccessful endeavour.

With the morning having been given to equipping his car with a Bodmin purchased towing hook it had been three at least before the ten-minute drive from Dinham had brought him into Rock with an initial intention of seeking out Bira's former house. He'd asked first along the small parade of shops that flank the one principle road before its last steady half mile drop to the waterfront...... but could any of the assorted staff in the Post Office-Newsagents, the filling station, the butchers or bakers, say where their famous sporting celebrity had once lived? Not one.

From the girl who sat alone at her desk in the Jack Bray estate agency there was, though, at least some assistance...... for it had only been the day before that another person (neglecting to leave name and number) had telephoned with the same enquiry. She hadn't herself been able to help then anymore than she could now, but it did occur to her later that amongst the more venerable members of the local Sailing and Golf Clubs there had to be some who might still recall this guy from his prime.

And so it was on her gladly given advice that to the Golf Course Eamon had then made, motoring up into the dunes, hope intact still, to find the St Enodoc Links clubhouse. The steward there was welcoming and pleased that this off-season visitor should stretch to ordering for himself the day's local fish special as an early evening meal. If the cook turned up on time it could be readied for six, he was told, so in the two hours until then he might make the most of the pleasant late afternoon light...... with a walk down towards Daymer and the quaint little Church of St Enodoc, or there was the stiff climb to take in the view from Brea Hill.

Carroll had then explained his quest, mentioning as he did the advice offered at the estate agency.

"Then that could be your man," the steward had said, pointing the back of a window facing chair that Eamon hadn't realised was occupied. "Stan must know. Another twenty minutes and he'll usually be awake."

Taking the counter top *Telegraph* with his half-pint glass of Guinness, Eamon had slipped carefully into a nearby vacant chair to watch and to wait for his flannel-and-blazered veteran to stir...... and this he did, waking as scheduled to survey his lush domain with all the self posessed sagacity of Wodehouse's oldest member. Here was a man who would be only too pleased to expound on the personalities of the past. Progress was assured, Eamon knew.

A well oiled taxi-man's charm was smoothly invoked, and by the time supper was served the vivid image of a dashing wartime Bira had been lovingly raised from host of fond memories. A clever man, was the Prince, a courageous man, a cultured man, with not an ounce of conceit. For Stan, merely to have trodden the same paths and driven the same lanes as this figure was nothing less than privilege...... a highlight, indeed, in what had been a far from uneventful life. If the Prince had arrived in Rock as a sporting hero then he'd departed as an outright legend, if only for his war work, an invaluable contribution to the development of the kind of glider technology utilised so effectively in the capture of the Orne crossings.

The house, *Lynam House* it was named, was in fact a fair sized residence, and this he'd vacated soon after the war, but then would frequently stay with his cousin across at Tredethy. That was until the early '60s when Chula succumbed to terminal cancer. After that, Bira's trips down to Cornwall became rarer. He'd made a home in the south of France, but there were regular visits to London...... and this was where he'd suddenly died, no more than a couple of years ago.

A unique charisma is what Bira had. A vivid charisma, said Stan, strong enough to last and linger in these haunts, in his own memory and that of others.

Eamon heard how when the house had been split into holiday apartments, perhaps dozen years ago now, there'd been found in the loft two hefty trunks brimful of Bira artefacts. Carefully wrapped in one were items from the model railway that he'd constructed and operated, to the delight, obviously, of the children of those friends that he loved to entertain. Found in the other were photographs, journals, other documents, and even trophies associated with his and Chula's motor racing exploits. Bira was in Thailand at the time, and on being contacted he'd instructed that all should be auctioned with the proceeds to be given to a local hospice movement.

In the event, Eamon was told, the full lot was secured by a collector who'd established a toy museum close to one of the main car parks in Tintagel. To supplement his display of tin plate he was making a corner of his small gallery over to a commemoration of motor sport in Cornwall, and in particular to a series of events held on the nearby Davidstow airfield during the ten years that followed the war. Bira, at this time, would have been competing in the far grander international arena, but nevertheless, with his strong local connections those sporting treasures amounted to an excellent acquisition. Yes, said Stan, for those interested in the evolution of the modern Grand Prix format here was a collection to savour.

As it had to be for anyone interested in Bira and Chula the men, thought Eamon. Indeed it was a must-go-and-see.

Lynam House.
Rock.

*

114

Wednesday a.m. Wadebridge, Cornwall……

…….. where a spright if elderly lady emerges from the compact Co-op supermarket, clinging to her two plastic carrier bags, the one holding onions and mushrooms, the other a fresh pineapple. A brisk walk through the adjacent car park will take her to her kitchen; she must pause, though, to allow a large motorised caravan to ease itself from a barely adequate marked parking space.

The side windows are tinted. She can see nothing of its interior, except when the driver lowers his window and the wing mirror throws to her a brief of glimpse of what sits behind him, amongst the tailored fittings, and the plush fixtures. It has a face, and…….

……..and in that second her head is spinning, atop shoulders rooted to feet of lead; and those bags, they slip to the ground from fragile fingers of ice. She cannot move. She cannot speak. She can barely watch, but, with haunted eyes, she must. Fearfully they follow as the vehicle pulls smoothly away, turning now for the old stone bridge which, arch by arch, it must cross slowly before taking the climb for Camelford, or the coast maybe, and at last passing from sight.

*

Wednesday (early afternoon); Perth.

"So were those three hours with the Youngs sufficient?" Chas was driving. They were moving out of Perth on the A9 Pitlochry road. The Highlands loomed near and large.

"Ample…… thanks Chas. You missed a good meal."

"Maybe….. but I couldn't have skipped any more sleep. It's a hundred rugged miles yet to Inverness, and I've said to Peg we can be there by five."

"So you found a call box……"

"…… and got through." The boy pointed to a slip of paper on the dash. "See there, the directions he gave me to his lodge."

"Looks simple enough."

"And he'll be by his phone after four, lest we should be unsure as

115

we get nearer." Chas glanced down towards his companion's shins and the brief case still propped between. "Put that in the back, you'll be more comfortable. I trust those letters from *Monsieur Boulle* did not disappoint."

"I can read you one now," offered Helen, fingers moving from handle to catch. "Or more than one should you wish."

"Well let's hear the first...... and see if we're grabbed."

A click of the catch ensued, and a grunt then as the case itself was slotted rearwards between the seats, followed by a shuffle of papers. Chas drove on, seconds stretching to minutes.

"Ah, now *this* would appear to be the first," muttered Helen, as if eventually sorted.

"Dated?"

'*October 1959,*' read Helen.

'*Dear Mr Young*

Thank you for your recent letter. It was both interesting and moving to read of your Japanese prison camp experiences, and of your being put to work on the Thai-Burma Railway.

Having spoken to others who endured similar treatment I have the utmost respect for your fortitude and also your opinions. I too served the Allied cause in the far east. Before the war I worked on a rubber plantation in Malaya, then, with its outbreak I enlisted with the French army. They sent me into Indo China where, at that time, Thai militarism was perceived as the principal threat.

Following the fall of France to Germany I chose to join a small Free French unit based in Singapore. From there we strove to disrupt a Vichy collaboration with Japan, and despite the fall of Singapore early in '42 were able to take our fight into Indo China. I was involved in a number of sabotage missions performed to varying success before being captured and imprisoned by the Vichy people in Saigon, and later in Hanoi.

I managed to escape, though, to help a Calcutta based British special forces unit mainly in an advisory capacity. I met a variety of personalities during these adventures, some comrades, some enemies, and many influenced my subsequent storytelling both in terms of characterisation and plot.

This said, I must remind you that 'The Bridge over the River Kwai' is merely a novel (rather than a historical account), and that my original story differs significantly from its film version.

I enclose a copy, hopefully for your enjoyment.

Best wishes

Pierre Boulle.'

"And our Mr Young must have read that book and responded," said Chas. "I suppose we'll never know what he wrote."
"But Boulle's side of the continuing exchange can give us an idea." Helen was flicking through the pages. "Here's his next, written a couple of months later......listen."

Piere Boulle.

Lean's bridge over the River Kwai

The real bridge near Tamarkan.

*

Bath

"So Kate gave you my address."

"She did, Jeremy...... and worry not, I bring you her tender regards. Wants you to know she's looking forward to having you down there again for the weekend," Gareth pecked cautiously at a hastily rustled cheese sandwich, avoiding the hint of mould on a slightly warped lower crust.

"And she told you how we....."

"How you managed to settle your differences, yes...... and it was quite a little adventure, I understand, with that Grigson boyo having found himself in a tight spot. But he's back at work now, I'm told."

"Quite an adventure, yes, from which issues could yet remain." Bringing a mug of tea apiece the lecturer now joined his visitor at the end of a never more than partially cleared kitchen table. "Have you been introduced to Mr James Busbridge?"

"I have, an interesting character. A curious man you could say."

"And what about a Mr Eamon Carroll?"

"Not yet, Jeremy, though I have been told a little about him. I'm told that for more, then you're the guy to speak to."

"So is this why you're here?"

"Partly, yes."

"But only partly......"

"....... because I was given the impression that *you* could be interested in what *I* might have to say."

"Concerning.....?"

".......this predicament of Carroll's. I understand that there might be a Royal dimension to it."

"Go on."

Gareth was choosing his words carefully.

"I allowed Busbridge to wheedle it from me that a former comrade of mine, another ex-Guardsman, had secured for himself a position in Kensington Palace..... home of the latest generation of Mountbatten-Windsors, and also the youngest issue of George and Marina of Kent."

Grigson owed him a beer for this, thought Gareth, as the lecturer cast a dubious glance at his own sandwich. Never before had he tendered so regal a bait.

118

But would Jeremy take it?

"I would like you to meet our Eamon," said the lecturer, "and I'm sure he would like to meet you. Why not join us at the weekend?"

He had, in a single gulp.

*

Later, heading south from Inverness.

"So worthwhile?"

"Long way to have come if not," smiled Chas, now the passenger. "Could be lucky. There *were* things, like charts and other documents that were removed from the boat."

"So they would have escaped the fire......and does he remember where they are?"

"A variety of places were mentioned. One needs to know the lie of the land." An evasive answer this for, on listening to Chas, Peg had insisted on nothing he was to say being divulged to anyone, save perhaps to his father, or Kate and Jeremy, or to Declan at St Erney. If this created an awkwardness between the boy and a companion who'd been kind enough to bring him so far then in the veteran's view this had to be borne as an unfortunate consequence of her having been told too much already.

Conveniently, though, Helen appeared to sense this. There was no pressing from her, and as a topic of conversation *The Bridge over the River Kwai* offered itself as an agreeable cushion.

During Chas's hour with Peg she'd continued to scrutinise Boulle's letters and could say now that that his imaginary bridge over an imaginary river had probably been inspired by actual aerial photographs he'd seen towards the end of the war in Calcutta, whilst working there for British intelligence....... photographs of where the death railway bridged the *Kwae Mae Khlong* river near Tamarkan, the construction of which had certainly relied on the forced labours of allied POWs and captured Malays.

Then, after the war the seeds of a tale had been further nurtured as he spoke with a number of those who'd survived the exhaustion, disease, and wanton cruelty that had claimed so many. And in this tale, stressed its author in one letter, unlike in the film that was made of it, the bridge actually survives its attempted demolition by the saboteurs who on being captured are led away for an interrogation which can only be thwarted by their comrades' purposely directed lethal mortar attack.

As for the Colonel Nicholson who has overseen the construction and prevents the detonation of their explosives, he, in the book, will survive with his pet project ..... but not so the train, which having crossed the river is de-railed by a second charge laid further along the line.

And the real crossing at Tamarkan.....? This was used by the Japanese until June 1945 when it was at last successfully bombed by American and British planes, this having little effect on the course of a war which was to end within two months with the nuclear assaults on Hiroshima and Nagasaki...... leaving the railway, built at such cost, to be repaired by the victors for their own use.

The debate over whether the fictional Colonel Nicholson amounted to a defamation of the real Philip Toosey only arose following the release and success of the film, claimed Boulle, who in one letter had been adamant that in this particular respect no one had ever previously complained about his book. Yes, he'd heard of the man prior to starting it, and mainly from those who'd survived Tamarkan. Always, though, their words had expressed admiration and affection and gratitude. As a character this real Colonel was simply too good and too balanced, for the story he'd had in mind.

Darkness, fast falling in the Spey Valley, prevented Chas from reading any more of this for himself, the dicussion turning instead to why changes should have been made for the late 1950s cinema audience, changes that hadn't prevented the movie from winning a number of Hollywood Oscars. Films were Helen's subject, and despite his creeping fatigue Chas made sure she stayed with it across the Forest of Atholl. Only as they began the steady descent through Glen Garry into the Tay Valley with a petrol gauge nudging half empty was he ready to tilt back his seat and insist on the sleep essential before his next stint at the wheel.

*

Later that evening….. and a phone call

"So you can report progress, Gareth."

"I can, Alan……. progress on two fronts. I left Bath at six, and was back here in less than an hour."

"And you found Jeremy at home?"

"I did, I'm invited to join him in Cornwall this coming weekend. I look forward to meeting Mr Carroll, your taxi driver friend."

"And they're all keen to see more of you….."

"……and keen to hear more of what currently might be afoot in Kensington Palace. David Evans is alive in their imaginations."

"As he is in mine, Gareth."

"Good, because this is where I can hand you a bonus. I've spoken to him tonight. I called at his parents' place, just to check how he might best be contacted, and by fortunate coincidence he was actually there….. having been given a day's leave to visit his poorly mother."

"So to which of the residents of Kensington Palace is he attached, or does he have a general role?"

"He's with Charles and Diana and their toddler sons."

"Excellent…… and having known him as a loyal soldier, how would you rate his loyalty as a servant?"

Gareth hesitated.

"I would say it was less than cast iron, for loyalty we know is a two way thing."

"And he's feeling short changed?"

"When they took him on it was known that he'd had psychiatric problems."

"But he would have been over these, surely."

"By and large, yes, but after all he'd given to Queen and Country a measure of protection from a bullying tendency amongst senior staff should not have been too much of an ask."

"But sadly….."

"Yes, sadly it would appear that, if not actually condoned, the less than reputable conduct of these inadequates has been too often ignored by the head of the household."

"Hardly a King-like attitude."

"Which is David's view, Alan, a view that has equipped him to detect a similar disillusionment in the Princess herself."

"So he can find some comfort in that."

"On the contrary; for with her, separately caused and more deeply felt, the disillusionment is far less stoically borne.....to a degree which causes my friend positive alarm. It seems that she is prone to moods, extreme moods. On one day she can be half crippled by self pity and, by the next, doubly energised by a sense of mission, feeling it her duty to clean out what she perceives to be a sort of institutionalised malaise, something which if allowed to persist might blight the lives of her precious youngsters, William and Harry. Their father, she feels, has already been irreparably damaged."

"The *Heir of Sorrows* thing."

"Quite, but for the boys there might still be a chance......of this she is convinced."

"So when you say clean out, Gareth......"

"..... this suggests exposure. Media contacts are being cultivated. We can anticipate unattributed briefings, with all the attendant *aimed at* embarrassment........ for *Queen*, which won't bother my friend so much, and also for *Country*, which most emphatically will. For he feels that what then becomes at issue is security for all, as manifest in the integrity of the Nation, a Nation for which, like me, he is still ready to fight to the death......."

"........against hostile forces, forces that prowl abroad ever looking to seize upon top table indiscretion, and it's to these that he's sensing that the attitudes prevailing within the Wales's household offer an Achilles' heel."

"This is the mind set, Alan. One that leads him to observe, almost as an implied term of his employment, a duty to fathom ahead those murky waters into which the Princess might be tempted venture."

"So that when it appears she might be lured beyond her depth he can see her and the Country steered tactfully to safety."

"Exactly, and while such a steering might have to be left to more professional hands, he fears that too precipitate an intervention might double resentment. It's in the nature of the thoroughbred to be skittish, he reckons, and correction will be all the more effective for being proportionate."

"And this will depend on an his early assessment of the potential mischief, Gareth, early and accurate."

"An assessment that can require further quietly marshalled fact and opinion. Now I've mentioned you before to David, and I've also mentioned Jeremy....... in quite glowing terms. He trusts me as a former comrade, and he respects my judgement of talent and character."

"And you've sold us to him, haven't you, as agents who can perhaps bring an as yet vague concern more sharply into focus. I think he's told you that the Princess might be on to something to do with those Thais."

"He has, oiled by what from me would have sounded quite a knowledgable response."

"Primed as you'd been by our friends down in Cornwall earlier in the week......."

"....and also by you and Jeremy over in Bath. The Browning link went down particularly well; mention of this officer who'd served under Mountbatten in the east during the war, then afterwards worked at the palace, whilst throughout knowing Chula as a Cornish neighbour. For with this, David was recalling how less than a couple of years ago the princess had grown extremely inquisitive about Chula and Bira and their country. At that time he was reassured by her readiness to share this interest with her protection squad officer. While guarding her safety, you see...."

"....the fellow could also exert a scruitiny over her activities. He was ideally placed."

"This was my pal's initial assumption.'

"So perhaps not?"

"Perhaps not Alan....anxieties have grown, not withstanding Bira's death at the end of '85."

"And he's kept these to himself?"

"He has."

"After being stirred by what, Gareth?"

"By rumours surrounding that bodyguard. Officially, in the Spring of last year he was moved on to another post. And then this year he was killed in a road accident."

"In North London...... came off the back of a motorbike."

"You know something about this, then Alan."

"A little, Gareth, but tell me about those rumours."

"It is whispered that he was moved on because of a fear amongst his masters that he might have grown too close to the Princess. "

"And while most take this to mean a romantic attraction, not David."

"Not David," echoed Gareth, "who is compelled to quietly suspect that this poor fellow might have been charmed by the Princess into being her own personal spook."

"So where once he'd been ready to assume that Diana's enquiries and activities had been adequately monitored, he has to now wonder if in fact they might have ranged more widely and more freely than thought."

"And if they might be continuing to range so, Alan.... for on my telling him about the emergence amongst my associates of a tape recording believed to have been retrieved from the scene of that accident, then out this concern did tumble. He even spoke about having access to documents she's gathered. I can have copies, he said."

"And you can collect these when, and from where?"

"It happens that the Royal couple are away at this moment, and he expects to be able to put an initial sample in the post before the weekend. I gave him Kate's address. Should it come any sooner then it can wait for me there."

"Where you can put it before her regular panel of experts. Good work Gareth, bloody good work. And you'll be back in Wales by when?"

"By next Wednesday, when David said he will be across again to see his mum."

"Excellent. Show the others what he sends down, as I said, but when coming away bring that stuff with you."

"Because you'll be wanting to check it over."

"I most certainly will."

*

And from a call box......

"CAVAN?"

"Speaking......"

"SLIGO here," confirmed Eamon. "to report satisfactory progress......so far. Former contacts have been revived, and we're starting to piece together the Thais' time in Cornwall. Useful enquiries made at

Tredethy Manor and Rock. Hoping to find out more in Tintagel."

"And you're staying where?"

"In my caravan."

"And its location?"

"Will continue to vary," answered Eamon warily.

"So you won't tell me."

"I heard what happened to Kellegher and Conlon."

"Well maybe when you find out that wasn't down to me," countered McBeamish, "so long as this doesn't turn out to be too late."

"Perhaps if I'd been given certain assurances," faltered the cabby....... and sensing that weakness, McBeamish took firm grip of what hitherto had been a fairly balanced exchange.

"In our game, SLIGO, assurances are never given. They will only be earned, or not, on the strength of our information."

"And strong this will be," claimed Carroll. "As strong as it was last time, I'm confident of that."

"Good, but this time I won't want it brought to my lair. That caused problems. This must be just for me, so when the time is right I'll be looking to come to you, just you. Would you not feel honoured?"

*

To Hamilton services…...

.......where both are ready for a freshen-up, Helen after her turn at the wheel, Chas after his sleep; fitful this but just about adequate. Food is due (as well as fuel) but the staled remnants offered at a partly closed late-evening food counter threaten to suppress hunger rather than fortify. There is the shop, though, where the more durable fillings amongst the chilled sandwich selection look to be a healthier bet.

Making her choice, Helen leaves Chas to queue and to pay. She has a phone call to make, she says. She'd promised this to a friend.

Male…..? Chas wonders, his thoughts turning then to Sally who he might have called before now but hadn't.

And with just the single till operating the queue is not a short one, so neither need this call be, to whatever recipient. Would she say? Could he ask?

He comes out of the shop, and the phone is still at her ear as she looks across, watching for him it seems, as if his emergence might be the signal to hang up..... which she does, without great haste, but with a certain firmness. Throughout, the eyes stay with Chas, implying strongly that he'd perhaps been a feature of that conversation. So no, maybe he shouldn't ask.

*

Thursday; mid morning.

"And you'll be pleased to know, Jim, that thanks to this old boy up at the local golf club I was able to locate the house in Rock rented by Bira during the war. Like you I'd enquired at the local estate agent......"

"Like me?" Busbridge was driving. At his prudent suggestion they'd met at the quiet village of St Teath where Eamon's car might discretely remain while they went together with just the one into Tintagel. Knowing the north coast well he was cutting to the west of Delabole, along the little used lane that would take them through the hamlet of Trebarwith. The road was greasy, made so by the drizzle sprinkling from the low cloud that had totally obscured Roughtor away to their east. "Why *like me?*"

"Because I was told of a phone call to their office only the previous day, by someone wanting to know the same thing. No name....... but that's got to be James Busbridge, I thought."

"Then you thought wrongly Eamon."

"So who else?"

"You tell me..... and let's hope that from being a step behind them you're now a step ahead."

"If we can strike lucky again today, then more than a step ahead...... and I have the feeling we might."

Busbridge slowed, selecting a low gear for the acute right hand bend which would slot him, he knew, into the stream etched canyon behind Trebarwith Strand. A right at the brake testing junction at the bottom saw them briefly along the broader beach traffic road before the next lane to the left led them into a facing climb, no less severe than their descent, up through Treknow onto that final level, if twisting, mile into Tintagel.

And what an enchanting spectacle is Fore St, Tintagel ....Delabole del Mar! Given the true beauty of a surround that abounds in genuine archaeological interest, can there be anywhere else in the world that chooses to embrace phoniness with such wholehearted vigour? Do people really prefer that Camelot hokum, or is it merely that a better living is to be drawn from ignorant and the suspicious? Ask not. Let it suffice that the prostitution of natural charm will ever be a demand led business, and that those who would cavil at the cynicism of the supplier are best averting their eyes.

Mercifully, though, the toy museum offers sanctuary from things Arthurian, and also an extremely obliging proprietor..... aged early sixties, as well preserved as his cheery exhibits and, seemingly, of personality no less colourful. His home is a small converted disused chapel, the museum being what was formerly the attached Sunday School room.

"Mr Busbridge......," a hand is offered, "Mr James Busbridge, it has to be."

"It is," confirmed Jim, "and Mr Eamon Carroll, my friend. And you're Mr....."

"Brian George. Call me Brian."

"How do you do Brian," joined Carroll, hoping with his perfunctory nod to encourage the fuss this man was clearly wanting to make of his companion. George obliged.

"Yes, Mr Busbridge, the famous Mr Busbridge, I've read many a letter of yours in the newspapers, and many a magazine article too."

"Well we're here to do a touch of research, Mr George."

"Excellent, and in that case do allow me to waive my entry fee. I'm sure you can be relied upon to acknowledge your sources when going to print."

"Of course, delighted to, delighted to," oiled Busbridge.

"So is there any particular model, or range of models?"

"Actually it's a person. We've been told, Mr George, that you have material here on Prince Bira, the Thai racing driver......"

"....... who lived over at Rock during the war. Yes I do. Then his cousin, who'd financed what before the war had been quite successful *White Mouse* team, he moved into Tredethy Manor, a place even nearer. Follow me. Bira's corner is over here. I've got more on him than I could ever use. Look at this for a moment while I fetch the box from my garage."

Not unsurprisingly Bira's corner was dominated by Bira. There was just the one image of Chula (in Home Guard uniform) showing him in what was termed 'the train room at Rock' standing between Bira (RAF) and an understandably bereft looking Princess Marina of Kent......... while to the fore, operating what is clearly an extensive model layout, is her young Edward, fresh inheritor of the Dukedom.

Of the other ten prints one has Bira displaying his sculpted bust of Lord Tredegar and a second has him in the cockpit of a glider, leaving a remaining eight to show him in race overalls and goggles in or beside a variety of single seat racers. Featured prominently in the pre war selection was an ERA named *Romulus*, and of his post war cars, a Maserati in which he was to come to display his undoubted ability and courage in the newly developed Grand Prix format.

The celebrity sportsman.

To complement the photos die cast models of both vehicles shone from a wall mounted display cabinet, resplendent in their pale 'Bira Blue' livery. The more important details of the Thais' sporting records and their lives in Cornwall were presented through a number of boldly printed wall mounted paragraphs interspersed amongst the pictures and the models.

These were being examined as Brian George reappeared, cardboard box in arms.

"Most of the train stuff has been put out in the general displays, for that's what I was trying to build up when I bought it. What's left in here are more photos than I could ever use, and you'll find letters and a journal. The impression I have of Bira is that he was something of a spendthrift, these ways perhaps having been indulged by the older cousin with his Thai based fortune. But during the war they are suddenly beset by uncertainty, for who's to say that those estates of Chula's won't be confiscated by a pro Japanese government? Their place in Rock has only been taken on a short term lease, so what then should they be given notice?"

"But they did come through, obviously." Carroll pointed to the Maserati. "It's not long before Bira's at the wheel of this beast, and Chula's once again entertaining Royalty over at a freehold Tredethy. Clearly, things didn't turn out so badly as might have been feared."

"Well feel free to sift this lot at leisure," said the proprietor. "I'll bring you some chairs."

*

M5 Southbound (Gloucestershire)

Where, as Helen accelerated from Michaelwood Services, why should Chas be bracing himself to an endeavour to stay awake?

The girl had slept well through the early hours and was confident of reaching Plymouth without further interruption, a confidence shared by Chas....... so what had rendered him so determined now to forego the deserved shut-eye that he had been so looking forward to just two hours before?

A creeping suspicion, that's what. One some fifty or so miles old by the time he'd pulled in for their best part of an hour long stop. He'd sensed a follower, just the one man in a worryingly anonymous silver grey Honda Accord which he was coming to feel had too closely matched his own variations in speed and switch of lane, even to the extent of following him into the Services car park.

Yes, by the time they'd emerged he was gone....... but what had there been to prevent him from fixing a tracking device, under the back bumper for instance, so as to enable a more discrete shadowing to be resumed a junction or two further along?

He'd said nothing to Helen, for she would think him paranoid, he thought, and perhaps justifiably, for even he was tempted to dismiss all this as a symptom of fatigue. But maybe not, so for as long as he could he would attempt to remain watchful.

*

Tintagel

"Hey Jim, look at his July entry...... July 1945." Eamon passed the journal, allowing Busbridge to reciprocate with a handful of photos.

"Ah yes." Adjusting his glasses he flicked at the previous pages. "Bira getting towards the end of his notebook......"

"......and towards the end of his time at Rock. *Where next?* he was thinking, and *what shall I do?* OK, as we've said, things turned out well, but I'm not sure this was anticipated."

The curious man was already reading:

July 1945

And, having been given notice that we must vacate Lynam House by the end of September, could this be our last summer in Cornwall? With Victory in Europe secured the local RAF presence is already being substantially reduced and, having proved itself as a weapon of war, the glider can resume now as my second favourite sporting chariot, provided of course that there can be a future for me in motor racing.

It is for this that drivers such as I have fought and survived, and we know that across the continent a public, too long starved of entertainment, waits eagerly to see their heroes of old wrestle with new machinery. Already the invitations arrive for the White Mouse team to attend this event and that, many of them on improvised circuits using disused airfields.

We need have no fears for the sport. It is alive and it is kicking. For the White Mouse though, matters are very different, so reliant are we on the resources of Chula. Without his time and energy, his organisational flair, and of course his money, the team would be nothing. He well knows this, and whilst ever regretful he has recently had to warn me that other duties might preclude any repeat of his pre war commitment to our sporting venture.

We must be mindful that Britain is still at war in the east, he says, and that in our homeland Pibul's Japanese friendly militaristic party still clings desperately to power and also to those parcels of land annexed for them from Burma and from Laos by way of reward for their collaboration. But its days are numbered, we know, for sooner or later Tokyo must capitulate, so overwhelming now is the superiority of the British-American Force.

And it will be later, agree most, aware as they are of the ferocity and determination with which the Japanese soldier can be expected to conduct a rearguard defence of his homeland however ill equipped. Most though will not be so well informed as Lord Mountbatten.

Having spoken to the Supreme Commander of British forces in that area Chula detects a sense of optimism within the topmost ranks. It might be that with the development and deployment of a knock out weapon such as might reduce the whole of urban Japan to uninhabitable rubble in the space of a mere week, a resolution of the conflict could be forced within days of such cataclysmic force being demonstrated.

Were this to happen we must appreciate that the political situation in Bangkok can be so suddenly and radically altered as to render the whole nation an easy snatch for whoever might be best prepared and placed to seize that hour. This might sound dramatic, but, as Chula says, who in the area could speak with more authority than Lord Louis, the top man in the campaign to clear Burma and therefore one naturally supportive of our Free Thai movement?

None, thinks my cousin. And accordingly, in response to a suggestion from Lord Louis that together with Pridi (leader of the Free Thais) he might suddenly be required to radically re structure the Thai administration, Chula now holds himself in readiness to lend appropriate assistance. Such a fresh new Government, he has been warned, could need to find for itself a fresh new King, an abdication by the young Mahidol boys being widely predicted given that young Ananda's accession, ten years ago, was strongly promoted by Pibul.

Perhaps too clumsily I attemped to warn my cousin against his being in turn seen as a symbol of western imperialist puppetry. To this he flew into one of his 'moods', berating me for my ingratitude to our British hosts, and adding that a lack of co operation on his part could well see his fortune, and mine, coming under the severest scrutiny of the His Majesty's Department of Inland Revenue.

If all this were not enough I am hearing from many involved in the organising of a calendar of racing events across Europe for next year that France will be imposing entry restrictions on those of Thai nationality until such time as a Bangkok Government (however constituted) agrees to hand back the provinces taken by the Japanese from French Laos and Cambodia.

Busbridge looked up.

"What a superb snapshot of that time, Eamon, the brief episode between VE day and VJ. Well done, so much better this is than anything I've seen amongst those photos. And so intriguing given how things turned out in for Pibul, Pridi and the Mahidols in Bangkok, and for Bira and Chula here in Cornwall......such a turnaround! In the event, no throne for Chula......"

"...... and a spanking new Maserati for Bira," added Eamon."What a turnaround indeed......"

"....... with not the slightest indication in July '45 of all that was to transpire."

"Save for the bomb."

"OK," nodded Busbridge, "but how wrong they were in their predictions of its consequences...... Chula keeping his wealth and happily living as to the Manor born over at Tredethy."

"This enabling Bira to develop further his career as a Playboy of the Western World," added Eamon with Syngesque relish. "Everyone's a winner!"

"Save for the doomed young King," reminded Busbridge, looking hard at the page, and after a pause adding, "yes, and maybe Lord Louis Mountbatten. I want a copy of this."

"Mr George looks the kind who wouldn't mind, if he has a copying facility. Now what about these photos....... anything of interest here now, in the light of that which we have just read?"

They were passed back, and Brian George reappeared as Busbridge shuffled though them once again.

"So these are surplus to requirement," said Jim.

"Most are of Chula," said the proprietor, as if in confirmation. "Any there any of interest?"

"I'll give you £5 for this one." It was held up, and there was Chula in his prime, impeccably suited, on the steps of what Eamon recognised to be the clubhouse where he'd eaten earlier in the week. Around him stood a group of four....... two attractive women fashionably suited in the tweedy *new look* style of that time, and with them two younger looking men, the taller being of stern visage, the other markedly less kempt.

"Chula of course, with his wife, Lisba, and Bira's then wife, Ceril, and the men with them....... I'm afraid I don't know. Perhaps you recognise them Mr Busbridge."

"Yes, perhaps I do," smiled the buyer enigmatically. "I'm not sure...... but I'll tell you when I pass again, once I've checked. In the meantime I wonder if you could let us copy a page or so from Bira's journal."

"No problem, Mr Busbridge. In fact if one or both of you would care to come by tomorrow I can get the whole lot copied. There's a machine down at the Spar shop." He glanced at his watch. "But for the school party I'm expecting later I could have done the job this afternoon" Jim produced his wallet and successfully fished therein for a £5 note. George waved it away. "Take the photo now, pay me for it all tomorrow."

Twenty minutes later, and Jim and Eamon are back at St Teath. They can celebrate a successful morning with lunch at the Inn. And both can more closely scrutinise the former's as yet unpaid for purchase.

"Yes," agreed Busbridge, "the photo over at Tredethy attempts to give a far more formal record......."

".......of an altogether more formal gathering, I would say. By comparison one would have to say this was quite amateurish."

"But my guess is that it would again have been Bira behind the camera."

"Making it three couples in all."

"Two married and this pair at the back," pointed Jim

"The two blokes you mean, as a couple...... a recognisable couple? You appear more sure now than you were ready back there to let on."

"This fellow on the left, Eamon, quite smart, as you see ...... I'm thinking that a forty years older version of that very same face filled a week's worth dailies some seven or eight years ago. By then he'd cultivated remarkably strong connections with the Royal Palace, indeed so durable that since his death it has even been suggested he could have been a half brother to the Kings Edward and George, and the Dukes of Kent and Gloucester. He'd made the papers, though, on the strength of his having been belatedly exposed as a *fourth man*. And as for this other character, he with the crumpled ill-fitting suit, the fag in hand, and the gravity defying neck tie, well according to the same sequence we are best regarding him as the *first*, given that the names of the initial pair will almost always be ordered alphabetically."

"So we're looking at one of Cyril Connolly's eponymous *Missing*

Diplomats," nodded Eamon. "The one who went on to outrage Washington during his posting to the British Embassy. How often they will crop up in so many lives! So what, to you, would a wartime call on Chula and Bira imply?"

"Now, with the benefit of hindsight, and a glimpse of that later written journal of Bira's, we might conclude that no self respecting great power was ready to leave Thailand's future as a matter for the nation itself to sort out. This said, at the time there might have been other *Kings across the water* who would also have attracted scrutiny. We've spoken of Marina of Kent being a frequent wartime guest down at Rock. She might have confided to her hosts about this clique of fervently anti-communist Free Poles whose intersest in George might, with his death, have settled on the young Edward."

"Sounds as if this pair could have been spoilt for choice," chuckled Eamon, "dear Marina being in it up to her elbows!"

"But more as a passive listener than as an active intriguer," stressed Busbridge. "Olga, Louis, Philip....... just plain family gossip would at that time have carried so much of political moment."

"But you say we needn't bother ourselves too much with that, Jim, appreciating as we now do how volatile a situation was brewing in Thailand, with the Japs about to be sent packing."

"I do, Eamon, because the resurgent Stalin was making sure that the likes of George of Kent and Paul of Yugoslavia were never again to be in the running, even had the former not flown into a Scottish mountain. With Chula, though, the situation was very different."

"As a Thai pretender you mean."

"I do, for his accession so as to help legitimise a Pridi led post war, post Japanese administration for Thailand would surely have been encouraged by Moscow. Seen as less of a fascist than Pibul, Pridi would have been much preferred, if only as the easier prospective push over."

"But they obviously didn't encourage Chula sufficiently," said Eamon.

"Unless he was more successfully *dis*couraged by others."

"So are we talking threat?"

"Not necessarily, Eamon. We're also in the realm of inducement, remember."

"I suppose we are. Now there's food for thought."

"And to take with you I'm afraid. Join me for supper tomorrow

134

evening. And if you would, Eamon, I'd like you to call up to see our Mr George on your way. We can show the journal, then, to the others."

"I'll be there, Jim. Worry not."

And with that they were away on their separate journeys, Eamon's the shorter, to his caravan at Dinham, Jim's to his cottage at Tremorebridge. And it is he that we can follow....... down the A39 to Wadebridge, then out on the Bodmin Road to Sladesbridge and the turn off there into the lane that finds Polbrock Bridge, Ruthernbridge, and eventually Tremore.

On reaching Jasmine Cottage he is ready for a nap, but first it will be to the phone, to check his message tape.

'Jim...... Tony Cross. It's one thirty. Me and Chas are needing to speak with you urgently, hopefully before the lad begins his night shift. We can be at Jamaica Inn for four this afternoon. If you can be there, then confirm no later than an hour before.

He glances down. By the phone's digital display he has twenty minutes to call back. Twenty seconds is enough.

At St. Enodoc
Chula stands between Lisba (his wife) and Ceril (Bira's), flanked
by friends Antony (l) and Guy (r).

*

Jamaica Inn

They meet in the car park, and settle for the spacious and, at this time, near empty dining area. Coffee is sufficient, certainly for one who'd not so long ago dined at St Teath, and as Busbridge fetches from the self serve he notices straightway how watchful are both father and son, how they edgily check for followers, and how cautiously they select the remotest available table offering a sight of both bar and the car park entrances.

"So......developments?" probed the curious man.

"Chas" prompted Cross senior, "this is your story to tell." *Tine to own up lad*, he meant.

"I've spoken to Peg," commenced the boy awkwardly.

"On the phone...... you'd been given his number?"

"Not on the phone. I travelled to Scotland, leaving on Tuseday evening......."

"........being dropped back in Plymouth just a few hours ago," added the father.

"So you had a lift .... for part of the journey?"

"For the whole of the journey, with someone who'd intended to go most of the way alone. If I could assist with the driving she was ready to go on for the couple more hours that it took."

"To get to Inverness," nodded Busbridge. "So this *she*, she had business in Glasgow/Edinburgh area."

"It was the Helen that I got talking with last Saturday, the grand daughter of Edward Trembath. Her job was taking her as far as Perth."

"Mr Busbridge will want to know what kind of job," said Tony Cross.

"Research...... she works as an assistant for a film production company. They're hoping to bring out a made for television piece on the Burma-Thailand railway. There was this survivor of the death camps who, before he'd eventually died of old age, had taken issue with those he'd considered responsible for the impressions of people and events conveyed in the movie *The Bridge on the River Kwai*. Alec Young he was called, and his family had kept the letters he'd received in the course of quite a lengthy correspondence maintained with the guy who'd written the book from which the screenplay was adapted."

"Pierre Boulle," said Busbridge with authority. "And you saw these letters?"

"Copies of them, yes."

"Interesting...... I have Monsieur Boulle's story at home, and also his address and contact number. I've dropped him a line to say I'm thinking of doing a book, myself, about the entry of Japan into the last war and our woeful state of readiness in respect of the defence of Singapore. He'd been recommended to me as a source, I told him, living as he did at that time in Malaya. A card came back, and yes, he would be pleased to help it said. But do go on. You spoke to Peg, and were rewarded, I trust, for having journeyed so far."

"He was understandably grieved by the destruction of the boat, but no less intrigued than the rest of us when I came to this photograph of his old boss and friends....."

"....... which you said had found its way back to where it was taken, to Tredethy," said Busbridge.

"Subsequent to it having been trimmed," continued Chas. "For I was there in pursuit of the possibility that an intact negative, or perhaps even the actual trimmings, had been saved amongst a wad of documents that Peg might have inherited with the boat. We might imagine a collection of navigation charts, or mooring fee and repair work receipts."

"Or a mixture of all and more," approved Busbridge. "As you say, a possibility. And did you strike lucky?"

"I think I might have. There was a wallet of documents, Peg said, which he removed from the boat....."

"......to leave it with his possessions at the cottage over at St Erney?"

"No. He remembers taking them to a shed he used on the Port Eliot Estate, where there was already a collection of maps, these concerned mostly with the layout of the covers and the rearing pens over which he had the manage, plans he would need to consult when briefing the beaters as to the expected progress of shooting parties along this path or that......"

"...... and, once in with that lot, the boat things were going to be neglected."

"This possibly being to our advantage," continued Chas, "for there they might still lie, neglected and undisturbed. If we can get in there, Jim, then we could give the contents of that wallet a closer inspection than he, Peg, ever did."

"But the actual getting in might be a problem, is this what you're saying?"

Chas hesitated.

"Go on," prompted the father.

"For the final part of the journey, from the other side of Bristol to Plymouth, Helen drove. Having done eight or nine hours worth down from Scotland I was ready to sleep....... and sleep I did, Jim, even though I'd set myself to remain awake."

"You were *anxious* to remain awake, is this what you mean?"

"I suppose I do, because towards the end of that previous stint of mine at the wheel I started to sense we were being followed."

"And you wanted to confirm this growing suspicion. Did you mention this to your companion?"

"I didn't, not wanting to appear paranoid."

"And there was the possibility, also, that she might have instigated the tail," added Tony Cross.

"But I wasn't thinking that way at the time," protested Chas.

"At the time, yes," echoed Busbridge, "but now, on less than half a day's reflection…..."

"More than mere reflection," said the father. "I'm used to being watched, and well before he's back I'm noticing that something's up. The spooks are out in force, and not only in my Plymouth neighbourhood. Declan McDaid calls me from the pay phone in the *Buller's*……"

"…….. to tell you that they have Landrake covered."

"Quarry Cottages, the boat yard, St Erney Church, the lot."

"So everywhere and anywhere associated with Peg Willis," nodded Busbridge.

"Including the Port Eliot," joined Chas. "From Tideford around to Polbathic there's not a lane into the place that won't have its watcher, and I suppose there'll be more of the same around the Menabilly estate, over at Fowey."

"It looks, then, as if a section within the security service was quickly made aware of the purpose behind this spur of the moment journey to Scotland," said Busbridge, "and that they're intent now on grabbing a slice of whatever dividend your enterprise promises to yield."

"And to me it's sounding as if the girl is in cahoots with them," said Tony Cross. "Even if my son, here, remains reluctant to admit as much."

Chas shifted in his seat, exuding an uncomfortable mix of embarrassment and tacit exasperation.

"Chas," mediated Busbridge, "you want to give your companion the benefit of the doubt, and that's your entitlement as well as hers....... but, in fairness, I think we ought to know what she has been told."

"On the way back, very little," mumbled the boy, limply. "On Peg's insistence the Port Eliot stuff was to be strictly for ourselves."

"And you've complied," said Busbridge positively, approvingly.

"Which probably explains why they're not in there already." The father was relentless. "So what did she learn during your journey up?"

"I told her about the group photo at Tredethy, assuming this to have been broached in Carwinion House."

"I'm not sure that it was," snapped Tony Cross.

"But go on," coaxed the curious man.

"And I said about Peg working for Browning down at Fowey before coming to St Erney and Port Eliot with his former boss's boat."

"And what about this suspicion that the photo might have been trimmed?" probed Busbridge gently.

Chas shook his head, but not in denial. The eyes were cast down. Here was self-reproach. An admission was unnecessary, but it came nonetheless.

"This was mentioned. Briefly, though, because she wasn't making much of it."

"At the time, to you....... of course not," scoffed the father. "She merely had to sit tight and wait for the next service station pay phone."

"So was she continuing on to Carwinion" asked Busbridge, "or turning back towards London?"

"She'll be at Carwinion," replied Chas, "for tonight at least. Is this of consequence?"

"It could be that Helen has been used solely by her folks down there, and that rather than her, it's either the father or grandfather, or both, who are in cahoots with the watchers around Port Eliot. If it's through Carwinion that this guard has been raised then I'm thinking that it's to Carwinion we might go to effect a lowering."

"And how does one do that?" questioned Tony Cross.

"The security people will have a two step plan," explained Busbridge, "step one being to allow Chas to find what he seeks."

"And step two?" asked Chas, not without trepidation.

"Will be to gently but firmly dispossess you of that prize before you can fully appreciate its significance. As I see it, though, their strategy is not without its weaknesses."

"Which are?" said Cross senior.

"Firstly, they don't know that we're aware of their lying in wait, and secondly, while they might have Port Eliot covered they can't be so sure as we that this is the place we're needing to get into."

"And we can exploit these flaws?" Chas was doubtful.

"Maybe, but for my idea to work we would need to move quickly."

"And that idea?"

"Is to fool them into thinking they've already obtained what they're after."

"How though?"

"You take them something else, pretending it to be what they want and that it's been recovered from somewhere other than Port Eliot. This is accepted, the watch there is stood down, and for as long as they remain deceived we have a window of opportunity."

Tony Cross nodded approvingly, the implied use of Helen Trembath seeming to him as just as it was safe.

"So what have you in mind as a decoy," he asked, "and from where might you claim it to have been retrieved?"

"If you've a pair of scissors in the Volvo then out there in my car I could have the ideal thing, and where better than here, at *Jamaica Inn*, for it to have lain dormant? Out there, on the edge of the old courtyard there's a room given over to the display of things du Maurier, ranging from movie posters and theatre programmes to manuscript drafts and research notes. There's a few items of personal furniture too, and of course a number of photographs, family photographs......"

"......such as could have been brought here by the likes of Peg," continued Chas, "having been sorted from the kind of miscellany that could easily have accumulated on our boat."

"The choice of here for this rendezvous was inspired," smiled Busbridge. "If it's been noted that you're headed this way then *so what......* our credibility is merely enhanced."

"So you'd better show us what you have in the car," said Tony Cross, rising from his chair...... and within half a minute he'd led the others out into the car park.

*

Tintagel

A minute this, during which Brian George had finally managed rid his establishment of the last of that tiresome party of school children. For no more than an hour they'd infested his museum, but to him it had seemed like twenty....... and now there was the finger smudged glass to be polished and the floor to swept of sweet papers.

Changing his door sign 'closed' he made a start with a broom, carefully avoiding the two customers who yet remained, a pair of late arriving Japanese tourists who, having given their money, couldn't now be begrudged a further half-hour's peaceful perusal of the exhibits. Courteously they'd made to leave when George had paused at the door..... but he'd bade them stay, confident that they were of a sort that would never seek to stretch the little latitude that he was pleased to allow. It was interesting to see how they too were drawn to the Prince Bira corner where, on a chair close by, lay that journal he'd promised to copy for the next day.

They were moving towards it, he noticed, as he swept on at a discrete distance...... and lifting it now, to inspect the pages. They would ask questions, he knew. He was prepared, though, to the extent, even, of being ready to offer to make for them a set of copies extra to that promised to the gentlemen who'd been in earlier..... for these guys now, they looked the kind who might tip well.

And as that long neglected journal was receiving its second examination of the day, so, sitting in the Cross's Volvo, James Busbridge took a pair of borrowed scissors to the photograph he'd earlier eased into his possession. Four careful snips and it was just the three figures, Prince Chula, his own wife and that of his younger cousin who were left to grace the entrance to the nineteenth at St Enodoc Golf Club. Their guests lay sequestrated on his lap, retaining even as mere shadows their notorious talent for deceit.

"Now Chas," Jim held his recruits up so that the boy in the rear might see, his palm shielding them from the father who sat at the wheel. "Can you identify this pair?"

"I'm afraid I can't."

"That's good, for you'll sound all the more convincing when you show them to your friend, asking this same question."

"And you think she'll know?"

"I don't, but I'm hoping she might suggest they be waved in front of her father and grandfather, something I want you to agree to."

"You intend, then, that these be left with her."

"I do, and she must understand that in accordance with what you'd been told by Peg, in Scotland, you managed to locate them here at *Jamaica Inn* this afternoon. With any luck she'll pass this on and, for a while at least, those who've set the watchers to wait will think themselves to be in possesion of what they want."

"And the guard around Port Eliot, this will be stood down," said Tony Cross, "giving us a chance to creep in and secure for ourselves the real deal. I'm not sure, though, that I'm comfortable with Chas venturing into Carwinion alone."

"He doesn't have to," said Busbridge. "There's a pay phone back there in the inn, and Chas must have the girl's number to hand. Give her a place and a time and just a hint at what you've got to show her and she'll come out, I'm sure. There's a pub in Trispen, just a few miles this side of Truro...... *The Clock and Key*, the ideal place."

"So I would go alone in the Volvo." Chas looked tentatively towards his father. Tony Cross raised no objection. "And you, Jim, you wouldn't mind me leaving these cuttings with her."

"If that's what it takes, young man, then not at all. I'm thinking the sooner she's back at Carwinion the better, so an hour with her in the *Clock and Key* would probably be too long. By then, using my car, your father and I will have met up with Declan, at the *Rod and Line*, say, over at Tideford, and with the benefit of his local knowledge we can be plotting the best way in and out of a soon to be unguarded Port Eliot."

"Take what you need," said father to son, producing from his pocket a palm full of change.

Chas did, making the call then to find Helen every bit as obliging as Jim had predicted. Of course she knew the *Clock and Key*, and she would be delighted to join him there.

So delighted, in fact, that it would be he that joined her, for it was she who arrived at their rendezvous first. As Chas rolled the Volvo into the pub car park there she waited, in that now familiar XR3.

Out she hopped to lead him smartly through to the lounge bar and there insist that she be the one to stand the first drink apiece. The *only*

142

drink apiece, Chas informed her, claiming that he would be late enough in getting back as it was.

"Then briskly to business," prompted the girl as they chose their table. "The long trek to Scotland has borne fruit, you tell me."

Chas laid the clippings before her.

"These characters I picked up at *Jamaica Inn*."

"Interesting."

"But as to identity, I would only be guessing. Any ideas?" Helen shook her head. "But what about your father, or your grandfather? They might know."

"If they were here.....but they're not."

"You said earlier that you'd be returning up country tomorrow. Take these chaps back to Carwinion for the night. Show your folks, then, in the morning, leave Cornwall by the Plymouth road. I can meet you at the car park up at the bridge and there hear what, if anything, they've made of them."

Within twenty minutes they were back in their separate cars, heading in opposite directions. It had been too easy, feared Chas. While matched by hers, his eagerness to be away must have seemed suspicious. All he had to do now was to drive to St John and wait, as arranged, at Sally's for the phone call from his father saying where and when he would be best collected.

Easing himself onto the on to the A30 at the Garland Cross roundabout he glanced down at the dashboard clock. He should be through Trerulefoot by eight, he reckoned, by which time Helen will have been back at Carwinion for a good half-hour at least, and perhaps already presenting the bait. It might be taken at any minute. He hoped they were ready at the *Rod and Line*.

And they were, McDaid having re-activated the local network of contacts through which he'd been alerted to the extent of the watch around Port Eliot. Should it be stood down then here in the main bar of Tideford's 'local' he was well placed to again be promptly and quietly briefed.

Eight o' clock came, but, as yet, no word of any slackening of that guard.......eight-thirty, nine, and still not so much as whisper. Nothing, not until nine-forty five, when there came into the bar a four man group evincing an almost palpable squad uniformity, less with their attire (apart from the general robustness of footwear) than with the commonality of age and build, the distinct trim of hair and severity of countenance. Declan recalled this kind of presence earlier in the year, an absence this time of any visibly toted firearms making it only marginally less menacing.

He sat tight, listening with his friends to the warm-down nature of their conversation, cautious this initially, then, with a round of drinks, progressively relaxed and for a pair of keen eared listeners, more revelatory. This was just part of a larger team assigned to Port Eliot, they gathered, the rest almost certainly exercising a preference for the Eliot Arms over in St Germans.

Then started the trickle of telling phrases; mention of
'word from further down west......'
then
'turned up at Jamaica Inn......'
followed by
'dropped into our laps......'
and even a
'no more left for us to do here, not now......'

It was time to make their move. As planned, Busbridge would take Tony Cross up to Trerulefoot, to the Windyridge transport café, on the Torpoint road just across from Kernow Mill. There they could summon and wait for Chas, and perhaps between the three of them and the two vehicles concerned, draw such attention that might have otherwise have followed Declan's homeward stroll to St Erney.

For this time he would be taking a less direct route than usual. Having been told what Peg had said he'd left on the estate McDaid knew exactly where it was to be found. And if he could go in alone, he'd persuaded the others, then with his knowledge of the brakes and the hollows and the maze of paths therethrough he could easily confound any attempt made to follow, however professionally mounted. If allowed now to address this task in his own way, in his own time, then he was confident he could have something for them by the morning.

"I can be at *The Notter Bridge* for eleven," he suggested.

"We'll be there," promised Cross, "both Chas and I."

"The pair of you being en route to Tremorebridge," insisted Busbridge, "and I would be delighted, Declan, if you could come along with them."

*

St John

"Because at the time, Sally, that opportunity of getting to Inverness seemed too good to miss." Chas knew that the girl deserved a better explanation and he, to be fair, would like to be providing one, but following those in-car indiscretions with Helen he was wary of compounding the resultant embarrassment.

"And you've agreed to meet her again tomorrow?"

"Because now we're into a double game. We've fed her disinformation, in the form of a loaned item. She wants to return it in good faith."

"And credibility demands that you accept it likewise. How convenient, Chas! And the real information?"

"Isn't yet accessible, hence the deception and my being so vague. I wish I could tell you more." The phone rang. "That should be Dad." He sounded a little too relieved. Sally answered, and he'd been right. She passed the receiver, and within seconds it was back on the hook. Chas had to be going.

"They're waiting for you I suppose," she pouted, reaching for the video control to restart the film she'd been watching when he'd arrived. "You needn't worry about me." A black and white picture returned to the screen, the characters momentarily frozen until lurching with their soundtrack into scratchily orchestrated life. "I've the last hour of *Great Expectations* to keep me entertained."

Within fifteen minutes the rendezvous at Windyridge had been made, father and son then returning eastward via the bridge to urban Plymouth, Jim taking his opposite direction for rural Tremore. Reaching Jasmine Cottage by eleven thirty the curious man looked to the morrow with glee. Eamon would be bringing the copy of Bira's journal, and Declan, hopefully, would be in possession of those clipped from the wings of the Tredethy *ensemble*. And later, of course, that Jeremy would be with them to lend his interpretation to what might be pulled together.

Excited, he had little appetite for sleep. Instead he set about putting faces to the figures sketched by Kate. Most were available on his bookshelves. Snipped from their pages they could be dragooned into a Sergeant Pepper style montage. That they might not be groomed and dresed appropriately for an eastertime lawn mattered far less than the progress they signified.

He could add to them that print of Chula himself at the St Enodoc clubhouse acquired earlier in the day....... but finding faces for the remaining figures, the Mesdames *A* and *T*, this was going to be more problematic. Perhaps, after this night's foray by moonlight, Declan might bring a lead.

*

Declan

A foray so far proceeding without hitch. Having successfully wormed his way to the heart of the Port Eliot estate, and his target, a copse-shielded lakeside shed, McDaid had quickly located the likely sheaf of documents that he had been tasked to retrieve. Now, tucking it securely beneath his jacket, he could make for home by the quickest, most direct and discreet path, a route that would *not* return him to Tideford and the main road.

Instead he was following the widening river southwards towards St Germans, leaving the main house with its lush lawn to his right, and likewise the village with its magnificent Norman Church. By ducking into the wooded spur where once stood an old Priory he could edge along to the embankment which lifted the main railway line onto its elegantly arched stone and brick viaduct. Climb through the bushes to the track, follow the up-line across, and in no time he would be over the Tiddy and safely back in his home Parish.

*

Friday a.m.

.... and at Ruthernbridge Kate opens the door to her postman. He has knocked so as to hand her an uncommonly large envelope, one of dimension too important to suffer being bent through the letterbox.

> '*For the attention of G Thomas*
> *c/o K Rogers,*'

146

begins the address. It is accepted with polite thanks, and taken through to the kitchen where it must wait for the addressee's anticipated later arrival. Anticipated by herself, yes, but by who else she wonders. This thing had a London postmark What might this mean when Gareth was based in South Wales and Jeremy in Bath...... a wider involvement? Neither had said, so who could be trusting her to look after this before passing it on? Alan......? she asks herself intuitively. Whether so or not, she would learn later, perhaps, and consider such enlightenment due reward for the day's work that lay ahead.

Eamon, meanwhile, dozed on at Dinham Field, eventually stirring at ten for a leisurely wash and shave. A good late breakfast, he decided, should see him through to the promised supper at Jasmine Cottage....... so where better for a couple of freshly caught, freshly grilled mackerel than Port Isaac?

And no less tasty to follow on this bright morning was a brisk climb to Lobber point with its stupendous Devonward view, past Tintagel, to Hartland, and even Lundy beyond. The haven below, with its harbour and tangle narrow lanes, could have been a scale model, and his own car, there below the slip on the low-tide stream washed shingle, just a toy.

A toy....... reminding him that it was time to move on now to the museum lest Mr George were in the habit of closing for lunch. If, in light so clear as today's the distance seemed walk-able, he still had before him nothing less than a twenty-minute drive. But once on the road he felt no great need to hurry. He could gently cruise Delabole main street and then pick his way carefully through that swarm of traffic which will persist, albeit lightly, around Tintagel even into low season October.

He was almost there now, and preparing to swing into the parking area....... but wait. Indicate not, Eamon, for already standing therein are two police cars. If the light shining within suggested the officers had entered, the door looked to be firmly shut. The place was closed, it seemed, and an enquiry was in progress. The cabby drove steadily on, striving to make it look as if he were passing on an every day journey.

A junction ahead appeared to offer access to an inland ridge, so he took this lane, winding his way upwards until finding a gateway that offered a panorama of the town, the toy museum included. Pulling a small pair of binoculars from his glove pocket he climbed out and from the cover of the hedge set himself to watch.

After twenty uneventful minutes four uniformed officers emerged, two for each car, but there was still no sign of Barry George, the fastening of the museum door being left to the last of the constables. One set then went on their way, the other pair staying on in response to the arrival of what appeared from their equipment to be a two-man television outside broadcast team. In no more than twenty further minutes their work was done, a reporter having spoken briefly to the camera before allowing it to pan slowly along the outside of the museum.

Intrigued, Eamon returned to his vehicle, tuning its radio to the local station, *Radio Cornwall*. He had only two songs to wait, and then, in the lunch time news round-up;-

Police have this afternoon confirmed the identity of a man whose badly mutilated body was found just after dawn by the side of the main A39 at Collan's Cross, between Davidstow and Slaughterbridge. He has been named as Mr Barry George, a local man best known as founder and proprietor of the Tintagel Toy museum.

It would appear that he might have been struck and dragged some distance by a large fast moving vehicle, either a lorry or a coach. Drivers of such who travelled that section of road during the early hours of today are asked to check for, and report, any sign of their vehicle having been involved in such an incident. Enquiries continue, meanwhile, as the Police endeavour to build a picture of Mr George's movements during the 24 hours prior to his death.

Eamon was stunned, the absence of even so much as a hint at foul play working perversely to intensify the unease. His background demanded that such a presumption be positively countered. In that report it had been simply ignored, and feeling exposed he was suddenly anxious for cover. This whole stretch of Cornwall, from Morwenstow down to Pentire was too elevated, too treeless. He needed the wooded valleys of the inland Camel and its feeders. There was shelter there, and there were friends. Tintagel could be left to brave King Arthur, and if Jim still wanted Bira's journal then it was up to himself to make representations to the appropriate authorities.

Driving on, Eamon's continued climb away from the town brought him to a crossroads. Left it was to Boscastle and right to Camelford, his intended direction. A signpost, though, persuaded him across to stay with the lane. 'Davidstow', it indicated, and soon he was emerging on to the very stretch of the Bude-Camelford highway that had supposedly claimed George's life. The road was wide. It was fast, and, even at mid-day, isolated. He paused for a line of traffic. A jaywalker here, during the early hours, this was barely imaginable. So did this make a hit and run incident excusable almost ...... or merely less likely? For this particular driver it had to be the latter.

Turning southward, he followed the main road down into the heart of the neat little township of Camelford, a welcome crumb of something just a little more urban. The shock was subsiding, he could begin to think ahead. Would Busbridge share his misgivings, he wondered. Certainly there would be frustration, for a man less fearful and more curious would have surely ventured an enquiry about access to that journal, if only to know that it hadn't been removed from the premises.

But now, without so much as that to report, Carroll could only feel inadequate. He would be a disappointment, he knew, unless he could somehow concoct a sweetener along the way. And perhaps he might, he thought, as he forked off the A39 onto the Bodmin road. In less than ten minutes he would be passing within half a mile of Tredethy...... Tredethy and the picture in which sat that wordly companion for the young bachelor Prince.

'*A*' was the clue, and she had been vaguely familiar. An identity would come to him eventually he was sure...... so perhaps with another quick look. He glanced at his watch.

*

At the border

It was almost one, the time also noted by Chas as he stood in the small car park to the Devon side of the bridge. He'd stepped off the bus just five minutes before and yes, this was her distinctive moter crossing now. With no toll queue she would be impressively punctual. Through she came, filtering right for the roundabout with its car park exit, and eventually growling to a halt on the front rank overlooking Brunel's grand design.

"Don't look so surprised to see me!" she quipped, leaning to open the door so that Chas might join her in the car. He did.

"And you can drop me back at the yard?"

"Of course I can," smiled Helen, "but not before I've returned these." She passed an unsealed envelope from which Chas eased the two images.

"So any luck?"

"My father couldn't be sure, but my Grandfather, he's pretty certain that this one," she pointed first to the smarter figure, "is Anthony Blunt, and that the other chap, here, is Guy Burgess."

"So, a pair of traitors caught together on camera," smirked Chas, realising now what a crafty little ploy he'd helped effect, "both men at that time working for Moscow. So what kind of task might they have been set, across there in north Cornwall. Did your folks speculate?"

"They did, and I heard that Chula had a Russian mother, and that Bira was engaged in the development of airborne assault techniques. Also there was mention from my grandfather of the uncertainties then surrounding the destiny of the Thai crown. He spoke of a boy king who lived at that time in Switzerland, along with an elder sister and a younger brother, this at the insistence of their mother who was determined that they should have the benefit of a full European education."

"So the Royal duties in Bangkok....?"

".......had been left to a Regent. The boy King had been just nine when he came to the throne, and this after his predecessor had been as good as forced to abdicate, the consequence of a constitutional crisis."

"And he also lived in exile?"

"Forced exile in his case, which he lived out in this country, somewhere up in Surrey. Grandad spoke of visits made to him there by his friend Walter....."

"Walter Monckton....."

"......who it seems was a something of a specialist in the abdication business. The impression gained was that the while living in the same country, the old King and Chula were not on the best of terms, the uncle being particularly critical of his nephew's indulgent guardianship of a young cousin."

"And do we know when the old King died?" asked Chas.

" '41, and this might have simplified things for the lad in Lausanne but for the fact of his country then being over run by the Japs."

"And with their defeat, we're into the Cold War contest, the communist hordes versus the big dollars."

"And during a visit to Bangkok the young King suffers a violent death, in circumstances still far from clear."

"But the younger brother," continued Chas, "he then rises to the responsibilities thrust his way and wears the Crown to this day. One must suppose, though, that for a while Chula would have been in the mix. Did Sir Edward go into this?"

"He didn't."

"Because he couldn't...... or just wouldn't?"

Helen started her motor. "All the same to me, Chas. I merely listen. I'll get you back to work."

*

Camel valley

Turning into Tredethy, Carroll edged slowly across the broad gravelled forecourt. And something had changed here, to the front of the house. A boarded across ground floor window was disturbing the building's pleasing symmetry. There'd been a break-in he suspected, with entry having been forced close to the office. Ominous this, but having come to the door he would have to press the bell.

It was the proprietor who answered. A fierce glare confirmed recognition.

"You were with Mr Busbridge," she scowled. "It surprises me that you should show up like this."

"Alone this time, and I was hoping to beg another glance at that photo you have on the wall of your office."

"You've not seen your friend today, then?"

"Not yet. Has he been around too?"

"Not this morning, but during the night...... well who knows? We've been burgled. That picture went, and nothing else. I've given his name to the police. He 's been in trouble with the law before, I've heard."

"So when I catch up with him he'll have been interviewed, you think."

151

"One hopes the constabulary would have done their job."

"But there's been no loss of life?" An earnest enquiry this from Eamon, but received as sarcasm. Retreating, the proprietor readied to close the door.

"There's nothing for you here. I'll thank you to be on your way. Good day."

The cabby sloped back to his vehicle, disconsolate and perturbed. These unexpected turns of event, at Tintagel and here at Tredethy, they had to be somehow connected, he felt, by an as yet hidden link that carried implications for his own safety. He needed time and space to think. He could take an hour now, so to where for a place? Helland Bridge, he decided, just below here. He could park and take himself for a stroll...... twenty minutes, upriver this time, and then twenty minutes back.

*

Devonport

Having been dropped back at the Yard entrance in good time Chas does not immediately check in for his afternoon stint. Instead, on Helen's characteristically brisk departure, he crosses to the nearby side turning where, as arranged, his father waits in the Volvo. They are at a critical juncture. Telephones are not to be trusted. Opening the front passenger door Chas slips in next to his father. He produces the traitors.

"She was fooled, dad, I'm pretty sure of that. Our Jim, he's a devious as they come. You know yet who these are?"

"I feel I ought to," squints Cross senior, "this guy, the smarter one, particularly."

"Well 'this guy' isn't a Guy, he's an Anthony....... Anthony Blunt, no less. While here," Chas holds up the scruffier, "we have the real thing...... Mr Guy Burgess."

"And both men identified for us by the former member for Plymouth North. What an excellent pair of red herrings."

"Unless, by unhappy coincidence, the same pair actually did feature in that other photo"

"Taken at another time, at another place?"

152

"Unlikely, yes, but we can't ignore the possibility. If they were entertained at Rock then why not also at Tredethy? Has Declan phoned?"

"He has, and I've said I'm picking you up after work then driving on over. We'll meet him at *The Notter Bridge*, and then travel on to Jim's."

*

To Jasmine Cottage, Tremorebridge

........where it will be mid afternoon before Eamon eventually turns up, fully expecting to find a police car in the lane outside, attendant upon a rigorous search of the premises. But there is no sign of such, and he is welcomed by the curious man who can extend a cordial and relaxed greeting.

Busbridge will note, however, that Carroll is a degree edgier today, and he sees too that the man is empty handed. Disappointing news is anticipated, but not the initial question.

"Have you had the police here this morning?"

"I've not, Eamon...... does that surprise you?"

"It does, Jim. I was told they'd been given your name."

"By whom...... when, and where?"

"By the woman in charge over at Tredethy. I was speaking to her just a couple of hours ago. I called there on the way down from Tintagel, hoping for another viewing of that photo. Another glimpse of that 'A' woman and a name might have come to me."

"And did it?"

"I was told there'd been a break in, and the thing had been taken."

"So the police were summoned, and they've been told of our interest."

"First thing this morning, the break-in having occurred during last night." Eamon took a deep breath. "And there was something else, also during the night, up at Tintagel."

"Concerning that museum?"

"You've not tuned to the local news this afternoon?"

Busbridge shook his head. "Tell me."

"Our friend Mr George is no more. His mangled body was found

153

at day-break by the side of the main Bude-Camelford highway, just a couple of miles inland from Tintagel."

"So what we were promised from him......"

"...... hasn't materialised, Jim, at least not in my hands. When I reached the museum this morning the police were there. I didn't hang about. Parking outside the town I tuned to Radio Cornwall......"

".......and you learned of Barry George's death. Any suggestion of foul play?"

"Not on the radio."

"But you're thinking that these two incidents of last night, at Tintagel and Tredethy, might in some way be connected."

"Because in terms of our interest in the Thai princes they inescapably are, and in a way, Jim, it begins to bother me that the police haven't turned up here. One's reminded of that Holmes story......"

"........ in which the dog supposedly set to do so fails to bark." Busbridge was sorting himself a pen and writing pad. "Despair not, Eamon. Others are on their way to contribute to our understanding of these events. In the meantime, we would be failing them if we didn't now commit to paper all we can remember of Bira's journal."

*

Ruthern

Leaving work at the same time as Chas, Kate could be back at Ruthernbridge before the Crosses had even reached Notter....... and this was as well for, on the A30, Gareth was already within sight of Bodmin's stone Beacon. Jeremy, now rounding Exeter after his relatively late start from Bath, he would be a good hour behind. Time in which the Welsh Guards veteran would closely inspect the contents of the envelope waiting upon his arrival.

Three good photocopies of three enlarged photographs, each one portraying the same two figures, both male...... one of relatively slight, adolescent build, and oriental of feature and hue, the other displaying the fuller build and paler skin of the white middle aged Saxon. Unclothed, the pair shared a bed, and thereon three varieties of consensual intimate

154

embrace. They were lovers it appeared, and if the older less passive figure appeared the more experienced, the younger was certainly compliant.

"Interesting," remarked Kate, as she might perhaps on a sequence of casualty department X rays. "Is there a note to say when they were taken?"

"Here...... on the reverse of theis we have a when and where. '*1944*,' it says, and '*Lausanne*', with David adding that '*The Princess enjoys a uniquely privileged access to the private papers of the late Viscount Monckton of Brenchley.*"

"David?" The name was new one to Kate.

"A former comrade of mine, a fellow Falklands veteran now holding a Royal household position, at Kensington Palace."

"So this Princess...... are we talking Margaret Windsor, Michael of Kent, or Diana of Wales even?"

"Any of them, I suppose," replied Gareth evasively. "This Viscount Monckton, though, he's Jeremy's man. I'll be interested to know his thoughts on the matter." Kate glanced across to her mantle-shelf clock.

"Well he shouldn't be too long now."

*

Also heading west

Tony Cross was at the wheel. Declan now had the front passenger seat, Chas having moved to the rear.

For fifteen or so minutes little had been said, not while they skirted the Eliot estate, awed as they were at their own overnight audacity, and wary lest something to arrest their progress might suddenly rear out from behind the trees and the hedges to their left. Only on their turn away at Trerulefoot could that lip locking anxiety lessen with each westward mile.

"So Declan," began Chas, "am I to be allowed a preview of this evening's picture show?"

"You're that desperate, eh?"

"Apprehensive might be the better word. A matching pair and our bluff fails."

McDaid reached for his wallet, producing therefrom what he'd been sent to retrieve, the two cut out figures. Transferred carefully to thumb and fingers of his left hand he held them up at ear level, above his right shoulder.

"Recognise these? I don't."

"And I don't," said the boy, relieved to be seeing neither Blunt nor Burgess."This is good, for somebody might....... Jim, Jeremy, Eamon......"

"Or even me," smiled Tony Cross, driving on, eyes firmly ahead.

Half an hour and he was through the Glynn Valley, crossing the River Fowey for a third time at Bodmin Parkway to climb past Coleslogget and smoothly join the A30....... some ten minutes short of having had to give way for Jeremy who with due regard for Gareth's parked motorcycle, was now rolling to a careful halt at Ruthernbridge.

*

Ruthern

"Just the man," glowed Kate, warmly opening her door. "Come and see what the postman brought today. Gareth can't wait to show you. We're in the kitchen. The kettle's on."

The lecturer followed her through, and any travel weariness was quickly dispelled by the spread of pictures on the table.

"Steamy enough already, you might think," quipped Gareth. "These have been sent down for me by a former comrade in arms. He now works at Kensington Palace. I've told him about Eamon's tape and the riddle of the Denning's *Desert Island* selection from *The King and I*. Clearly he thinks this lot might have some relevance."

"And is this explained?" asked Jeremy. "Was there a covering letter?"

"The briefest of notes, that's all. My friend isn't looking to make trouble for himself."

"He wishes to preserve anonymity."

"A proviso, I'd say, should we be wanting him to send more."

"And the note tells us what?"

"Here." Gareth had it in his hand. "Read it."

Jeremy took it.

'1944: Lausanne
The Princess enjoys a uniquely privileged access to the private papers of
the late Viscount Monckton of Brenchley.'

"Walter again! I suppose that shouldn't surprise me. So could this be the King?" he added, scanning the pictures once more. "Not quite twenty he would have been in '44."

"The young King of Siam, you mean."

"Who then lived in Lausanne, his mother having insisted that he should complete a European education."

"And some finishing school this was!"

"It was a trap, Gareth."

"So you're talking blackmail," joined Kate, handing to each a mug of tea.

"Attempted blackmail at least," nodded Jeremy, with a perfunctory 'ta'. "And we know that this evidence of un-regal conduct came into the hands of Walter, an expert in the art of smooth dethronement."

"But this lad was shot," said Gareth.

"He was," acknowledged Jeremy. "By his own weapon, though, held perhaps in his own hand...... the ultimate abdication."

"So which Princess might be dabbling into this sort of stuff, Jeremy?" asked Kate. "If this is from Kensington Palace then one has a choice...... Margaret, Michael, Diana."

"I think I'd put my money on the last, if only because I know her to have struck up a close frienship with Rosa Monckton, she a grand daughter to our man Walter."

"So would Diana be trying to make some kind of point, or some kind of trouble" said the nurse.

"For her father in law, perhaps," suggested the lecturer, "or even for her husband, who held his great uncle Dickie in such famously high esteem....... absurdly high esteem, many would say."

"Put with the bombing that Eamon narrowly missed, and the burning of Browning's boat this looks to be dangerous stuff," said Gareth.

"Perhaps she won't know what she's triggered...... but even so, is young Lady Di really going to be so desperate?"

"Come to where I work," answered Kate grimly, "and you'll soon enough see what a combination of post natal depression and an unfeeling spouse can do. It could be that she's feeling locked in, that her cries for help are being muffled by the façade that is *Majesty*. Wanting to hit out she'll be delighted to sling a bit of muck around. I've seen it happen, the husband's family can become a prime target. It's seen as a formative influence, and as such a threat to be nullified."

Jeremy went again to the table, to the pictures and note.

"*1944*," he muttered. "If we're to conclude that this older fellow is connected *our* Royal Family then we can safely eliminate the Duke of Kent. By then he was a couple of years dead. Browning will be the key to this, I'm sure."

"He and that female companion of Prince Philip," added Kate. "The 'A' perhaps for Anna, who could still be alive."

*

At Jim's

It took a second, firmer knock on the door of nearby Jasmine Cottage to jerk Busbridge from the desk at which he and Eamon had been attempting from memory to re-assemble the bones of the Bira '45 journal entry read and left and probably now lost at Tintagel. Good, he thought. This would be the Crosses, hopefully with a successful Declan McDaid.

Eamon stayed with the freshly made note, which was coming to focus more on the youger cousin's personal anxiety at that time, than any broader political uncertainties. If they were relevant (as they surely were) they could be discussed later, at supper, in Jeremy's presence. More to be stressed now was Bira's concern over money. Could Chula, the generous pre war patron, ever again provide the kind of backing that might ensure post war racing circuit success? Clearly, at the time Bira had doubted this....... and yet, as things had turned out, that understandable pessimism seems to have been weirdly unjustified. *White Mouse* was re-launched, and the career of its star driver went from strength to strength.

Declan meanwhile was being ushered into the cottage, his entry commanding a mix of deference and expectation worthy of a World Champion Boxer. He knew it, and while giving nothing away from his own expression, the Crosses who followed beamed as confidently as would a pair of corner-men convinced of their man's infallibility. Chas in particularly saw little cause for reticence.

"You can take this pair back now, Jim," he said brandishing Blunt and Burgess as if each were a ticket for a ringside seat. "You are as a devious as you are curious, sir, and I will ever consider myself privileged to have played a part in such a crafty little ruse."

"Thank you," nodded Busbridge, slotting the characters into his wallet. "Do I take it, then, that you can report some success?"

"Declan?" prompted Tony Cross.

McDaid reached into his pocket, producing once again what he'd shown to Chas in the car, the cuttings this time being lain on the table for all to see.

"There you are," he announced, "freshly garnered from the depths of a moonlit Eliot Estate..... pictures, but I'm afraid no names. As pleased as I was to get them back to Quarry Cottage, I regret to say that I there found myself looking at a pair of total strangers. I'm sorry. For all the fuss surrounding these men I would have thought that just one might have been at least half famous."

"Apologise not, Declan," said Cross senior. "Your specialist role in this enterprise is splendidly achieved. I wouldn't have been able to place them either....... Jim?.......Eamon?"

A huddle had formed over the fragments.

"From the backgrounds I'd certainly say they were off that same picture that was hanging at Tredethy," observed Eamon.

Busbridge tapped at the younger looking of the men. "Yes, and we've spoken of this before as a possibility. The fellow would have stood just within the left hand margin of the print, and therefore to the right of the sitting Princess Marina. He looks to me like a young Jack Profumo."

"Aaha, yes," joined Eamon. "Now you say...... and perhaps the man's later conduct can explain the later excision. A combination of Jack Profumo and the country house party came to be associated with a particular kind of woman......"

"...... and a particular word," joined Tony Cross, "*scandal.*"

"And it wouldn't have done for the Princess Marina to have been tainted by such," said Busbridge, "renowned as she'd become by the '60s for her effortless Majesty. And likewise, in the same frame, we have a young Prince Philip...... another whose future role, like that of Caesar's bride to be, was to require that he be above suspicion."

"So in his capacity as a former Palace minder, you think that Browning might have wielded the scissors around the early to mid '60s time," ventured Chas, "post Profumo."

"And perhaps at the suggestion of Lord Denning," offered Eamon, "master of the whitewash rollers. But how is any of this to be connected with *The King and I*?"

"Because it won't just be about Profumo's conduct as a Government Minister," answered Busbridge. "Indeed, we needn't assume this to have been the primary issue. The Keeler business was sordid enough, you might tell me, but no military or political catastrophe ensued. Loss of life was limited to Stephen Ward, in the run of things a death so inconsequential as to perhaps underline my point."

"Which is?" asked McDaid.

"That maybe the Profumo scandal threatened to lift the lid on an even bigger can of worms, something that had been festering since the time that photo was taken, something that involved the Royal families of both Britain and Thailand......"

".......in which a younger Profumo would only have had a minor role," nodded McDaid.

"Quite possibly," answered Busbridge.

"So who were the major players?" asked Eamon. "And of these, who the major casualties?"

"*Some have been deposed*," declaimed Busbridge, sonorously
"*some slain in war,*
Some haunted by the ghosts they have deposed,
.... some sleeping killed.
All murdered."

"So you're talking life and death," said Chas.

"I am," confirmed the curious man. "Life, death, the destiny of Nations, then...... and perhaps even now."

"Accordingly must our realm of speculation widen," grimaced Eamon, "and just as we were hoping to get things little more narrowed down."

A further shrug from the cabby and the three just arrived might have heard right then of what had passed in Tintagel and Tredethy, had there not come the further knock at the door, a lighter knock recognised immediately by Jim as Kate's.

"Do come in," he called, and they did….. the nurse followed by Gareth and then Jeremy. While having met Busbridge before at Kate's, for the Welshman this was a first visit to Jasmine Cottage. "Welcome Gareth," continued the host. "As you've probably been told, you join some fellow guests this evening…… Mr Declan McDaid from Saltash, Mr Tony Cross and his son Chas, both from Plymouth, and Mr Eamon Carroll who hails from London."

"We were just listening to Jim doing a fine impersonation of Sir John Gielguld," smiled Tony Cross.

"Prompted by a first glimpse of the missing pair," said Busbridge.

"Chopped from the edges of a group photo you'd seen," nodded Gareth. "I've been told about this. It was up at some manor house where it had been taken, back when it was owned by a Thai Prince."

"Tredethy the place, Chula the Prince," said Carroll. "Jim has re assembled the more famous characters using other snaps scattered amongst his library. Here, look……. a freakish assembly I know, but to each side we can add this man, and this, like a pair of bookends."

"And are they too identified?" asked Gareth, his graft scarred eyes glancing from one figure to the other.

"The younger fellow to the left, with Marina, I'm fairly sure he's Jack Profumo," answered Busbridge.

"And over here, this other character," pointed the Guardsman, "can you again venture a name?"

"On that one we're stumped."

"But I'm not," said Jeremy. "That's our friend Walter…… Walter Monckton. We spoke of him the other day, down at Carwinion. Monckton and Edward Trembath shared a close and lengthy professional association, going back to the '30s when they both worked for the Duchy."

"But if this was '46," said Kate, "neither would yet have been into parliamentary politics."

"Granted," nodded Jeremy, "but Walter was certainly into his specialist niche, that of pilot to the royal figure having to navigate uncertain waters. His counsel for David Windsor won high regard from an establishment pleased to have the former Monarch safely tucked away in exile…… and come '46, out in India, the dear old Nizam of Hyderabad was enduring a similar pre-squeeze softening, notwithstanding his touching loyalty during the war."

"So it's your view," checked Busbridge, "that for all his surface indignation Monckton was supportive of the Viceroy in his scuttling of India."

"Because this was what Westminster wanted," confirmed Jeremy, "and where a hard-cop/soft-cop routine was appropriate then Walter was a natural for that latter role."

"And by the time he got into politics he had this down to a fine art," said Kate. "And what we've been told before by Sir Edward is that he was being steadily and quietly groomed by J Edgar's people over in America."

"We've learned that they recruited Walter during the war," nodded Jeremy, "and that they used him later, in the '50s, when he attained Cabinet rank. This isn't to say, however, that he would have been *active* on behalf of Washington during the years between. In fact, if he was under strict orders to further ingratiate himself with the British establishment, we might be wiser to assume the contrary......"

"......that he was quietly burrowing, silently sleeping," joined Gareth.

"Maybe," said Carroll, "but the the very fact of his excision from that photo would hardly suggest a benign presence at Tredethy."

"That was my point," said Jeremy, sharply. "A calculated inactivity on behalf of American intelligence doesn't preclude calculated activity on behalf of the British establishment. Churchill might have made Mountbatten a top military commander, and Attlee may have been lining him up as the last Viceroy but this didn't mean that all were convinced of his scruple......far, far from it."

"You're right there," agreed Jim. "For all his undoubted charisma this was a man who could play fast and loose with the lives and the reputations of others. If to be openly critical then was to risk being dismissed as jealous or disrespectful, he nevertheless needed to be watched......."

"....... and he was," reasoned Jeremy, "in the military sphere by the likes of Boy Browning, and in the diplomatic by the likes of Walter Monckton, figures who could be trusted not to be drawn into any half-baked scheming."

"But there's no Mountbatten in that picture," said Kate.

"There's a Philip Mountbatten," said Gareth, "and Marina, a cousin, but can we really believe that just keeping an eye on that pair could warrant Monckton being snipped away..... Jim?"

"At that time Mountbatten would have probably been at his Singapore HQ, and possibly attempting to stir the political mix in post war Thailand."

"Just his kind of headstrong frolic," nodded Jeremy.

"And while we might say that for busy Cabinet figures in London and Washington, Bangkok was a side-show," continued Busbridge, "I'm not sure that a matching disinterest prevailed in Paris and The Hague. For the French and the Dutch, eager to re assert mastery over their former neighbouring colonies, any meddling in matters Thai would have been rated an impingemnt."

"And come the 1950s when a summit was convened in Geneva so as to at least attempt a sorting of Vietnam," offered Gareth, "and the '60s when its makeshift provisions were to ultimately unravel, it can be imagined that what went down in neighbouring Thailand back in '46 could have started to attract retrospective scrutiny.......".

"........ prompting Browning to snip these figures from his photo," said Jeremy.

"And despite this a concern would appear to be persisting to this day," added Eamon, "for why else this destruction of Peg's boat?" He could mention also those further events in Tintagel and at Tredethy, but not yet. His moment would come, he knew.

"Might be a good time for me to have a quiet chat with Sir Edward Trembath," said Jeremy. "Just to hear what he might recall of Walter from back in '46."

"So you have your Monckton and you have your Profumo," said Gareth, ready to move on. "Now take a look at what's been sent down for me." The envelope, hitherto held unnoticed in hand, was pushed onto the table. "They arrived down at Kate's this morning, addressed to me."

Busbridge duly slid out the contents, spreading them for all to see.

"Where did these come from?" The curious man was intrigued.

"From a former comrade, currently working in Kensington Palace."

"And you've mentioned to him about my tape?" asked Eamon.

"Which I'd heard about from Jeremy here, and Kate. *Desert Island Discs*, as chosen by Denning, and there was something about his selection of a particular tune from *The King and I*, the musical about a King of Siam."

"*I Whistle a Happy Tune*," confirmed Eamon.

"Well as it says *Lausanne 1944* on these pictures we think it a strong possibility that the younger fellow, he of the more oriental extraction, could be the then King of Siam....."

".......he of the still unexplained sudden and violent death, in his Bangkok palace, just two years later."

"We can check," said Busbridge, "I'll have another picture of him somewhere, just give me a moment in my library."

"Hardly a regal spectacle," remarked Eamon.

"If this was some kind of trap then the boy could well have been drugged," offered Kate.

"A mean trick," said Tony Cross, "and one that might possibly strengthen the suicide theory. Difficult thing, this, for one so elevated to live with."

Busbridge reappeared, brandishing Ziegler's official biography of Lord Louis Mountbatten. "I've had this out already, looking for reasonable print of nephew Philip. I'm pretty sure I saw a good one of Dickie with young King Ananda." Flicking through the pages he settled on the second of four blocks of plates, and yes, there indeed was the youthful king, spectacled maybe but incontrovertibly the same lad whose naked image was now spread across the table. But to justify the biographer's selection of this picture, it had to be the imperious Mountbatten who was dominating the picture...... and the caption beneath;

With the King of Siam- 'a rather pathetic and lonesome figure'
wrote Mountbatten -at a garden party in Bangkok, January 1946.

did nothing to alleviate the condescension in the Supreme Commander's haughtily struck pose.

"That's him right enough," said Chas, "a couple of years older....... and a few more clothes on of course."

"Leaving us to identify this bed-mate in Lausanne," said Kate, "and wonder if these pictures are linked in some way to a completed version of that which hangs over in Tredethy."

"Except that it is no longer there," said Eamon at last.

"No longer where?" Jeremy asked.

"Over at Tredethy," repeated the cabby. "It's been taken. There was a break in last night. I called at the place today. The police had been, and there was some surprise that their enquiries hadn't brought them here."

"Sounds like we could be lucky to have what we have." Having taken the biography from Jim, Gareth was glancing back at some of the other plates in which Mountbatten was pictured with the likes of Churchill, the Chiang Kai-sheks, the Duke of Windsor, and an array of crippled warships. Then there was the wife, Edwina, and the daughters Patricia and Pamela, and even the young Princess Elizabeth........ and what was this? He blinked amazement, for just as the photos looked to be becoming less and less official, here was one of a certain Peter Murphy. And while in this picture he might have been equipped more for an afternoon on Polzeath beach, this Peter Murphy was still unmistakably he who cavorted before them on the table, snapped with the King, in Laussanne, in '44. "But hey.......just take a look at this! See the scar on the forehead, and the hint of a dimpled chin. Surely the same man........ Jim, have you read this book?"

"Parts," said the host. "Murphy gets frequent mention but I'd never before noticed that photo, tucked as it is in the family album section amongst so many others."

"So what does Ziegler tell us about the fellow?" asked Jeremy.

"That he and Mountbatten met in the '20s whilst students at Cambridge," began Busbridge. "That he was Irish and of exceptional intelligence and charm, multilingual, and a talented pianist."

Having consulted the index, Gareth stepped in. "It says here, page 51, that;

He had been in the Irish Guards, and had a wealthy mother who allowed him enough money to live in comfort but not luxury...... and......*since luxury is what he liked, he looked to the very rich for friends; he was a generous, tolerant and amiable man who gave as much pleasure as he received.*"

"One would hope that the young King of Siam could have endorsed that last bit," smirked Chas.

"Turning over," Gareth ignored the boy's facetiousness, "it says that Murphy's politics tended to the extreme left wing, and that while friendship with such a figure might have been acceptable at Cambridge it attracted distrust and suspicion as Mountbatten's career led him into positions of ever greater power and responsibility. *In 1952,*" he read, "*he was denounced as a Communist agent. "*

"Probably by the Yanks," said Jeremy.

"While not believing a word of it, Mountbatten felt that he had to ask the Security Service to investigate his friend. They did so, and concluded that there was no reason to believe that Murphy was a member of the Communist party, still less that he was working actively on its behalf. They also reported that he was homosexual and had been so for many years."

"Well it seems they were right enough there," nodded the lecturer. "Does it say anything in there about Murphy having influence over Mountbatten's performance in South East Asia?"

Gareth went again to the index.

"Murphy," he muttered to himself, *"role in South East Asia; pages 307,314........* here we are. We're getting well towards the end of the war for this bit.

Peter Murphy's role on Mountbatten's staff was one which caused confusion and distress to those who prized hierarchical good order above all else. He had been smuggled out under the auspices of the political intelligence department of the Foreign office to act as a kind of odd job man......

While the fighting was on Murphy's importance was trifling; when attention turned to civil government of the reconquered territories there were those who maintained that his influence was over-powerful and malign."

"Remember that Mountbatten was a man of odd contradictions," said Busbridge. "If he was heard to champion the impoverished native, at the same time he was seen to enjoy a notoriously opulent South East Asia Command Headquarters in Colombo, Ceylon........ well away from the fighting of course."

"On the same page, down here," pointed Gareth, "we are told that over Christmas 1944, he and Murphy entertained Prince Philip and Boy Browning, his nephew's ship at that time patrolling the Indian Ocean."

"Two guests who, less than eighteen months on, meet again at Tredethy," observed Eamon, "under the watchful eye of your Walter."

"Listen to this piece," resumed Gareth, "outlining Mountbatten's stance in the Autumn of '45 when, following the Japanese surrender, the HQ was moved to Singapore;

' *He needed urgently to establish his attitude towards the burgeoning nationalist movements which had sprung up in the shadow of the Japanese occupation and now thrived in the sunshine of liberation. Mountbatten was influenced by two main considerations. The first was practical and military: it was his job to maintain stable government and he could not do that by waging civil wars which he lacked the resources to conduct. If the independence movements were too strong to ignore, then the only course was to come to terms with them. The second was personal and idealistic. He believed that people should be allowed as far as possible to control their own destiny.....Both these considerations led him to take up positions which, to the more conservative of those who served under him, seemed radical and misguided."*

"Sounds a fair minded man," quipped Eamon, "with the Irish mate, and the Home Rule instinct."

"But there were those contradictions," cautioned Busbridge. "He would often seek to manipulate those to whom he was relinquishing power, a trait that the Americans were quickly on to......"

"...... they being into a similar sort of game," said Jeremy.

"Yes," continued Gareth, "for on the next page we have this:

Some accused Mountbatten of being an unconscious servant of international Marxism, probably under the malign influence of Peter Murphy. Mr Ulius Amoss, who ran an organisation in the United States known as International Services of Information, went still farther and announced that he had positive evidence that Mountbatten himself was deeply involved with the Communist Party."

"So how would all this pan out as regards Thailand," asked Jeremy, "with its indigenous Pibul versus Pridi power struggle and that so, so precarious throne?"

"Mountbatten was very much a Pridi man of course," said Busbridge," Pridi being the leader of the Free Thai force and, as such, code named RUTH, co-opted into that region's British SOE saboteur group. His rival, Pibul, by collaborating with the Japs in their seizure of Singapore had made himself a declared enemy of London."

"And what about the Monarchy?" asked Eamon.

"See this," said Gareth. "Very interesting..... in his account, the author is in absolutely no doubt. We've heard it said that the young King might have either accidentally *or* deliberately shot himself, or *perhaps* even been murdered. Here, on page 330, there's no maybe about it. Ziegler states *categorically* that he was mysteriously murdered."

"Intriguing," said Jeremy. "How can Ziegler be so definite?"

"Tell them about Bira's journal, Jim," urged Eamon, "and about our efforts to equip ourselves with a copy. Vain efforts I fear."

"A hoped for photocopy hasn't materialised." Busbridge picked up the note he'd made earlier. "But never mind, we do have this. The essence of the thing for us was an entry made between VE and VJ days. With war in Europe at an end Bira was anxious to restart what had been quite a successful motor racing career "

"So he would have been writing just prior to the atomic bombing of Hiroshima and Nagasaki," said Tony Cross who, with his son above and behind him, sat crammed on the narrow staircase that opened down into the well filled reception room.

"Attacks that are vaguely alluded to as he writes of his cousin Chula having been in conversation with Louis Mountbatten," continued Busbridge.

"Top secret stuff," remarked Jeremy. "I'm not sure of its relevance to motor sport?"

"Bira's pre war career had always depended on Chula's money, most of this being derived from the latter's estates in Thailand. By staying in Britain, and assisting our war effort, the pair had alienated themselves from their native country's pro Jap wartime masters......"

"..... but these, we now know, were on borrowed time," said Jeremy. "I start to see the link. Some of Bira's anxiety would have been allayed by hints from Mountbatten that devastating new weaponry might force an early capitulation in Tokyo. Regime change in Bangkok would naturally follow, and the flow of wealth resumed."

"You can be forgiven for thinking so," smiled Busbridge, "but actually the opposite was true, for it seems that the Supreme Commander was at that time attempting to bend Chula to his efforts at shaping this imminent regime change to his own liking. Mountbatten, it seems, was as good as convinced that the Mahidols would be keen to relinquish a throne they'd taken at the behest of a now disgraced pro fascist chief minister....."

"....... because even at such a distance, in far away Switzerland, and at such a young age, they were not immune to the taint of collaboration," followed Chas.

"And it was to be borne in mind that two significant precedents had been set by their accession back in '35," offered Jeremy. "Firstly, this had been precipitated by an abdication......."

"....... and secondly," prompted Declan, who while saying little had been following the discussion closely.

"That by being offered to and taken by a young Mahidol it became accepted that a Prince need no longer be disqualified from the Crown by reason of having a mother who was not fully Thai, or even fully Royal........ Mama Mahidol having been a half Chinese slum girl."

"Good point, Jeremy," beamed Busbridge, "for this second precedent overturned the principle that had previously disqualified Chula from the Crown. It wouldn't matter so much now that *his* mother had been half Russian."

"I think I see where this is leading," said Kate. "Anticipating that the Royal palace in Bangkok might fall vacant, Mountbatten could well have been attempting to line Chula up as the next tenant."

"And were this to happen," nodded Busbridge, "the *White Mouse* racing team would be left without its organising genius and principal sponsor. Hence the anxiety of the star driver. What's interesting, though, is that it for all this fretting before VJ Day it would appear that Bira needn't have worried. Chula in fact stayed Cornwall, at Tredethy, a bigger and better house, while his cousin went on to participate in the revived European racing calender, in bigger and better cars."

"Because there was no abdication in Bangkok," added Jeremy. "Instead there occurred this strange violent death of the elder brother, Ananda, followed by the enthronement of the younger, the present King Bhumibol......"

"......who must have been petrified, poor lad," added Declan, no stranger he to youthful trauma.

"Yes," continued Busbridge, "he high-tailed it back to Switzerland for a few more years."

"Understandable," said Eamon.

"But less so perhaps was the non-abdication," said the curious man "By all accounts Mama Mahidol had been rocked to the core. Surely she wouldn't risk another son."

"But she has,"said Declan.

"Confounding many a wide expectation."

"Including that of Lord Louis Mountbatten?" wondered Jeremy.

"Maybe not, for he is said to have written to Buckingham Palace to tell GeorgeVI and our present Queen Mother stating that in his view Ananda had been murdered by Mama Mahidol and her youngest son," continued Busbridge, "a suggestion generally thought now to have been wild and preposterous......."

"......but then?" posed Kate.

"One consequence was Chula's attendance at the Coronation of our Queen in '53 , he presumably having been invited to represent Thailand......"

"......rather than a Mahidol, and this would have been taken as a snub."

"Very much so," said Jim "Inter-Palace relations took some time to repair. Interestingly it was the Kents, Marina and Alexandra, who did most to effect the mending."

"So there's no record of Mountbatten recanting or apologising?" asked Tony Cross.

"No public record," shrugged Busbridge, and for more than a moment the room fell silent...... so much was there to consider.

"Perhaps," began a tentative Chas......

"Go on," encouraged Kate.

"Perhaps Mountbatten hadn't discounted the possibility of an honour killing within the Mahidol family, either suicide or homicide, committed so as to purge conduct unbecoming........for that's what you would appear to have there in those pictures. Is this not part of the Hindu tradition, a tradition that, through his work, Lord Louis would have understood better than most."

"Sounds a reasonable point," said Eamon.

"Except that the ways of the Hindu are not those of the Buddhist," scotched Jeremy. "The latter finds remedy for dishonour in transcendence, in achieving that state of grace termed Nivarna. It is an improved life that must be sought. To choose death is to invite further ignomony."

"And the Thai culture is built around the Buddhist way," added Tony Cross with that degree of authority, half presumed, half second-hand acquired that will guarantee the resentment of any son. Here, though, amongst these others, it had to stay unvoiced. Chas could bite his tonge, and in this same silence vow *not* to abandon his infant theory, whatever the views of those more better informed...... or less.

"But in the end," said Gareth, "whoever might have been responsible, it would appear that Mountbatten gained nothing from the killing, and even less from this attempt to pin the crime on the mother, sister and younger brother. That said, while missing out again on the

Crown, Chula himself wasn't to emerge from this a loser, and neither was his cousin who by his own account had for a while been anxious that he might."

"I'd certainly like to see more of that journal of Bira's," said Jeremy. "but you were saying, Eamon, that it's likely now to be beyond us."

"Another death," responded Carroll bluntly. "Another death occurring in the night, last night, the same night as this burglary over at Tredethy. We left the journal with its owner, a Mr George, the proprietor of a toy museum up in Tintagel. He was to procure for us a copy. I was to pick it up this morning. There was a police presence, though, at the museum and tuning into the local radio I was to hear that a mangled body found that morning by the side of a fast stretch of the main Bude-Camelford highway was that of Mr George. I decided not to bother the police."

"But there's no indication, yet, of foul play," checked McDaid.

"Not yet, for the police," continued Kate, "but for us, Declan, there is this *King and I* thing running as a common theme, through the two-death blowing up of that London pub, the destruction of Peg's boat near where you live, the burglary of the picture at Tredethy, and this violent death of this pleased-to-assist Mr Barry George. With what we have before us from '44, who are we to say that this isn't all connected to events in Bangkok two years later?"

"And Bira's death in '85," said Busbridge. "That was sudden, and followed shortly after a rare return visit to Tredethy."

"And I can remind you," said Eamon, "that back in '79, up in Classiebawn, Earl Mountbatten himself suffered the same fate recently visited upon the pair in the *Earl of Connaught*."

"So you're putting it to us, Eamon, that the death of a particular Kensington Palace protection officer on a north London road has prompted a recent surge in a forty year old body count," said Chas. "One that begins in the Bangkok Royal Palace, and ends in a roadside ditch on the edge of Bodmin Moor."

"I guess I am," acknowledged the cabby, "and I'm wanting none of us to become a further addition. The enemy, I fear, is getting closer...... an unidentified enemy."

"What about contacting Alan Grigson?" suggested Kate

"OK," agreed Jeremy, "but I'm not sure how one might do that."

"I was given a number," said Gareth, "but it's at home, and I can't remember it. I'll travel back now though."

"But you've only just got here," protested Kate. "You'll wait for supper at least."

"For all our sakes, the sooner I'm out of here with those photos the better," insisted the veteran. "We need to keep them and that tape of Eamon's well apart. Together they make a magnet, a force field that draws mischief."

"I'm curious as to what's going down in Kensington Palace," said Jeremy. "Some one in there will have the originals I guess."

"And probably more besides," said Tony Cross rising from the foot of the stairs to again shake Gareth's hand. "You might encourage your old battle comrade to find out for us. Good luck."

"Thanks….. I'll be in touch Kate."

*

Saturday a.m. ….. Elvira's

"So between you all you managed to throw your *piece* down at Carwinion off the scent," said Sally, suspiciously.

"More than that," smiled Chas. "We were able to use her in the feint by which Declan got into Port Eliot and actually came out with the goods. Quite a clever dodge it was…… Jim Busbridge's idea."

"But what about when she and her folks come to realise they've been fooled. Won't you be seen as a principal perpetrator?"

"So clever was this ruse that my part in it can just as easily be construed a well intentioned mistake, and there's a chance that they won't realise anyway. The picture to which they might be hoping to match what I gave them….."

"…….which hangs in this Tredethy Manor….."

"…… well it no longer hangs there. Apparently, the night before last, someone broke in and took it. And did you hear on the news about a body being found on the roadside up towards Tintagel?"

"I think I did, now you remind me."

"Well we're wondering if there might be a link between both

172

incidents and this *King and I* business."

"But Chas, focus for a moment just on that burglary. Who's to say that this wasn't the people using the Trembaths ……. possibly a security agency? Their picture and those that you've passed them don't match, so suddenly your involvement comes under the closest of scrutiny."

"But they still can't be sure my role wasn't that of an unwitting tool, as was Helen's."

"So if she were in contact again you would attempt to keep the bluff going."

"I would have to, if only for the sake of the others……"

"…… rather than any taste you might have for attractive young ladies who drive fast cars!"

"And here you go again, Sally," scoffed Chas. "I reckon you've been over-dosing on that Dickens."

*

Phoning from Wales

"So I told them, Alan, that I had a number at home and would be phoning you."

"And it was Kate's suggestion that I should be contacted?"

"Prompted by that Mr Carroll. He'll have consorted with some pretty ruthless people in his time, I can see that, but a death down there in Cornwall seems to have left him more than slightly rattled. But it was suggestion endorsed by all present, and that made a good crowd I have to say. Jeremy, the father and son diving outfit from Plymouth, and an older chap called Declan who'd been key in bringing the figures missing from the picture at Tredethy out of Port Eliot……. plus, of course, our host."

"Mr James Busbridge, the curious man. One easily underestimated. You and I, Gareth, we must meet, and soon. I have to see those pictures."

"Well why not Jeremy's place in Bath? Say 7pm Monday evening. We both know where he lives. He'll be back there by then and done a day's work. I'll phone Kate's later and tell him to be there to receive us."

*

St Enodoc Golf Club.

"I was hoping to speak with Stan again, actually," said Eamon as the steward waited for the customary voluminous head to subside before topping the first drawn draught Guinness of the morning. "Are you expecting him today?"

"Wish I was, but I regret to report that the old boy has passed away. When were you here?"

"Tuesday afternoon."

"I don't come in on Wednesdays, so it would have been Thursday evening that he died. He was taken ill here, after lunch. He didn't wake from his usual sleep. Looked like a stroke. We called an ambulance, and he was just about alive when they took him off....... but this said, it was no surprise to hear later that he'd expired. Couldn't have known much about it, so perhaps not such a bad way to go. The steak and kidney he'd had. Nothing wrong with that, though. I tried some myself."

"After I'd left on Tuesday, or even on Thursday, you can't I suppose remember if anyone troubled him with a similar enquiry to mine."

"A couple of Japanese looking gentlemen also took lunch on Thursday. This isn't so unusual, they're all so keen on the sport in that country. They'd hoped to play, but with the ladies' team having a match on they said they would book for the next day. They spent perhaps twenty minutes in conversation with Stan, the last conversation he probably had."

"And the topic?"

"That I can't tell you. I was busy..... but they would have been polite, their kind always are."

"And you saw them again on Friday?"

"They didn't come in here, but if they played they would have checked in and paid around at the pro shop. Ask there if they turned up."

*

Truro Cathedral

"Thank you, Sir Edward, for coming at such short notice. I do so value the kind of privacy we have here. How much more focussed it can make our conversation....... how much more productive." A noon-sharp shaft of autumnal sunshine cut down and across from opposite tower window giving those commemorated by inscription on the wall above their side pew a brief moment of seasonal radiance.

"When you whistle it seems that I will always come. So if you can spare me the curt niceties, Mr Barnes, I don't have *all* day."

"Of course you don't, Sir Edward. And neither do I". The lecturer glanced at his watch. "My companion will be waiting for me outside Marks & Spencer's in twenty minutes so, coming to the point........ it's Walter again."

"I thought it might be."

"Easter '46....... we know he was in Cornwall. He visited Tredethy, we're sure. Did he come this way, or did you meet, perhaps in Plymouth?"

"Very briefly we met, for he was a very busy man..... as I was too. Just days later, before the end of that April, he was to travel out to India, there to resume his attempt to sort the predicament of the Nizam."

"A lost cause."

"Sadly, yes, but by sticking at it for best part of two years he did win the gratitude of the Labour people, and it was whilst in India, I believe, that he met his second wife."

"But at that time he wouldn't have been active for the Americans."

"Certainly not on the issue of Hyderabad."

"What about Thailand, Sir Edward?"

"Ahh yes, now I see where this is headed. You're wondering what he might have been up to over at Tredethy."

"Keeping a watchful eye on the wider machinations Mountbatten perhaps?" tested Jeremy.

"If so then almost certainly on behalf of our Establisment, as with David Windsor five years earlier....."

"........ prior to you and he being despatched to the Bahamas."

"Yes, and while Washington did come to show flair in the black arts of subversion, this wasn't really until the blockade of Berlin and the invasion of South Korea spelt out the consequences of sitting idly by."

"And you say about Walter being so, so busy with the Hyderabad issue."

"I do Mr Barnes. It's one of those things that few people remember now........"

"........but at the time was quite big. So with regard to those Thai Princes living in this county, might Walter have briefed one of his *firm's* more junior partners to serve as eyes and ears during his absence abroad."

"If you're talking about the Duchy, Mr Barnes, and suggesting that I might have been asked, then I'm afraid that on this occasion I must disappoint."

Jeremy raised an apologetic hand, for actually he hadn't meant the Duchy. It was a different pond he'd had in mind, the Party, from which he'd been hoping to angle himself a bigger fish. After a moment's regret at not having made himself more clear he decided that this, perhaps, was the wrong man to be asking anyway........ and that the few minutes left to them might better be given to matters less distant.

"Your grand daughter Helen, she uses your flat up in London, I'm told. Do you have much involvement in her activities?"

"Very little, Mr Barnes. Insofar as she might be said to be under anyone's control then that person is my son, her father."

"And your son, Hugh....... he is his own man?"

"He's certainly not mine, Mr Barnes. To him, now, I'm an embarrassment, thanks mainly to you. Being merely helpful to the Americans was fine, as far as his understanding of that *Kampala* business originally went....... but for him to then learn that virtually the whole of my career, plus the best part of his, and the estate too, had been nurtured largely so as to facilitate some of the murkier tactics by which Washington had furthered its foreign policy, this came as quite a shock."

"I had that impression."

"And of course it must grieve him still to know that amongst those whose opinions matter to him there persists a somewhat jaundiced view of his assiduously cultivated respectability."

"But, as a man of action, Hugh would never be content to just sit there and take this," prompted the lecturer.

"Youi're right, so what we have now in my son is the *super patriot.*"

"Because, again thanks to me, you're now clear of the Americans....... now that they've squeezed Carwinion for every last inch

176

of mileage, much as they with the *Kampala.*"

"Yes," sighed Trembath, "ready for the breakers, that's me, but at least Hugh is free now to convince himself, and anyone ready to listen, that he's ready to vigorously defend the beleaguered integrity of our still great nation. The fruits of that long tended local grapevine of his will now tend now to be passed upwards, rather than hoarded for personal delectation."

"There's a weary cynicism in your voice, would this be telling me that you think he could be trying overhard?"

"Probably," sighed the retired MP.

"And when you spoke just now of Helen being under her father's control, was I to infer that she has been incorporated into his network?"

"There have been occasions, yes......"

".......but not all of them with her knowledge."

"As a general rule, Mr Barnes, none of us will be told more than we need to know. Why should we think her exempt?"

"Because we speak of a father-daughter relationship, trusting father-trusting daughter.......ideally."

"Yes, ideally," echoed Trembath. "Full trust all round, but that's not how it was between me and Hugh, so what can I say when it comes to him and his child?"

"But her interest in the boy we brought to Carwinion, the lad from Plymouth......."

"...... will have been encouraged."

"And was there a topic that we brought up that prompted this...... the Thais perhaps, or Mountbatten?"

"No topic required, Mr Barnes, the mere appearance of yourself and Mr Cross would have been quite enough. Don't think that each of you aren't known to the security people, if only for having previously worked closely with that Alan Grigson guy....... the one we learned was a professional."

"So it wouldn't have mattered if all we'd come to discuss had been the weather prospects."

"Just presenting yourselves as a duo....... that in itself would have set alarm bells a-jangle."

"And Hugh will have acted."

"Probably, Mr Barnes, but no longer am I to expect him to confide to me the nature any such response. I can say that a couple of interesting figures clipped from a group photo passed through Carwinion during the week, but as to from where they might have emerged........ I would imagine that you might be better informed than I."

"Fair enough, Sir Edward, I'll not press you on that."

"So is that all?" Trembath gathered himself to leave.

"One final matter."

"If you can be quick about it."

"Can you remember Walter ever metioning the name *Ullius Amoss*?"

"One like that's once heard never forgotten. Sounds to be of Jewish Greek extraction."

"So........?"

"A new one on me, Mr Barnes......but not, it would seem, on yourself."

"I turned it up yesterday evening whilst looking at Ziegler's official biography of Mountbatten. He was an American, as you say, probably Jewish American and apparently he ran an agency over there known as *International Services of Information*."

"Sounds to be of the sort designed to feed Washington's anti Red paranoia."

"More than possible, for according to the author this fellow was able to announce that he had positive evidence that Mountbatten was deeply involved with the Communist Party."

"His friend, Peter Murphy, was unapologetic in his Marxist views. Your Mr Amoss wouldn't have needed Walter to tell him that. And then there was the wife, Edwina, who would readily try any kind of extremism on for size. Dickie, though, he was never a party man....... too much the individualist he, a born maverick."

"So I understand, and for me this points up the nature of his dealings with the leader of the wartime Free Thai movement."

"Another said to be in the pay of Moscow? I hope you're not expecting me to know his name."

"Pridi Banomyong," obliged Jeremy, "and yes, we can guess that the likes of Mr Amoss would have wanted to paint him a vivid shade of Red."

"To misrepresent him also, you're saying."

"I suppose I am, and this leads me to ask why...... and whilst doing so, to reflect on the circumstances surrounding his fall from grace."

"Together with the circumstances surrounding Mountbatten's death...... how many years later? thirty? More than thirty. I'm sorry Mr Barnes, this time you've come to the wrong man." Trembath rose. "Must go I'm afraid, I wish you good day."

And that was it, Trembath was on his way, striding the transept for the north door, leaving Jeremy to turn more hesitantly for the west. But what was with this mention of Mountbatten's *death*, he wondered.

Pridi.   Pibul.

Saturday pm, Jasmine Cottage......

......where James Busbridge, returning from a light soup and roll pub lunch this time taken alone over at Lanlivery, finds himself in receipt, this time through his own machine, of a faxed letter from one *Monsieur Pierre Boulle*, a prompt response this to the brief phone call made to the man's Paris home just two days before. Detaching the three page document from the scroll he settles into his favourite easy chair to read;

Saturday am
Dear James

Thank you for the phone call of earlier in the week. I trust that you progress well with your books on Pearl Harbor and the Surcouf, each a fascinating subject. Having read a number of your articles, I eagerly anticipate what I'm sure will be a fearless and penetrative accounts.
How interesting it is that you should also be enquiring about the building of the Burma-Thailand Railway by the Japanese, and the somewhat erratic career, at that time, of Pridi Banomyong.
On Pridi first, for the course of his career had a bearing on the overall usefulness of the Railway.
In the '30s, when I worked on a plantation in Malaya, the politics of Thailand were dominated by two figures, Pridi Banomyong and Pibul

Songkram. Each had emerged from The Promoters of Political Change, the party that had successfully forced the revolution of '32. Thereafter, Pibul, the more right wing of the pair, looked to take and hold power by nurturing a military elite while Pridi, by contrast, took a more egalitarian position which many, at home and abroad, regarded as nascent Marxism. Their natural rivalry came to be polarised by the Second World War, and in particular the Japanese strike southward to Singapore.

Opening the borders to the Imperial army, Pibul adopted a Quisling-like stance and was duly rewarded by the Tokyo warlords who invited him to enlarge his country at the expense of French Laos and Cambodia to the north.

The outlawed Pridi's response was to ally himself with Britain and America who, while initially having to retreat, were to eventually rally and prevail. Pridi became the leader of the Free Thais, and, as such, an agent of the British SOE code-named RUTH.

It must be added, though, that those wary of a softness towards communism within the British High Command, were far from enamoured of one who was suspected of being under the influence of Moscow.

Nevertheless, with the Japanese surrender Pibul had to go, and with the encouragement of the likes of Mountbatten, Pridi did step in to take charge.

Completing the first page, Busbridge pauses. He has learned nothing new so far, but is not discouraged. Further enlightenment might be to hand, he senses. He reads on;

Having suffered little war damage Thailand remained a relatively wealthy nation and there was every indication that Pridi was capable of forming a prudent and progressive peace time administration that would avoid such doctrinaire crusading as might entail hardship for the ordinary citizen........or perhaps 'subject' should be my term here, for the country had its King still, the doomed young Ananda whose tragic fate in '46 was also to ruin Pridi's political career.

The poor lad's violent and still unexplained death had the effect of unleashing a tide of largely unfounded rumour which was to engulf Pridi's fragile civilian based government, and shortly afterwards a de-Japped Pibul found himself re installed.

Outlawed yet again, Pridi was as good as forced to seek sanctuary in

Russia, this giving further ammunition to those who'd long whispered that he'd been dangerously Red at heart.
But was he?
In my opinion, no......and neither do I believe that this man, by act of commission or omission, was responsible for the death of his King.

On the Railway.

You ask if I ever corresponded with a former soldier and POW of the Japanese named Alec Young, a Scotsman, on the subject of the film made of my novel 'The Bridge on the River Kwai', the fellow having been a survivor of a death camp similar to that presented by the story.
My answer is no.

This is more like it......but he is far from surprised. Better will follow, he is sure.

Those who claim to have seen such correspondence purporting to be from myself can be told that they have been looking at a forgery.
I say this with certainty, for over the years I have received numerous letters from comrades of this Mr Young and all have been scrupulously saved. They still come and I still answer each and every one.
Most were written in response to the film in which my story was significantly altered (a point that I have made countless times in my replies) and many have a particular concern to defend the reputation of a Colonel Philip Toosey whose organisational genius, they say, saved the lives of thousands suffering the privations in the death camps near Tamarkan, close to where the the railway bridged the Kwae Mae Khlong River.
Toosey is rightly revered amongst the survivors who will be commonly outraged by the film's portrayal of my Colonel Nicholson, a role played to the hilt by the actor Alec Guinness.
You will remember that for him, the bridge and its preservation becomes an obsession, to the extent that an attempt to sabotage the structure is caused (at least in the book) to misfire.
I will repeat again, now, that from all I spoke with whilst researching my story I heard nothing but praise for Colonel Toosey. The man was a true hero, and it would indeed be a shame if his deeds came to be obscured by

what has essentially been a work of fiction.

But this does beg the question as to where else I might have found the inspiration for a story which points up a theme of divided loyalties at high command level......a question that I've often asked myself, and never found easy to answer.

Your enquiry about Pridi, though, prompts me to try once again.

Pridi took to the jungle during the Japanese occupation, organising therefrom a Free Thai force somewhat perversely named the 'White Elephants'. He was encouraged in this by the British from their SE Asia Command HQs in Delhi, and later in Ceylon.

Pridi's resistance organisation was amalgamated into the Allies' Force 136, an outfit largely overseen by Churchill's Special Operations Executive but which included American and French specialists in behind the lines infiltration. It was at this time that Pridi became SOE agent RUTH.

I actually worked with Force 136 in Calcutta following my escape from Vichy policed French Indo China where I had suffered capture, imprisonment, and torture. My role in Calcutta was to help interpret aerial photographs of areas familiar to me on the ground.

During this work I became acquainted with the kind of tensions that must always , it seems, develop within any multi national force.........in short, divided loyalties.'

Excellent, thinks Busbridge as, in the space of a few lines, this freshly arrived epistle becomes as pregnant with revelation as any conjured by St John the divine.

The importance to the Japanese of their Thailand-Burma Railway was obvious. If their conquests in Burma and, hopefully, Northern India were to be held their armies would have to be supplied by land. While they'd captured Singapore, control of the Andaman Sea was, as yet, beyond them.

Once completed the line could become a major artery, and accordingly from amongst the SOE sabotage specialists there emerged many a daring plan to disrupt the project. From the photos put in front of me I could gauge both the progress of the Japanese and also the urgency a frustration of those wanting to inflict upon then at least temporary delay.

I say 'frustration' because as repeatedly as these plans were put to the

182

High Command so they would repeatedly be rejected, a pattern that became particularly pronounced during the final three or four months preceding the destruction of Hiroshima.

Of course with hindsight it can be imagined that those who exercised these vetoes did so in the privileged knowledge that the Japanese home soil was about to be atom bombed, and in this light considered a disabling of the railway to be of much lessened importance to an impending surrender.

At the time, though, as underlings with neither privileged information nor powers of foresight, some of our speculations as to why there should have been this odd reluctance to go for such an obvious jugular tended to range in a variety of directions.

Some suggested, for instance, that Mountbatten and Pridi were looking ahead, and agreeing that while they might take another year to drive them back to their islands the Japanese were definitely on the run, and that before an eventual surrender they could, between the pair of them, liberate Thailand and together assume the mantel of Kingmakers.

As such they might then shape the country as they wished, perhaps to include some of the northern provinces given to Bangkok by the Japanese, or even a wedge of Burma where it seemed that whoever could install the strongest army would have the loudest say.

Remember, a vast swathe of good poppy-growing country was up for grabs, where possession would mean nine tenths of the law and ten tenths of the proceeds.

In this context, ran the argument, a ready made railway with which to first consolidate one's military presence, and then facilitate one's commercial transactions was not something to be blown to pieces, even if had been put together by an enemy using prisoners of war as slave labour.

I have to say that the hypothesis impressed me until, with the quick surrender in August '45, it was buried beneath an assumption that Mountbatten, for one at least, knew what was about to happen at Hiroshima and Nagasaki.

This said, although the Tamarkan Bridge was hit by a US air attack shortly before the end of the war the resultant damage was quickly repaired by the victors who were of course soon putting the trains to work for themselves.

Against this background it is possible to see my story as an allegory in which the attitude of Colonel Nicholson, who so wants to preserve the *railway in working order, merely reflects a degree of restraint perhaps being observed within the High Command in Ceylon. It may be that the joint ambitions of Mountbatten and Pridi for Thailand were never fully realised, but this isn't to say they never existed, or indeed that they did not facilitate the completion of a slave labour dependent project.*

Do write back and tell me what you think.

Yours truly

Pierre Boulle

And this, now, is better than excellent, thinks James Busbridge....... for how intriguingly well Boulle's words fit alongside those recalled from Bira's journal.

Yes, it had long been noted that Lord Louis liked to dabble in *Kingmaking*, a hobby that was said to have emerged even here in Britain during the 1970s when, reputedly, he allowed himself to be associated with a plot to oust Harold Wilson, the elected Prime Minister. So could he have been honing those techniques thirty years before, in Ceylon...... and could his efforts have in some way led to the death of the young Ananda, he who'd featured with Peter Murphy in those damagingly candid photographs from Switzerland?

Here was something to show Jeremy. He had been invited down to Kate's for later. Returning from Truro they would be getting in some Chinese food from her favourite take-away over in Wadebridge and there would be enough, she was sure, for the three of them to share.

*

Take-away

"Only standard boiled rice this evening," said Zhou Jingzhi, proprietor of Wadebridge's sole Chinese take away, *The Silver Pagoda*.

"Well *that* I can do at home," said Kate. "There's plenty in my pantry waiting to be tidied up." She looked again at the menu card. "We'll take two more portions of mixed vegetables instead, one in the black bean sauce, the other in the *gan sheow*. Shame though, for I always look forward to sampling from Madame Zhou's selection of fried rices. I tell people it's the best in the county. It's unusual not see her helping you on a Saturday evening........ she is well I trust?"

"She is well........ but not so her mother. She in hospital."

"In Truro, you mean, as an emergency admission?"

"Emergency yes........ but not Truro."

"Not Truro........ so into Plymouth are you saying? To the new place up at Derriford?"

"She go to Bodmin, into St Lawrence. You work there, I think I hear you say?"

"I do," confirmed the nurse, momentarily taken aback, "but not with the acute cases. I can't remember her having been ill before."

"Never before...... not like this."

"Like what?" asked Jeremy firmly, but not without concern.

"She has bad, bad dream. It come to her in daytime, very sudden, very clear. She have big fright."

"Here, in the house?" asked Kate.

"In the town, just four days ago. And for three nights and three days, then, no sleep, no eat. She shake. She sweat. She stay in room, beneath bedclothes, where she wets and she soils herself, and moans and moans about having seen the devil."

"The devil," repeated Jeremy, more puzzled than alarmed.

Kate nodded sympathetically. "Sounds like a psychotic episode," she soothed, giving the men to understand that she was far from unfamiliar with the phenomenon.

"So where in Wadebridge would she have seen the devil?" asked Jeremy.

"She was found in car park behind Co-op, by river. She point across to old bridge. '*The devil*,' she say, '*of Shanghai*'."

"And were there people on the bridge," asked Kate.

"Just traffic."

"But no one's said about anything unusual, like the kind of striking logo which sometimes will get painted on the side of a large lorry."

"No lorries seen, only cars........ and an unusually large motor caravan, someone say."

"And this was headed for the far side of the bridge," pressed Jeremy, "going northward......like it might have just left that car park just a minute or so before?"

Zhou shook his head vaguely.

"One way or the other," he said, "I cannot be sure."

"And your mother-in- law, Zhou, would be how old?"

"Easy over seventy."

"Yes," confirmed Kate, "pushing eighty even."

"And did she ever live in Singapore?" Jeremy was sleuthing.

"Yes, she flee there from Shanghai with my wife's brother when he just twelve."

"And your wife being......?"

".......not yet born. She born in Singapore."

"And they would have fled there from the Japanese."

"They had killed her husband......"

"......who you cannot be sure was your father in law."

Zhou Jingzhi winced. "Because while husband was bayoneted to death, my mother in law was raped and raped again by the invaders."

"But she and the boy stole aboard a boat heading south, and they joined the exiled community in Singapore, trusting there in the protection of the British. A trust that in early '42 was to prove misplaced."

"Again the Japanese invade," nodded Zhou, "and, with many thousands of Chinese, this time my wife's brother is butchered....... he not yet seventeen."

"Leaving his mother, now twice bereaved, to bring up the four year old girl who you will eventually marry."

"We meet here in England, in '55, where they come to live after they try to go back to China. But they not wanted, not in Red China, and not in Formosa."

"So what we can say," ventured Jeremy, "is that there has been no shortage of trauma such as might have fuelled a psychotic episode."

"Quite," agreed Kate, as Zhou left them briefly to sort the right vegetables in the kitchen. "Only so much can be repressed for so long, beyond that and the right detonator can trigger the chain reaction to blow the whole lot."

"Like what happened with the youngest Wakeham over at *Jamaica Inn*. You know, McDaid's brother, who emerged more recently at St Lawrence as Gordon."

"Except that he saw an actual cigarette card, something of substance seen by others, which for all the anguish it uncorked carried nothing fearsome in itself. To see *a devil*, though, is to be entering a very different dimension. The woman's mind seems to have conjured an apparition."

"And one vivid enough to have frightened her clean out of her wits........"

*

An hour later, Ruthernbridge

"A fascinating letter, Jim......very intriguing," Jeremy returned it to the recipient. "And Monsieur Boulle invites you to write back. You will, I take it."

"I'm going to ask if, later, he ever encountered Bira either in Thailand or France. The Prince took homes in both countries after leaving Cornwall. I'll tell him, of course, about the gist of Bira's journal...... and I'll be querying that little piece about the railway being put to use by the victors. I've been of the understanding that much of the track was subsequently torn up, and the levelled land allowed to return to jungle."

"Later, yes, that would figure," said Jeremy. "Reinstated and favouring a fortress-Thailand stance, what use had Pibul for a backdoor into Burma?"

"And a matching attitude would surely have prevailed in newly independent Rangoon," added Busbridge. "The line would have been seen as a symbol of old fashioned armed imperialism...... Japanese, British, it mattered not whose. While it might have briefly figured in the plans of Pridi and the ambitions of Mountbatten, these, in a matter of months, were to be swept away by the tide of history......."

".......as, it seems, was the life of the young King Ananda." The rice now ready, Kate could lift the Chow Mein and the vegetables from her warming oven and invite her guests to take a plate and make their selection. "Tell me, Jim, about the Chinese in Singapore, back in '42," prompted the lecturer.

"They were many," said Busbridge, spooning for himself a

succulent lump of chicken, "thousands having fled there from the Chinese mainland after the Japanese invasion of five years earlier. Regarded as allies of the surrendered British they were treated accordingly, with even less regard for any Geneva protocols. Men not massacred were enslaved and most worked to death on the construction projects undertaken before the railway, the rebuilding for instance of the port's destroyed defences."

"And the women......?"

".......became brothel fodder. It was either that, or starve. You ask as if this might have significance."

"Might have, might not have, for what Kate and I have just learned is that there lies in St Lawrence a woman who endured those cruelties."

"Of less than sound mind, I'll assume."

"Until just a few days ago she was fine," joined Kate, shaking her two thirds empty bottle of rich soy sauce, "helping her daughter and son-in-law in *The Silver Pagoda*."

"Then, in a Wadebridge car park would you believe, there did appear unto her in a vision none other that *the Devil of Shanghai*, whereupon normal mental and bodily functions are thrown severely awry."

"You say that, Jeremy, like it's some kind of joke," scolded the nurse. "This is a soul in living torment."

"So age....?" intervened Busbridge.

"Late seventies," pouted Kate.

"And that of the daughter?"

"Late forties," obliged Jeremy, sensibly dropping the flippancy. "Possibly conceived during the plunder of Shanghai, during the winter of '37/'38. The husband had been put to death by the Japs, then, four years later in Singapore, she similarly lost a teenaged son."

"So what could she have beheld?" asked Busbridge.

"Outside her local Co op?....... Only she can say." Jeremy looked to Kate. "So might she, do you think, with the appropriate treatment?"

"I'll get on to her case...... first thing on Monday."

*

188

Sunday pm........ Mount Edgcumbe Gardens

"So have you heard again from Helen Trembath?" probed Sally as she and Chas climbed onto the wide stone 'garden' emplacement from where once a full twenty strong battery of cannons were trained across the mouth of the Tamar. Sky and Sound were greying. Rain had been forecast. It was yet to arrive.

"No reason to," replied the boy, the curtness perhaps betraying a tinge of regret.

"But you'd like it all the same, were she to make contact."

"Only because of what I've heard this morning from Jim Busbridge. He tells us that Pierre Boulle faxed him a letter yesterday, and it says that the correspondence that she'd chased up to Scotland for, the letters supposedly sent by Boulle to one Alec Young, these amounted to a fabrication. He'd written to many former POWs, he said, but never any of that name."

"So had she be taken in too, do you think, or was she part of the deceit?"

"Can't be sure, yet, but I've reason to veer towards the former."

"And that reason?"

"Is her swallowing just as big a whopper fed by us."

"So she's not yet tumbled this?"

"I don't know. She might still think me to have been fooled also. All this has a certain neatness."

"Provided you can believe that it really was Boulle who faxed our Mr James Busbridge," smiled Sally as, keeping within a pebbles throw of the water, they moved past the ancient blockhouse and into the shadow of the celebrated 30 foot high ilex hedge. A hundred yards of this and they were entering the landscaped bowl of the 'amphitheatre', replete with its sheltered cove and decorative temples. From high to their right, falling leaves fluttered across them towards the shore, swept gently on the balmy westerly.

"So how are you going with *Great Expectations*?" Chas was groping for a fresh topic.

"OK now...... the film was quite helpful."

"So remind me again of the story."

"We follow the fortunes of a flawed hero, Pip, and also a flawed heroine, Estella. It's a puppet show, each being manipulated by a scarred

189

adult. For Pip it's the convict who he first encounters as a child......."

".......and for Estella, that mad woman in the wedding dress. The famous role in the film and telly productions."

"Yes, Miss Havisham......and on their parallel journeys, Chas, each must find out the hard way that there's more to life than living out the thwarted aspirations of others."

"Lending them hope, yet, as a couple."

"A hope that the reader must draw on as he is left to speculate on Pip and Estella's future. It's one of the great untold stories of literature."

"Someone will pick up the tale, I'm sure, and give it a more modern twist. Estella will be discovered to have had a born out of wedlock child, perhaps, sired no doubt by a sea captain."

"Or even a French Admiral," quipped the girl.

"Who will of course be party to some nicely ripened political scandal."

"I'll lend you the book, Chas, if you want."

"I'll try the film first..... if we could perhaps watch it together one evening?"

*

Monday evening; Bath.....

......where prompted by Gareth, Jeremy has started to explain as best he can why he and those others who'd met at Jasmine Cottage were wishing once more for the presence in Cornwall of a Mr Alan Grigson. The supplicated listens attentively...... for while he could say that he is already on the case, he needn't, at least yet. Yes, he might have to, in due course, but by placing a measure of trust in the Guardsman's discretion, he can wait.

"It's Eamon who's feeling the heat," said the lecturer. "He'd ventured west again at the behest of what sounds like a couple of renegade nationalists, and within twenty four hours hears from me that these have been blown up in that same London pub where he'd met them and been briefed on his task."

190

"And this errand?" feigned Grigson

"Concerned the possible significance of a radio programme, an edition of *Desert Island Discs*, a tape of which was recovered at the scene of a fatal road accident. The victim, from whose jacket the cassette had spilled, was an off duty policeman, his duties having at one time included protecting the members of the Royal Family at Kensington Palace. It's thought that for a while he might have been officially attached to Diana, Princess of Wales, and that when moved on she might have asked him to continue working for her in a less regular capacity."

"By that you mean less formal....... and it's thought that the cassette might have something to do with this little piece of moonlighting."

"Thanks to Gareth, here, we have strong indications that this could indeed be the case."

"There's a former comrade of mine currently working in the Wales's Household," added the Guardsman, with convincing earnestness. "He has sent me what looks to be associated material. I'll show you this later, but let's first listen to our friend."

"Go on then, Jeremy," urged Grigson, happy to sustain the pretence.

"Our suspicion is that Princess Diana could have uncovered a scandal involving prominent members of the Royal Family, a scandal stretching back over forty years, and one which might have come close to having been revealed by the judicial enquiry conducted into the Profumo affair......"

"..... by Lord Denning," nodded Grigson, "towards the end of '63, I think. But he kept the lid on things......"

"......as we must assume he was trusted to," continued the lecturer. "It seems that the scandal might have touched on the control of post-war Thailand, and the dealings between the former colonial powers as they strove to re-assert influence in the area."

"As well as the Anglo-American *special* relationship, effective enough in Korea but less so a bit later when it came to the Suez thing." Now Alan was priming the lecturer, quite cynically.

"Before being re-stiffened by Macmillan," obliged Jeremy, "for the heightened east-west tensions of his era, over Berlin, Formosa, Cuba, Vietnam."

"So who in the Royal Family might we be talking about if we're looking at forty years ago?" asked Alan. "Charles hadn't been born then, in fact his parents were barely married. Would this about his father, Prince Philip?"

"He is in the frame, literally, and at one time so were a young Jack Profumo and our old friend Walter Monckton, a true specialist when it came to sorting the Windsor laundry basket."

"*At one time?*"

"Before someone for whatever reason attempted to cut them out of the picture."

"A picture that we're attempting to re assemble," added Gareth neatly. "Our view is that Philip might have been at the margin of things, bearing it in mind that prior to his marriage he was very much the protégé of his Uncle Louis."

"Of course," pretended Grigson. "Dickie Mountbatten, who by dint of his remoteness from the succession was able to attain a military and political clout far in excess of that which could be allowed to accrue to any son, grand or great-grand, in the exalted line of Saxe Coburg."

"And far in excess of his talent, some do say," remarked Gareth.

"Dead now of course," continued Jeremy, "a victim of the troubles, but, perhaps because of that, big enough still in the public memory to be singled posthumously for a second assassination...... that of character."

"By the young Princess, you say. Would she be capable of such," Grigson affected faint scepticism, "after hearing so much over the years about how her husband idolised the man?"

"It's too easy to imagine that Wales's household is a bed of roses," countered Gareth. "The word from the inside is that this could be a woman scorned. She might smile for the camera Alan, but make no mistake....... this one can be spiteful. The more she hears of her Charles's fondness for lauding his 'Uncle Dickie' then, possibly, the more she's wanting that reputation demolished."

"OK," conceded Alan, "but how can taped edition of *Desert Island Discs* lead one to Lord Mountbatten?"

"Gareth," said Jeremy, "time, I think, to get those pictures out." The Welshman reached for the rucksack he'd brought in. Out came the prints to be spread across Jeremy's table as they had across Jim's, in Cornwall, three days before. "Now the guest on *Desert Island Discs*," continued Jeremy, "is Lord Thompson Denning. He chooses a selection of tunes which reflect a number of important aspects of his life, all being reasonably straightforward....... save perhaps for one; *I Whistle a Happy Tune.*"

"Rodgers and Hammerstein," remembered Alan.

"From *The King and I*," nodded Jeremy, "their musical about a King of Siam."

"And you've asked yourself what significance this might hold for in respect of Denning's career," said Grigson.

"We think it could be a teasingly brief comment on his enquiry into the Profumo business."

"Saying what?"

"Saying that while admittedly his published report might have sheltered more than just a few establishment reputations, this wasn't to mean that he should be taken for a fool."

"So he'd known more than he let on." Alan straightened the pictures on the table. "And what that might have been is thought, in Kensington Palace, to be to some extent illustrated by these. Can we identify either of the unclothed?"

"The younger of the two was the King of Siam," said Gareth. "*Lausanne, '44*, we are told on the back, and that would put him ten years into a soon to be violently curtailed reign. Domiciled and schooled in Switzerland, the still young King Ananda was to visit his country in '46, and there be found dead in his Bangkok Palace bed...... the recipient of a single pistol shot to the head."

"For a photo of the King *not* in the altogether, try Ziegler's official biography of Mountbatten," offered Jeremy. "They abound in charity shops, after for a while being a popular gift for the octogenarian who still liked to read. But they don't live for ever, and their houses must be cleared......."

".......and so they fetch up on the Oxfam shelves," smiled Alan, "tempting a last few bob from the likes of Mr James Busbridge."

"Very likely," said Jeremy, "for he obliged us with a copy from his personal library, and as well as enabling an identification of the young King it carried another photo by which we've identified this other guy."

"The King's partner, you mean...... the older bloke."

Jeremy tapped at the man's shoulder.

"Mr Peter Murphy, Alan, a close companion of Dickie's from their university days in the '20s right up to his death in '66. Irish, homosexual, communist......."

"Plenty there, then, for Lady Di to get her teeth into..... and not, one would hope, in the manner of this young King of Siam!"

"But it looks more and more a can of worms," said Gareth. "That you must agree."

"And I suppose you're asking if there's a link between these pictures and the death of the King...... were it murder, suicide or whatever."

"What we're asking, Alan, is who might be working to ensure that any such a link is never exposed," said Jeremy. "Are the security services watching Kensington Palace? Were they watching the *Earl of Connaught*, the pub in Cricklewood, visited two Fridays ago by Eamon Carroll, just prior to the murder of its two occupants? Could they have been responsible for the destruction of a boat in St Erney the next day..... or for a burglary at Tredethy Manor during Thursday night, or even for a further death near Tintagel during the early hours of the next morning? We recall too well the ruthlessness of those entrusted to keep the lid on HIGHLAND CLEARANCE. Eamon could have been killed were it not for Declan McDaid...... and your career might just as easily have been finished."

Grigson hesitated, as if to be considering. The others waited.

"That's quite a list," he eventually said. "As a start I might enquire around this other death, near Tintagel you say. There'll be transparent procedures invoked, and a post-mortem certainly. What you can do for me now, Jeremy, is to phone Kate. See if you can get from her the name of the pathologist who's likely to be involved. She's well enough placed to track down the body, so it shouldn't be a problem to track down the man."

"And you're going to come in on this," pretended Gareth.

"I will," answered Alan, "but in my own way. In the meantime I'd like you to continue cultivating that friend of yours on the inside."

"David, in Kensington Palace."

"Who would appear to be on to our old friend Walter," added Jeremy, moving towards his phone. "I've read that Diana has made a close friend of Walter's grand-daughter. If this is how she came by those photos then perhaps he should be watching out for anything similar." He dialled and waited, leaving Alan to scoop together the pictures and, with a discrete wink, pass them back to Gareth. A contrived cake of an evening had baked up nicely. A successful phone call and the icing would be complete.

Jeremy was through.

"Kate," he began, "I've got Gareth and Alan here now."

"And is the latter coming aboard?"

"Yes, and actually I phone at his request. We told him of that road death up near Tintagel, and he's wanting a word with the pathologist entrusted with the post-mortem, ideally before what's left gets passed on to the undertakers."

"I'll phone up to the hospital. There'll be someone there who'll put me on to the right guy. Give me half an hour and I'll call back. And by the way, lest I forget later, this afternoon I went down to the acute ward to check out Madame Jingzhi's mother."

"And she's been sedated, I would think."

"She was, but no longer. Having put her under for forty-eight hours they've allowed her to gently come around, and while hardly as right as rain there's been a quite remarkable improvement. She's lucid. She's relaxed. She's eating, and back in control of bodily functions. She remembers things and people long term, but, this said, no one's yet dared raise that last shopping expedition....."

"...... or the *Devil of Shanghai*. So what next?"

"The usual tests..... the EEG, the scan for a possible tumour."

"Let's hope then for further good news. I'll let you get on now for Alan...... speak to you later."

*

In Chapel Amble meanwhile......

.......Eamon is also on the phone, in the call box close to the village green.

"CAVAN is that?"

"It is."

"SLIGO speaking."

"With a measure of progress to report, I trust."

"A few interesting developments....... something else has come out of Kensington Palace. We've a man on the inside, it seems, an acquaintance of a patched up Falklands veteran that the nurse and the lecturer know from before the HIGHLAND CLEARANCE business. He's come up with these photos, and they point to this being to do with the boy King of Thailand who was found shot back in '46. We suspect Lord Louis Mountbatten to have been somehow mixed up in it all. Shame he's not about. He could have been squeezed for an account, perhaps."

"It is a shame," agrees McBeamish, leaving Eamon to wonder at the mix of frustration and regret carried in the man's tone. He was supposed to have been in charge then. If, now, he was truly wishing things otherwise why had the assassination been sanctioned? "Anything else?" the voice now demands.

"A security branch has a team in the field, we're fairly sure of that, and the suspicion grows that what they might lack in competence they more than make up with their ruthlessness."

"And as you've mentioned Kate the nurse and Jeremy the lecturer, I have to ask if we're likely to encounter the third element of this blessed trinity....... he who calls himself Grigson, the fully indentured spook."

"They're trying to rope him in. The soldier, Gareth, claims to have a contact number, and my guess is yes, at some stage he'll show. Remember, though, that back in the summer he'd been suspended. Like me then he was something of an outcast...."

"...... and just as you might be less so now....."

"...... he too will be less of a free agent, and accordingly moving with care."

"Again, like yourself."

"Like myself," repeats Eamon, hoping thereby to deter the natural enquiry anticipated from McBeamish as to his exact whereabouts....... and he succeeds.

*

Tuesday 7a.m; Tremorebridge…..

……and James Busbridge is woken from a gradually shallowing slumber by the familiar chatter of the downstairs fax machine. Strange sort of time, he is thinking, until a rather grumpy descent of the stairs confirms the arrived document to be a letter from Tasmania, from his cousin Peter Bright……. formerly of MI5, recently in dispute with the UK Government over the publication of his memoir *'Molehunter'*. Already, there, it would be early evening, so maybe this was forgivable. Lifting the missive from the machine, he reads;

Dear Jim,

I write, as promised, in response to your enquiry about Tania Gaubert, with particular reference to the friendships with the Princes Chula and Bira of Thailand.
   As I've mentioned before, I interviewed this woman in 1971 when she freely admitted to me that while she'd arrived in this country ostensibly as a White Russian émigré during the early '30s she had in fact agreed to work as a minor information gatherer for the KGB.
   By the end of the war this work was largely done, and as a Mrs John Crocker (m. 1942) she was content to settle to being a wife of a farmer and mother to his children, initially in Devon before moving to Ireland. After that it was Somerset before, on retirement, taking a flat in London. This said, her testimony contributed to the case I was then constructing against the far more important figure of Edith Tudor Hart, an Oxford academic.
   As regards Tania's visits to Lynam House and Tredethy Manor during the 1940s, she told me that her brief had been two fold.
   Firstly, merely by listening, she was to gauge how impressed Chula and Bira were by the efforts of the Free Thai force which, under Pridi Banomyong, at that time sought to disrupt the Japanese hold on their country.
   Secondly, again by listening, she was to help monitor the activities of another regular guest of the Princes, the widowed Princess Marina, Duchess of Kent. At the bottom of this lay Stalin's paranoia over Poland, and the clique therein who'd sought to establish a constitutional

monarchy for their country as part of an early negotiated peace between the western powers and Berlin.

It had reached him that George, Duke of Kent had been offered the Crown, and although this Prince lost his life in an air crash, two sons and a daughter still survived as possible 'young pretenders'......their willingness or not to play such a part, then or later, depending almost wholly on such encouragement or discouragement received from Marina, their mother.

My information is that she, quite understandably, didn't want to know...... but Stalin, a man famous for believing only what he wanted to believe, remained watchful to the end of his life.

I must admit that the Thai issue, to me, was of secondary importance. Clearly, for you, it is not, and perhaps you suspect me of having been deceived by a Kent smokescreen.

If so then the best I can do is to give you what, to me, is Tania's last known address, and hope that she remains alive and well enough to perhaps grant you a personal interview.

Best Wishes

Peter

The address:

21a Cleveland Square
Bayswater.

Crocker, thought Busbridge.... so that *T* would indeed be Tania. This was progress, and that address was so conveniently close to Paddington Station. Here was a call he wanted to make himself, in person....... and why not today? If he could get himself down to Bodmin Parkway for the eight fifteen then even with the walk at the other end he might be knocking at the door by two.

The decision swiftly made, he reached the station with time to spare, sufficient indeed to enable him to take his car to the furthest reach of an elongated car park that stretched beyond the down platform. It would less likely be noticed, thought the watchful owner, daring not to speculate who by...... and un-noticed it did stay when, some five hours later, Alan Grigson stepped from a Penzance bound express with eyes solely for the blue '86 registered Cavalier that he'd been told would be there by Dr Simon Burrows, the Home Office pathologist he'd eventually managed to contact by phone the previous evening.

He would be driving down to meet him, Alan had been assured, and yes, there by the gate from the platform was the vehicle with, behind the wheel, presumably the man himself.

Alan hesitated by the lowered window, and that was enough.

"Mr Grigson?"

"Dr Burrows......you're obviously a busy man. Thanks for coming out."

"Looking to save a bit of time, that's all. If I can take you around to Lanhydrock then I can hear you out over a spot of lunch. Jump in."

'*Hear you out,*' pondered Grigson as Burrows negotiated the narrow lane to Respryn before climbing from the Fowey valley so as to enter the estate grounds by its northern 'cricket field' gate. There was something dismissive in that choice of phrase. Had this man been fore warned of this enquiry, he wondered. Could he even be under instructions to stonewall? Whatever, Alan had not come this far to relent.

Lordly Lanydrock glinted beneath the October sun like a multi faceted jewel, backed vividly as it was by the gold of the beech-hangered ridge to the west. The National Trust tearoom offered ample room and an appropriate selection of thoughtfully garnished toasted sandwiches.

"To business Mr Grigson," began Burrows. "Yesterday evening, at home, I receive a phone call from yourself about the gentleman from Tintagel whose corpse was recovered from the side of a nearby main road. Mr Barry George was the man's name, I can tell you. Being a local figure, he was identified quite promptly."

"I'm sorry about the out of hours call. I feared you might be close to releasing the body for burial or cremation."

"That you should have gone to the trouble of obtaining my number speaks of a certain determination to stall this. Is there something you fear that I might have missed?"

"Possibly........"

"......rather than probably?"

"To say that would be to question your competence, Dr Burrows."

"The lunch is on me," countered the pathologist. "In return I'll thank you *not* to mince words."

"So cause of death.....?"

"Multiple injuries consistent with having been struck and dragged some distance by a large, fast moving vehicle."

"And you would say instantaneous."

"As good as..... if not from brain damage beneath a fractured skull, then certainly from the catastrophic chest cavity bleeding occasioned by the rupture of the main pulmonary and coronary arteries."

"And what about the abdominal cavity?"

"One didn't really need to look that far...... not for a cause of death."

"But perhaps, as a matter of routine, you might have investigated stomach contents....... to see, maybe, if he'd been drinking."

"A blood test showed that during the twelve hours prior to death he'd taken no more than a glass of wine's worth of alcohol...... and bearing in mind that the deep laceration of soft tissue areas included a partial disembowelment, little remained to indicate otherwise."

Alan gulped, his appetite fast fading, but those sandwiches were here now and Burrows was tucking into his with relish. Effort was required, and effort duly made.

"And the pancreas and the spleen?"

"In pieces."

"And likewise the liver?"

"I've had to bag up the lot up together, as a butcher might do the giblets of a goose."

"But did you inspect the liver, Dr Burrows," Alan persisted.

"Not closely, Mr Grigson, but there is time yet. Would you suggest that I should?"

"Let me first tell you about the findings of one of your fellow practitioners. He works up in London, and this cropped up barely more than a week ago."

*

200

Bayswater, London......

......where James Busbridge has reached Cleveland Square and found flat 21a, an impressive property enjoying an impressive location. He sounds the bell and, after as well as possible identifying himself and his purpose to a security microphone, the lock releases and he is invited to push through.

Before him in the hall stoops an elderly well dressed man who can only move, it would appear, with the aid of zimmer- frame.

"Come through Mr Busbridge," croaks the frail voice.

"You are Mr John Crocker, husband to Tania Crocker?"

"Widowed husband, sadly, Mr Busbridge...... I've been on my own now for the best part of the year. From the way you've just spoken, I anticipate an interest in my late wife rather than me. Have you travelled far?"

"From Cornwall."

"A good way then.....״

"......yes, but by train, which brings me virtually to your doorstep"

"We'll sit. Do take a chair. I've a housekeeper, but having fed me my lunch she won't be back until four. The next pot of tea won't be brewed until then......"

"......by which time I'm hoping to be on my way back."

"And that's to which part of Cornwall Mr Busbridge?"

"A small hamlet near Withiel, plumb in the middle......close to a small stream that feeds the Camel, just to the west of Bodmin. Know that part?" The curious man was a master angler, and John Crocker rose to the bait.

"Tania would have. When we met she would frequently visit Cornwall, often staying with her friend Bira, Prince Bira. A racing driver, you might remember, and during the war he had place down there on the Camel estuary."

"Then, afterwards, his cousin Chula bought himself an old manor not so far from where I live."

"My wife once or twice went there on her own. That was when we were in Devon just after the war. Then we took our first farm in Ireland. A dozen or so years later we came back to Somerset, but by then Bira had given up motorsport, making him less reliant on Chula's money. Most of his time then he spent in France. He was an accomplished pilot too, and for a while operated a small freight airline between Thailand and Europe. It seemed to me that he could handle a car or a plane far better than he could his business affairs."

"So did Tania and Bira keep in touch?"

"Not really."

"Not really?" queried Busbridge, unsure as to his hosts meaning.

"Not for a long time."

"Until yourselves and he came to be both living within strolling distance of Kensington High St. I understand that when he died he had a place down towards Earls Court."

"This is so, and just prior to his death he did contact us, totally out of the blue. Tania invited him around, and was so looking forward to his visit...... but then we read of his sudden death. She was most upset."

"Christmas '85, wasn't it, that he died?"

"Christmas '85, and Tania struggled on to October '86. It's been a lonely year, but I have the three children still. I must count that a blessing."

"So by *not really* you mean that an attempt was made by Bira to end a long period of estrangement, but in the event this was foiled by his own sudden death."

"In putting it like that, Mr Busbridge, you imply that there was something deliberate in the sequence. Was it not just a fatal heart attack, as might happen to me or to any one of his age...... or even to yourself?"

"I guess it was," acknowledged the visitor, not wishing to worry an old and lonely man. "I'm sorry. I've no good reason to suspect otherwise."

"*No good reason to suspect otherwise*," repeated John Crocker with a wry smile. "Now you're starting to sound like Tania, who, to the end, however unreasonably, was niggled by doubt."

"Have others come to you voicing similar?" The curious man was wary.

"None, so worry not," replied the host. "You're the first, and because you may well be the last, perhaps it is time for some plain speaking."

"I'm listening," Busbridge gently urged.

"And so am I," countered the old man firmly. "I'm asking you first to be open with me. Say the right kind of thing and I might well have something for you."

"And were I not to?"

"Then at least you'll have lost nothing by coming. Either way, be assured, nothing will go beyond these four walls."

Busbridge considered for a moment. Was this fair? It wasn't unfair, he decided. He hadn't come this far just to lie to the man.

"A week ago," he began, "I was in Tintagel, in a small museum. There I was given an opportunity to sift through a bundle of personal papers and photos recovered from Bira's wartime residence in Rock, these having lain neglected in its loft for a good thirty years. Amongst these was a hand written journal which offered what for me was an intriguing picture of those times."

"And there was mention of Tania?"

"Probably there was, but with the time I had I could only briefly scan through an entry made in the middle of '45, Between VE day and VJ."

"When the Japanese were still running things in Thailand."

"Yes, while hard pressed in Burma and in the Philippines, they were just about hanging on. With hindsight we can say it was borrowed time."

"And Bira, did he know anything about how soon and suddenly the war did in fact end, and the likely destiny of his nation?"

"I doubt it, for the tone of the entry was far from optimistic. It was almost fearful."

"*Fearful?*"

"Not like scared frightened....... more that he was fearful for his future sporting career. Anticipating a resumption of motor racing in Europe, he wondered if the financial backing and management acumen previously supplied by Chula might be available still."

"But we know he did get back into it.......so was this anxiety justified?"

"According to Bira, his cousin had been warning him.... drawing his attention to an uncertain situation in Thailand. A Japanese withdrawal could be expected to create a power vacuum into which he, Chula, was likely to be drawn, or even pushed. Those who'd collaborated with the Japs, Chief Minister Pibul and his pals, they would be looking to make themselves scarce...... and given that they'd installed the reigning Monarch and his family, the Mahidols, it was widely predicted that they might abdicate." Busbridge hesitated. Old Crocker had been listening closely, but was this what he was wanting to hear?

"But, in the event, just as Bira's career was to flourish on after the war, so, after a brief interlude, likewise did Pibul's."

"....... and to this day a Mahidol rules in Bangkok," capped Busbridge, encouraged by his host's perceptive comment. He was meeting with the man's approval, he sensed, and maybe he could hold back on a few things, on those photographs taken in Lausanne of the young King Ananda for instance. But there was one snap he could mention. "And one of the more interesting photos amongst this box of goodies at the museum was that of Chula at St Enodoc golf club flanked by Anthony Blunt and Guy Burgess."

"And you have this with you?"

"I'm afraid I don't..... I didn't think," stuttered Busbridge. What was he to say should the old man demand that he bring it?

"Well never mind," sighed Crocker, to the caller's relief. "I'm taking it that you wouldn't have mentioned that pair had you not read somewhere, or been told, that for a while Tania herself passed information to the KGB."

"This is so."

"That Peter Bright fellow, he of the *Molehunter* book...... during her final months she spoke of being interrogated by him and were she here now she would tell you the same. That back in the '40s she had no idea that the likes of Blunt, Burgess and Maclean were in the same business."

"This would figure," conceded Busbridge. "But between Bira and Tania there developed an estrangement, you've said. Might this have been because he'd been quietly warned that some of his guests in Cornwall were fellow travellers ....Tania included?"

"This is what Tania was expecting might emerge when he came around to visit but, as I said, he never made it."

"How thoughtless of him to die."

"Indeed, but she was sure that it all went back to the standing of the Mahidols in Bangkok, in '45 and '46."

"And also to Chula's position," nudged Busbridge.

"And also to Chula's position," old Crocker quietly confirmed. "And it is important, here, to know that Chula was an honourable man with a refined sense of duty. Were the throne to have fallen vacant and he then to have been legitimately invited to take it then yes, out of duty rather than ambition he would have felt obliged to step up....... such was his respect for his country's traditions. By the same token, were there *no* vacancy beneath the nine ceremonial umbrellas, then this sense of duty would compel him to desist from joining any plot to undermine or even overthrow an incumbent. Chula could draw a firm line between the two positions......."

"....... which others, perhaps, could not."

"Because while a firm inviolable line in Chula's mind, to those others it could by turns appear blurred and challengingly narrow."

"One only has to read Bira's journal," nodded Busbridge.

"Tania would have told you that the Mahidols probably considered the option of abdication," said Crocker, "and that knowing this, Chula would have been concerned to ensure that whatever the decision made, it was reached under a minimum of outside pressure."

"And what would she have made of the ambitions of Pridi, arch rival to Pibul?"

"As a politician, Pridi was allowed to have ambitions....... when it came, though, to his attitude to the Mahidols, this, Tania would say, differed little to Chula's. As leader of the Free Thais he replaced Pibul as chief minister, and if King Ananda wanted to stay then an important aspect of this role was to respect and protect the boy."

"And that last, he failed to do."

"But not for want of trying...... this Tania firmly believed. And, sadly, the tragedy ruined the career of this true patriot, his enemies moving sharply to recycle all the old stuff about his being an agent of Moscow."

"And this is when it would have been whispered to Bira that he would do well to distance himself substantially from your wife."

"Not least, Mr Busbridge, because the King's death re-ignited the abdication question, the younger brother this time being left to wonder if he should tempt the sort of fate met by his elder."

"Now what would your wife have said if she were here now to hear me say that I have evidence that at the time of the Japanese surrender a close associate of Lord Louis Mountbatten could have been exerting pressure on the Mahidols to go."

"She would not have expressed surprise, Mr Busbridge. A revelation of this sort was anticipated from Bira, just from the tone of his preceding phone call. She would have still defended Chula and Pridi, though. Nothing would have persuaded her of their complicity. Mountbatten was a rogue, this is well known now. By contrast, Chula's integrity stands all the more pronounced. If Bira was finally on to this then we can imagine him wanting to settle things with Tania......"

".....by way of an apology, you mean, for having ceased to ask her and you down to Tredethy."

"Yes, for in this changed light it needed to be asked why Chula hadn't been just as selective when it came to not re-inviting a few other regular guests, guests who were friendly to Mountbatten......."

".......rather than friendly to the ambitions of Joe Stalin. I get your point Mr Crocker, but my attention has been drawn to one man who by repute was friendly to both."

"I think, Mr Busbridge, I know of whom you speak. You sound like you might have read Ziegler's book."

"I have."

"And the fellow who springs to mind is that Peter Murphy."

"Did Tania ever mention him?"

"Not as a fellow guest down in Cornwall, and this figures for it was regarded as bad practice in the KGB to have separately controlled agents turning up at the same place at the same time. But he comes close to being identified in a final letter she wrote, one that she left with me to pass on to any that might express the kind of interest you've shown."

"So have I earned a chance to see this, with what I've so far said?"

"You have, Mr Busbridge. Otherwise and I would have made no mention of it. And not only do you see it, you can take the thing. Relieve me of it, please, for I'm just too old now to be doing with this sort of stuff. You see that atlas on my bookshelf...." He pointed.

"I do."

"Fetch it down and you'll find the page showing Thailand, Indo China and Malaya to be book-marked by an envelope. "Busbridge complied. "That's yours," instructed the host. "It holds a letter. Take it away with you, and know that I've helped you all I can."

"Thank you Mr Crocker." They shook hands, and within fifteen minutes our day-tripper was back at the terminus, gazing up at the clattering indicator and calculating when he would be back at Jasmine Cottage.

*

206

Bodmin

"Kind of you to look me up Mr Grigson," said Kate warily. "You can see I'm busy, but if we can keep it to just a few minutes then they can easily be made up later. Now we're outside, perhaps you can tell me what brings you to the St Lawrence Hospital?"

"A body, Nurse Rogers," smiled Alan with a mischievous down and up glance. Kate blushed..... then rallied.

"So the honour of this visit we can attribute to an urge to flirt."

"A dead body, Kate," the expression changed, "and this is serious. With your help yesterday I was able to contact the local pathologist and, though you might not know it, sometimes he will avail himself of the mortuary facility here for his more general duties. The examination in this case is of a road accident victim, the unfortunate having been pronounced dead at the scene."

"Are we speaking of this fellow that Eamon hoped to see the other day? Ran a museum up in Tintagel."

"We are. My visit concerns the remains of Mr Brian George."

"And you've found the pathologist helpful?"

"Exceedingly....... met me off the train, bought lunch for me at Lanhydrock, and then even brought me here so that I might know how promptly and thoroughly he could respond to my query. When do you finish work?"

"I can be out in an hour and a quarter."

"And your car is where?"

"Just over there." Kate pointed. "With this block we get our own spaces."

"So it is. If I come back then, will I be OK for a lift to Parkway Station? I can say what needs to be said on the way down."

*

Heading west

With his train through Reading and easing itself gently up the Kennet valley, the curious man tackles the late Tania Crocker's letter for a third time. It is that kind of testament, each reading compelling a re-reading...... some parts being so definite while others so vague. So once more, he mutters to himself, once more from the top;

Cleveland Square
January 1986

I leave this letter with my husband, trusting him to pass it on my behalf to a worthy recipient or, if need be, to instruct our children to do the same. It concerns Prince Bira, a friend from the past whose acquaintance I hoped to renew late last year. At his instigation we were to meet, but sadly, before we could do so he suddenly died. I write this now because as I myself become increasingly frail in mind and body, I fear that the many things we could have spoken of might soon be lost forever.

I was a frequent guest at Lynam House, Bira's rented residence in Cornwall during the war years. Prince Chula, an older cousin (but effectively a guardian) lived there with him for a while and then, just after the war, moved to nearby Tredethy Manor. More than once I visited Tredethy, but then the invitations stopped, and seemingly at their wish, communication with the Royal pair dwindled away to nothing.

I've long assumed that on being told that behind my rumoured White Russian credentials there lurked a minor KGB informant they were persuaded that I was best avoided, particularly in view of political developments in their native Thailand.

The violent death in 1946 of the young King Ananda could only have made them more wary, a pro-Pibul faction in Bangkok using this as an opportunity to revive the career of a champion severely (but not terminally) discredited by his collaboration with Tokyo. Here, for this group, was an opportunity to bring down he who had ousted Pibul, the former Free Thai leader Pridi. An assassination had been organised from Moscow, they claimed, and Pridi had been at best neglectful, at worst complicit.

208

Chula and Bira, so supportive of Pridi during the war, would now have had to exercise extreme care.

Over the years, from a distance, I tried to let it be known to the Princes that while accepting that Moscow might have observed the situation with interest I was far from convinced that a murder would have been ordered by the KGB, stability in Bangkok being prized by them above all else. Instead I voiced my suspicion that the regicide had stemmed from an attempt to de-stabilise the Thai monarchy by a roguish clique of eminent Britons, an element that while possibly including a maverick strain of Marxism answered only to itself.

I put it to them that in their concern to curb this element's tendency to embarrassing excess, the British Establishment had set their own watch on these people, calling on Service colleagues and those who frequented the same social circles to report on the progress of their scheming. I held (and hold still) that aside from the likes of me, informants of this home grown species were also well represented in the Tredethy guest list and that it was was more likely that as a consequence of THEIR selectively channelled reports reaching a ruthless agency deployed by a major non-Marxist power that Ananda took the fatal hit.

Beyond my family, any reader of this letter will have been heard to express an awareness of the ambitious and scheming nature of Lord Louis Mountbatten. Had they not then on my strict instruction it would have been withheld. While saying this, though, lest there be any misunderstanding, I can happily accept that Lord Louis would no more have ordered the lad to be shot than would have Pridi, or even Chula himself.

My view is that those others were responsible, acting out of alarm at Lord Louis' antics. Those others who were (and still are) far more adept at concealment. Be warned that THEY REMAIN DANGEROUS. If an option remains of letting the sleeping dog lie then this must be seriously considered. If it is awake, though, and in pursuit, then perhaps it might be better to carefully get to know the enemy so as hopefully to better counter its menace.

And how might such knowledge be acquired? From familiarity, I would suggest, with those who could be deemed my rival informants, mentioned above to have been well represented in the Tredethy guest list.

Actual names, though, I must not give for fear that any such list might invite danger on my family. To lessen the risk for them (and anyone else who might hold this document) I will instead suggest that the connections of THE QUEEN'S GENERAL be scrutinised, and also those of a STELLA whose company was enjoyed by the young P.

Good Luck

Tania

Again the two hand-written pages are re-folded, returned to their envelope, and re-pocketed. Constructed with care, this letter is obviously to be guarded likewise. It isn't to be left lying on the table, or even on his lap, lest he should sleep.

But sleep……. how could he? For what an acquisition this looks to be! How frustrating it now was not to have Bira's journal to hand, having come so close to the thing…… and yet how fortunate he'd been to have had that glimpse he'd enjoyed. And then there was that picture at Tredethy, again snatched away to leave him reliant on memory. But how vivid the memories had now become, sharpened to such colour by this letter which offered, surely, to further link those vanished items.

It would seem that the cloud which had settled over Pridi following the King's death in Bangkok had, by association, threatened to dim the prestige of Chula amongst his countrymen, and his response had been to question Tania's loyalty as a friend…… his suspicion being that she might have been complicit in a Moscow inspired intrigue which, to his embarrassment, sought to activate his claim on the throne.

And Bira had gone along with this view……until just before his death, when it seems he was ready to rectify matters with some sort of apology for Tania, and perhaps an explanation which might sit better with this alternative scenario cautiously outlined in her letter. Here a failed attempt to destabilise the Thai monarchy by a characteristically ambitious, scheming, and incompetent Lord Louis is held to be distinct from a successful attempt on the King's life made by *others, more adept at conceament,* who *remain dangerous* ……. and to the extent that these *non-marxist* others had also infiltrated informants into Chula's circle, it had to be they rather than she who'd been deserving of the Prince's opprobrium.

So who were and are these others, Busbridge asks himself. *The Queen's General*, might tell him, the letter says...... and he has a candidate for this one. Surely it would have been General Frederick Browning, Tommy himself, pictured in the group at Tredethy. Moved out to Ceylon after the Arnhem fiasco he could well have been briefed by Stuart Menzies to keep Mountbatten under rein....... Menzies, of course, having been the eminence who had entrusted the execution and subsequent concealment of HIGHLAND CLEARANCE to GUSTAVE, alias Shimi Lovat, another army officer.

Then, after the war, Browning had been attached to Prince Philip and his new bride who, within a few years, became Queen Elizabeth....... *The Queen's General* indeed. But unlike Lovat, 'Boy' Browning was long dead. If he was to speak then it would have to be through those *connections* as, in a manner, he already had.

For it could be assumed that it was he who'd trimmed that photo at Tredethy, those snipped from the group having been secreted in his boat before being moved by Peg Willis to Port Eliot. And what a brace had from there been spirited, Jack Profumo and Walter Monckton..... the implication of Tania's letter being that the reason for their excision lay not in the all too public career-closing pickle that engulfed the former when a Minister, instead in their clandestine machinations of fifteen years earlier, exposure of which might have brought even greater embarrassment to the likes of Princess Marina and Prince Philip.

So what, then, was there to be added by this *Stella whose company was enjoyed by a young P*? If Philip, Mountbatten's nephew, could certainly qualify as a *young P*, there'd been nothing so far to suggest that the companion of his pictured a Tredethy might be a *Stella*. 'Mrs A. Allen', this was the only lead so far, the A perhaps being for Anna, the Anna of 'Anna and the King', around whom the *The King and I* was devised. If Tania was here asserting that this woman might also have been known as Stella then there'd been nothing hitherto from elsewhere to suggest this. So far it was just Tania alone, but the word of one who'd *actually been there* wasn't to be ignored, far from it.......for unlike Tania, even if slightly older, this 'A' woman, whether also a *Stella* or not, might still be alive. If she could be identified and traced, then here might be someone to provide an even better testimony.

*

In Kate's car

"And you can't say when you'll be back, Alan? We'd hoped you might be volunteered for one of those roaming briefs which tend to keep you in Cornwall for longer." Kate was emerging onto the Carminnow Cross roundabout, her detour towards the Beacon having lifted her around the town centre traffic.

"You forget, Kate, my last foray came as a consequence of my being pushed out. Then, cast as the scapegoat, I could roam more freely."

"Whereas now you're wanting to sticking with the herd. Safety in numbers I guess."

"Partly that," responded the passenger, declining to rise to what he felt was intended as a mild taunt. "But do bear in mind an opposite view......... and for down here, one no less valid."

"Be more clear."

"Consider, for a moment, how many of you gathered for supper over at Jim's. You, Jeremy, and Gareth, Cross the father, Cross the son, McDaid, and then the host as well...... that's seven, making it a lot to keep under some sort of control."

"Maybe, but is *control* so important?"

"For me, Kate, it is vital, lest there develop conflicts of interests."

"In the sense that a duty to your employer could cut across the loyalty you might want to show to the likes of us....... mere friends."

"I'm saying that the best efforts and intentions of all, me included, won't guarantee that this *us* you speak of will not fragment." Alan was choosing his words with care. "Yes, you've gathered together and that's fine, but this isn't to say you'll be hanging together."

"You didn't include Carroll, the eighth. Was that a deliberate omission?"

"It was, for why should I assume that he doesn't already have a handler? Is he a fugitive like last time, or is he now an informant? He might even be both. Jeremy didn't say."

"And you're thinking that I might?" asked Kate, carefully negotiating the Coleslogget bends.

"Well you live around here, twentyfour-seven......unlike Jeremy, unlike Gareth. And considering your line of work, perhaps you're better placed to assess Eamon's state of mind."

"Eamon is nervous, and little wonder," said the nurse. "He speaks to this person and then that, only to find within days they're dead. The guy's beside himself. Who's to say which way he'll jump...... it might even be over a cliff"

"And at this stage I'm afraid that prompts me to question his reliability. Just to be feeling sorry for the bloke isn't enough."

"So you want more on him and his situation, but what am I to offer when all to me remains so shadowy and contradictory."

"In what respect shadowy?"

"Eamon and his Fenian pals are on to something, it's significance still being obscure. Its potential, possibly known or guessed at in Kensington Palace, will become clearer if he can find out more, and for this he has been sent to the right place and the right people."

"And *contradictory*, you said," pressed Alan, as the driver slowed to bridge the Fowey, indicating her intention to take the immediate right into the station.

"By turns it seems that your people might at times be tailing him, and at other times obstructing him...... occasionally resorting to what I feel to be a disturbing degree of violence. Could it be that the Home Office has two teams in the field, two specialist teams, one evolved to counter the IRA and its various splinters, the other devoted to keeping the Monarchy in servicable nick......"

".......with neither being clear as to where the other might be treading, eh?"

"The kind of thing we sometimes get in the Health Service," smiled the nurse.

"And certainly not unknown in my world," conceded Alan. "A surveillance man can be assigned to this unit or that whilst never being admitted to their highest counsels of any so........"

".......so your guess still has to be better than mine," said Kate sharply, sensing a characteristic evasivenesss.

"What I have learned, Kate, is that Royal Protection, that is the guarding of Royal personages, Royal reputations, and Royal prestige, concerns itself with more than the menace *without*. Also to be countered is the menace that can sometimes arise from *within*, a task reserved for the true elite operating at a rarefied level way above any that I've ever flown to".

"From within?" queried the puzzled driver, moving into a vacant parking space close to station entrance and turning off her motor.

"As when a mix of individual trait and broad circumstance can spur a Royal Family *member* to such folly or mischief, or both, that measures are deemed necessary such as might forestall lasting damage."

"Measures of what kind, Alan?"

"Restricting their access to those people and places and things that could encourage and thus further this mischief......"

"...... and this can entail removal?"

"Of the people do you mean, or the things?"

"Eamon would suspect both, pointing for a start to the sudden death of Prince Bira a couple of Decembers ago. This was less than a month after he'd visited Tredethy for the first time in years, and shown a close interest in a photograph that hung there, a photograph sniffed out by Eamon on his first morning down here, prior to its theft earlier this week."

"Now that's interesting, Kate," said Alan, "for it's been in response to a word from the Irish section concerning our friend's sudden disappearance from London that the Palace Guard, as I shall term it, has placed itself on heightened alert....... a smallish problem, previously deemed under control, suddenly having become quite large."

"On heightened *active* alert, Eamon might say, and ruthlessly active at that. Two recent deaths in London, he could point to, and another to follow in Tintagel, plus the destruction of Peg Willis's old boat over at St Erney....... as well as the burglary of that photograph from Tredethy Manor. That's a lot of things in a short time, Alan. And now we have you dashing down to Bodmin today, something to suggest more than a mere passing involvement. What did you find out about that body?"

An old style semaphore signal at the end of the 'up' platform dropped, and with it a little of the passenger's reserve.

"Enough to now suspect that those killings were unlikely to have been the work of any domestic agency," he said grimly.

"So Irish...... maybe?" ventured the nurse, opening her door. She wanted this conversation to continue.

"I don't think so." Alan stepped out too, to be accompanied across the quaintly roofed wooden footbridge.

"Why not?" Kate pressed, hoping that the train had stopped at Lostwithiel and that its departure was being delayed a few more minutes by the level crossing there.

"There are indications, less than clear I add, that the victims were put to death in a ritualistic manner." Kate's jaw dropped. "For the moment that's all I can say. In a day or so I might have a better grasp of the implications." Suddenly the nurse was breathless, the worn staircase seeming to steepen. Alan, though, was starting to flow. "The boat and the burglary we can put down to my people, Kate. I'll admit that, just on the in-house chatter I've picked up. The existence of that photo was long known, as was the fact of its alteration by Browning, the owner, but not until a few days ago was its recent whereabouts. Before that, when it was realised that Eamon was heading for Cornwall......"

"........then finding the bits had to be the next best thing," mumbled Kate, her tongue at last re-found.

"This was the logic. Menabilly and Kilmarth they'd searched before, more than once for each, but the boat was overlooked.......until it's realised that the thing sits at St Erney, being stripped down by people that Carroll might soon be talking with."

"So they destroy it as a belt and braces precaution," nodded Kate. "The consensus at Jasmine Cottage holds this to have been inadvisedly clumsy. But then, within a few days, the picture itself is known to be at Tredethy."

"This came up from our friends at Carwinion....."

"....... where Jeremy kindly led a delegation that included the Crosses......"

"......who should have been forewarned that the walls there have ears. Hugh Trembath, is always keen to impress, and this time, yes, he did the business."

"You speak as if he wasn't totally reliable."

"He means well, Kate, but a question mark over the House will remain, certainly for as long as Sir Edward lives. Washington invested heavily in that place, and such a stake can never be discounted."

"And I suppose the son senses this still......"

"...... making him try perhaps a little too hard," nodded Alan. "He'll even attempt to use his daughter, but with all that time spent at her grandfather's other place in London no one's sure how trusty a tool it is that's been fashioned." The engine rumbled past, gliding its carriages to a measured halt.

"So you're abandoning us," fluttered Kate.

"Because a little time and a little distance is required, but I will be in touch....... one way or another. Say to Eamon from me that he needs to be very, very careful; careful in where he goes alone, careful with

215

whom he speaks, and careful with what he says."

Into the train Grigson climbs, the few doors used slam and away it growls, steeling for its stiff climb to lofty Largin. The last of the half dozen disembarked passengers reach the footbridge, but Kate isn't yet following. The island platform, now deserted, offers solitude and with this a welcome sense of security. Here is a moment to gather an alarming range of thoughts. A bench beckons. She sits.

Ritualistic manner, this was enough, for with those two words the concern seeded by the initial mention of the Chinese woman's hospitalisation, then nurtured subconsciously by talk of a sharply improved condition, sprouted now as pernicious anxiety. What might have been dismissed as a probable hallucination loomed now as a possible memory, no less dark than that restored so painfully to the Wakeham at *Jamaica Inn*...... except that in this instance, at Wadebridge, the trigger would appear to have been something far more fearsome than a cigarette card.

An image returns to her own mind, one seared therein when, as a teenager, flicking through a volume of history found in her old school library, she'd happened upon a photograph taken at the time of the pillage of 1930s Shanghai. A shortening line of prisoners knelt before a Japanese officer, his ceremonial sword held high...... whilst behind him grew two piles, the larger made of decapitated torsos, the smaller of disembodied heads.

A steel blade taken to a warm neck, this was what *ritualistic manner* means for Kate Rogers. She shudders. Eamon needed to be warned. Alan had said as much...... so she would call on Jim and suggest that they might seek him out together.

But James Busbridge, of course, is not to be found at home. He is still two hours the wrong side of Plymouth, and with the Jasmine Cottage door unresponsive to her knock the nurse must re-consider. Knowing where to find Eamon's caravan she can just as easily drive herself across to Dinham, and this she will do, but with it being a little early yet, perhaps there might be something to be gained by calling in at *The Silver Pagoda* on her way.

*

Bath

A decision this, that, were he to have known of it, Jeremy would have quietly applauded, for he at this moment is in the Bath City Library checking the history shelves for what they can offer on Imperial Japan's militarism of the '30s and '40s. That a relatively small island nation could so rapidly subjugate so vast an area of so full and varied a population was, however reprehensible and long-term disastrous, a remarkable feat of arms, one that required exceptional talent in its planning, and ruthlessnes in its execution. Kate's brief mention over the phone of Madame Jingzhi's mother had been the prompt. Just who were these commanders, he'd wondered, and what had happened to them as individuals once they'd eventually been disarmed?

The cruellest were dead, this was the popular belief, either killed in battle, or by their own hand, or executed as un-recanting war criminals. In the west, the odd prudent Nazi might have secured for himself a safe conduct to deepest Paraguay on the strength of his hoard of treasure, of secrets perhaps, on communist networks, or rocketry, or biological warfare, all this obtained by diabolical device....... but not so in the east. There, under a stricter honour code, nothing of the plenty gathered to Japan by comparable means had been offered up so pragmatically.

But what had *popular belief* ever been to Jeremy Barnes? A gaudy and unsubtle bloom, tended by a succession of vested interests, each bringing its own barrow of manure...... a plant that could too easily run riot if not constrained.

For might there indeed be a *Devil of Shanghai*, one young and resourceful enough to have survived and prospered well enough to reappear fifty years later in Cornwall? A far out possibility, maybe, but not one to evade so sharp a nose for concealed rottenness as carried by our lecturer.

Except that so far he is finding little to assist him amongst this particular selection of books. It seems from these that on their surrender the Japanese top brass did indeed struggle to find buyers for their talents and insights, unlike the more anonymous rank and file. Here was an unexpected paradox. The foot soldier so graphically vilified in the action comics of Jeremy's youth, was emerging from these accounts as a quiescent, almost co operative species which when deployed under American, British and French orders proved an effective and useful policing device for vast swathes of its relinquished empire. With the GI and the Tommy chafing for their return to anxious families a parlous post-war stability from Indo China to the Philippines had to be built, it seemed, largely on this resource.

Interesting this, but not what he is seeking, and he is left to reflect that this is but one section in this one public library, and incomplete in that some books would be out on loan. He needn't give up....... not at all. If he travelled further then surely he would do better. And besides there was another avenue, he shouldn't forget, along which young Chas Cross might be of help. Yes, he would phone the boy later. And perhaps there is someone else he might also contact. He turns, making for the reference section. Details could be here, in the *Who's Who*.

*

Wadebridge

Kate approached *The Silver Pagoda*. The door would be locked, she knew this, for it was forty minutes yet until 6.30......but she would knock nevertheless. She did, and a window curtain moved. It was Madame Jingzhi, possibly alone. If so then would she answer, wondered the nurse....... hoping so, for if it could be just she and her then all the better.

Seconds passed....... then the latch was lifted, and the door opened sufficiently for a tilted face to nod the caller through.

"Thank you Madame Jingzhi," said Kate softly as the lock was firmly re-set. "I bring encouraging news of your mother."

"Then I must thank you, Nurse Rogers. You think she can make full recovery?"

"One can be more hopeful now, on Tuesday, than say Saturday night. But something or someone has given her a bad, bad scare."

"Bad, bad memories, I fear." The proprietress offered one of the soft chairs available for waiting customers, she herself retreating behind the counter. Kate sat.

"And have these surfaced before? Can you recall any previous mention of this *Devil of Shanghai*?"

"Rarely, and only in fevered sleep."

"And what does the term mean to you?"

"It is a Japanese soldier."

"Not '*was*'."

" '*Is*', for if not in the flesh, this one will ever live in the memory."

"And is it a particular one?"

"I have no name..... but yes, a particular one who held high command at both Shanghai and Singapore."

"So you would have had no positive news of his death."

"How.....with no name?"

"But rumour perhaps?"

"The occasional will reach my husband......"

"...... but you do not speak of such things in front of your mother."

"Quite....."

"So these stories.....?"

"Some say that this man flee into Thailand at end of the war, and few that he never come out again. He is put to death by communists, they say, who see through his disguise as monk. Others say this is lie, spread on purpose to cover further escape into Vietnam where he operate as jungle mercenary. This until he goes to Laos, and there is eaten by tiger."

"And throughout he has been spoken of only as *The Devil of Shanghai*," added Kate. "So how old would he have been now?"

"He born say 1900, at earliest," said Madame Jingzhi. "So no more than 37 in Shanghai....."

".......and 87 at the most, now. A good age, and if your mother really recognised him from 50 years ago we must assume him well preserved."

"Some saying this down to unique feature of diet...... his taste for human liver, taken ideally from freshly bled corpse of an enemy." Kate almost retched. Might this be the indelicacy that Alan had been alluding to when speaking of a *ritualistic manner*? If so then a devil did indeed lay in the detail. She couldn't speak. "I can bring you a glass of water Nurse Rogers."

Kate nodded. Madame Jingzhi went to her kitchen.

"I must be busy now," she said on her return.

Kate, standing to take the glass and gulp back its welcome content had heard enough. Her eventual words were few.

"Thank you for your time, and for being so frank." The glass returned she moved to the door.

"I tell you so you will better understand my mother should she speak of these things. Before then I trust you not to cause her alarm." Madame Jingzhi held the door.

"Of course," said Kate, finding a measure of reassurance in the gentle hum of early evening Wadebridge.

*

Jeremy phones (i)

"Chas?"

"Speaking."

"Jeremy here, Chas, in Bath. I've just been down to the City Library looking for anything on, or even by, the high-ups in the Japanese army during the last war."

"Any luck?"

"Not really, it was a pretty meagre selection."

"So you're thinking our Plymouth Library might offer more? I wouldn't count on that. Naval stuff maybe, but the Burma Campaign and all that......I don't think so."

"Fair enough, but there's somewhere else I thought you could try for me. Back in the summer I was told of a military bookshop down in the Barbican area, one piled high with second hand stuff on just about every aspect of warfare you might imagine."

"*Rod's* that is, and yes, he's an expert in that field."

"When you have a spare moment, then, I'd like you to pick his brains. What I'm after are characters....... the Americans had their Patton, we had Monty. With the Russians it was Zhukov; with the Germans, Rommel. There have to be books on, or by, the Japanese equivalent. See what he has, or what he can suggest."

"And you're hoping to be down when?"

"By Thursday evening."

"Two days then......yes, it should be possible."

"I'll call from Kate's when I get there."

*

Jeremy phones (ii)

"Mr Ziegler...... Mr Philip Ziegler? "

"It is.....and you?"

"A Mr Jeremy Barnes, speaking from Bath. You don't know me, but as you've furnished your *Who's Who* entry with this number I'm persuaded that you're not going to over mind me making this enquiry."

"That might depend on its nature Mr Barnes..... so if I could ask that you come to your point."

"Your biography of Mountbatten, Mr Ziegler..... very interesting."

"Thank you." The tone was that of one weary of faint praise.

"And for me, nothing more so than your unequivocal assertion that the young King Ananda of Thailand was murdered in his bed. Is this your conclusion or merely an echo of that reached by your subject."

"The latter I suppose, for as intriguing as it might be for the likes of yourself I must admit to not having studied the episode to any great depth. I simply wouldn't know enough about any of the competing theories. Mountbatten's letters, and relatives and friends I've spoken to, all indicate a preference for murder......"

".......rather than accident or suicide."

"Rather than either," endorsed the biographer, as if to conclude the exchange. Jeremy, though, was merely drawing breath.

"So did those sources hint at all at a perpetrator?"

"They tended to be guarded in this respect, but there was the occasional mention of this letter written by Mountbatten in Singapore shortly after the crime and sent to Buckingham Palace."

"To George VI and the current Queen Mother...... I've heard of this. It holds that Ananda's mother and younger brother together conspired to commit the murder, a somewhat far fetched theory. Was any motive suggested?"

"Merely implied, Mr Barnes. We are to believe that the young Monarch was perhaps felt to be wanting in Majesty."

"Without which the Mahidol succession was, I suppose, vulnerable." Ziegler hadn't seen those photos of Ananda and Murphy cavorting, Jeremy was sure, but the mother and the brother..... perhaps they had. So could he now admit that young Chas's suggestion of the honour motive had merit? He couldn't, for even leaving aside the sanctity

221

of life ethos so central to Buddhism, in its very act such a murder was simply too unnatural. Whatever the dishonour the Mahidols would have chosen to go down together, he was sure, and he was no less certain that this had been the outcome hoped for by the scheming Mountbatten. But Dickie's plans had miscarried, and if somehow he'd been thwarted then who by...... and how? "So Mama and younger brother Mahidol wouldn't have been too impressed by Lord Louis," continued the lecturer.

"On learning that he'd branded them murderers...... decidedly not, and thanks to *that* letter the relationship between Buckingham palace and the Royal Palace of Bangkok was, quite understandably, to remain strained for some years. There was no King of Thailand at the Coronation of our Queen in '53. Instead the invitation went to a Prince Chula who was living in Cornwall at the time."

Jeremy had heard as much from James Busbridge.

"Is that so?" he responded ingenuously. "But things have since been repaired, I'll assume."

"Largely due to Marina of Kent and, more latterly, her daughter Alexandra...... a task eased of course by the death of Lord Louis. And I'm afraid that's as much time as I can spare you this evening Mr Barnes. I hope I've been of assistance."

*

Pentireglaze, Polzeath

"So I'm to be careful."

"Extremely careful Eamon."

"In where I go alone, with whom I speak, and with what I say."

"Alan's very words," confirmed Kate, as a haze reddened sun sank slowly over Stepper Point giving a pinkish tinge to the rumbling breakers that were rewarding the patience of the last half dozen sea-silhouetted surfers with a final worthwhile set. High to the right the pale grass of Pentire Head had taken the deep grey-green hue of the sea whilst, beneath, the slate-grey cliffs darkened by the second to a curtain of black. Turning from the water's edge only the firm damp sand held something of the evenings dying glow as the pair retraced their shallow shaddowed footprints back into the sheltered cove and the winding path by which they would climb to the road above and Kate's waiting car. "Too much has been said already, he reckons, not so much by yourself as by those whose curiosity took them down to the Trembaths. He admits that it was his people who placed a guard around Port Eliot, after word came up from Carwinion."

"The route by which they were subsequently tricked into lowering it."

"But not disuaded from burgling Tredethy…..."

"…….and taking that picture, from which they must have learned of our ruse," muttered Eamon.

"On noticing the mismatch between the photos, you think? I'm not so sure, for just how much could they firmly conclude? Merely that there was an *attempted* ruse by *someone.* That's all, with suspicion falling just as easily on Carwinion House and its occupants as on anywhere or anyone else. OK, they will have the Tredethy photo, just as they will have destroyed Peg's boat, but they'll have had nothing yet to confirm that anyone got into Port Eliot, let alone if anything was found."

"Hence Grigson's advice to be careful," nodded Eamon, "but what's with all the urgency? Am I imagined to be touring the local pubs each evening, bragging Jim and Declan's achievement to all at every least opportunity?"

"Other things are being imagined, Eamon, and imagined with alarming vividness. We fear that there could be a second outfit in the field…….. an alien agency this, possibly better briefed than anything raised domestically, and probably more vicious."

"But working to a similar agenda, the suppression of these awkward truths which could otherwise threaten the prestige of the British Monarchy."

"Awkward truths, yes, but who in the wider world will be caring too much about the Palace? It could be that these more parochial concerns are incidental to a *parallel* agenda which, while fashioned in response to the same sequence of events, perhaps addresses issues more global."

"More global and also more grave, and, as such, outside the domain of our Home Office." They were at the top of the beach, and for the narrow path Eamon let Kate climb slightly ahead. "So when you say more *vicious*…….."

"Those associates of yours who were blown up in London, and

that Mr George over at Tintagel...... having spoken with those whose duty it has been to make sense of the remains Alan is ready to hint at there having been a ritualistic aspect to the manner of their deaths, and perhaps even to the treatment of the corpses."

"The removal of trophies?"

"And not merely to ornament the walls, Eamon."

"So for stocking the larder too, Kate, ... is this what you're getting at?"

"We are."

"And you answer 'we' because Alan had you sounding out the local pathologist."

"No, I've had nothing to do with that."

"But this is a joint suspicion, nonetheless."

"My share having been arrived at independently."

"So who *have* you been talking with, Kate, and when?"

"A woman in Wadebridge, this last weekend, just after her mother had to be admitted into St Lawrence."

"Something age-related?" gasped Eamon, lagging slightly as the path steepened.

"In the sense that the mother's old enough to remember Shanghai before the last war, and Singapore during....... yes. Daughter and son-in-law operate *The Silver Pagoda*, the local take away."

"So Chinese."

"Chinese, yes Eamon, a people who for a full ten years suffered unspeakable cruelties at the hands of Imperial Japanese Army."

"And you have in your wards now a survivor?"

"A survivor of two particular atrocities, the first in Shanghai from where, having been widowed and raped, she was to flee with her son....plus this daughter in utero to Singapore...."

"......where the boy, by then a teenager, was also butchered."

"And this daughter is half Japanese."

"Forcibly conceived, as I said." Kate stopped climbing, turned and put a finger to her lips. A lone figure above on the path was moving towards them, a woman, seemingly in a hurry, as if following an unleashed dog....... except there'd been none, and as they stepped aside to let her pass she paused briefly.

"You need my help," she whispered loudly, but I won't stop here. "You're parked around by the Atlantic Hotel, I see. You'll find plenty of tables in the *Doom Bar*. Buy a drink apiece and wait. I'll be back up in five minutes to order one for myself. I'll then use the Ladies'. Follow, and I'll explain….. now on you go."

And on Kate and Eamon watchfully did climb, with neither word nor backward glance, the silently shared inference being that danger might lie ahead. Around to the bar they went where, with table taken and drinks purchased as instructed, they could only wait with a creeping sense of trepidation.

"So younger than you, or older?" asked the cabby.

"Older……. and going on the voice rather than looks, I'd say by a good five years."

"Moving briskly enough though."

"Thank you, Eamon," chided the nurse, glancing doorwards yet again and missing the opening of an interior door that gave access to the bar from the small Hotel's reception foyer….. an oversight promptly remedied by a nudge from her companion.

The woman was at the bar now, confirming Kate's estimate with a confident, almost brusque bearing and a nicely fitting combination of boots, coat and pearls that evinced comfort and confidence, financial and social, rather than any regard for fashion. The neat hair shone still and, in this light, seemingly without artifice, skin and figure retained a tautness of youth.

A brief glance across won confirmation that her entrance had been noted. She paid for the drink, and leaving it untouched on the bar withdrew through the same door.

The Ladies' room, Kate remembered, was off that corridor leading to the reception desk. She counted slowly to ten, then followed. She found the right door, and after checking the length of the corridor behind and ahead for anyone following or watching she slipped smoothly through to find the instigator of this furtiveness waiting at the sink with a faintly embarrassed smile.

"Stephanie," she said proffering a hand.

"Kate," returned the nurse warily, "and my companion out there in the bar, Eamon. You're not about to suggest I need help in handling him?"

"No….. but."

"But?"

"You live locally?"

"I do," Kate confirmed.

"Then perhaps you know something of the tragic death of a Mr Barry George....."

".......the museum man from Tintagel. A road accident, that's my understanding. Would yours be any different?"

"If not already, I think you ought to be aware of more than one visit made to that same museum, around the time of the proprietor's death, by a person or persons using your friend's motor vehicle. My assumption is that he would have been behind the wheel."

"And you can be no more positive in your identification than that? Convince me that it's been the same vehicle."

"I live in the old town of Stratton, near Bude, and work at the Morwenstow Tracking Station, one of the main listening posts of GCHQ, Cheltenham. They have been recently alerted by their people in Ireland to a short series of phone calls received at a number in the Northern Province, each having been placed from one of the spread of public call boxes serving the pocket of countryside that stretches northward from here between the River Camel and the coast. Our task has been to attempt to assemble a satellite shot overview of those particular boxes......"

"........ at those particular times; cloud and daylight conditions permitting. So any luck?"

"A particular individual won't ever be thus identified.......at least not by us."

"......but a particular car has featured," guessed Kate.

"Repeatedly," confirmed Stephanie.

"And are we saying also that you've been privy to what has actually been said in these phone calls?"

"No, again I'm not included amongst those who need to know."

"And yet you appear fairly sure of a link with Mr George's death. Is this not somewhat speculative?"

"It might be were it not for the prompting I've received from a second source."

"You mean not from GCHQ."

"From a totally separate agency, and this is something you must allow me to explain when we've more time. What I must tell you now though, Kate, is that this afternoon someone attached a bug to your vehicle."

"A listening device?"

"Not to eavesdrop......merely to track your movements. Having the appropriate gadget in my car, I too can lock onto its periodic bleep. This is what brings me here. At a discrete distance I followed you out of Wadebridge, to the site where you collected Eamon, and then on."

"Who, then, would be behind this, and why, and since when?" Surely not Alan, thought Kate. "Are you talking a Government agency?"

"Home Intelligence.....? If I thought that, I probably wouldn't be saying."

"More than you job's worth," nodded Kate, "so.....?"

"I've checked, and they're in a hire car, Im told, and I'm thinking this could be linked to what I'll later explain."

"Which must wait, you say. But I also asked 'since when' ?"

"Since 3.30 this afternoon."

"Give or take quarter of an hour?"

"No more than a minute either way," narrowed Stephanie. And this, recalled Kate, would have been during the twenty or so minutes that she'd left her car to accompany Alan to the up platform at Bodmin Parkway Station, there to wait for his train, to see him off, and loiter for a few minutes following his departure.

"So if you think we've been followed here, how do you see our immediate situation? You offer help. Have you a proposal?"

"There's just the one road into and out of New Polzeath and this they'll have this covered. If not outside now, watching for you to emerge, they'll probably have pulled into the camping field next to turn off into Lundynant Lane, the cut through to Polzeath itself."

"So we can't use that as a bolt hole."

"We'll not get away from here un-noticed, Kate, so for the moment I suggest we play along. We'll not even attempt to disturb the bug, not yet. Our first step has to be to get Eamon back to his caravan......"

"......and after that I'm on my own."

"Don't think that for a minute. What we then do is to attempt to properly shake them off, as a team."

"And if we can't?"

"Then I'll certainly see to it that they're set back a bit."

*

Devonport

"And have you heard from the posh piece down west since the weekend?"

"Down west?" responded Chas, with telling discomfort.

"The Trembath girl, her of the big house to the other side of Truro," pressed Sally as the vehicles filed steadily past them down the Devonport side slip-way onto the fast filling Torpoint Ferry. As a foot passenger she could wait until just before the ramp was drawn up, but board she would.

"Nothing from 'down west'," fenced the yard apprentice, failing to convince.

"You're holding back on me," challenged the girl, "playing for time, knowing that I've a lift over there, expecting me to be on this crossing."

Chas relented. "She did phone, asking me not to say to anyone."

"And I'm just 'anyone'," pouted Sally. "I suppose I'm to be grateful that that lie didn't trip off your tongue too easily."

"I've heard nothing from down west, Sally."

"But she did phone, you say now."

"From London, from the flat the family have in Belgravia."

"A huge house, a flat in Belgravia.......what's the difference? I hope you told her where to get off."

"You needn't get so middle-bloody-class-jealous about it all," protested Chas. "As it turned out she was useful to us."

"Maybe....... but not intentionally. What's she wanting to rope you into next? When's she coming down again?"

"Might not be for a while. She was sounding more than a little cross at her father......"

".........because?"

"Those letters we picked up in Scotland were less of a coup than had been hoped. In fact they are an embarrassment. If they were to be used, thought her project leader, then authenticity needed to be verified. Boulle himself was contacted......"

"......... and he says they are forgeries. Oh dear."

"It seems too that the people she visited in Scotland were phonies. The telephone number through which the arrangements were made to collect the things no longer exists."

"And didn't she get that from her father? What does he have to say on it all?"

"Very little....... much to Helen's understandable annoyance. But while she might not know it, there's a strong chance he'll be smarting too, for thanks to Jim he has himself bought a couple of dummies. I told you, didn't I, about how we got those cuttings out of Port Eliot."

"But you're ready to believe that in that first deception she was an unknowing tool."

"Because she's so cross, and expressing this annoyance to the likes of me," claimed Chas. "She can't yet suspect that she's been similarly used for our counter deception."

"So, as yet, feeling betrayed on just the one side," shrugged Sally, "but with humiliation waiting upon humiliation..... oh dear again. I don't see, though, that we owe them any sympathy. Just desserts, I'd say, with father and daughter best being left to sort it out between themselves."

*

Leaving Dinham

With Kate's assistance Eamon's caravan had been quickly hooked. Now he was set to go, and she in her car ready to follow. At the end of the lane they were to join the St Minver Highlands road, and as they turned eastward thereon towards Wadebridge they could expect to be shadowed, initially at a distance, by a vehicle that would be listening and watching for their emergence. Then, half a mile or so along the road Stephanie would be waiting for the convoy and, before Trewornan Bridge, looking to slot in between, behind Kate. Eamon would lead them across the single lane bridge in accordance with the traffic lights, and once across they were to allow their new friend to overtake and lead them on. Their followers will have been seen to, she'd assured them....... without detailing exactly how.

In just minutes they were at the end of the lane and soon dropping into the Gutt Bridge gully. A glance up at her rear view mirror just before the hairpin and yes, briefly for Kate they were there, those anticipated headlamps, for the moment at the predicted respectful distance. A short climb now and they were cresting the spur, giving Eamon a view of

Trewornan Bridge, low and narrow ahead, and also of Stephanie's vehicle against the verge, waiting as promised, to follow Kate's through the lights and over.

Green, beckoned the control, inviting Eamon to proceed. Kate kept close, glancing rearwards in her mirror to catch a glimpse of the tailing lights......now at a distance less respectful and closing with every second, clearly determined not to be left the wrong side of a changed signal.

But suddenly she has up-close headlamps flooding her mirror.....Stephanie's.

'I'm in and right behind, as promised,' they announce vividly, *'anything further back can be left to me.'*

Eamon rolled on, as instructed. The nurse followed, sandwiched front and back, walled to either side, and more than a little relieved. But that rearguard was dropping back now. In fact it was drawing to a mid-span halt, effecting a firm block. Eamon towed on, unaware, off the bridge now and climbing towards Wadebridge, slowing only with his belated realisation that Kate had drawn into the layby on the opposite verge. By the time he'd stopped with the van, a good fifty yards on, she was out of her car and hearing from the bridge an impatient double toot from the stymied rearmost vehicle.

But Stephanie's motor was staying there, and by doing so eliciting a more prolonged blare of escalated annoyance. Was it about to be abandoned, wondered Kate. Should she be preparing for the driver to be suddenly out of the door and making a dash off the bridge towards her? She was here for Stephanie were she to elect so to do, but surely something like this might have been better explained earlier. For what if those antagonised pursued, likewise on foot? Yes, she was sprightly, and would have the advantage of surprise, but for how far might this count in any contest with masculine youth?

But her door was indeed being opened, and vaguely lit by the interior light the woman now stood beside the car. Had she taken flight then Kate would have perhaps sat back in to restart and reverse to assist, but for the moment it was best, maybe, to wait a second or so, and that was all it took....... before four shots rang out, quickly and evenly spaced, the first two hitting the front tyres of the blocked car, the second two taking out the pneumatically dipped front lights. And might that pistol of Stephanie's hold two more bullets? No one down there was taking a chance on finding out.

The woman was back into her car and away, past Kate before she'd even turned her ignition, and on then to pull in ahead of parked Eamon, the arm from her window beckoning him to follow..... which he did, leaving Kate now to bring up the rear. Over the Atlantic Highway Stephanie took them, to the edge of Wadebridge and then out on the Bodmin road, through Sladesbridge and up to Washaway, eventually to stop in Old School Lane, the cut through to the Camelford Road, close by the entrance to Pencarrow House.

Out of their vehicles, the others walked back together to meet a slightly lagging Kate...... and an understandably cautious Kate, for she'd noted an item in the right hand of their pilot, being carried much as a pistol might be. And a small gun this was, but this time not of the bullet loaded sort. It was a hand-held scanner, and already it was guiding her to the driver's side rear-wheel arch and the tracking device that had been affixed beneath.

"That's where it is," declared Stephanie. "Eamon......if you wouldn't mind reaching for it."

The cabby obliged, rising from his knees with the prize comfortably gripped between a thumb and just two fingers.

"And to render it inoperative?" he said, holding it aloft.

"Put it under your boot," said Stephanie. "Grind it into the road, and then we move on."

"To where?"

"We need to get this caravan under cover before daybreak. I have this farmer friend. His place is the other side of St Breward."

"So against the Moor," joined Kate, "not a lot of cover there."

"He has a barn with space enough."

"And he'll be expecting me?" checked Eamon.

"He will," confirmed Stephanie.

"And you have a gun," challenged Kate, "which you were not afraid to use, and use effectively. I trust you carry appropriate authority."

"My guess is that with the likes of those characters back there a bullet is the only authority. They'll not respond to anything less."

"So who were they?" demanded Eamon. "And why should we deserve your protection?"

"Later," replied Stephanie, returning to her car. "First we need to get to where we're going."

"Take just Eamon," suggested Kate. "Get that van tucked away and then come back to my place. It's not far from here. He'll know the way. We can perhaps introduce you to our friend Mr Busbridge."

"*The* Mr Busbridge?"

"Mr James Busbridge....... almost a neighbour."

'*THE Mr Busbridge*', pondered Kate, now back on the main Bodmin road and dropping to cross the Camel at Dunmere. An interesting inflexion that .... maybe betraying a familiarity extra to that available from the local media. Would she have the benefit of inside information, as well as that lethal hardware?

Climbing past the *Borough Arms* and turning right now, the nurse had chosen this more circuitous route back to Ruthern with a view to calling at Jim's. Told of the evening 's events he would surely be delighted to follow along, meet this bold Stephanie, and take a share in whatever kind of explanation she might offer.

But the tenant of Jasmine Cottage was not at home, nor was there any sign of his car. Not until she was almost to her own house....... and there it was, parked outside. He'd been waiting, and climbing from his car he was clearly pleased to have her arrive. Instantly he was across to her lowered window.

"Late for you, Kate...... I was getting worried."

"Long story Jim...... allow me to get out and I can take you in and get it told. Been here long?"

"Ten minutes, that's all, not long ago having come back from a couple of hours in London....... fruitful hours though. I left the car down at Parkway and on ny return my first thought was to nip over and try to see Eamon. But there was this traffic hold up on the bridge just past Wadebridge. I had to detour through Chapel Amble, then, on eventually getting to Dinham......"

"........ you found Eamon no longer there." Unlocking her door she led Busbridge through.

"So you've been looking for him too?"

"I was with him earlier, when he was actually advised to move." Kate beckoned her guest to a kitchen table chair.

"Advice that he's promptly followed."

"Indeed, as a matter of urgency." The nurse sat also. "And I helped him."

"So move to where, and just who might be so persuasive with their advice?"

"Stephanie is the name, and if we give them forty minutes she and Eamon should be here. In the meantime I must tell you that Alan has been in Bodmin today, on an *Awayday* deal that would appear to have mirrored yours. He'd arranged to meet the Home Office pathologist who'd taken charge of the remains of your friend up at Tintagel, Mr George. As he sometimes will, the Doctor had used one of our slabs in at St Lawrence. He met Alan off the train, and after a light lunch across at Lanhydrock brought him up to the hospital for what I must assume to have been a last look at the deceased's injuries."

"And it was while you were at work that you saw him."

"Where he persuaded me to meet him when finished, to run him back to Parkway."

"And this you did."

"Leaving my car in the station car park and crossing with Alan to wait with him on the up platform. It was in doing this that the rest of my evening seems to have been shaped. Any account is best left until the others arrive."

"But Alan left on his train."

"He did."

"And his enquiries with the pathologist, was there progress for him there?"

"I sensed there was."

"Meaning he wasn't keen to divulge...."

".......I think mainly out of a wish to protect me from the worst of his suspicions, forgetting that work as a casualty nurse leaves one well hardened to tales of blood and guts."

"But he must have said *something*," pressed the curious man.

"He said that I was to tell Eamon to take extreme care, both in what he says and to whom he speaks. We all must, and that's ironic. For while his train rolls in and obscures any view I would have had of my car, it seems to have attracted meddlers."

"Who'd been following, you mean?"

"Awaiting an opportunity to effect a modification."

"Of what sort?"

"A small transmitter was attached, to signal my movements. I'm assuming that a watch placed initially on the pathologist was transferred to Alan before being switched to me at the station......but all this, I hope, can be better explained in a moment. Until then, you might tell me about your day. I'll just fill the kettle."

As she did so Busbridge drew out his letter, giving it a further scan through before laying it unfolded on the table before Kate's chair. She turned to pick it up, preferring to read it whilst standing as the water came to the boil.

"Tania..... of course," she said as the kettle switched itself off.

"Tania Crocker, nee Gaubert," acknowledged Busbridge, "now dead, like Bira. But not her husband........ I called on him today. He gave me that."

"Which you've had most of the afternoon and evening to pore over. What do you make of it, this mention of *connections* that might be *scrutinised*?"

" *'The Queen's General'*....... I think we can take that to be Browning."

Kate nodded. "So what about this *'Stella'* and her young *'P'*.

"When my return train reached Taunton this woman took the seat opposite me and produced a book, a du Maurier title......*My Cousin Rachel*. After Exeter I ventured to open a conversation on the author. She was pleased to tell me that she'd read most of her novels, and that story, a particular favourite of hers, more than once. I'd read a few, I told her, mentioning *Jamaica Inn* and *Rebecca*, and then I asked her if she knew of a *Stella* in any of the tales."

"And did she?"

"She thought long and hard, as if considering each story by turn, and mentally ticking off the casts one by one. The name was in there, she was sure, but for some time at a loss to say exactly where. As we passed through Dawlish I started to regret asking her, such was her distraction and frustration. With her book now closed she was looking out at the sea as if the answer might lie there........ and it did."

"In the sea?" prompted Kate. "On the sea? Under the sea?"

" *'September Tide!'* she exclaimed, her note of triumph straightway allaying those misgivings of mine. I hadn't heard of that title, I said, and this was no surprise to her. For it isn't a novel, she explained, but a play, written not long after the publication of *The King's General* and staged in the West End with Gertrude Lawrence in the starring role."

"A *Stella*."

"A *Stella*, yes, and this woman had actually seen this play."

"All those years ago?"

"No..... apparently it was revived in Edinburgh for a short run about ten years ago. She caught it there, being in the city by chance."

"And there was a '*P*' character?"

"The lead man, he, according to the plot the son in law of *Stella*, is a painter...... of the portrait artist kind."

"Rather than an interior decorator," smirked Kate. "And while painting a portrait of the older woman they fall in love, is that right?"

"Something like that," conceded an embarrassed Busbridge. Such a dramatic device felt appallingly dated.

"And would he have been called *Piero* or *Pietro*?" scoffed the nurse.

"A *Painter* of *Portraits*," said Jim weakly. "And that's about as far as any association can, for the moment, be stretched. It's just a possible lead, the *kind* of thing we might be looking at. We could check on the names of the actors involved."

"I suppose we could," said Kate, not wanting to patronise while fearing she too easily might. "Indeed hasn't Gertrude already been mentioned, and not only on account of an intense friendship with Daphne. Did this not blossom a little later in America when Gertrude was starring there as Anna in the *King and I*?"

"Very much her swan song," sighed Jim, obviously wanting to lower the curtain on this particular avenue of speculation. One production at a time was quite enough. Kate sensed he needed to change tack.

"So what about this mention of *a ruthlessly active non-marxist power*, one that *remains dangerous*? Are these just the loose jottings of a geriatric woman, or do we take this seriously?"

"You've spoken to Alan today," answered Busbridge grimly. "Also you've met this Stephanie woman. What do you think?" Kate stirred the mugs, without a word, without a smile. She had to think, and realising this, her companion stood. "I've got my Ziegler out in the car. I thought earlier to take it on the train, but on reaching Parkway decided against. Now, though, with this, perhaps it might offer a further clue or two. I'll fetch it while my coffee cools."

Kate re-read the letter. *The British Establishment*, what would this Russian woman mean by that? More solid, more enduring, clearly for her it was distinct from the Mountbatten clique, a loose cannon he; and also far more permanent than the Labour Government elected in' 45 to take over from Churchill's wartime coalition. So to whom then might such an entity have been answerable for the forty years that this letter looked back upon? Or was this another such matter as HIGHLAND CLEARANCE, an exception to received constitutional law, derived from a necessarily obscure diplomatic gambit to afterwards endure in a protracted end game...... and did this mean there might be another such as GUSTAVE?

Could Denning have a hand in such a project, she wondered. Surely not........ for playing jury too would be an anathema to such an eminent judge, and any suggestion that he might condome in the task of executioner a ritualistic element was totally absurd.

Busbridge returned, with book already opened. "Here," he began, settling back at the table. "*Chapter 26...... The Return of Empire*, which can be taken to mean the spectacularly gained but short lived Japanese Empire; conquered Malaya, Singapore, Indonesia, and Indochina, plus occupied Thailand, all eventually liberated on the strength of the two fell atomic swoops against distant Hiroshima and Nagasaki. Plenty of countries, plenty of people, all landing in the lap of our Lord Louis."

"Sort this lot out mate......."

"...... and, sadly for us, this Mr Ziegler shows little interest in his subject's response. While Malaya alone might have warranted a full book this whole episode is crammed into just fourteen derisory pages." Busbridge flicked forward, through and past the chapter. "And India looms, that's why. The biographer is hungry to get to the truly meaty part of the sandwich. See.....India gets ten times that amount, well over a hundred pages out of a total of more than eight hundred."

"But what can we learn from those fourteen pages?"

"That Mountbatten was disposed generally to give an emergent Nationalist leader his chance, an approach that was to initially find favour in Washington where, by tradition, there had been little enthusiasm for old style European colonialism. If Pandit Nehru was to be trusted with India and Chiang Kai Chek with China, then why not Sukarno in Dutch Indonesia and Ho Chi Minh in French Vietnam? The Dutch and the French, though, had other ideas."

"Ideas that, with Chiang's inability to contain the Chinese Reds, started to find some sympathy in America, a sympathy which within a few short cold war years was to snowball into outright enthusiasm."

"Indeed, home rule for the old colonies wasn't such a good idea after all, they were to conclude, not where this meant handing the intiative to the Maoist hordes. But that was to come three or four years later. Back in '46 Chiang was felt to be secure within his borders, and the French in Vietnam and the Dutch in Indonesia were widely assumed to be capable of re asserting their pre war dominance without too much too much of a struggle."

"But struggle it became."

"It did, Kate, and it was struggle entered into with vigour. With their action to assert control in the port of Haiphong the French forces killed thousands. And of course this is when the port of Bangkok attracted the attention of the combatants....."

"......for it was from here that the blockade runners would load up and set sail."

"Thailand had never been a colony, that was the key thing, and certainly for the time it suited the Communists *not* to foment revolution there."

"So for as long as Bangkok promised to be the key to success elsewhere......."

"........ the Reds would have been happy to spare the Mahidols the Romanov treatment," said Busbridge. "Such designs they had on Thailand would have been strictly for the long term future. In fact letting the young King continue his rule from Switzerland while Pridi stayed in charge was, for the immediate purposes of Moscow, as good an arrangement as any. If Mountbatten or his acolytes were thinking that by precipitating an abdication they might be doing Stalin's strategists a favour then I would say that they were sadly mistaken."

"And Tania's testimony would tie in with such a scenario," observed Kate. "The desirability of a stable Bangkok is mentioned, together with a *roguish clique of eminent Britons* featuring *a maverick strain of Marxism*. This said, we are alerted to an *anti Marxist power* that leaves nothing to chance. One that to this day, it seems, will have little qualm in drawing on all the ferocity of the Japanese warrior caste. How stood the Japanese army during the year after the war, Jim?"

"Remarkably intact, as thousands of the rank and file were re-deployed by Allied Command in a policing role, such was the wariness of a slide towards anarchy in the surrendered territories."

"And some Kow Towed to the Yanks and some to the Brits."

"So MacArthur and Mountbatten needed to liaise," said Busbridge.

"And you say Ziegler makes scant mention of this episode."

"Even with it lasting for more than a year......"

".......the year in which Ananda was killed," said Kate Busbridge turned another page.

"Here's an interesting snippet. We are told here of anti-French riots in Saigon in September '46, before the Paris Government could get troops there in any number. Though he'd been instructed to support the French we read that;

Mountbatten tried to play as minor role as possible. On 2nd October when forced to use Japanese troops to keep order, he told the Chiefs of Staff that:

'We shall find it hard to counter the accusations that our forces are remaining in the country solely in order to hold the Viet Minh Independence Movement in check.'

All Mountbatten could do was to present British activities as palatably as possible.

'I was most distressed to see you had been burning down houses in congested areas too,' he wrote to his field commander, General Gracey. 'If they were really necessary, could not such unsavoury jobs be left to the French?'

No, replied Gracey; the French did not understand minimum violence and would have burnt down not twenty but two thousand huts.'

"So with that, plus Haiphong to the north, there's a definite sense of the French moving back in with a vengeance. A ruthlessly active non Marxist *force*, certainly, so might not the *power* that Tania warns us against be a lethal remnant of this," asked Kate, "with what, for her, was a sleeping dog now, for us, being a prowling beast?"

There was a rap at the door...... but, thankfully, no beast. Here was Eamon with Stephanie. Kate let them in and, leading them through, introduced Stephanie to her friend from the neighbouring hamlet.

"Mr James Busbridge, a pleasure....... I've heard much about you."

"Complimentary I would hope....... Mrs?"

"Wild, Ms Stephanie Wild, but Steph will do."

"And you would have heard, I guess, from the radio," Busbridge rose from his chair, offering it politely. "You live locally and tune to the regional programmes? Do call me Jim."

"Thank you Jim." She sat. "I do live fairly locally, and yes, I have heard mention of you over the air...... but more recently from an acquaintance."

"A mutual acquaintance?"

"One with whom you've certainly had correspondence. I speak of Monsieur Peirre Boulle. Speaking on the phone he has suggested to me that you might need assistance."

"Armed assistance?" asked Kate.

"That was left to me, and given the circumstances I felt a couple of warning shots not inappropriate."

"Certainly put them off the scent," added Eamon.

"Who exactly?" enquired a naturally curious man.

*

Meanwhile
(i) in Plymouth

.... a solitary male, barely adult, kicks wide the door of the the Barbican call box and strides towards the Mayflower Steps, there to gather his thoughts. Three people figured; Jeremy, Helen, and Sally.

For the first he'd made his afternoon enquiry at *Rod's Books* ......and met disappointment. Such books, on the IJA top brass, did pass through, and not infrequently. At another time there might be two or three on his shelves, but rarely would any linger for more than a month, in fact they would usually find a taker within a week.

Indeed, had he called just a few days before then a campaign memoir produced by one of the more infamous players in the far-eastern theatre, *Japan's Greatest Victory*, could have been his....... at a price, of course, for finding a reasonably well kept edition of that particular account of the fall of Singapore was becoming increasingly difficult. But it had been spotted and taken by a young lady, he'd said, and recalled when gently pressed that it had been on Friday *and* in the afternoon. *And yes* she'd had dark hair and been well dressed, and, to make an initial enquiry prior to parking, *had* drawn in against the kerb outside in a sporty sounding red soft top. And he was right, also, about her having an interest in Japanese operations in Thailand, focussing particularly on the construction of what's become known as 'the death railway'.

This was Helen. She had that book...... and its author? A former Colonel named Masanobu Tsuji. So could he be alive still, Chas had asked, to be told that the man's death had been repeatedly rumoured and even reported, but never confirmed. A companion memoir titled *Underground Escape,* an even rarer acquisition, served to underline the old soldier's talent for elusive survival.

Having just tried and had no reply, he would be attempting again to contact Helen on this, the decision to phone having been reached promptly enough back in the bookshop. But was he to tell Sally or Jeremy? Here he was uncertain.

If one was to know then probably it had to be both he realised, sucking on the sea air so as to clear his nostrils of the phone box reek....... so for the while at least he would tell neither. He glanced at his watch. Another hour he would give Helen, and during that time....... why not some fish and chips?

*

Meanwhile
(ii) in London (Paddington Station)

"Worry not, David. The South Wales line offers a frequent service. Getting here at such short notice was no problem...... but why so urgent a summons? I'm intrigued to know."

"I have something for you, Gareth. You'll find it between the pages of this newspaper that I hold. I'll leave it on the bench when I go. I don't have a lot of time."

"You're catching a train."

"No, I'm having to report to the coach station down at Victoria in....... " he glanced over to the grand clock, "......well in less than an hour now. A special bus is being laid on."

"For you?"

"And the rest of the Wales's household. We're being taken out to Sandringham apparently, in the clothes we happened to be wearing when told.......just three hours ago. Our part of Kensington Palace has been sealed off."

"You've been locked out, you mean."

"It's a security sweep of some sort. They're looking for things."

"Like what sort of things."

"Possibly those pictures of which I let you have copies...... and related items such as this that I have here."

"More copies?"

"Three, of one document, taken earlier today, plus the original which I'd planned to return."

"And now can't."

"But as she's away at the moment she won't, on her return, be placed to ascribe their permanent removal to me."

"I suppose not," agreed Gareth "at least until she might be persuaded to co-operate fully with the spooks, finding then to her surprise that they don't have everything."

"And it'll be some time before that happens, if at all. So make the most of this opportunity. I can't promise any more." David stood. The newspaper stayed. "Until I can, you'll not hear from me again. Good luck."

"And to you, old friend."

*

Back at Ruthern

" 'ODESSA'," nodded Busbridge, "in the Forsyth story it's an acronym for an organisation which shielded former Nazi SS officers in western Europe for almost three decades after the war. 'The ODESSA file', the document which drives the plot amounted to a register of the false identities under which the fugitives were cloaked."

"Well to understand my emergence into your not so uneventful lives you must understand that following their surrender an organisation similar to ODESSA was developed on behalf of the officers of the Imperial Japanese Army," continued Stephanie. " 'UNIT 4', we can call it, but unlike with the Nazis an incriminating document was let slip quite soon after the war, while the International Military Tribunal for the Far East was still in session. Before it could be submitted, though, it was lost. It was in the possession of a British officer, a Colonel Cyril Wild when his plane crashed shortly after take off from Hong Kong in September '46. Cyril Wild was my father, his widow carrying me until my birth in April '47."

"And has there been an equivalent to the fictional agency dedicated to secretly chasing down the members of ODESSA?" asked Eamon.

"There *is* such a group," confirmed Stephanie, "into which I was inducted when it was seen that my career could be taking me into Signals Intelligence. That was in 1970. It was Monsieur Boulle who approached me, he having been a member since the early days. He actually knew my father......"

"......and was able to explain the circumstances of his death," finished Kate.

"As far as they could be explained, yes," acknowledged the other woman. "Speculation persists to this day."

"And those Japanese Officers," said Eamon. "Some, Steph, will have lived on to this day."

"A few, yes, with amongst them some extremely unpleasant characters...... war criminals, perpetrators of atrocity."

"And it's Pierre Boulle who's put you on alert," said Busbridge, "subsequent to receiving my enquiry about a supposed correspondence with a survivor of the Death Railway labour camps."

"Forged correspondence, I understand. There's been a further separate enquiry on this matter."

"From here in Cornwall?"

"From London I believe, but we needn't dwell on that....we can move to those palace intrigues of Bangkok. Visualised so as to place and order the events of those times Pierre holds in his mind a map, and in a corner of this, prominently marked, stands Tredethy. He sets me to watch and to listen and then almost immediately I'm hearing of the sad death of Mr George. Then we get the fun and games of this afternoon and evening."

"So why should that trace have been attached to my car?" asked Kate.

"I think there might have been an initial concern for an uncomplicated disposal of Mr George's body."

"And this was at the hospital, where my car was just one out of hundreds."

"But say they were watching the pathologist," said Eamon, "and he goes down to the station and meets with Alan."

"The pair have lunch," resumed Kate. "Then it's back up to the hospital for a further look at the corpse......"

"........ and they're going to be interested in who might be offering a second opinion," continued Stephanie. "They watch him leave with you, Kate, follow to the station and take an opportunity fasten that bug, just to see where you might lead them."

"Sounds a big ask for a gang of geriatric Japanese war veterans," said the nurse.

"Could be just one, tucked away somewhere and sending out henchmen to patrol. Their car would have been hired"

"So I would have led them to Eamon."

"That Eamon was at Dinham might have already been known," said Stephanie slowly. "Bear in mind that it was Mr George who was killed, and was there not an old boy down at the golf course who expired not long after you'd been in there talking with him? In each instance you, Mr Carroll, sailed on unharmed........"

"....... which was what happened in London also," added Busbridge. "So what you're saying is that perhaps Kate here is being lined up as the next target."

Kate mustered a sardonic smile. "In which case I'm to thank you, Steph, for your intervention........ and perhaps take this opportunity to come clean." She drew a deep breath. "I'm onto something, I think, and were they to have known of this it might have had them truly sharpening their knives."

"And you're ready to trust us with this?" checked Stephanie.

"In gratitude for your timely intervention, and also because of a compelling relevance to your expertise."

"We're all listening," said Eamon.

"A Japanese war criminal has been seen and recognised, over in Wadebridge."

Eamon it was who bravely broke the incredulous silence. "By whom?"

"By someone known to me, who I'm told more than just witnessed first his devilry in Shanghai and then, later, his butchery in Singapore. She lives with her daughter and son in law, Zhou Jingzhi, the proprietor of *The Silver Lotus*, the town's Chinese take away. Her husband was put to the sword in Shanghai, where she was raped by the invading troops, the resultant daughter being half Japanese. She'd fleed to Singapore, but in '42 the IJA was to follow and this time kill Madame Jingzhi's teenaged older brother. The sighting, only last week, threw the poor soul into a state of shock, necessitating an admission into St Lawrence. She was thought, initially, to have sustained permanent or at least long term brain damage as a result of some kind of stroke or haemorrage."

"But there's been a marked improvement," suggested Busbridge.

"And what were thought to have been hallucinatory ramblings about a *Devil of Shanghai* and a *Butcher of Singapore* I've had to take more seriously."

"So Steph," asked Busbridge, "are you at all familiar with those labels?"

"Not so as I can fix them to a particular officer...... but Monsieur Boulle, like your patient, he was out there at the time. We can put them to him." Stephanie turned to the nurse. "But now tell me about this Alan, Kate. Eamon said something about the guy on the way over. Did you mention your Chinese lady to him?"

"I didn't, Steph, because I felt he wasn't levelling with me about the state of Mr George's body."

"And he's some kind of professional."

"More than any of us," said Eamon.

"Apart, perhaps, from yourself Steph," added thte nurse tactfully. "But where you sit and you listen, he roams and he watches. Get the pair of you harnessed and equipped with a sniffer dog and everything's covered."

"And *not levelling with you*," pressed the woman.

"He alluded to people, one of them Mr George, perhaps having been put to death in a ritualistic manner....."

"....... but beyond that declined either to elaborate or stay and protect. Sounds a real gentleman! What called him away?"

"His duties, on which again he declined to elaborate."

"Am I supposed to be impressed? It appears to me you've been left to fend for yourselves, just when he could be useful."

"It was my decision to see him on to the platform down there at Parkway," defended the nurse. "He can't be held responsible for what happened to my car. You might see these things from a distance, but the kind of equipment you have access to isn't available to us."

"So now you just wait, until *he* decides to turn up again." Stephanie was almost scornful.

"Well if by his neglect we gain an access to your talent then perhaps we stand strengthened," joined Busbridge with a placatory smile. "Where now from here? That's the question."

Kate turned to Stephanie.

"Well if I can assume that while driving over Eamon has briefed you on his recent adventures with us."

"The tape he's mentioned."

"Good, for I'd like you to meet Jeremy, and Gareth too. They're on their way. We don't know how, yet, or in which direction, but they'll have made progress for sure. I'm hoping they can add to that we've so far gathered, stuff about the Princes Chula and Bira and their circle of friends, and about Lord Mountbatten and his sidekick Mr Peter Murphy."

"And these things that you already have..... am I allowed to be inquisitive?"

"Jim, here, will expound for you, equipped as he is with his Ziegler, the essential primer for anyone with an interest in that last pair."

"Also, obtained today in London, I have this very intriguing letter," added Busbridge. "And Kate, those prints that arrived here for Gareth, taken in Laussane back in '44........?"

"........ are with Gareth, which perhaps is as well, for if they'd been in my car this afternoon I might have handed them to Alan."

"Good for Gareth," said Stephanie. She would make up her own mind about Alan.

*

Contact

"Chas...... how nice to be hearing back from you so soon. To what might I be owing this pleasure?"

"I'm hoping, Helen, that you might be of assistance to me."

"Go on"

"Further to his continued interest in 1940s Thailand our friend Mr Jeremy Barnes asked me to look into *Rod's Books*, the military specialist down here in the The Barbican.That's where I am now, in a call box."

"But he'll be closed."

"He is, yes, but he wasn't earlier and we were able to discuss my enquiry."

"Made on behalf of the lecturer."

"Yes, and it concerned books written on, or by, top ranking Japanese army commanders......"

"......of the 30s and 40s. Funny you should say that......"

"......because you went in there, didn't you, after we met the other day over at the bridge."

"So Rod remembered me."

"He certainly remembered your car, and he remembered your purchase."

"*Japan's Greatest Victory.....*"

"......written by a guy named Tsuji, quite an interesting character by all accounts."

"I'll bring it next time I come down. We can meet up again. I'm hoping to have more on him......"

"........because you know he wrote this other book. You think you can find one up there in the capital?"

"Not only that, Chas. You remember me saying how livid I was with my father and grandfather over that Alec Young nonsense. It was just so, so embarrassing for me at work."

"I do remember, yes," answered Chas warily.

"Well that evening, while truly seething still, I did something that I'd never before dared. I rifled through my grandfather's office, checking through some of the filed information he'd saved on his old Parliamentary colleagues. Some of them still live quite local to here, and if any had served out in the East, or even been taken prisoner by the Japanese, perhaps an opportunity might be engineered, I thought, to pick their brains."

"On this Tsuji character?"

"Or on the 'death railway', or......whatever."

"And....?"

"And one particularly fascinating entry featured the career of Profumo, the famous Profumo of the scandal in the 1960s"

"The Keeler business, and all that....... do go on."

"Well whilst an MP during the war he served with distinction in North Africa, but then, despite returning a hero, he lost his seat in the '45 election."

"So he had to wait until the next, and for a safer seat."

"Which he did. But in the meantime, for a while anyway, the army was ready to keep him on....... and this is the good bit. He was sent out to Japan, his task there to liaise with MacArthur's American Forces Headquarters, sorting out the deployment of British and American units, as well as that of Japanese troops put under Allied Command."

"Interesting." Given Profumo's place in the Tredethy line up, probably then on leave, it was more than interesting. But this wasn't for Helen to know

"And perhaps more importantly for us, with our interest in the railway and in the likes of Tsuji, he would have been also concerned with the bringing to justice of perpetrators of atrocities against civilians, as well as those whose conduct towards prisoners had breached Geneva convention rules."

"And he lives just around the corner, you say."

"Up the road, just off the other end of Sloane Street, I called there this afternoon, spoke to his wife."

"Introducing yourself as Sir Edward's grandaughter.....and?"

"She was very nice...... said that Jack was busy today with his Toynbee work, an East End charity, but if I'd like to come around tomorrow evening then fine."

"And did you mention Tsuji?"

"I had his book with me. I showed her that, and mentioned I had a project on to do with Thailand. If the man meant anything to her, she didn't say."

*

247

Eamon's priority…..

…….the next morning was to find himself yet another vehicle, and accordingly he was on the road and through the Trerulefoot roundabout before 8.30. From his time at Whitsands he could recall inspecting the line up of used vehicles at a roadside garage in Polbathic. The proprietor had seemed as honest as any in that game, and likely to give a fair allowance on a trade in.

In the absence of anything suitable he might then drive on to see what was available in Torpoint and, if need be, move on to Plymouth using the ferry. Which is how it happened as, by 9.45, no-one to the south of the Lynher had been able to offer him anything remotely appropriate. Power had been available, yes, but with the kind of performance that commanded too heavy a price. There would be something more economical across the Tamar, he told himself and after buying for himself a *Western Morning News* he joined the ferry queue for what, by his estimate, should be no more than a twenty minute wait.

In fact he was embarked on the ferry inside fifteen, time in which he'd quicky scanned the classified ads' *used vehicles* section, and also had his attention arrested by a small inside page photo of an elderly gentleman……. frail, but bright eyed, sitting at a table with pen in hand and before him a stack of books.

'*Autumn Leaves; Lord Denning at Trebah*,' explained the caption beneath. Then;

The former Master of the Rolls delighted fellow visitors to Trebah Gardens yesterday by taking an opportunity to sign copies of a recently published anthology of his favourite prose; 'Leaves from my Library'.

Staying locally for the first time in a number of years Lord Denning expressed delight at being back in an area that holds for him many a fond memory.

A useful snippet maybe, he'd thought as he'd stowed the paper into his door before boarding. Now, though, with car firmly slotted too, he was ready to stretch his legs and draw on some of that brackish Hamoaze air. Only as he returned to his vehicle, the crossing by then almost complete, did he notice and recognise the pedestrian who'd positioned herself to be off the vessel as soon the now lowering ramp grounded on the Devon slipway.

"Sally," he called as he opened the driver's door. She turned and smiled recognition. "Late for school?"

"Depends on the buses."

"I can give you a lift. Jump in."

"That's kind," she said, coming across.

"I can take that," offered the accomplished cabby, reaching over the bonnet for the bag that she needed to slip from her shoulder, opening then his side's rear door so as to slide it onto the back seat, but not without a moment's hesitation. For once supported an unzipped top gaped so as to reveal much of that within.......... books mainly, but nestling amongst them a video.

"So you're studying Dickens at the moment," he said as with all doors now closed they fastened themselves in the front. "*Great Expectations* did I see...... book and video?"

"The old David Lean black and white version," said Sally.

"As apparent from stills on the case."

"Have you seen it?"

"I've not, but if you could spare it for a day or so, I'd very much like to play it through."

"In your caravan?"

"If I may, I'd like to take it down Jim Busbridge's. If he doesn't have a player then he'll know someone who will."

"Kate perhaps........OK, take it and go as soon as you've dropped me. I need to have it back in my hand at four, when I come out. It's promised to a classmate." They were off the ferry now. "Go left here, then we take the road up through Stoke, following the signs for Tavistock."

"And then your school is just past the football ground."

"Drop me there, then carry straight on up the road to the Manamead interchange. The Parkway will take you down to the bridge and with any luck you should be around Bodmin within the hour."

The Milehouse traffic lights slowed them temporarily.

"Seen anything of Chas this past couple of days?"

"We're supposed to be meeting after school," sighed the girl, as if beset by doubt.

"Well I'm sure he's looking forward to it," smiled Eamon, again flexing that taximan's charm. "I certainly would be."

*

Gareth......

.......meanwhile stops to refuel his motorcycle at Sourton Cross. Having returned to Wales by train the previous evening he'd risen early, determined as he was to be in Cornwall before mid day. He'd contacted Kate, and she'd alerted Busbridge. Both, he knew, would be keenly awaiting his arrival at Ruthernbridge.

*

While Alan, in London.....

......had decided this might be a good moment to exploit the access he'd long enjoyed to the Northclffe Group's news picture library, a central image bank to where would be wired everything and anything presented to the 'family's' provincial as well as national editors. And what a sound decision this was to prove for one specifically seeking to update in his mind the visage of Alfred Thompson Denning, a figure who, since his rather ungainly slither into retirement back in '81, had been the beneficiary of a merciful degree of media inattention. For it was to be while Alan waited, as the Denning file was being brought out for him from the archive, that a clerk was to come to the same desk with that same photograph seen by Eamon only an hour earlier.

*

Chula's own words

Gareth was by some minutes the first past Bodmin, Eamon on the A38 having the much slower road. Expecting the Welshman, Kate had suggested to Jim that he should await her summons, and this was as well, for it left him at Jasmine Cottage long enough to allow him to greet Carroll's surprise arrival at his front gate. This was convenient, for together they could travel down to Ruthernbridge in Eamon's car.

"Gareth's down again," explained Busbridge. "He's already at Kate's, and we think he's got something."

"I think I have too. Do you know if she has a video machine?"

"Not sure, Eamon..... we shall soon find out."

Having welcomed Gareth and settled him into a seat far more comfortable than that he'd straddled for most of the previous three hours, Kate could now unfold and inspect the two-page document flourished with such pride by her visitor...... David Evans's *piece de resistance*. And what a prize it was! No copy this, instead she had before her something handwritten by the sender, in authentic fountain pen ink.

She read;

HRH Prince Chula Chakabrongse
Tredethy Manor
Cornwall

March 1946

Dear Monckton

Recently in the course of a private conversation enjoyed with General Frederick Browning it was quietly mentioned to me that the decidedly brittle nature of Thailand's monarchy had attracted the attention of what he termed 'a major power', one with a concern, I was told, to consolidate its position in that area. It was put to me that, having last year responded positively to a suggestion from Louis Mountbatten that I might hold myself in readiness to mount the steps of a vacant throne, I could have unwittingly undermined the legitimate standing of the current occupant.

My response was to state unequivocally that for as long as the Mahidols were ready and willing to address their challenging duties then they could count on my full support.

This was a pledge, the General said, that he would be pleased to pass on, adding that this 'major power' understood well the degree of financial hardship caused to my cousin and I by the Japanese occupation of our homeland, and that any conditional assistance being offered by Mountbatten in this respect could be more than matched.

There was a realisation, for instance, that once Tredethy was fully paid for then I might be more happily placed to proceed with the kind of renovations appropriate to making it my permanent home; and likewise it was noted that, if not in driving expertise then certainly in costly equipment, my young cousin Bira needed to be better equipped if he was to resume a successful career in motor sport.

Whilst resisting any implication that my already freely declared loyalty to the current Thai Monarch was subject to price I was ready to agree that our joint contribution to the anti fascist war effort in Europe might merit recognition. I did cite Bira's work in training glider pilots and he, as an Airborne Army Commander was happy to acknowledge, notwithstanding the setback at Arnhem, how valuable this had been to the liberation of Holland and, in particular, France.

Gratitude was certainly due, the General agreed, and further to this he suggested that the person to have an informal chat with might be yourself, one with unique skill and experience in arriving at negotiated accomodation between Governments and Royal Figures.

He has told me that later in April you will be travelling to India so as to hopefully smooth a settlement between your client the Nizam of Hyderabad and the Indian Congress movement, in all likelyhood a protracted task. With this in prospect I would very much like to invite you to join the gathering that I hope to be entertaining at Tredethy over the Easter weekend. The Duchess of Kent will be coming, as well as the young Prince Philip of Greece, together with such companions as they might wish to accompany them.

Whilst staying with his family at nearby Menabilly, General Browning will himself be driving across to dine with us on the Saturday and the Monday. We look forward to hearing that you can join us all.

Yours truly,

Chula

"Wow, Gareth, full marks. Note that *particular* mention made of France. Jim will love it, for how neatly it complements Bira's journal and Tania's testimony....."

".....and also your montage reconstruction of Browning's picture."

"You're right. This is one hell of a find.... and filched from the possession's of the Princess of Wales, you say."

"Who's currently abroad."

"But due back when? How long before this must be returned?"

"The Prince and she will back within the next 48 hours, but that needn't matter. I've been told that a specialist unit from Alan's department will be going through her stuff at this very moment. They won't know of its removal."

"And when she gets back?"

"How can she be sure that it's not them who'll have taken it? Convoluted reasoning you'll say......."

"........but sound enough," agreed Kate afer a momemt's thought. There was a rap at her door. "That's Jim now, and with Eamon too by the sound of it. I'll let them in."

"There on the table," indicated the guardsman as the newly arrived were shown through. "A last drop siphoned from Kensington Palace, before Wales's apartment gets well turned over."

Busbridge read the letter first, leaving Eamon to pass the video to their host as he waited his turn.

"You have a machine?"

"I do," nodded Kate. "If you're wanting to play it now I'll go and load it up."

Busbridge passed the first of Chula's pages, picking up the second in the same movement.

"Excellent, Gareth," he said. "This must have been retrieved from Monckton's personal archive, heightening a suspicion that those Lausanne prints were obtained from that same treasure house."

"Though we shouldn't assume," cautioned the Welshman, "that they were sent to him way back in '46, as was the letter."

"I guess not," agreed Busbridge.

"But some letter this is!" enthused Eamon. "It looks like that Tania was pretty spot on with her reading of events. We have it here from Chula himself, that 'Boy' Browning, was in cahoots with Walter as together they moved to thwart Mountbatten's scheming. It could start to explain why at some later time the *Queen's General* was moved to lop the Royal lawyer who rose to Cabinet Minister from his framed photo."

"But not why, to the other side, we have Jack Profumo sharing the same fate," said Kate, coming back into the kitchen with the montage.

"But one could suppose this to have been done at a different date, and for a different reason."

"Like in the '60s," offered Gareth, "so as to spare Marina and Philip embarrassment."

"Odd, then, that Declan found the sequestered pair pouched together," mulled Busbridge. "And odd, I suppose, that Tania makes direct mention of neither, instead drawing our attention to the mysterious *Stella*."

"Who *wasn't* Gertrude Lawrence, you decided," said Kate, looking down at the faceless ones in her sketch.

"But for every star in every production there will be an understudy," said Busbridge, "and maybe this could be her. It shouldn't be beyond us to check back to see who might have occasionally stepped in for Gertie in *September Tide*. There has to be a record somewhere."

"But hardly in Cornwall," remarked Eamon, almost superciliously. *So let's hear your better suggestion*, demanded the ensuing silence........ and, to his credit, the cabby was ready to oblige. "Time for us to look at this video, borrowed this morning from Sally, young Chas's friend, who I met by chance on the Torpoint Ferry. Can we go through, Kate?"

The nurse led them to the screen and started the player. Eamon handed the empty cassete box to Busbridge.

"Recognise any of those pictured on the front?" asked Carroll.

"*Great Expectations*, so this is a young John Mills of course, and........ and maybe, Eamon, maybe. John Mills and Valerie Hobson it says here, and now, the more I think back to that morning stroll of ours up to Tredethy, the more I'm sure. You'll have to wind the film on, Kate, for when the story begins *Pip* and *Estella* are children, played by a child actor and actress. In fact, take it almost to the end, for that's when any likeness will be at its most apparent."

Kate fast-forwarded the tape then, with her third attempt, found a sccene featuring *Estella*.

"Yes," said Busbridge, "that's her all right. We can say that Valerie Hobson was at Tredethy, possibly during in a break in the filming of that very film. And in hearing the name *Estella*, our Russian born Tania could well have failed to pick up a relatively muted first syllable."

"So what of this *A(nna)Havelock-Allen?*" posed Eamon. "Is this our mistake, or will it mean something as yet obscure?"

"A question perhaps for Ms Hobson," said Jim. "If alive still she'll surely not be too difficult to find."

"Jeremy is something of a movie buff," said Kate. "He'll be the one to put us on the trail. I'll speak to him later. How long can I keep this tape, Eamon?"

"You can't. Sally asked that I should be there with it when she comes out of school, promised as it is to one of her chums. In fact if I'm to do in Plymouth what I first intended, that's to look for a different car, then I must leave now."

And within four minutes, with tape politely re wound, Carroll was gone.

"So Jim," declared Kate, "we have some progress."

"Significant progress," agreed the curious man. "Well done Gareth, and well done to that friend of yours up at the Palace......"

"........who having excelled himself with that letter has probably forwarded as much as he can," said the former guardsman. "His stint in Kensington Palace has been curtailed, he told me. For anything more from that quarter we'll need to look to Grigson."

"And we're not to hold our breath according to Stephanie Wild," said Kate. "With the original Lausanne prints in their hands, plus the framed photo nicked from Tredethy the security people will be equpped to confront our Princess.

Look Ma'am, we're wise to this barrow load of dung you're about to start spreading;

this is what she'll be told.......and she'll be persuaded to stop, thinking of course that it's they who'll have searched out this letter written by Chula, her prize exhibit."

"Then, with the immediate risk to the Monarchy eliminated that's their job done," said Busbridge, "irrespective of what dangers have been loosed in these parts."

"And you're saying that Alan is tied in to this strategy," said Gareth who then, after a moment's hesitation, fixed Kate. "So tell me..... who is this Stephanie Wild?"

"If you're planning to stop the night here....."

"Two, if you can fit me in."

"........then I can perhaps get her across this evening, or at least as far as *Jamaica Inn*. With that letter to show her she'll be no less delighted to meet you, and if she can assist with the pinning down of this *major power* then all the better. Already she has shown herself to be alert to its threat."

*

Chas gets back

"Jeremy?"

"Speaking."

"Chas here, Jeremy."

"Good to hear from you…..but a second, please, I'm just bringing in a bag of groceries. My key's still in the door."

Chas was encouraged. Unless she'd got through to his college, Kate wouldn't have yet phoned him……for this, according to Sally, was what was going to happen, she having been told as much by Eamon when returning to her that *Great Expectations* video. And the cabby had been full of it apparently……. brimming with this tale of how, from this old black and white picture, he first, and later Jim Busbridge had identified the third lady who'd sat in the group at Tredethy. Valerie Hobson was the name, and Kate was intending to put it to Jeremy at her first opportunity, knowing his knowledge of cinematic history. The response was keenly anticipated.

But this wouldn't stop Chas, as he now realised that he was through to the lecturer before the nurse. He could casually drop the actress's name alongside this other that he had…….

"Chas?" Jeremy was back. "Any luck down at Rod's?"

"No books for you……at least not yet."

"*Not yet*……..what's that meant to mean Chas?"

"I'm on to an account of the capture of Singapore, *Japan's Greatest Victory*, written by one of the IJA officers involved. Someone got in just ahead of us….."

"……. into the shop, and bought the book?"

"Yes, but from the description given I think this might be someone I know."

"Someone you could approach?"

256

"Someone I could approach."

"Good...... but how soon? I was hoping to come down tomorrow, so......."

"......so be assured, I'm working on it. The name to remember is Masanobu Tsuji."

"I'll write that down."

Chas spelt it out.

"And there was something you mght be able to help me with." The boy continued. "A few months back I remember you priming me and Sally on British made films, to get us under Clark's radar."

"And it worked too, didn't it?"

"Very well...... so what if I threw to you the name of Hobson, Valerie Hobson?"

"*Great Expectations* opposite John Mills, *Kind Hearts and Coronets* opposite Alec Guinness."

"And would she have been known by any other name?"

"You mean apart from *Estella* in the first of those films, and *Edith* in the second. I think she married Anthony Havelock Allen, one of the big British producers. He and David Lean were of the partnership that set up *Cineguild*, the compny behind the *Great Expectations* project. It's a good film......comparing well with the epics that Lean would do later, *Kwai* of course, and *Lawrence*. Mills, interestingly, was to return for *Ryan's Daughter*, but by then your Valerie had been long retired."

"With her husband, I guess, who sounds to have been substantially older."

"With her second husband, by then, who while famously retired was not, this one, substantially older. In fact we were speaking of him only the other day, he having been pictured at Tredethy in '46, in the company of the Princess Marina."

"Profumo! You're telling me that after being styled Mrs 'A for Anthony' Havelock Allen, she became a Mrs J Profumo......"

"I *am* telling you that, and, furthermore, that she has stayed married to the lucky fellow to this day......."

"......despite his name becoming a by word for deceit and infidelity. So how long had they been married when......"

"......when the scandal erupted? Barely ten years, I'd say....... '53, perhaps '54, when she gave up performing and he was testing the first rungs of the Ministerial ladder."

Seven years, at least, after they were pictured together in '46, thought Chas, Valerie seemingly then a companion of the young Prince Philip. He needn't raise this now, though, for he was suddenly anxious to make a second call. Helen in London ought to know this. She was intending to call on the Profumos, and maybe the comings and goings at their flat were being scrutinised.

"Intriguing, Jeremy, but I must leave it there. If I'm to get hold of Tsuji's book for you there's another call I have to make."

*

Belgravia

Japan's Greatest Victory, the book, and at this moment it lay before Helen as she stood at her grandfather's desk. Should she or should she not take it along to the Profumo's nearby flat? Though not all, she'd read enough of it now to demonstrate familiarity with the content, and even to suggest she'd also dipped into *Underground Escape*, the companion volume which surely had to be more germane to her host's stint in post war Japan.

So maybe she didn't need to wave it in front of these people, and risk seeming tactless.....particularly after the wife had been so warm in that invitation to call. Yes, she would leave it she decided, and rely instead on a little feminine charm, to which, for all his years, many of them difficult, it was said that old Jack had never quite developed an immunity.

And as a sweetener to begin, a classy box of chocs maybe, so if she gave herself an hour and went now she could go via Harrod's. After a last brush of her hair, and check of her bag and watch, she slipped on her coat and was out...... to allow just thirty seconds to elapse in that empty silent flat before the phone began to ring, continuing so to do for a further thirty seconds, and then cease, unanswered.

*

Plymouth

So where to now, thought Chas, replacing the phone. He glanced at his watch, frustration sharpening his concern for the too distant Helen. Mrs Jack Profumo now, Mrs Anthony Havelock Allen then; and there was a chance that in '46, on matters Thai, this Valerie might have known *more* than the man who was to become her second husband. This was what he should be telling the girl, and perhaps better late than never.

5pm it was now, so a fast train leaving soon could get him into Paddington before 9, from where, by cab, he might be delivered to Belgravia inside fifteen minutes. He had cash enough for that. They would take plastic at the station.

Would there be a train though? He had to get up there now.

*

Travelling

And boldness found reward, for a train there was. In a little over an hour he was watching the empty platforms of Taunton station slide from view, wishing to himself that this were a faster service. It was just about keeping time, though, and at least now it had made the last of its scheduled stops.

If she wasn't there already, these two people on whom Helen would soon be calling had been guests at Tredethy back in the spring of '46, responding separately to separate invitations. Indeed it might have been their first ever encounter, the first, obviously, of many. She ought to know this, and also that there'd been an attempt to expunge the future husband from the photographic record, an attempt possibly made in the '60s to protect others in the group, perhaps at the suggestion of Lord Denning. But why remove that Monckton character also, pondered Chas. What sort of enbarrassment might they have represented as a brace?

A Rosa Monckton was a pal of the Princess of Wales, he'd been told, and the grandfather had, like she was now, been a confidante of Royalty........ as maybe Profumo had been too, given his proximity to the Duchess of Kent, and maybe also the Mrs Allen, given her pictured proximity to the young Prince Philip. Since the Profumo scandal this woman had been popularly perceived as a victim. Wronged big time, she'd nevertheless stuck it out, holding the family together despite, showing herself to be as moral as he was immoral. But was this the true picture, he wondered, or could that which had not so long ago hung at Tredethy have been suggesting otherwise.

How much was she able to confide to handsome Jack back in '46, and how much had she felt able to confide since.....during courtship and then more than thirty years of marriage? These were the questions.

Helen would be hoping, naturally, to hear something from Jack on his time in Japan, and he might be happy to tell her all that he might remember, which could be a great deal, but still she might be missing plenty by assuming Valerie to be a mere adornment, subsequently gathered .... an asumption that might even now, forty years on, prove dangerous.

So Chas feared.......

*

Belgravia

...... where Helen, almost an hour now into her appointment, was finding it difficult enough merely to get Jack to talk about his own career. Prompted by a gracious and attentive wife he'd spent most of this time enquiring after Sir Edward, an old friend and colleague with whom he'd regretfully lost touch.

Just a few kind words in one's hour of need went a long way, said Profumo, and from Sir Edward he'd had more than just a few........ whilst from other so-called friends there'd been nothing.

But the good moments were what he remembered best, and now with apparent glee. The campaigns of '51, and '55, and '59, were great campaigns he recalled, looking back on the General Election triumphs of Churchill, Eden, and Macmillan. For each a one-off victory, perhaps, but what satisfaction there'd been as Anthony and then Harold had skated home with increased majorities for the Party of Government.

Yes, these had been heady times, times that held many an anecdote....... but of Valerie's equally colourful career there was sparse mention, leaving her, to Helen, as unremarkable a politician's wife as had been her own vaguely remembered grandmother.

"And your work, Helen," said the husband at last, "which, my wife tells me, is what has brought you here."

"I've read that just after the war, following your election defeat in Kettering, you took a military posting in Japan......"

"...... that's right, working alongside the Americans as we and they sorted our options for policing the former Japanese posessions, an extensive empire even if short-lived. For two years I was out and back, out and back, sometimes feeling to be little more than a glorified courier."

"But all the same, this might have involved you in discussions over the future of countries such as Thailand, who'd been occupied by the Japanese without, technically, sustaining defeat."

"Very much a case on its own was Thailand," nodded Profumo.

"But it was through Thailand that the Japanese built that which we know as the *Death Railway*, at the cost of thousands of British POW lives."

"It was."

"And there's this book that I've found written by a former IJA Colonel, *Japan's Greatest Victory* by one Manasobu Tsuji."

"Really."

"At the end of my edition the publisher puffs up the author's next volume, *Underground Escape*, wherein he gives an account, I'm to understand, of how he found sanctuary in Thailand after the Japanese surrender....... this while a number of fellow officers were captured and executed."

"Thailand certainly presented a tricky problem." Profumo looked hesitantly at his wife, who rose from her chair.

"Perhaps a glass of water Jack? I'll fetch you one from the kitchen."

"Thank you dear," resumed the suddenly aged husband. "Yes, a tricky problem, mainly because Thailand's state of war with Britain, a consequence of the country's assistance to Japan in the attack on Singapore. There was a parallel hostility towards France, from whom whom a corner of neighbouring Laos had been annexed, but not towards the US, the Japanese action against Pearl Harbor having been a far more distant matter."

"So whereas Mountbatten had scores to settle in Bangkok, not so MacArthur."

261

"I suppose so," acknowledged Profumo....... less sure, it seemed, without his wife at his side. These people were old, realised Helen, and if not past a little nostalgia then certainly beyond any kind of interrogation that she might devise, subtle or otherwise.

Valerie returned with that glass of water for her John. He took a sip as she re-settled.

"Helen mentioned Thailand my love," he said.

"It's a pity then that our old friend Bira is no longer with us. He had a place not so far away, until he dropped dead down at Baron's Court Station."

"Would this be the Prince Bira who raced cars, cousin to the Prince Chula who made himself into a Cornish country squire," Helen affected no more than a vague familiarity. "I forget the name of the house, but it was up on the Camel."

"Tredethy," said Valerie. "I've stayed there with them, once encountering my John, but that was long before we started courting. He's always been a bit coy about it, but I think, at the time, he was offering companionship to the Duchess of Kent."

"And I'll be as coy as I like about my life before we married," smiled Profumo, "particularly where Royalty might be involved, and particularly too as you've divulged nothing to me of whatever busniess had taken you there."

"Nothing to you John," teased the wife. "Nothing to you."

"And Bira never said, of course........ but then he was even worse for the ladies than I."

"What are you saying, Jack?" Valerie reached to playfully smack her husband's wrist in mock outrage. "He had a wife then, and I had a husband."

"So, latterly, how often did you see Bira?" asked Helen unaware of how closely the conversation had drifted to the subject of Chas's Scottish quest.

"He'd been scarce for years, while living abroad, but during the year prior to his death, after he'd taken that flat just a few stops down the line, then it became increasingly often."

"Lovely man," added Profumo. "Wonderful company."

"So what might he have told me about post war Thailand?" Helen wasn't letting this go.

"He was pleased when Bangkok sorted its differences with Paris," answered Valerie after some thought. "The villa he was to acquire in the south of France and the resumption of his racing career on the continent, for a while these things looked to be in doubt."

For a while, reflected Helen. How might this *while* have been determined? This was the question to ask, but the former Minister was suddenly looking weary, and his wife, concerned.

"That's interesting, Mrs Profumo, as it has all been. Your husband is tired, I can see. I'll thank you for a super evening......if you could just get me my coat."

*

At Paddington

Chas had again tried Helen's number, again to meet no reply. This was frustrating, but there was at least some consolation in the punctuality of his train. Into the terminus before time he was now, in the quickly hired taxi, being whisked southward through Hyde Park. Over the Serpentine Bridge they arched as from away on the right, through the trees of Kensington Gardens, came the twinkle of the Palace lights.

*

At the Palace

Yes, Kensington Palace where, for tonight minus her Prince, the Princess of Wales was back in residence with her two young boys. And now that William and Harry were at last fully asleep, their mother could give full attention to the senior security officer and his companion who, having arrived un-annouced, had been required to wait a full forty minutes for their 'urgent' audience.

Both rose as she entered the reception room. Acknowledging their shallow bows she bade them sit, firmly closing the door before taking the vacant chair that they'd made sure was suitably positioned.

"We've had to make changes Ma'am," began the senior officer.

"So I've noticed Captain Daniels....... in personnel, as well as in the arrangement of my personal effects."

"All in the interests of State security, Ma'am. As servants of this Nation we all have duties, and ours would appear to include having to remind you of yours, Your Highness."

"My duties."

"To keep you, your sons, and the rest of the Royal Family safe, and in the manner to which it is accustomed, the Government is ready do dip deeply into the public purse. In return Ma'am it must expect co operation."

"Naturally, Captain Daniels...... so if you're here to make a specific point then please do come to it."

"Alarm has developed, Your Highness, at your interest in the difficulties endured more than forty years ago now by the Royal Family of Thailand. If you haven't already, you'll find that certain items formerly in your possession....... "

".......no longer are, because they have been deemed troublesome must I assume?"

"They have been deemed downright dangerous, Your Highness, an assessment that we've had to make clear to your friend Ms Monckton. Both of you would appear to be unaware as to the explosive nature of that with which you dabble."

"And her response?"

"Has been to agree to close off the independent access you've enjoyed to her family's archive."

"So I no longer get to delve amongst her grandfather's papers."

"In future you would have to expect close supervision, and close advice. Those Lausanne photographs you turned up, which were found here, we've had to destroy........ a matter of regret this to Rosa who will, I'm sure, be anxious to preserve other heirlooms from a similar fate."

"So the posthumous reputation of my husband's great uncle Dickie," said the Princess sourly. "Am I to understand that this is as precious to the State as it is to the Prince?"

"In effect, yes," confirmed Daniels, "for to unravel that could be to unravel too much more besides."

"Too much more? Explain."

"Fully?...... I'm not sure that I could, Your Highness, even were

264

it within my authority so to attempt. What I can say, though, is that for us this is about more than family strife. To allow this to be exacerbated further might, we fear, invite grave international and even global repercussions."

"The involvement of other countries, you mean...... so which ones?"

"Trading partners within the Eurpoean Community, the super powers, nations on the Pacific rim....... we're not sure where it might stop. Also we have a range of terrorist movements to consider, amongst which information will often be traded for arms. One such is the IRA, a gang that, as you know, we listen to and watch very closely. You've attracted their attention also, and it's feared that if we don't move then they will."

"Is that what this clearout of our domestic staff has been about........ suspected Republican sympathies?"

"As it happens, no. You'll remember Sergeant Mannakee, I know."

"Of course, such a kind man......"

"......who you kept on, unofficially, even after his being assigned elsewhere."

"Until he was killed......yes."

"Killed in a road accident in North London, whilst carrying a copy of a tape made of an edition of *Desert Island Discs* featuring a selection made by Lord Denning." The Princess blushed. "I must tell you that this fell into the hands of an IRA member who, in an innocent attempt to return it to the deceased's wife, was referred to here and, in effect, to yourself. We too now have a copy of that programme, together with a framed photograph that was once the property General Frederick Browning. We found it hanging in a manor house down in Cornwall....... Tredethy Manor, the former home of Prince Chula of Thailand, cousin of the Prince Bira who died suddenly here in London not so long ago."

"We were acquainted," admitted the Princess.

"Well even if we can't now be certain as to the circumstances of his death, I think it wise to perhaps let it stand as a warning to us all. Only a couple of weeks ago an explosion in a pub not so far from here took the lives of a couple of IRA men, one of whom we know to have been at the scene of your Sergeant's fatal motorcycle accident."

"And you would compare my situation with that of a couple of IRA minions?"

265

"Your Highness, just eight years ago Lord Louis himself, together with a number of his close family, was blown to high heaven, supposedly by the IRA."

"Most, Captain Daniels, will say this was for what he represented......."

".......while others ask, still, if it might have been for what he knew."

*

Close by (Belgravia)

Chas, had found the entrance door for Helen's flat, barely fifty yards behind the *Royal Court Theatre*. He'd rang the bell and been unsurprised at the lack of response. '*The other end of Sloane St*', she'd said, for the Profumo's, so if he crossed the Square and slowly walked its length then maybe he could intercept her return.

So away he set, keeping to the left hand, Brompton, side of the street so as to give himself a better view of the opposite pavement along that stretch where it fronted Cadogan Place.

And yes, on that side, in the distance now but closing, that could indeed be her, striding purposely for home. He stopped and, checking the traffic approaching from behind, prepared to cross. He would have to wait a vehicle or two, so he glanced again across the street to pick up Helen again and noticed two figures, both male, emerge stealthily out of those Cadogan trees.......only about ten paces behind her, and now closing, even as he watched, waiting for his break in the traffic.

And now, suddenly, she was walking faster, as if she sensed pursuit, yet still they gained. In fact they were running, and so was he, dodging traffic to the blare of horns, wanting his eyes to be on Helen and her assailants, needing them to be on the cars. They had her down now, and were hauling at her bag which she clung to grimly, but in vain, for they had it free now just as Chas leapt for it too....... only to receive an expertly delivered chop to the throat, rendering him unable to breath, unable to move, unable to stand let alone follow.

The victim, thus, was left to tend to her rescuer, as slowly his respiratory seizure relented, and gradually others gathered around. Helen was now on her feet and urging Chas to his. The police should be called, said someone....... or an ambulance said another, but these suggestions the girl resisted, as likewise did the boy when, unsteadily, he at last rose too.

"We live around the corner," said the girl. We can report this when we get in.

"Your keys are here." Chas was bending to pick them off the pavement. "Spilled in the tussel maybe."

"Thanks Chas. Great to see you."

"Something I've found out," he gasped. "Sorry....... couldn't make it earlier."

"Save it until we're inside. We have the keys, so your intervention counts for something. We can get in. We can use the car."

"For you, though, no cash....... and no cards."

"I might have some change, plus the odd fiver." Helen was feeling through her pockets. "Wait a minute.......what's this?" She drew a folded piece of paper from her pocket. It was a note, but not of currency. "I don't remember this." She held it up, trusting the street lighting to make things clearer......but no. Pencil written, the words were still too faint. This would also have to wait.

*

A call to St John

"Sally.......this is Tony Cross."

"Hi Mr Cross..... all OK over there?"

"I'm not sure. I've not seen Chas since this morning, and there's been no word either. He's not at your place?"

"He isn't, I'm afraid, but I did see him at the ferry after school. He looked to be fine. He made no mention of doing anything special......"

".......or of no one further down in Cornwall?"

"Like who do you mean?"

"Busbridge, Kate, Eamon?"

"I told him I saw Eamon earlier in the day, on my way to school. That was on the ferry. He gave me a lift, then I saw him again, at the school gate this afternoon when I came out. He returned a video that I'd lent him for the day……..as he said he would."

"And might this have caused the lad to dash down there?"

Sally hesitated, trying to recall exactly what she'd passed on……..before deciding that either Kate or Jim might be best doing that, as well as confirming positively whether or not Chas had made some sort of contact since.

"Do you have numbers for Kate and Jim?" she asked.

"I do."

"See what they say, then. In the meantime if I hear anything from your son then you'll get a call either from him or me. That, I promise."

"And if I hear anything then, likewise, you'll know. Hope to be speaking to you soon."

Sally replaced the receiver. Where would Chas have got to, she asked herself. Why hadn't he said? Who might he be with?

*

Kensington

In that their paths had led them through the same square mile of west London, Alan Grigson might have been best placed to say…… were it not for his having been ordered to accompany Colin Daniels' into Kensington palce and there listen to and gauge the Princess's responses to each of the Captain's firmy made yet tactfully put points. Here had been an object lesson in how a young but increasingly significant Royal figure might be advised. Out now and away they strolled southward along Exhibition Road, barely one tube stop from Belgravia.

"So you think my message got through Mr Grigson, and the source of this nonsense is now truly plugged."

"If you've secured Rosa's co operation then you'll have Diana's, I'm sure. You've confiscated those photos, that's the main thing. As well as clarity they had a dangerous authenticity. Age testing of the paper would have verified the date thereon….."

"……and now without this, little else can stand up. Diana will be told as much I'm sure, as will the mischief makers from Ireland."

Except that there might be an even more ruthless team operating out there, thought Alan. And whilst not letting on, Daniels was maybe by now aware of this and in line with orders from the top, leaving it to complete whatever business it was engaged upon.

If this were so then he too had to hold back. The predicament of his friends in Cornwall, and his use of Gareth and, by extension, Gareth's friend were matters to be kept close.

"A fresh infusion of carefully selected household staff will, I'm sure, seal things to your liking," he smoothed.

"Quite," said Daniels, his self-satisfied nonchalance suggesting complacency to Alan, and also opportunity. This could be the moment to raise an enquiry, one prompted by his most recent telephone conversation with Gareth and the Welshman's repeated mention of the name 'Profumo'. Care was required though, care and stealth.

"And while clearly you have plenty to do looking out for Royalty, can I assume you keep contact with the Division whose remit it is to watch over our VIPs?"

"With the top politicos, you mean?"

"And the Judiciary I suppose," said Alan, cautiously. "Take old Denning for instance, well into his eighties by now. Would he have a minder?"

"Not at the moment," chuckled Daniels, "but with the kind of opinions he's been heard to bandy around in private it's perhaps something to consider."

"No fool like an old fool, eh?"

*

Close by (Belgravia)

"Sshh!" Helen put a finger to her lips. "Say nothing, Chas," she then whispered, passing the note. "Just read it."

He did;

We have long thought our room, and also our telephone to be bugged. We suspect that Sir Edward endures likewise. Accordingly, on the

Tredethy business, I had to be guarded.

You must understand also that my husband can tell you little more than he already has. I try to protect him, so some things I have never mentioned within his hearing, and never will. I must insist, therefore, that you DO NOT contact me again.

If you seek more then try this telephone number (using a call box). Say to the gentleman who answers that I gave it to you. All that I knew I told to him. What he remembers he might be ready to share. He might not. It will be his decision.

0293 68492

Good luck
Yours,
V. P.

"I think we leave this place now," he concluded.
"To go where?"
"We can discuss that ouside."

*

Bolventor

"Well Kate," Stephanie Wild announced grimly "if your Chinese lady down at Wadebridge is speaking of a *Devil of Shanghai*, and of a *Butcher of Singapore*, then according to Monsieur Boulle, with whom I spoke earlier today, you might well have hooked yourself the grand-daddy of them all." Kate said nothing. Perhaps one of the three others gathered around the fireside table in this quiet corner of *Jamaica Inn*, Gareth, Eamon, or Jim, might muster a reply. And naturally it was the curious man.

"And my friend Pierre, he has given you a name?"

"Colonel Masanobu Tsuji, a nightmare incarnate; to this day excavations in the course of road building and high rise development around Singapore will exhume the grisly remnants of his killing spree. If the burden of the Chinese refugees was instrumental in the British defeat,

270

the likes of Tsuji made sure that the IJA would never be similarly encumbered. The young and the infirm were put to the sword, often quite literally, while the fit were worked to death, by the thousand. If, taking all nationalities, say eighty thousand POWs slaved on the death railway, then these were more than 2 to 1 outnumbered by civilians. And where perhaps a fifth of the soldiers died, amongst those civilians barely half were to survive."

"So Madame Jingzhi's mother has good reason to remember *the Butcher of Singapore*," nodded Kate.

"And there is a further aspect to this man's infamy," continued Stephanie, "and this touches upon what was said in your last conversation with the guy you took down to Parkway Station....... Alan his name, I think. The guy I've yet to meet."

"Alan, yes." confirmed Busbridge. "Go on, this further aspect being........ "

"...... a penchant for cannibalism, reputed to have been displayed after an American air raid against a Division under his command that had been pressed back to the China-Burma border. A shot down American pilot, one Lieutenant Parker, is said to have taken the full brunt of the Colonel's ire. Following his execution it was ordered that his liver should be cut up, roasted on skewers, and served at the officers' table."

"So come the surrender in '45, up go the *Most Wanted* posters," contnued Eamon, "and this, Stephanie, is where your father enters the fray."

"After having suffered enough, himself, as a prisoner of war."

"And with the Americans he set about attempting to hunt this character down."

"Which was what he believed himself to be doing when his plane came down and he was killed," confirmed the daughter. "On that very day he was thought to have been carrying information on Tsuji's where abouts."

"Information that would have been lost also," added Gareth, his sympathy taking a pinch of suspicion. "But when you say '*Which was what HE believed himself to be doing* ', are we to understand that *others* have come to think differently, including Pierre Boulle maybe?....... including yourself?"

"While having read Tsuji's books, including *Underground Escape*, the author's own account of how he evaded those like my father seeking to bring him to justice, Boulle has also spoken with......."

"...... others," prompted Eamon.

"Yes others...... former friends, former enemies, who knew something of the man's movements."

"So Pierre is aware of gaps and discrepancies," said Jim, "and....."

".........and one of the more intriguing concerns Tsuji's predicament when, on the Japanese surrender he found himself having to seek sanctuary in Bangkok, where he'd happened to be in command of the IJA garrison. By his own account he laid low, disguing himself as a Buddhist monk before making his way northward temple by temple into Burma, then on to China.

After that his career during the cold war years was distinguished by a certain quick footedness insamuch as he found ways of finding takers for a renowned expertise in jungle military campaigning on both sides of the ideological divide....... in China, in Vietnam."

"But back to Thailand, please, and that immediate post year," said Kate. "We have the gist of Tsuji's story, Stephanie, but those others say what?"

"Others will claim that Tsuji's disguise was not so effective as he would want us to believe, and that in fact he was recognised and captured by a group looking to effect a regime change in that country, an integral part of this planned overthrow being the removal of the King. The theory holds that Tsuji himself was engaged to perform the deed......"

"......his payment being a renewed opportunity to escape," said Eamon. "And when, forty years later, on the other side of the world, a prying Princess starts to set a few long cupboarded skeletons a-rattle, then who better to seal them in whilst keeping the dwindling number of those *in the know* to an absolute minimum."

"Our prying Princess, though, can be left to the British establishment," continued Gareth, "which had showed itself adept at letting all this lie when once before, in the early '60s, there were fears that something might then emerge. We catch them locally in the trimming of that photo up at Tredethy; while nationally in old Denning's trimming of his report on the Profumo scandal."

"And see how your friend Alan scuttles back to London," said Stephanie.

"Where today he and his mates will have given the Wales's

apartment a good turming over," added the Guardsman. "Rogue elements within the IRA, though, are less well protected."

"And must consequently pay the ultimate price for their folly," said Busbridge.

"Except you, Eamon." Stephanie glanced quizically into her wineglass, before swirling first then gulping back a last mouthfull.

"Thanks to yourself, I guess," responded Carroll.

"Maybe," nodded Stephanie, her whisper a blend of modesty and scepticism, "but to accept all this is naturally then to speculate on just who it was that struck this deal with Tsuji." Her voice rose. "The assassination happened for sure, but did the regime change? Was this intent realised, or was it not? Either and the schemer requires a cover up."

"Moutbatten was certainly a schemer," said Kate.

"But I go with Tania," countered Busbridge. "I don't see him hiring the likes of Tsuji. Hire a trusted photographer to take a few kinky shots, yes....... but a gunman? No, and certainly not from the ranks of his vanquished enemy."

"OK," accepted Kate, "but within this Free Thai Force you've spoken of, the movement used by Mountbatten, there might have been infiltrated a hard line Moscow-directed cadre of the sort seeded about amongst the-anti fascist Resistance movements of occupied Europe. Can we not imagine Tsuji being collared and then used by such in the furtherance of a long game which might, as a first stage, have sought an installation of Mountbatten's placemen into the Palaces and Parliaments of Bangkok, placemen to be toppled at a later date."

"This might be *imagined*, Kate," allowed Jim, "but if this is how it happened then, from their standpoint, what a total calamity this strategy did prove...... given how this rationale was quickly and gratefully seized upon by supporters of the disgraced Pibul. Suddenly, despite his recent collaboration with the Japs, he was looking the safest pair of hands, so impeccable had been his record in the persecution of the Reds and also in the protection of the legitimate King, those very areas in which his rival, Pridi, could now be painted as decidedly suspect. Add to this the determination of Ananda's youger brother to keep the Mahidol line alive......"

"........and, all in all, the fall-out from the episode turns out to be more in tune with the hopes of Dutch and the French," added Gareth.

"And one must suppose," reasoned Eamon, "that back in '46 old style colonialism wasn't so discredited as an aspiration."

"And that certain aspirants might have then ranked still as the *major power* mentioned by Chula in his letter," said Jim. "Is this what you mean?"

"You sound doubtful."

"Because I have this other letter which carries near enough the same term."

"And your problem......?"

".......is that it was written 40 years later, and that's 30 years after the humiliations sustained by French in the once theirs Indo China, and by the Dutch in the once theirs East Indies......"

"...... and by us at the hands of a badly underestimated Gamal Abdel Nasser," chimed Gareth.

"So leaving aside the Dutch, you're wondering if now, in the late '80s, France can still be termed a 'major power'," said Kate, "Opinions anyone? Gareth perhaps."

"What would Jeremy say?" countered the Guardsman. Kate considered. The others waited.

"Jeremy would say that France was and is still a *major* power." Kate was emphatic. "There are two *super*powers, he would say, the US and the USSR, with China coming up fast to join them. Beneath these there are the other nuclear powers, France included, Britain included, India, I suppose, and Pakistan soon perhaps. Yes and all, to a greater or lesser extent, he would term *major powers* ....probably adding Japan for its economic clout alone."

"And France's ability to deliver an intercontinental weapon independently would arguably make it the stongest major power of all," said Gareth. "So who then would be the relegation candidates?"

"We look for nations which relinquished colonies but declined to build themselves a bomb," said Eamon. "Belgium and Portugal for instance who pulled out of Africa, and in the context of South East Asia we have The Netherlands......."

"........and that's about all," nodded Busbridge. "I think we have to remember too that in March '46, when Chula wrote his letter at Tredethy, the French had not yet returned to Indo China in any great force. Their true intent wasn't to be publicly declared until the November of that year, eight months later, at Haiphong."

"Haiphong.....?" queried Carroll. "Remind me Jim."

274

"Think of the British in Amritsar, India, 1919, and in Dublin the following year, at Croke Park. Total score.....? Say four hundred deaths. For the French in Haiphong, as a postscript to the second great war of this century, we can times that number by at least twenty."

"Policing with a capital P," whistled Gareth, "*and* with the UN by then up and running. It's only a major power that can get away with that sort of thing."

"That would have been two months after my father was killed," said Stephanie.

"And five after the death of King Ananda," added Jim. "So events that Tania, in early '86, could regard as history hadn't yet happened in Chula's world of early '46."

"And Tania's later assessment would have taken into account the forty year development of France's nuclear capability," said Kate, "achieved, I remind you, largely through a testing programme conducted within the Pacific rim."

"Good point," agreed Stephanie, "very good point, for Tania wrote early last year of these people remaining dangerous, a comment maybe on events in New Zealand some six months before."

"So barely two years ago....... in New Zealand?" now Kate was puzzled.

"The Green Peace ship," esplained Stephanie, "The *Rainbow Warrior*, blown up in Auckland harbour two Julys ago, a crime the French Government were subsequently forced to admit had been its responsibility."

"They'd hired the murderous thugs, you're saying."

"As they might well have done back in '46, in Thailand. And think....... were this tale to emerge now to compound the propaganda disaster of '85 then they could find themselves well and truly in the mire." Stephanie was surprising even herself, so speculative was this linking of the Bangkok Palace shooting of '46 with the blowing up of a ship in Auckland in '85. Across all that time and all that distance, could she really stretch such a thread? But the others were listening, they were following......she could lead on!

"But look," she continued, "if your old lady in St Lawrence has correctly identified Tsuji then, rather than any sponsor, our immediate concern has to be him and his running dogs. If, as seems, they're in the field, then to achieve their remit they'll be a law unto themseves. Be watchful in your movements. Lock doors. Lock windows. Lock vehicles."

"Now you're sounding like Alan," smiled the nurse.

"Except that I'll be sticking around, Kate. If I'm alert enough, then there should be clues again at work, of the sort that got me down to Polzeath on time the other evening."

Her speech made Stephanie drained her glass, shoving it then to the centre of the table as if to offer notice of imminent departure.

"You might ask amongst your older colleagues for any memories they might have of Valerie Hobson, the film actress who was later to marry John Profumo," suggested Busbridge, watching her reach to the floor for her bag.

"I've a few myself, actually." She was pausing in those preparations to leave.

"So you'll have seen *Great Expectations*," Eamon said.

"I have, yes, but better than that, when I was girl my mother took me up to London to see her perform on stage. I couldn't have been much more than eight."

"In a children's show, then, and, at a few years older, with a role more matronly than that of *Estella*," deduced Kate. "Mrs Darling was she, in a production of Peter Pan?"

"No, this was a main part. She played Anna, the governess in the first London production of the *King and I*. It was a matinee at the Savoy, Drury Lane, and being my first trip to a West End theatre, and such a colourful production too, it made a vivid impression.......unforgettable. I've seen the film with the mighty Brynher, and Deborah Kerr miming to Marnie Nixon's note perfect voice, but somehow it's never matched up even though Hobson's singing was less than precise."

"In the tradition set by Gertie," chuckled Jim.

"*Getting to know you*," trilled Kate softly. "*Getting to know all about you*........."

"Herbert Lom was the King," continued Stephanie, unaware of any significance these recollections might have for the others, "and of course he had all these children."

"But can you remember if an original London cast recording was made?" The curious man wasn't ready to let this one go.

"One was, I know, for my mother was so taken by the songs and the performance that she bought the LP. When she died I kept it. It's at home....... a bit scratchy now, as you might imagine."

276

"We're interested in the arrangement of *I Whistle a Happy Tune*," said Kate, singing then......

" *Tumtummytum-pompompom*

Tumtummytum-pompompom ...... can you do us a tape and bring it over for tomorrow evening? Jeremy should be down. With this and Chula's letter, plus the *Estella* link to Tania's, he's going to be well impressed."

"I'll be over, definitely," promised Stephanie, " and I'll have the whole thing taped."

"And perhaps there's something else, whilst you're at work." Busbridge was hesitant. "I don't know....."

"Spit it out, Jim."

"Before coming out I had a call from a concerned Tony Cross. Chas was a good three hours overdue for the evening meal. He'd last been seen by the girl, Sally, at the ferry, shortly after you'd seen her at the school gate Eamon. She told him what you'd said to her about *Estella* becoming Mrs Jack Profumo."

"Go on," prompted Gareth.

"I think he's still in touch with the Trembath girl, and she uses her grandfather's flat which I'm sure is fairly close to where the Profumos live."

"So what's Stephanie supposed to do?" said Kate.

"I'm wondering if t boy might have shot off up there, on impulse, by train."

"And if he has?"

"Then he could have used a credit card," nodded Stephanie, "at Plymouth Station. And Charles Cross would be the name on the card. Yes, it's worth a try Jim. I can put it to the relevant desk. We might find out if he's in London."

*

Belgravia

"So tell me now, Chas, before we move off, what is it that you've travelled so far to tell me?" Helen sat at the wheel of the car, her ignition key inserted but as yet unturned.

"Nothing that you don't already now know, as it's worked out. You will have noticed my lack of surprise at the content of that note. I was hoping to pre warn you of Jack Profumo's familiarity with Tredethy......"

".......something you've perhaps known for a while?", .

"I suppose so," admitted Chas, "but not this separate individual involvement here confessed by Valerie. A first inkling of this came only late this afternoon. I tried to phone, more than once. Unable to get through I dashed for the train. I was wanting you to be better prepared, an attack of the sort you've just endured suddenly seeming more likely."

"We don't dismiss that pair as mere handbag snatchers, you're saying. So if not then what else might they have been after?"

"In our last telephone coversation, with you at your granfather's flat, we spoke of this book of Tsuji's. They might have been wanting to relieve you of that."

"Well I've packed it now with the rest of my things. Staying there tonight doesn't appeal."

Chas placed a hand on hers.

"You needn't," he said tenderly. "There's an old school friend of mine with a place just the other side of Shepherd's Bush. He'll put us up."

"And this number on the note.....?"

".....will have to wait until morning."

*

Book Three

1950 Bangkok....
where, four years after Ananda's death,
Little Brother Lek is carried through the
streets, as part of his ritual proclamation
as King Bhumibol, Ninth Rama.

20 years on, and he and Prince Philip
enjoy a firm friendship.... one
encouraged before her death by Philip's
cousin Marina.

The next morning

"*The Lawns*," answered the voice, a woman's voice, well spoken, and of no great age.

Chas hesitated.

"I'm sorry," he began, "I was told that I would be speaking to a gentleman."

"By whom?"

"By the person who gave me this number."

"And this was?"

"A Mrs John Profumo."

"Just a moment, while I check the list......" Twenty seconds elapsed. "This name, yes, it is here, so on another day you might have got through to Lord Denning. I'm at his desk where you've come through on his special line, but on this occasion you speak instead with his daughter in law."

"So might there be a more convenient moment today?"

"He'll be away for another week, I'm afraid, Mr......."

".......Cross. Has he been taken into hospital? He's no longer so young, I know."

"Nothing like that, Mr Cross, in fact he's taking a holiday. He has gone down to Cornwall again, for the first time in a number of years. Like the old days, really, when he would go regularly...... but, as you say, he's no longer so young."

"And he has a favourite part, does he?"

"Don't we all........ his is the Helford, and now is his favourite time of year, Autumn, with the waterside woods dripping with gold."

"So another week you would say." Chas was giving the woman every opportunity to give another number, but it wasn't forthcoming.

"Yes, give it another week."

*

St Gennys

And James Busbridge has also taken a phone call......
a brief invitation this, from Stephanie Wild, to join him for lunch. She
would have information for him, he guessed, information too urgent for
the page, and too sensitive for the wire. She wouldn't have long, but he'd
been ready to drive most, or even all of the way. And this, now, to the *The
Wainhouse Inn* at St Genny's is what he is doing.

'Easily found', Stephanie had assured him, whilst for her it was
sufficiently far from work to preclude recognition by a colleague. Jim had
set off almost immediately, knowing that traffic will sometimes need to
queue to get through Camelford.

But not today, thankfully, and he can use the resultant twenty
spare minutes to drop down to Crackington Haven and take in some of the
best cliff in the county, topped as it was now by the rich gorse-specked
autumnal brown of heather-cushioned bracken. A brief stroll onto the
deserted beach wasn't to be resisted, for what better way could there be to
sharpen both appetite and curiosity?

And still he was early, and ready outside to greet Stephanie who,
somehow predictably, rolled up precisely on time. Knowing *The
Wainhouse*, she was pleased to recommend the soup of that particular day,
a dense but sensitively herbed concoction of carrot, courgette, and
cauliflower ..... with the locally baked bread and locally churned butter, a
speciality of the house.

"And now, Stephanie, you must have news."

"As we'd imangined a card bearing the name Chas Cross was used
to purchase a rail ticket at Plymouth station yesterday evening."

"A ticket to where?"

"London Paddington......"

".......and back?"

"Yes, but that part might be superfluous."

"How can you say that?"

"The same card was used less than two hours ago at a service
station in Hampshire. The till record together with that provided by a
CCTV camera links the transaction to an XR3 convertible headed in a
westward direction."

"That would figure," nodded Busbridge. "Can I tell his father?"

"Over the phone?..........Well just say that you have it on good authority that he spent the night in London, and that you believe him to be now on his way home. We might pick something up from by satellite, but you'll appreciate how cloudy it has stayed over the past few days. My guess is that he'll be at work tomorrow anyway."

"And you mentioned before how Eamon's motor had been picked out from above. I suppose he'll have been likewise obliterated. He was keen to change that vehicle, I know, and this was probably what he was out to do yesterday, in Plymouth."

Stephanie straightened, placing her spoon onto the side plate, next to her roll.

"The response of a man who doesn't know who to trust, Jim, of a man who knows what it is to be used, and knows also the torture of being uncertain as to when that usefulness might expire and whether, come this time, he might be marked for a brutal disposal. I've been surprised somewhat at Kate. At my first opportunity of speaking alone with her, this in the women's room in the *Atlantic Hotel* over at Polzeath, I did say to her that Eamon could be making phone calls to a number in Ireland. If not alarm then I thought this might provoke some kind of reaction......but......"

"......but no," affirmed Busbridge, "and by this she's actually saying that you too needn't be surprised. There's a little history to this, you see, recent history, which for want of time I couldn't even start to explain now. I'll just say that as we groped through the fog of an earlier conspiracy, it was on the dubious strength of Eamon's far from tightly ravelled connections with the Republican Movement that we came to a clearer view."

"So there was an Irish dimension to that adventure."

"As there would appear to be to this," confirmed Busbridge. "And throughout it would appear to be Eamon's fate to inhabit this limbo state of non acceptance."

"So he's on borrowed time."

"Teetering, you might say, on the very brink of foreclosure."

"But he survives."

"He does, Stephanie," sighed Jim, "while a guy like Barry George comes to a sticky end. One of the good and brave, as were King Ananda and your own father. Why, why, and why...... that's how many questions, Stephanie?"

"Three."

"Three, yes, but with so much that overlaps maybe there's a single explanation that covers all."

"And Eamon Carroll…….. you think that he's the one to stumble across the key to this."

"Perhaps, Stephanie, he holds it already, without knowing."

"Well you make of it what you like, Jim, but know from me now that a further call was made to Ireland late yesterday afternoon, this one of longer duration, and from a call box in Plymouth………. one not so very far from the girl's school."

*

Helen and Chas…..

………had followed the A303 to Honiton almost, a stretch during which the passenger was, to some extent at least, able relieve his conscience of the part he'd played in that after-Scotland deception that Helen had endured, the coup by which Profumo and Monckton had been rescued from Port Eliot. Busbridge's reourcefulness was to be admired, Helen had acknowledged, as well as Declan's diligence and his own nerve. They'd spoken to Profumo now, but the significance of Walter was surely best discussed in the presence of Denning, it was decided. She would have to wait.

The A30 they'd followed almost to Exeter, and now, briefly, to skirt the City, it was the M5,…….three lanes of westbound traffic hurrying them across the Exe to a fast looming point of decision. Were they to take the A38 Plymouth road next, or the faster and more direct route into Cornwall, the rejoined A30?

End of Motorway was already signed, but it was the driver's shout thought Chas. He glanced across, and she reached for his hand. Could she sense his thoughts, he wondered.

"Coming with me all the way then?" she at last said, giving him no more than a furlong at eighty to decide and respond.

"Only if you want."

"So long as you do too, Chas."

"Of course." This was an adventure to see through.

"It could be that Denning stays at Helford Passage on the north bank, so rather than going straight around to the village and risking having to back track, we'll enquire at *The Ferryboat* first. If they tell us he's on the other side then we can still get there in the light."

"I get it," nodded Chas, "at a cost of twenty minutes we might save ourselves what?"

"A possible hour, were we to get it wrong on the far side. The lanes over there are never easy."

*

On the phone

"Cross speaking....... Bovisand."

"Tony......Alan Grigson here. Is Chas about?"

"Not yet."

"So not back from work."

"My understanding, Alan, is that he never went in."

"But you've been told he's on his way."

"I have, yes, but not by Chas himself. I get this somewhat guarded call from Jim Busbridge, and he tells me that my son went to London yesterday evening by train, and he's coming back today by car. How he could know this......" faltered the father, more puzzled than distressed.

"And you've not heard what prompted this trip to London?"

"Jim wasn't saying, at least not over the phone......."

"........lest this should betray his source, I guess."

"And where are you, Alan........ also headed this way?"

"Yes. A couple of hours and I should be with you, and if Chas arrives in the meantime then all the better. Don't let him shoot off again."

"So you want nothing from me?"

"Be ready in case....."

".....of what?"

"We can discuss that later, Tony. Petrol in your Volvo we might need, as well as in your quickest outboard; plus a trailer hicthed, and plenty of air in the inflatable secured thereto, as well as in your diving tanks."

*

The Helford

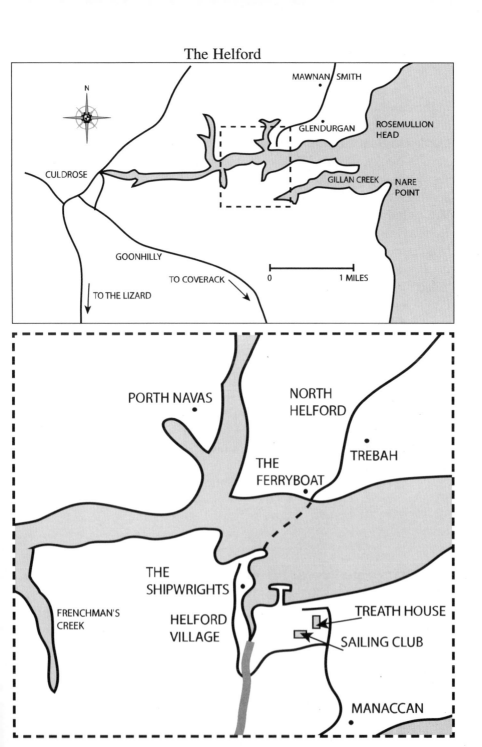

To come to Helford village…..

…….after a night in West London is to find tranquility itself, there in the easeful death of Autumnal light, and in the near still of an evening air seasoned by the whisp of bonfire drifting down from Glendurgan Garden to float almost on the smooth surface of a calmly filling estuary.

Select, decided Chas, in fact *very select*…….. an assessment easily made, even through the branches of the trees which mask the approach carpark. The village itself, hugging the small inlet down to their left, tailed out past the *Shipwrights Inn*, eventually to the ferry slip on Helford Point with its yacht moorings beyond. Across to their right, along from the wooden walled sailing club, fronting a widening estuary, began the *Bosahan Estate*. This, they'd been told at *The Ferryboat*, included the lodge that was being used, as it had often enough before, by the Lord and Lady Denning.

"That way," indicated Chas, "two or three hundred yards which from here which, I'd say, were best walked. You've got that note from Valerie Profumo… ?"

"I have," confirmed Helen. "I'll take Colonel Tsuji's book too."

And thus armed, having locked the car, off the pair did purposefully then set, neither taking a backward glance.

The careful arrival through the carpark entrance of a second, substantially larger vehicle, rolling slowly, engine cut and lights doused, therefore went un noticed.

*

Kerrow Downs (above St Breward)

With the first rap on the caravan door having jolted Eamon from a long overdue doze, an impatient second had him scrabbling for his wristwatch. It confirmed what he'd sensed. This was before the arranged time, by a good thirty minutes. He'd known similar earlier in the year at his London flat. He would wait for a voice, and……..

"Eamon……Eamon," it came, to his not inconsiderable relief. For while urgent, it was a familiar voice, and comfortingly so.

"Coming......OK, OK." On his feet now he little better than staggered to the door, to open up.......and find himself faced by a pistol, the barrel levelled at his head.

"Outside, Eamon, on your knees.......good, then hands together, held please as if in prayer. And pray you might as well, while you have opportunity."

"Let me explain first. Do listen, please."

"Unfortunately, Eamon, time presses......and I've already listend to quite enough."

*

Treath

"And you, you say, are the grandaughter of the 'Sir Edward' mentioned in this note," piped Lord Denning, a frail figure in his doorway, but forbidding still, even as an octogenarian.

"Helen Trembath," confirmed the girl, raising her voice unnecessarily, wrongly assuming deafness. "My friend, Chas, and I have driven down from London today. You might remember Sir Edward as a back bench MP for one of the Plymouth constituencies."

"Vaguely, yes....... and this Val P?"

"We think you might know who that is," Chas broke in boldly. "Knew Louis Mountbatten quite well back in the '40s, also his nephew, Prince Philip. She married one of Sir Edward's fellow MPs, for Stratford I believe, at that time. He was to make the front bench."

"He was, and she'd been an actress," nodded Denning, "who would occasionally sing......"

"......a happy tune?"

"Yes......... and I suppose you'd better come in, the pair of you."

"Nice place, Your Lordship," said Chas, his over-deference verging on the insolent as they were shown through to a spacious reception room, there to be settled around a gently burning log fire.

"Now," resumed Denning, "if you've been referred to me by Valerie I'm guessing that on certain matters Thai she will have admitted being more frank with me than she ever has been, or will be, with her husband Jack......."

"And that's about all," said Chas. "Clearly there's a reluctance to speak freely with the likes of us. Not wanting to provoke your displeasure perhaps?"

"Mmmm...... as if to have you knocking on my door is supposed to delight me!"

"Do I hear complaint," ventured Chas, "when but for that flash of vanity on *Desert Island Discs* these things might have stayed buried?"

"I'll thank you, young man, not to lecture me on the pitfalls that abound in the broadcasting media."

"I think what Chas might be suggesting," said Helen, "is that while not wishing to disclose more, Mrs Profumo could have felt that we might have already found out a little too much....... sufficient, that is, for her to be less than comfortable with simply sending us away."

"So what's to stop me from doing that now?" challenged Denning.

"Your curiousity." Chas wasn't to be intimidated.

"You're right," sighed Denning. "Yes, and the reason you're right is that while I might know more than Valerie, who in turn knows more than her husband, I still can't claim to know the full tale."

"Some one does, though." Chas was getting bolder by the second. "And we suspect that this person is doing his dammedest to make sure the whole sorry story can never emerge. A danger lurks, and if it's to be countered then all we can do now is to find out more. We're in too deep, we fear. There's no going back, and were we to stop swimming then the circling sharks might start closing in."

"So this starts, presumably, with a recording of *Desert Island Discs*," relented the former Master of the Rolls, "and leads you to Valerie Profumo."

"Not directly," said a puzzled Helen, as yet ignorant of the actress's staring role at the Savoy.

"So circuitously.....?" Denning was no less baffled, prompting Chas to again intervene.

"It was to Tredethy we were taken first, to a group photograph that hung on a wall there. It had been taken in '46, and pictured with Chula himself were Prince Philip, Princess Marina, a woman called Tania, a General Browning, and another woman who I only found out yesterday was our Valerie. We were told that the picture had belonged to Browning, and it was noticed that it might have been trimmed."

"Which it indeed was," admitted Denning.

"At your suggestion?"

"At my brother's actually......... had it been me there, I would have said burn the whole thing."

"Had it been you *where*?" pressed Chas, "and *when*?"

"At Menabilly, in '63, where I sent Reginald to ask Boy Browning about the Royal Family's connections to Jack Profumo."

"When you were set the task of producing a report on the Keeler business," said Helen. "So why didn't you come down?"

"I had to be careful about where I might be seen, and Reginald had served with 'Boy' out in the east......."

"....... under Mountbatten."

"Correct, and also at that time in '63 Browning had gotten himself into a spot of bother with the law.......drinking and driving essentially."

"So inducements could be offered," said Chas, "to help loosen the tongue......and this was when quite a bit of this came out. Obviously you would have spoken to Jack Profumo, but maybe Browning suggested a quiet word with Valerie."

"And it was a quiet word," confirmed Denning. "As she herself might have said, not even her husband knew."

"So it would have been through speaking with the *The Queen's General* and Valerie that it was all to come out," said Chas.

"Not all, young man......you've heard me say that already. Far from it, I must repeat, but enough to realise the potential damage that might be caused to our Royal Family and to the standing of this Nation in world affairs."

"And the key figure Helen mentioned just now," continued Chas. "Mountbatten.......the particular member of the Royal Family who, in '46, when that picture was taken, was assuming an active role in world affairs."

"Yes," agreed Denning, "so move on now to 1953, still ten years before Keeler aand Ivanov and Reginald's chat with Boy, to a nagging question raised amongst Royal watchers on the occasion of our Queen's Coronation, she by then being the wife of Prince Philip and mother of two of his children. Why, it was asked, was there no attendance at the ceremony by the King of Thailand, or by the Royal Sister or the Royal Mother in his place? In answer, it was placed on record that after the death of the King's older brother in '46, Mountbatten had written a letter to

Buckingham Palace offering his opinion that rather than suicide or an accident this had been a murder arranged by the victims mother and siblings........"

".......and that as a result of this letter, with its unproven allgation, the invitation to the Coronation was instead sent to Tredethy, to Chula," said Chas.

"A most unfortunate sequence, this, in the light of what was to be later made known to me about the kind of mischief that Lord Louis and pals had themselves been dabbling in just before the young King Ananda was found shot."

"So when you say '*made known to me*', this means from Reginald's conversation with Browning, in '63....."

".......and from the chat I had with Valerie shortly afterwards."

"So they shared their insights," said Helen, "but how had these been gained........by two characters of such contrasting colour?"

"By General Frederick Browning....... affectionately known to his friends as 'Tommy' or 'Boy', and by Mrs Anthony Havelock-Allen........ known to us now, of course, as Valerie? At this point we have to remind ourselves that over the pivotal months each was a close confidante of the young Prince Philip of Greece, soon to be Duke of Edinburgh, and later what he is now, a Prince of this Realm. To give him his due, this junior Naval Officer of then was quite perturbed, firstly at the calibre of some of his Uncle Dickie's close associates, and also at their appetite for Byzantine intrigue......"

".......as transposed to Bangkok," followed Chas.

"Exactly," squeaked Denning. "And when that photo was taken at Tredethy things were coming to a head."

"So why did Reginald suggest to Boy that Jack Profumo be trimmed from that group.......he and that Monckton fellow, both having been more to the edge of events back in '46?"

"With Profumo, of course, there was the notoriety he was to achieve seventeen years later."

"And Monckton?" pressed Helen.

"Well there was a fellow one could never be totally sure of."

"A fellow lawyer, was that the problem?" the girl teased.

"Probably," smiled Denning. "That role he perfected as a Royal go-between just about says it all.........*speak no evil*!"

"But as to what he might have heard, or seen......your brother clearly wasn't leaving anything to chance."

"Quite.......for while Walter might have had a safe enough pair of hands, those of his descendants couldn't be likewise guaranteed. To leave him there, thought Reginald, would be to leave a hostage to fortune."

"Because while Walter himself might not have been a worry, his archive was," said Chas, "a hoard of sensitive material kept as an insurance policy."

"Which he guards responsibly for as long as he is treated responsibly. But could his children's children be relied upon for the same vigilance and rectitude? My brother wasn't sure, and by that excision hoped to forestall the michievous and the curious who stand ready to exploit such laxity."

"And in the Tredethy scene, the curious might want to focus on what?" asked Chas.

"We suspected, Reginald and I, that Monckton maintained a channel of communication with Prince Chula, one by which those who'd brought this country through the war sought to curb the more wilder of Lord Louis' aspirations."

"And from what's been said to me of Walter's dealings with Royalty," continued Chas, "there would have been that persisting thread of preserving, so far as possible, the *Majesty* of the individuals concerned as well as the *Mystique* of the Monarchy as a lasting institution......and this, in the context of the Bangkok version, prompts me to mention a further set of images that it has been my fortune, or perhaps misfortune to have seen." He turned to his companion. "I've not told you of these yet, Helen, so listen well also."

For all his years, Denning was sharply to his feet, eyes alight, moving between the chairs in a kind of animated, if not agitated shuffle.

"I think I know what you speak of. It's that Irish wretch Murphy, and......."

"So you've seen them before?"

"Never...... I've heard them whispered of, that's all. The barely mentionable that's at the heart of all this, which I've always wanted to dismiss, sometimes as a cunning disinformation ploy, and at others as mere poisonous gossip."

"Well for me, your Lordship, seeing was believing. The originals, so I've been told, have found their way into Kensington Palace, having lain for some time in the Monckton archive. It's said that they were retrieved by our new Princess of Wales who is convinced that her husband has been too long crippled by his adulation for the late Lord Louis. It's a hereditary diease, she fears, and it might infect her children should she not move now at this opportunity to out Uncle Dickie as the scoundrel she's decided he was."

"Well at least Mountbatten is dead now," responded Denning. "This wasn't so back in the '60s when he, the Queen Mother, and Marina stood as pillars of the Royal edifice. To have this stuff leaking out now would be less calamitous, certainly ...."

".........but then again there is that closeness between between Valerie and Prince Philip to consider," contended Chas.

"I'm sorry," said Helen, "but I seem to be missing something here, something about an *Irish wretch* named Murphy, something *barely mentionable*. Would one of you please explain.

"Ananda became King in 1935," began Denning. "He was aged ten, and living in Lausanne, in Switzerland, which is where he continued to live as he completed his schooling, this including the period of Thailand's wartime occupation by the Imperial Japanese Army. Having been installed by the Party who collaborated with the Japanese many abroad regarded him as a puppet who might be pleased to abdicate come the defeat of Japan. This said, the majority of Thais, for whom the King is a Deity, prayed fervently that Ananda would yet rule long and rule wisely."

"But Mountbatten, the Supreme Commander of British forces in South East Asia," continued Chas, "he thought he knew better, and with what some would deem characteristic arrogance, ambition, and lack of scruple he hatched a scheme which was hoped might hasten the abdication of Ananda, plus close family, in favour of our Brit-friendly Prince Chula; he at that time living in Cornwall."

"And central to this quite diabolical trick were those pictures," said Denning.

"Containing?" urged Helen, looking to Chas.

"The young king Ananda, then aged 19, naked, on a bed with this Irish lackey of Mountbatten's, one Peter Murphy, he a notorious homosexual."

"So *in flagrante delicto*," nodded Denning, "just as those whispers did say."

"The boy had had been drugged, we decided," said Chas.

"But nevertheless Mountbatten was sufficiently armed to get Chula onto the throne by blackmail," reasoned Helen. "This, though, was precisely what didn't happen! History tells us that Mountbatten failed."

"History also tells us that Ananda took a bullet to the head," Chas reminded her.

"And also that Mountbatten had the temerity to impugn the conduct in all this of a distraught mother and brother," added Denning.

"Which meant that had those pictures surfaced in the '60s then his position would have looked really, really bad," explained Chas, "as his Lordship here has said. Even if one accepts that the King chose suicide before disgrace then Mountbatten is no less the villain."

"And was it suicide?" asked Helen.

"This wasn't the Buddhist way, apparently......so..." Chas looked to Denning for comment.

"I must repeat," he said, "you're not to expect me to explain the young King's death. Many have been forthcoming to me on the subject of Mountbatten's failed scheming, enough to persuade me that the shooting was a consequence of this....... but this isn't to say that he intended such an outcome, and not one of my informants has been as bold to suggest as much, even amongst the good few that had little liking for the man. As it worked out, the effect of the killing was to thwart Mountbatten."

"So if murder then maybe the perpetrators had this in mind," suggested Helen. "We heard just now of people who were concerned to rein in Mountbatten. Perhaps they've got an even bigger secret to hide. It could be that they deployed an operative who lives on to this day."

"Who, though, is going to walk into a Royal Palace and blow away a King?" mumbled Denning. "And then get out un-noticed."

"A professional, and a survivor," suggested Chas.

"Who would now be almost as old as me!" exclaimed the Law Lord.

"From what I've read, Thailand was crawling with them," said Helen.

"Hired guns or survivors?" Denning asked her

"Plenty of each, some who have been both..... and yes, a handful who might remain so, even to this day."

"You make them sound like London Lawyers," smirked the old man.

"You want a name?" Chas asked. "Show him that book of yours,

Helen, *Japan's Greatest Victory*."

"Manasobu Tsuji," she said, delving into her deep handbag.

"An IJA Colonel, who somehow evaded capture and prosecution as a war criminal," explained Chas. "Helen's work has involved research into the Thailand-Burma 'Death Railway'. As well as in the capture of Singapore boasted here, Tsuji demonstrated a flair for the enslavement of his captives. Following Japan's surrender he is said to have found sanctuary in Thailand, and also a means of escape into Indo China. Come the 1950s his immunity is sufficiently hardened to allow him to publish this book, and later a companion memoir, *Underground Escape*, which no less boastfully chronicles his journey of return to the changed world, one remarkably ready to fete him as an author. Perhaps Idi Amin might oblige us next."

"You're right to be cynical about the prosecution of war criminals," acknowledged Denning. "Too much depends on who you are......"

"......yes, and on what you can do and say."

"So am I hearing a suggestion that this one might have been employed and protected by those to who picked up the responsibility of policing post war Laos, Cambodia, and Vietnam?" asked Denning, "France, a loyal partner in our brave new European adventure?" His quizzical irony was not lost on Helen.

"The same country whose Secret Service blew up the *Rainbow Warrior*," she added. "The same establishment that sheltered Maurice Papon."

"But I don't think, dear, that we can pin these things on your Mr Tsuji," smiled Denning. "Just say, though, that early in '46 the French intercepted this man as he was attempting to slip out of Thailand into Laos....... under what *rationale* would they have turned a fugitive into an assassin and returned him to Bangkok?"

"A rationale derived presumably from an awareness of what Mountbatten was up to," explained Chas. "With what he had on King Ananda, Lord Louis would have been hoping that both the Mahidol brothers might go, leaving a vacant throne for his man Chula, under whom the position of Chief Minister Pridi, also his man, would become virtually unassailable. With the murder, though, Mountbatten's fox is shot, and it can be whispered to the younger brother that were he to the relinquish the throne then the next bullet might be for him."

"So Bhumibol sits tight," sighed Denning, "to this day, the Ninth Rama under a clamped-on Crown, as duty would require......."

".......and as duress would demand," added Chas grimly. "A victim of a different and third kind, after the brother who we know was killed, and Mountbatten, who we must presume was betrayed."

"So, again, who by?" asked Helen. "Someone who knew of, and who had access to those Lausanne photos..... surely."

"With these being held by Mountbatten under lock and key," suggested Chas, "at his HQ."

"A HQ which was moved from Delhi down to Ceylon," nodded Denning, "where we know Browning worked for him, and where Prince Philip visited when his ship was that way during the last year of the war."

"And Browning admitted to your brother that he knew *of* those photos?"

"He did," said Denning, "before denying adamantly that he'd ever having alerted anyone abroad to their existence."

"And he gave no hint as to who else might have been appropriately positioned," probed Helen, "as well as appropriately inclined?"

"There were a number of Royal figures invoved in all this," joined Chas. "Leaving aside the Mahidols out there in Bangkok, there were a several based in this country.......Mountbatten of course, and also Prince Chula, Bira as well, and the cousins' guests at Tredethy, Marina and Prince Philip, cousins themselves. My guess is that speaking with them in the '60s would have been a task strictly for your self."

"Chula first," obliged Denning, "Who, by the time I became aware of his significance, was a sick and dying man. Throat cancer claimed him at the end of '63. He was only 55, and I was too late."

"And Lord Louis?" asked Helen.

"He was able to coolly refute any suggestion that he'd put pressure on the Mahidols to abdicate. Yes, we know that he might have been *equipped* so to do, and even *hoping* so to do......."

"........ but in the event the opportunity was denied to him," said Chas, "by the murder of the King, a crime possibly instigated by a mishandling of those photos. Did you inform him that you'd been told of their existence?"

"No, out of a concern to protect my sources. I let him remind me that an abdication by the Mahidols was widely anticipated in diplomatic circles, and that he'd already placed on record his suspicion that the mother and brother could have had a hand in the shooting."

"So he was content to hold to that view," said Helen, "this man who was so famously good at believing himself always right."

"Quite," acknowledged the judge.

"And Marina?"

Denning hesitated. Words were being weighed, sensed Chas. He wouldn't interrupt.

"Marina was as straight as Dickie was crooked. She was genuinely fond of Chula and Bira, the Thais having been so good to her and the children after the death of George Duke of Kent in '42. With their decision not to abdicate firmly made, Chula showed impeccable loyalty to the surviving Mahidols and he strongly ecouraged Marina in her efforts to mend the damage wrought between them and the Windsors by Mountbatten's crude allegations. When Bhumibol brought his Queen to this country in 1960 it was she who entertained them, and young Alexandra was subsequently to make a number of visits to Bangkok."

"So how much would she have known of Mountbatten's scheming?" asked Helen.

"Not as much as Browning," answered Denning, evasively. "But this isn't to say she would have been surprised by the kind of stuff 'Boy' had let on to my brother. Marina was a shrewd and intelligent woman. She could see through her uncle Dickie well enough, and was capable of counselling young cousin Philip accordingly. It's a pity she didn't survive to provide a similar balance for young Charles."

"But to go back to '46," probed Helen. "You're saying that, then, Philip was too young and too junior to have been in the thick of all this."

"If that's what *you're* saying then I'll not disagree," replied Denning, so warily as to confirm for Chas that this was a duel of sorts. This man was guarding something....... but then, so too was he. If he was to tap the old man's reserve then he would have to give from his own.

"Well as expressed to you, this would appear to have been Marina's opinion," continued Helen, "and it seems she was anxious for us all to likewise believe that Chula's hands were equally clean."

"*Her* assessmet," confirmed Denning, looking across to Chas as if to almost invite contradiction.

"From a position of vantage do you mean?" fenced the boy. "Are we to infer that you knew her to have been better informed than perhaps

Chula, and certainly Philip......and that you discussed with her those matters which, but for his condition, you might have raised with Chula?"

"Such as," prompted Denning, eyes exhortingly a-twinkle, which Chas could not but reward.

"This impeccable loyalty of Chula's, we hear of......... you might have put it to her that, if not bought, then such devotion was certainly well compensated. My understanding is that after a struggle to make ends meet through the winter of 45/46 they were, within a couple of years, suddenly quite well-to-do again."

"A natural consequence of stability in Bangkok," countered Denning, "and of the French and Thai governments sorting their quarrel over the corner of Laos that the Japanese had annexed for the latter during the war. Be aware, please, that to attempt to draw one Royal on the finances of another was not, then, the done thing........ any more than it is now."

"And you're sure Chula's death wasn't hastened," pressed Chas brutally.

"I did put this to Marina," said Denning, keeping the Duchess of Kent alive in this conversation....... and this had to be for a reason, Chas knew.

"And her reply?"

"*Maybe*, but solely to ease the man's pain. I wasn't to allow myself to think that the man had been purposely silenced." Denning paused, as if in two minds. Chas waited. A revealation was to hand, he sensed, a ripening fruit that was about to drop. He needn't shake the tree. "Other lives, she went on to say, might have been less mercifully terminated in a hospital bed, but not this one."

"*Other lives*," repeated Helen softly, "other lives of relevance did she mean, and if so then other lives like whose?"

"Is this about that Stephen Ward character?" ventured Chas. "He that was brought to trial during the summer of '63 and supposedly took a fatal sleeping pill overdose before it concluded. Are we to understand that with better care he could have pulled through...... and that the lack of it owed something to his affiliation to the notorious coterie who styled themselves *The Thursday Club*?"

"No, it's not about Stephen Ward," said Denning. He hesitated. "But that wretched *Thursday Club* does feature. Marina was quite well known to a number of its members, and what she was inviting me to do was to consider the fate of one of its founding fathers, a figure so elevated by '56 as to have secured a cabin on the Royal Yacht for that world cruise occasioned by Philip's invitation to open the Melbourne Olympics. Three or four months it lasted, our Queen sitting it out, remaining in London for a difficult and lonely winter. Accepting Prime Minister Eden's resignation in the aftermath of Suez....."

"...... and inviting Macmillan to take on the tasks of first Minister," added Helen.

"But Marina would have us follow the Royal Yacht *Britannia* to the southern seas." Chas itched, now, to hear the name of this hanger-on.

"No she wouldn't," said Denning, "for this was her point then, and, accordingly, mine now. That cabin was never taken up. A month prior to embarkation the resrevation holder elected to enter hospital for minor surgical attention to an arthritic hip. There were complications it was said, and he died under anaesthetic."

"So do we have a name?" urged Chas.

"We do, and, perhaps more significantly, we have a profession. I've heard much from you this evening about photographs........some taken in Lausanne, and another taken a couple of years later in Cornwall. Now Marina couldn't have said this with any certainty, and nor could Valerie Profumo, but my brother was assured by Frederick 'Boy' Browning that all were taken by one lensman, the very same skilled exponent who, in '47, was hired by Prince Philip to take the official photographs of his wedding to Princess Elizabeth."

"A useful commission," said Helen

"The work was undeniably good," continued Denning, "and, seen all across the world, it was widely recognised as such. So much so that during the nine years that remained to him before that unexpected, suspiciously sudden and, at the age of 49, suspiciously early death, his services were in constant demand. Aristocrats, the stars of stage and screen, British and American...... hundreds would smile, pout, and scowl, for his camera. To this day, more than thirty years after they sat for him, his monochrome portraits of the likes of Marilyn Monroe and Rod Steiger carry iconic status."

"Please.......the name," pressed Chas.

Only to be denied a reply by a volley of rifle fire, automatic fire. Near, sudden, loud, it was at their door, the bullets ripping apart the handle and lock, the fragments forcing them to the floor, the elderly couple and the young, huddled together now, clutching for each other, clinging at the furniture.

Two figures entered; burly men, oriental of feature, each toting a gun and bristling intent.

"Take me," Denning nobly cried. "The youngsters know nothing."

A further burst was loosed........ three seconds worth of lead perforating the ceiling.

"You will speak when invited," barked he that brandished the smoking barrel. "Until then you listen, and you don't move."

Cord and tape was produced and each in turn bound and gagged. They were then to be guarded by just one, it appeared, as the other slipped from the room. What did this mean, wondered Chas. Were they hostages? They had to be, for if not then what else? What then might be the ransom; and of whom might it be demanded; and by who? And did this mean that a token might be taken and sent .... an item of jewellery perhaps, from Helen? Or was this a knife that now was being fetched, something that might carve a statement of intent as well as serve evidence of of identity?

Those departing footsteps could be heard, now, pacing across the gravel outside the window...... the surface over which they must have inched a stealthy approach. But now they stride as if to assert absolute command. The next move is ours, they state, as they slow and then swivel, and a vehicle door is heard to slide open. And there is certainly nothing lightweight in its mechanism, nor in that of an electric motor, of the kind that might drive the tail-lift of a smallish truck.

Something has been lowered, something wheeled and itself motorised, for it approaches with an altered whine, and to accompany the returning tread of footstep on gravel there is now the an unrelenting press off tyre. What was coming?

A voice might have helped, but there was none. Not until the wheelchair was in the room and its elderly occupant positioned to command all with stern gaze would their predicament be explained.

"*Japan's Greatest Victory*," he croaked. "And for Britain, her greatest defeat." Helen's book was gathered from the floor by one of the minders. "Do as I say and you may live to enjoy the prestige of having a rare signed copy. Lord Denning, Lady Denning, Mr Cross, and Miss Trembath........ Colonel Manasobu Tsuji introduces himself to each of you."

Alarmed glances were exchanged between the youngsters,

stunned as they'd been to have this apparition address them by name.

"In a moment, Miss Trembath," it continued, "I will have your gag removed. You will phone your father and relay to him my instructions......terms, these, which while by no means onerous will require putting with extreme care, given that there will be a knife at the throat of your young friend here. This satisfactorily done, I'm trusting that I can then retire to my motor home outside, due as I am for my evening's food and medication. As well as my larder and my pharmacy, the vehicle serves also as an office, one equipped so as to keep me in constant communication with those directing my mission. They have my progress reports from ground level, and also they have the benefit of an overview of the wider locality, placing them to provide, when required, immediate additional support."

Helford
Treath House (centre) from close to The Shipwrights.

An arrival

So traffic movemenent was being monitored, the relevant vehicle to be distinguished from the irrelevant, and of the former, those under control from those not.

For some were already moving to plan, one such in a specially provided Range Rover, modified this so as to register on the screen with beacon-like clarity.

It had been there as promised, on his touch down from Ireland, waiting in the carpark at Bristol Airport, glinting beneath an early afternoon sun with tank brim-filled with the finest performance petrol, plus, on the passenger seat, that neat little sketch map to guide him off the A30 towards St Breward and then out to Carroll's van.

More time might have better facilitated his business there, he thought, but now, if he was to stay on schedule then this would need to wait ....for a night and half a morning at least. He was expected in Helford, and his arrival there wasn't to be delayed. With the main event about to start he needed to be in the arena.

And his passenger.......?....... was keeping low.

*

Alan and Tony ....

........were in agreement. Coverack offered a good slip from which to launch the inflatable. Skirting Helston now, they could be there and un-hitched within twenty minutes. Cross had used the harbour before, having spent a month diving to the rusting carcass of the *Mohegan*, the liner that had famously and inexplicably wrecked itself on the nearby Manacles Reef with tragic loss of life. Familiar with the coast and the currents he was confident of steering them around to Gillan Creek and an access to the Bosahan Estate from the Manaccan side, an approach far less exposed than any made along the Helford River.

But were there really mischief-makers at large, wondered Tony Cross. Neither of them, not even Alan, could yet say for sure...... but with each step nearer so, through a shared sixth sense, the more strongly for both did a suspicion grow.

*

Stephanie......

......did know for sure, being acutely aware now of the critical moment that was upon her. Tucked low, as she was, between rear seat and hatchback she could do no more than guess at the driver's destination....... but they had arrived, she sensed, as McBeamish drove the Range Rover cautiously over Helford's main car park, passing on his way the one vehicle that remained therein, an unattended XR3 convertible.

It was an even chance, she'd reckoned. Were the driver, on halting, to come to the rear and open the hatch then she would need to drill him where he stood. Accordingly, silencer fitted, she held her pistol ready. And with not the slightest qualm, for she knew this to be a man who lived by the gun, and that come confrontation it had to be him or herself that so died. But she was prepared, so here it would be him........ *if* he came around to the rear.

So would he? Or, as she hoped, was he instead intent on a different direction...... and, unknowingly, on survival?

*

Later, at Kate's......

.......Jeremy had arrived from Bath, to be told by Gareth that Eamon would shortly be joining them, probably in the company of the intriguing Stephanie Wild. *Minutes*, the nurse had said, but that was an hour ago and as yet there'd been neither sight nor sound of either. And now Jim Busbridge would be waiting too, for when gathered they were to make their way up to his place. Kate had said that she would phone up to notify an imminent knock

But gathered, as yet, they were not. Perhaps it was time now to phone him anyway just to say as much. She dialled.

"Busbridge speaking."

"Kate here, Jim......."

".......and you're on your way?"

"Not yet, we're a couple short yet....... and I speak of the pair that had the least far to come."

"In which case I want you to allow me to look down."

"Do."

"And I'll be bringing a surprise guest. He's just turned up on my doorstep, and he has quite a tale for all of us. Five minutes?"

"Five minutes, Jim…….. I'll get the kettle on."

*

Mannacan

Their outboard now cut, the length of Gillan Creek was a comfortable tide assisted row for Tony Cross. Alan, at the stern, peered ahead through fast fading light, signalling the oarsman towards the oaks along the northern bank, at the same time listening hard between each gentle plop of the blades for anything on the shore that might have been stirred by their approach.

But nothing moved. Stealthily, quickly, they were ashore, and soon climbing the footpath past Trudgwell to crest the ridge behind Bosahan Barton. Then, on crossing the lane connecting remote St Anthony-in-Meneague to the rest of the world, they dropped into the wooded valley which would deliver them to the shore of the Helford River, less than a mile seaward of Treath, and Denning's holiday accommodation. If, as Grigson had been told, the old Judge was here in Cornwall, then this was where he was would be found…….. and perhaps already had been.

*

Ruthernbridge

Jeremy answered Jim's knock at the door, to immediately recognise the man's companion.

"Good evening Jim, and good evening to you also, Mr Hugh Trembath. Follow me through, do. A brew awaits. Mr Trembath, I believe you will already know those so far present."

He nodded to each. "Mr Hughes……. and Miss Rogers, I hope you can excuse my just turning up like this."

"If you bring something to share then you're welcome." Kate beckoned him into the spare kitchen table chair.

"But only after an explanation or two." Busbridge, ever curious, had had longer to marshal his questions. "That trip to Scotland made by your daughter…….was she party to that charade, or just another victim? And then there's the matter of a burglary over at Tredethy. We understand it was the security people, acting perhaps upon information passed by yourself."

"Explanations are due, I confess, and you shall have them when time allows. For the moment, though, you must listen to a demand." Trembath glanced at the kitchen clock. "Then, in twenty minutes will come your opportunity to check out what I'm having to say."

"Check out with who?" asked Busbridge.

"With the lad Mr Barnes here brought to Carwinion and introduced to us as Chas. I have a number, and briefly he will be by that phone. He will confirm what you're about to hear."

"Your demand?"

"Not mine, one that I merely relay."

"On whose behalf?"

Trembath glanced once more at the clock.

"Less than an hour ago, at Carwinion, I received a phone call from my daughter Helen. She told me she was at Treath, near Helford, at the holiday cottage of Lord Denning. I was to know that she and Chas Cross, together with Lord and Lady Denning, were being held at gun-point."

"Taken hostage, you mean," said Gareth.

"And 'demand' you mentioned," said Jeremy, "this suggesting a ransom. Do you come here because the price is one or more of us?"

"What they want," continued Hugh Trembath, "are two hand-written letters, and it's essential that they be the authentic documents and *not* copies. One, written by Prince Chula more than forty years ago, was sent to our old friend Walter Monckton. The other, less than two years old this, was written shortly before her death by a woman named Tania Crocker."

Jim and Gareth exchanged glances. They had these letters, yes, but how had this been made known to any beyond this cottage....... and what sort of significance could they be carrying to prompt the brandishing of fire arms? Stephanie would have said, thought Kate, for the woman herself carried a pistol, which the nurse had seen drawn, and used with impressive expertise. But she wasn't here, she was overdue, and likewise Eamon.

"Did the boy know about these letters?" asked Jeremy. "Could he have said about them?"

"Neither he nor his father have been this way since they appeared," said Jim.

"As Helen spoke over the phone," continued Trembath, "there was another voice in the background, quietly prompting."

"Male?" asked Kate.

"Male, yes, with what I'm pretty certain was an Irish accent."

"Perhaps explaining why Eamon's not here," suggested Gareth.

"Perhaps," agreed Busbridge, "but that's not to say that this was he. While there's plenty of Irishmen who'll tote a gun these days I've never reckoned Eamon Carroll to be one of them."

"Could he and your Stephanie Wild be in this together?" asked Jeremy.

"Another possibiliy," said Kate, "but no more than that. Tell us, Mr Trembath. Were we to agree to meet this ransom, how is it to be delivered?"

"I'm to cross the estuary on the first ferry of the morning. It runs from this, the Helford Passage side. I'll be met so that an exchange can be completed before boat makes its first return, hopefully bringing me, the youngsters and the Dennings to safety."

"*If* these people are to be believed," cautioned Busbridge. "Would they really release all prior to getting away? What makes them so confident of escape?"

"Because they know we'll be thinking they're the same ruthless bunch that did for Barry George," said Kate.

"And who would want to tangle with them, merely for the sake of a couple of letters," added Gareth. "I'm not sure that I would."

"And what about you, Mr Busbridge?" asked Trembath. "I understand that the *Tania* letter is yours, either to relinquish or not."

"OK, they've proposed this deal, and it's for us now to trust them to keep their side of it......... but I wish I could find this easier. I don't want to see anyone harmed, Mr Trembath, and least of all your daughter. If she's in danger then yes, I would hope that these letters might secure her safety, but I'm failing to see how simply handing them over guarantees that."

"Fair point," conceded Gareth. "Maybe this isn't so straightforward. I'm thinking it odd that there's been no mention of those Lausanne pictures. Each worth a thousand words, don't they say? Surely they'll have been told of them too."

"But they were mere copies," Kate reminded him, "whereas the letters you and Jim hold are originals. The *actual* Lausanne photos wouldn't have travelled far from Kensington Palace and now, from what you've been told by your old comrade, they're now likely to be in the hands of our security people, tucked away safely with that group photo raided from Tredethy."

"Also an original," nodded Jeremy. "And if, with the full collection now back under lock and key, the associated outbreak of Royal mischief making is checked then the good name of Mountbatten is upheld."

"And, so far," continued the nurse, "so all relatively harmless. But that far might not be far enough if we only have half the story. Alan as good as warned of this when last I spoke with him, and Stephanie has hinted likewise. There's another far from harmless agency out there, this they more than suspect. An agency with a parallel agenda......that was what Alan was suggesting. They might trust our Home Office to sit on those photos......"

"....... but these letters are a different matter," said Gareth.

"As are those rogue elements that can regularly sprout from the Irish Republican movement," offered Busbridge. "For them, Kellegher and Conlon were but one head of a Hydra."

"So how might we explain the Irish sounding voice we've heard of from Mr Trembath," asked Kate, "together, I suppose, with Eamon's non appearance here?"

"But that wouldn't have been he, down there on the Helford," said

Gareth, "not treating Chas so, surely."

"Then who?" pressed Kate.

"Someone acting upon information supplied by Eamon," reasoned Jeremy, "who I would guess to be a senior figure in the IRA, perhaps even McBeamish himself."

"So that would leave Eamon where?" Kate wanted to know.

"If no longer useful, then as a liability," said Jeremy grimly.

"Knowing too much to be allowed to live," nodded Jim. "He always had that worry. But we only speculate. He could be alive yet, and be just as baffled as we about what his top Command might have got itself mixed up in."

"But we're getting closer to knowing," said Kate. "Why else this deadline? They know we have the key pieces and they're out to stop us putting them together. Such time that is left to us thus becomes all the more valuable. We're not to relent."

"OK, so tell me the overview from Ruthernbridge," said Jeremy. "Think yourself to be in an operations room Mr Trembath. Listen closely. You start Kate. What *do* we see, and what not?"

"We know that during the time that his pal Pridi held political mastery over Thailand, Mountbatten hoped to supplant the Royal Mahidols with Chula and thereby consolidate his own influence in the area……. an influence that not all trusted. In this, though, he was thwarted…… by the death of the the elder Mahidol, by the resolve of the younger to take on the Kingship, and by a subsequent discrediting of Pridi. Certain people, we're not sure who, were sufficiently wary of Mountbatten to have the King killed. They'd been told of Lord Louis' plans, probably by a trusted confidante of his……."

"……… but again we're not sure who," joined Busbridge.

"Quite," continued Kate, "but were we to establish the identity of this informant, and his or her motive, then this must take us closer to establishing the identity of the informed."

"The latter almost certainly being a State agency. A ruthless executive arm granted a quite fearsome autonomy, for what else could field such a range of killing talent," said Busbridge, "from the IJA cannibal to the IRA executioner…….neither being your run of the mill hired gun!"

"So which State?" pressed Jeremy. "You must have a shortlist."

"We know that in Paris and The Hague there were concerns about the Pridi controlled Thailand," continued Busbridge. "Defeated in '40, driven from their far east colonies in '42, the French and the Dutch were anxious now to reclaim that on which they'd once drawn so freely. Against them were ranged those forces of Nationalism and Communism that had been agitating since the Great War and which now looked to seize their opportunity. Thailand, never once colonised, might have been immune to the virulence...."

".......but this wasn't preventing the country being a carrier, with no part more given to incubating and spreading this contagion than a too loosely policed Bangkok," said Jeremy.

"An open sore, for some" agreed the nurse, "to be poulticed by a return of Marshal Pibul, so recently castigated for being a pro Japanese Quisling. And this is indeed what happened, Pridi being unable to resist rumours of an involvement in the King's death."

"*Some* Dutchmen or *some* Frenchmen?" asked Trembath.

"Those letters now demanded, Chula's of early '46 and Tania's of early '86, they would tend to point to France." Busbridge was cautious. "And there were later events in '46, such as at Haiphong, and a much more recent event in New Zealand which reinforce that suspicion."

"New Zealand?" Trembath was puzzled.

"The *Rainbow Warrior* outrage," said Kate. "A propaganda disaster for the French such as they wouldn't want repeated."

"And we shouldn't forget how in the Far East the shaping of the post-war peace was left to a particular breed of warlord," explained Busbridge, "of the kind epitomised by MacArthur, the military supremo of the Caesar mentality. My friend Monsieur Boulle carries painful memories of the French equivalent."

So we shouldn't be thinking of Maurice Papon as a one-off aberration," said Jeremy. "But who would have betrayed to them details of Mountbatten's scheming, and why? Who would you put in the frame, Jim? Who might have been trusted enough to have been allowed access to those Lausanne photos?"

"Those already in the frame, Jeremy........ the frame that hung at Tredethy. For him or for her, why look any further?" Busbridge glanced at this watch and then at Trembath, an understandably anxious father. But he didn't need the man at his shoulder while phoning down to Helford for that brief word which might be allowed from Chas. "If you'll permit me to collect my thoughts prior to making this call," he ventured, as tactfully as the circumstances allowed "Jeremy, if Mr Trembath is ready to leave this to me you might show him Kate's montage. We can hear then what he makes of the true missing men, Monckton and Profumo, each a former associate of his father, and also of a final addition that could astound even yourself."

Jack P   Chula   Boy   Philip   Walter

Marina   Tania   A(nna)

*

Stephanie Wild……

……having gambled successfully, had no intention now of squandering the position and time won. She'd stayed low, she'd listened, she'd watched, and where she was and why was becoming more clear. The reality was hardening, displacing vague fear and conjecture.

Wriggling forwards between the passenger headrests and wary of what might have been an over-noisy door she'd slipped from the Range Rover feet first, gun still in hand, via the rearmost nearside window. On finding her feet, she'd then crept towards the Lodge that had drawn McBeamish, getting close enough to its main downstairs window to hear much of what was being said within….. including that initial phone call made to Carwinion. Enabled thus to identify those held, their captors, and their captors' demands she'd slid back into the cover of the most conveniently near of Bosahan's extensive proliferation of mature rhododendruns.

Shelter it offered, and also an unobstructed view of what was obviously Tsuji's mobile home….. so here she would wait, she'd decided, wait and observe. She'd overheard that soon he would be out to resume residence, and re-appear he did, McBeamish this time accompanying the chair and helping with the lift before following the invalid aboard.

That had been thirty fleeting minutes ago, through which she'd watched the screened windows for the silhouetted movement that might announce the Irishman's emergence. And this had to happen soon, she reckoned, if the man was to be back in the Lodge and set, there, to take the invited return phone call.

And yes, here was the anticipated movement…….and another, unanticipated. For her unobstructed view was no longer that. A crouching figure had moved across into her line of sight, and also reacting to the window blind was now backing towards her so as to unknowingly share her cover, under that same voluminous evergreen. A fellow interloper, it seemed, but would this figure be alone or accompanied? Should she shrink back further to remain unseen, or should she use her gun? A decision was required.

She stepped forward and jabbed her pistol between the male shoulder blades.

"This is a gun plus silencer," she said firmly. "Walk backwards with me, just six paces. Turn when I say, but not before." The man complied, raising his hands as he did so. Both looked ahead. Both saw McBeamish step from the van, re-fasten the door, and stride then for the Lodge. "Now explain yourself," the woman ordered.

"If I can turn?"

"Do, but this pistol will remain aimed at your upper torso."

"I'm looking for Denning and his wife. I'm with the Home Office. I do VIP protection."

"You're at the right place, but what they're needing now is a rescue specialist. Are you alone? Are you armed?

"No and no. I've one companion. The sea is his element, and it's by sea we've come. I've just sent him up to check out the carpark. We're looking for a red XR3 convertible."

"He'll find it, close to the Range Rover in which this fellow we've just watched arrived. I came with him, having stowed myself behind his rear seat."

"Chancy," Grigson glanced down at the pistol, "but I suppose you're appropriately equipped....."

".....and appropriately skilled." The gun stayed aimed.
"So whose is that XR3?"

"Belongs to a girl called Helen Trembath. Her father lives over on the Fal, she works in London. She might have a friend with her, a lad called Chas. He lives and works in Plymouth. My companion we spoke of, he's his father."

"And they too came here looking for Denning?"

"It seems so," answered Grigson.

"And this Chas....... trusting his father as you obviously do," tested Stephanie, "you would know that he maintains a close friendship with another young lady. *Younger* lady should I say, for I believe she still attends a Plymouth School."

"That would be Sally Shaw," confirmed Alan. "Have you met?"

"No.....but I have heard mention of her, while at *Jamaica Inn*, enjoying a drink in the company of a former Welsh Guardsman, a nurse currently working at Bodmin's St Lawrence Hospital, and a decidedly curious fellow........."

"........ called Jim, Jim Busbridge," said Alan needing no second invitation to confirm his credentials. "You speak also of Kate, and Gareth, and perhaps you had an Irish sounding Londoner with you too, a Mr Eamon Carroll."

311

"I do, and I believe I encounter, now, the fellow they'd almost given up on, even if still being held still in deepest esteem. Alan is it?"

"It is, and your name?"

"Stephanie Wild."

"Of whom I've heard nothing."

"And that, perhaps, is no one's fault but your own."

"Point taken, Ms Wild, and if I've much to catch up on then here's the place to start. You've been here the longer, and obviously got closer. I want your take on what's going on."

"Stay here, then, while I again drop around to the Lodge window. In just a few minutes you'll hear the phone. If I can get the gist of what's said then I'll be all the more useful. If I might leave you to watch that van."

*

At Ruthern.....

.......Jim and Gareth were as one. Nothing, they agreed, mattered more than the welfare of those youngsters. Those letters could be surrendered, even if their insights were thus to be suppressed........for given that what they touched upon might also be a *State* secret, who would be so un-patriotic as to claim any conflict of loyalty? Provided, of course, that the bargain was honoured with the safe deliverance of all four hostages, a point made loudly, if again somewhat emptily, by Jim, during the brief exchange he was allowed with the captors. But at least there was some comfort in this re-iteration for the removed but still listening Hugh Trembath, as there was in a conveyed reassurance that, so far, all held were unharmed.

Jeremy, meanwhile, quietly considered the montage, more than compensating for the anxious father's understandable indifference

"Valerie Hobson," he declared, "who at the time was the Mrs Anthony Havelock-Allen, the husband being himself a renowned film director. Certainly an intriguing addition........ "

".......particularly with this oblique *Estella* reference made to her in Tania's letter." said Jim. "Take this copy. I made three or four before I came down, on realising that my hours with the original might be numbered. I used my fax."

"So Tania is telling us what?" posed Jeremy. "After Jack Profumo lost his Kettering seat in '45 he was offered a short term army commission, a post that took him frequently out to Japan. Might this be something to do with that?"

"A possibility," said Kate, "but only that, given that he and Valerie were a good while yet from being the item they were to become."

"Yes," agreed Jim, "an outcome one certainly couldn't have guessed at from that picture at Tredethy. If that and Tania's letter together suggest anything it's that we shouldn't overlook Prince Philip as the possible Judas."

"And Monckton's involvement would, if anything, tend to support this," added Gareth.

"Rendering Profumo's presence merely incidental?" Jeremy was doubtful. "Just now, when talking of that framed photo, some one said *Why look any further?*"

"Because we have so little time for wider speculations," suggested Kate.

"Fair enough," acknowledged the lecturer, "but ought we not to consider who could have been *behind* the camera? Why should we be assuming his to have been an inert presence?"

"We thought it could have have been Bira," said Busbridge, "but for no better reason than his absence from the group."

"So hardly conclusive," said Jeremy. "I'll put it to you that it could just as easily have been another guest. Valerie would have known a number of photographers, as theatrical people do. They're all the time posing for the lens. I didn't see the photo at Tredethy, but you did Jim. Allowing for the passage of years, give it marks out of ten for professionalism."

Busbridge thought back...... and yes, the composition was far from haphazard, and the equipment used clearly good, far better than that used to snap Blunt and Burgess at the St Enodoc golf club. Jeremy had raised a valid point.

"Now you ask, I'd give it nothing less than eight. It was a fine piece of work, and understandably prized by the owner."

"And Gareth, those copies you had of the Lausanne prints, they were sharp enough to suggest that the originals might have been the product of no mean talent......agreed?"

313

"Agreed."

"So what if the *same* talent was responsible for both sessions? Would this not prompt a reversal of our whole approach to these images. Instead of taking the photographer's view to consider Chula's group of guests......."

"...... we might usefully take the guests' perspective," nodded Jim, "and consider the identity of the he or the her behind the camera. A character who, as you say Jeremy, might have been particularly well known to the film star."

"Or might *be* known," reminded Kate, "for if Valerie Profumo is still alive then why not also such an acquaintance?"

"Alive or not, it's a scenario that might better explain the distinct priorities of our separate adverseries," claimed Gareth. "Home Intelligence, Alan's mates, they've been concerned to secure the original photographs, those held by the Princess of Wales in Kensington Palace, and that which hung at Tredethy."

"Because a professional studio will endow its own prints with a unique forensic signature," suggested Busbridge, "for they will age at a specific rate, and in a specific way, according to the specific development techniques preferred by the specific practitioner."

"And as well as accurately dated, the originals could also be matched," reasoned Kate, "the Lausanne photos with the Tredethy."

"Which, together, might then be ascribed to a particular studio," said Jeremy.

"And the contrasting priorities of these other people, the IRA-IJA collaboration?" posed Kate.

"They've been after original *letters*, that can be put with an original *journal*," answered Jeremy, thinking this out as he spoke, "surmising correctly that the suppression of the pictures can be left, as Gareth says, to Home Intelligence."

"Those differing priorities reflecting different agendas," added Kate, remembering her last conversation with Alan. "The concern of the Home people has been to protect Mountbatten's reputation, Diana's target. The Lausanne photos are evidence of his scheming, but not of any muderous intent."

"But murderers there were," continued Busbridge, "and covering *their* guilt amounts to an altogether different challenge."

"And we're saying that that they might have been prompted in this deed by a close pal of Mountbatten," continued Gareth, "and that he might have been this photographer."

"And if so," said the nurse, "then for the purposes of the betrayal this professional wouldn't have needed to use the Lausanne prints he'd provided for Mountbatten, or any copies of them sneaked from Supreme Command Headquarters. He might simply have used more film in Lausanne than he'd let on, keeping some of it back so as to then secretly develop a few extra originals for his own use......when appropriate."

"So would that have been for naked cash, or for career advancement?" asked Gareth. "Are we looking for a photographer who suddenly became very famous in France, acquiring for himself a chateau or two in the proccess, or a Cote d' Azure villa maybe?"

Jeremy turned to Hugh Trembath.

"Your father," he said. "Is he at Carwinion?"

"He is."

"Sir Edward?" queried Kate.

"His era," explained the lecturer. "He'll surely know a few names. None of us will get much sleep tonight, and if we're to be down at *The Ferryboat* first thing why don't we take our pyjamas down to Hugh's......"

"....... and see if we can't profitably jog the old boy's memory," agreed the son. "Yes, consider yourself invited. I can take a couple in my car. If we're standing together on this then yes, the best idea has to be to move as one. Mr Busbridge, you said earlier that you would be phoning the boy's father. Invite him along too."

An attempt was promptly made, here on Kate's phone at Ruthern, then another a little later before their departure from Tremore, but in each instance, of course....... no reply.

*

While at Helford…..

…….. this was of little consequence to Tony Cross. Her eavesdrop done, Stephanie had re-met with Alan and together they'd retreated from the lodge to rendezvous with the latter's apprentice spook under the edge of the carpark trees. Now, listening closely, the boy's father was hearing as much as he might have learned through the phone in Plymouth, and plenty more besides.

"Comfortable they are not," stressed the woman, "but they'll be safe enough for the night, provided we don't alarm their captors. It's only a couple of letters that they're after and they've been led to expect that these will be delivered. I've heard nothing this evening to suggest they might not earn the release of all held…… the Dennings, Helen Trembath……"

"…… and my Chas," added Cross

"And your Chas," confirmed Grigson. "But Stephanie tells us that the old Jap running things from that motor caravan has announced himself to be one Colonel Tsuji, he of the notorious appetite for gruesome ritual……. a taste too recently indulged, we fear. Are we to merely hope that there'll be no repeat prior to an escape?"

"How he intends to get away will determine what he takes," said Stephanie, "and as to this I've so far had no clue."

"And to where he might be aiming to take those letters?" asked Cross

"Is similarly obscure."

"And this is where it might help to know just who it is that they have been hired by," said Alan. "It's a persuasive paymaster that can secure the services of Tsuji and McBeamish together."

"Persuasive, and powerful, and stealthy," listed Stephanie. "The hidden hand, but that's not to say it will stay so. If, for now, we see its agents pulling as one, my guess each will have been handed a separate job description."

"And if *you* suspect this then, singly, *they* will too," nodded Cross, "and with this would come a mutual wariness, each wondering if the other might be waiting for the moment to terminate the collaboration."

"So cracks of mistrust we watch for," said Stephanie "such as can only widen overnight, and perhaps, before morning, disclose what's behind this nasty little escapade." And, hopefully, a good deal more besides, she thought to herself. For having worked and waited long, an opportunity to learn more about her father's death might at last be opening.

*

Carwinion

"I said at the outset, Hugh, that you shouldn't be involving the girl in this. See, now, the fix she's in."

"Perhaps you might have made your point more firmly, Sir Edward," suggested Jeremy, "but what's done now is done. There's no harking back. If we're to face the consequences together then we can do without recrimination. Blame is worse than useless."

"Did she know she was being used?" asked Busbridge. "This might have a bearing on our next step."

"Hugh…..?" prompted his father.

"Not at the time of that trip to Scotland. She was to find out later though, and, as a result, our last telephone conversation was far from cordial. She'd been humiliated at work, she felt….."

"……where it had emerged that that Pierre Boulle correspondence was phoney," said Jim.

"But there could be a French dimension to this nevertheless," added Kate.

"Really?" said Sir Edward, his surprise being noted by Jeremy.

"More of that later," said the lecturer. "We were wondering, Sir Edward, if you had a contact number for Jack Profumo. We understand that he and his wife have a place near yours up in London……"

"……and thought that you might still be on speaking terms," added Gareth, "given that for many years you were Parliamentary colleagues."

Sir Edward hesitated, and then…..

"When we meet, yes, we are on speaking terms. But I would phone them only as a very last resort, particularly in circumstances such as these."

"You're saying there might be listeners?" pounced Gareth.

317

"I am."

"In which case we'll first see what's to be made of your own recollections," said Jeremy, almost hungrily.

"Concerning what?"

"Concerning *who*, more like...... we're after a photographer, a little older than yourself probably, but by no more than ten years. He would have had his own studio, and this would have been frequented by stars of stage and screen, the aristocracy, and even Royalty."

"So were he to have survived, we're talking of a man in now his eighties," said Hugh. His father looked thoughtful.

"And you're thinking he might have taken this picture that hung at Tredethy?" Sir Edward eventually said. "Remind me who was in it."

"Royalty aplenty," obliged Busbridge, "Prince Chula, Prince Philip, Princess Marina; then a brace of Royal minders..... 'Boy' Browning, and Walter."

"Plus the Profumos, Jack and Valerie," continued Kate, "well before they were married, she still a film actress."

"And there was also a Tania," completed Jim, "who I've tried calling on recently, only to learn from her husband that she died last year. He passed me this letter written by her."

"Part of the ransom being asked," explained Trembath junior, "so think, father, do."

"I am thinking, and several names spring to mind......"

"......but for your grand daughter's sake we're needing you to select just one," pressed Jeremy.

"In which case it would have to be Nahum, Baron Nahum."

"*A Baron*?" queried Gareth. "By birth is that?"

"Baron was a first name."

"His Christian name."

"Something I hesitate to say. For one thing he came from a family of Jews, well known to the City of Manchester where I studied. For another, he dropped his surname....... and by everyone and anyone who afterwards encountered him, professionally or socially, he was known and addressed simply as 'Baron'."

"Now *that* brings it back to me," said Busbridge with a snap of his fingers as he rose from his chair.

"What?" enquired Jeremy.

"It's been nagging at me since my return with Tania's letter, something her husband said which I've felt I ought to remember......"

".......but couldn't."

"Because at the time so much else was opening up, all seemingly of closer relevance. And it was barely an aside, in fact it was just one word."

"And that one word?" pressed Gareth.

"Was '*ironically*' .... the old gent was talking about the sudden death back in '85 of Bira, Chula's brother. He'd collapsed on an underground platform, I was told, and the actual station was mentioned......'*ironically at Baron's Court*'..... those were his very words and, intended as such or not, I'm now hearing a hint. I'm guessing that this name 'Baron' might have meant something to Tania, that it held a significance which she didn't dare commit to paper. What's the time?"

"Not yet nine," said Sir Edward, glancing across to the elegant mantelshelf clock.

"Well if you would allow me to use your phone I've got the old boy's number."

"Feel free," said Sir Edward.

Busbridge strode to the phone and dialled. All watched. None spoke...... only the curious man.

"Mr Crocker....... James Busbridge here, the fellow to whom you gave Tania's letter."

"And you're finding that helpful?" came a frail reply

"We are."

"Good...... because as I thought I made clear before you left, there's not a lot more I can add."

"One small thing, perhaps....... less to do with the letter....."

".......than?"

".......the way you qualified the train station platform on which Bira collapsed. 'Ironically at Baron's Court' were your words, and they've prompted us to speculate on the role of Baron Nahum in all this. Was he at Tredethy, behind the camera?"

A pause followed. Busbridge waited, as it lengthened. And then......

"He was."

"And two years before that, could he have been in Lausanne?"

"Not unlikely is it?"

"So does he still live?"

319

"More than thirty years ago he died......unexpectedly. He went into hospital for a minor op and died on the table, not yet fifty.........a sudden end for a spectacular career."

"What if he betrayed Mountbatten back in '46?"

"To whom and why?"

Busbridge blocked the mouthpiece. "To whom and why?" he repeated, looking to Jeremy.

"To the French let's say," obliged the lecturer, "and perhaps out of loyalty to his Jewish bretheren."

The answer was duly repeated by Busbridge "What would Tania have said to that......right path or wrong?" he then added.

"It's a dangerous path that you follow, she would have said," intoned the voice which, even at such distance, implied strongly that for any sensible person this ought to be answer enough. "I can say no more, so I would be obliged if you troubled me no more. I wish you goodnight."

The phone was dropped, leaving Busbridge to do likewise and turn then Jeremy.

"Well you certainly came to the point there. Left to my self I don't think I would have even thought of anything so......"

"..... so forthright, so specific?" Jeremy was unrepentant. "With that charm of yours, Jim, you're a master angler. We've seen that. What we must cope with now, though, is the bull. Cornered, we can only take it by the horns. *Right path or wrong*........ what was his answer?"

"We're on a dangerous path, he warned. Baron Nahum has been dead for more than thirty years, having failed to survive what I'm told was just minor surgery."

"Yes," Sir Edward broke in. "I think I remember now. That was during the build up to the Suez thing. Newspaper space was at a premium, of course, and for the front pages the story was just a one-day thing. His name was to crop up a few years later when Princess Margaret married Armstrong-Jones, now Lord Snowdon."

"Because he too was a photographer?" wondered Kate.

"One who'd actually made his name working under Baron. That would have been in the early and mid 50s when the studio got truly busy. But if we're talking about the full ten years between '46 and '56, something else that Baron cultivated over that time was the infamous 'Thursday Club', a kind of lads' night out for those who considered theselves above such concepts as austerity and rationing. Dickie

Mountbatten, his brother Milford Haven, their nephew Prince Philip, Iain Macleod MP, Fleet St editors, showbiz celebrities……

"…….a rare gang indeed," nodded Gareth.

"As well as taking the wedding photos, Baron also organised Philip's stag night."

"But on again to that death in '56." Jeremy was impatient. "This would have been against an intriguing political backdrop……. the Suez *thing* as our host put it. In this, again, we find a French dimension and a Jewish, the pretext for the Anglo-French grab for the canal having been cooked up with Israel."

"But your raising of that *loyalty to his Jewish bretheren* issue just now had little to do with the events of '56. This, Jeremy, is down to your historian's eye for what being a Jew might have meant ten years earlier, back in '46, the year in which Nahum might have betrayed his illustrious patron. The inference I took, and I'm sure that old Crocker did too, was that where they came into conflict, a superficial loyalty to the Thursday Club fraternity was likely to run a very poor second to a more fundamental sort governed by common ethnicity. Am I right?"

"Something like that," admitted Jeremy. "I'll piece together the political jigsaw far more readily than the emotional, so even for a personal betrayal I'll want a political explanation."

"But one derived from a firm identification with the aspirations of his own race," reasoned Busbridge, "rather than the aspirations of Marshal Pibul in Thailand and the French in Indo China."

"Such advantage that accrued there being merely incidental," joined Gareth, "So what was the kick back for Nahum if not of the *thirty pieces of silver* variety?" asked Gareth.

"Something that the French government might either give to, or withhold from, the nascent state of Israel," answered the lecturer with all the assurance that a barrister might display before a jury.

"The Zionists again," nodded Busbridge, thinking back to the summer. "And yes, why not? Except, I suppose, that in '46 there was no Israel. Britain governed Palestine on behalf United Nations, as previously mandated by the League of Nations."

"Granted, yes," conceded Jeremy, "but we must remember that the two pronged offensive which was to secure the Jews statehood within two years was by then gathering considerable momentum."

"*Two* pronged?" queried Gareth.

"The reputable and the disreputable."

"Meaning......"

"......the above board diplomatic offensive being conducted legitimately by The Jewish Agency offices in London, Washington, and the UN, as distinct from the terrorist campaign being waged by the armed militia groups mainly in Palestine itself, and mainly against the British, the policing power."

"And, at the UN, France had been given one of the five permanent seats on the Security Council," said Busbridge, "this making them a prime target of David Ben Gurion's..........is this your drift Jeremy?"

"As regards the reputable, yes, but I fear that the problems we face here tonight might be more related to the disreputable campaign and its never ending aftermath. You mentioned the name Ben Gurion, Jim, so I'll throw you another. A very recent Premier of Israel, this, who in fact still lives. Back in the '70s, on reaching agreement with Sadat of Egypt at Camp David, he was awarded a half share of a Nobel Peace Prize, only to return to bellicose type just a few years later when looking this time to tighten his northern border. I speak of course of......"

"........Menachem Begin," Busbridge put in.

"The very same," continued Jeremy, "but for the moment we must try to forget those recent '83 massacres facilitated in Beirut, at Sabra and Chatila, and even the atrocity actually perpetrated in the Jerusalem suburb of Deir Yassin thirty five years before. Instead, we must consider what in '46 he unashamedly represented. Now, his followers in the Likud party, headed by his successor Yitzhak Shamir, are reconciled to democracy .... but this wasn't always the case. For many years they were of the *Irgun* conviction, professing openly that elections were a luxury that the to fragile State of Israel could not afford. Military rule, they felt, was a prequisite to survival, and from without and within any Arab protest was to be met with force."

"Echoes then of Stern Yair," said Kate.

"Exactly, but things were never going to become quite so fascist for as long as Ben Gurion and the subsequent succession of elected Labor Party Premiers prevailed, and one reason that they *did* prevail for so long over Begin's hard line tendency was the manner in which the differences between the reputable and disreputable were brought to a head over the *Altalena*. Do you remember the *Altalena*, Sir Edward?"

"I do, she was a ship. The British mandate to rule Palestine expired, I think, on a day in May 1948. The world had been led to expect that the Jewish Agency would proclaim Israel's statehood on that very day, appointing David Ben Gurion as their democratically accountable Premier, he to exert civilian control over their *Haganah* defence force. The *Irgun*, though, had different ideas. While conceding that Ben Gurion's winning of the wider world's good opinion might have been essential in *establishing* a Jewish state, they were unconvinced, as you've said, that its subsequent *survival* wouldn't require something more muscular."

"Only the *Irgun* would see off the anticipated Arab reaction," repeated Gareth, "a stance that immediately undermines Ben Gurion. With his essential work done, he and his *Haganah* become, in Begin's view, a liability."

"And this ship?" prompted Kate.

"Had been purchased by the *Irgun*," explained Sir Edward, "I think in America, and then loaded to the brim in Europe with weapons to be shipped onto an *Irgun* controlled dock as soon as possible after British Naval patrols along the coast of Israel had ceased."

"So on the very first day of Ben Gurion's stewardship over his brand new State," said Kate, "and in defiance of the kind of civillian supervised order that he was hoping to establish therein."

"That was the plan," confirmed Jeremy. "Bear in mind that while Begin and Ben Gurion had seemed united in the struggle to oust the British and intimidate the Arabs, *at the same time each was plotting against the other*, knowing full well that once Israel was on the map only one style of self rule could prevail.

"But Ben Gurion emerged as the great father-of-the-nation statesman," said Gareth, "so we know now that Begin's plan must have miscarried."

"There were delays," continued Jeremy. "The *Altalena* was a month late in leaving for the new Israel, a critical month during which Ben Gurion was able to consolidate his position, cleverly using a UN imposed cease fire to spike the initial Arab offensive. He and the *Haganah* thus won time in which to show the doubters wrong, and by the time their ship appeared off Tel Aviv Begin's *Irgun*, touted thirty days earlier as the vital alternative administration, were being perceived as a potential international embarrassment."

"A month being a long long time in politics," chuckled Gareth. "So tell us Jeremy, what happened to the ship and its cargo?"

"Sensing, while waiting in Israel, that he'd lost his chance and that disaster loomed Begin, already had tried to signal the captain to turn around; he even attempted to negotiate a compromise with Ben Gurion....... but all to no avail. This was the latter's chance to put an end to his rival's totalitarian ambitions, and it wasn't passed up. By pretending to listen the vessel was lured into a cove to the north of Tel Aviv, and allowed there to be almost half emptied....... until there suddenly appeared on the cliffs and around the beach two *Haganah* regiments, complete with tanks and artillery, led by the Ben Gurion's redoubtable enforcer Moshe Dayan. Offshore, awaiting orders, stood three Israeli corvettes."

"So there was no escape," said Kate.

"Begin's people were surrounded," said Sir Edward. "Ordered to surrender he attempted to escape by rowing out to his doomed ship. Off the *Altalena* then set in desperate flight, hotly pursued by those corvettes. The relatively moderate Ben Gurion had out-manoeuvred and outlawed his more militant rival......"

"......and in the space of an afternoon had elevated himself from brigand to statesman," said Busbridge sagely. "A small step for man but a vast stride for a politician. Attempted by many, accomplished by few."

"So how did this end?" asked Gareth.

"Under bombardment the ship ran aground close to Tel Aviv," said Jeremy. "Begin was one of the few to escape, thanks to a plucky group of supporters on the shore venturing out to what had become a time bomb.......in a pleasure craft of all things. His bid for absolute power having failed, it was left to him to instruct what remained of his *Irgun* militia to henceforward take orders from the *Haganah* command in the continuing struggle against the common foe, the Arabs."

"And as a politician it was back to the bottom of the greasy pole," said Gareth. "He had to start again, this time holding a regard for the conventions of democracy."

"Yes, and to his credit he was eventually, thirty years later, to arrive at the top of the heap," said Jeremy, "and be internationally honoured, astonishingly, with half a Nobel prize! This wouldn't have been achieved, though, without Ben Gurion's firmness over the *Altalena*. It is a fact that previously, in British Palestine, the Jewish Agency had been happy to collaborate with the terrorists, but once a legitimised Party of government it needed to publicly repudiate what had overnight become an outmoded arrangement. This it did with the stand made over that ship, and by dissociating itself from the *Irgun* excesses it also sanitised a parliamentary opposition in which Begin's *Likud*, effectively a rebranding of his militia, was to eventually prosper."

"To the point of being elected to power ten years ago," nodded Hugh Trembath, "but now tell me how this relates to the current plight of my daughter."

*

Helford

How might these people be intending to get away? This was the question on Stephanie's mind as she crossed the wooden footbridge at the very heart of of the village, her route across the tide filled stream to its one pub, *The Shipwright's*, where she would find well earned refreshment, and a much needed toilet facility.

She considered the possibilities. *En masse* would it be, or in deliberately reduced number? By land, by sea, or by air even? As deadly as they might be they were mere agents, and, as such, one or more would be charged with either taking those retrieved letters to the principal, or supervising a verifiable destruction.

But who might those people be, that major power of whom Tania's letter had warned. Taking the lane, now, which rose past the Post Office before dipping again to the waterside pub she noticed a call box to her right, something she might use on her return.

Commited to memory she had a 'hot' line number to enable her, if need be to get through to her team leader at Morwenstow. The access was initially designed to enable information to be fed *in*, such as when an off duty officer noticed an irregular shipping or aircraft movement which might look to be potentially baffling for the deskbound at their screens. The channel could be used both ways though, and whilst at work she had herself occasionally fielded *enquiries* from others similarly privileged seeking to place a puzzling local perception into a wider and more understandable context, usually to leave them less perturbed.

Tonight there were questions she could ask, but how were they to be phrased? This would need to be thought through whilst in *The Shipwrights*

*

Carwinion

"Who might be desperate to hide what?" began Jeremy. "The question throughout....and my response is to suggest that the assistance secured by the *Irgun* in this doomed venture with the *Altalena* would only have been secured at a price, but obviously not with those official funds held by the Jewish Agency."

"So it would have been ill-gotten hard cash?" said Hugh Trembath.

"Partly, supplemented with ill-gotten hard information, together with a pledge to the payee to maintain a strict silence on how and where this might have been used."

"Ill-gotten by the likes of Baron Nahum," said Kate. "Is this what you mean?"

"That *facade* of the *bon viveur* might well have concealed something more calculating," continued the lecturer. "See him for a minute as a sponge and imagine, with his connections, the kind of information he might have been absorbing."

"And imagine how carefully he might have been squeezed for this by the English section of Begin's international network," said an enthusiastic Busbridge for whom Jeremy's logic clearly carried appeal.

"But merely banking this wouldn't have been enough," said Gareth, "given that they were in a race against time."

"An optimal immediate worth had to be secured, and this meant finding a buyer similarly pressed, and with something worthwhile to exchange," followed Sir Edward."

"Exactly," glowed Jeremy, "and I can tell you that while the *Altalena* might have been purchased in America in '47, it crossed the Atlantic early the next year with an empty hold."

"To be loaded where?" Gareth was intrigued

"*Port- de-Bouc* which is where the main highway from Nimes to

Marseille touches the south coast of France."

"Another French connection then," said Busbridge.

"Very much so," continued Jeremy. "For eighteen months before, in '46...... note the year....... Begin had been allowed to establish a headquarters in Paris and from here scour Europe for arms, many exhumed from the concealed arsenals of wartime resistance groups. Fighting men were also enlisted, and for a while an organisation already murdering Britons in Palestine was permitted to muster an army within the borders of *la belle France*, a country recently liberated at the cost of much British blood!"

"And when the *Altalena* docked, out it was all brought," followed Gareth.

"Munitions and men, from their scattered barns and billets," nodded Jeremy, "to be taken down to *Port-de-Bouc* and there loaded."

"But there was a critical delay, you said," remembered Kate. "Was this a kind of sabotage by officialdom?"

"There was a strike by French Muslim longshoremen, who, on learning of the ship's cargo and destination, came out in sympathy with their Palestinian co-religionists."

"And you don't think the French government had a hand in this," persisted the nurse.

"I don't think so, for by this time, with a UN imposed truce and arms embargo known to be iminent, they wanted the whole lot on its way and off their hands before any awkward questions were tabled by fellow Security Council members."

"Your point here being that the French authorities were ready to go out on a limb to assist the *Irgun*," said Busbridge, "in defiance of UN and home Muslim sentiment."

"And my question is *why*," replied Jeremy. "What was in it for them? Begin had dangled something, and they'd taken it......and perhaps knowing how this came to be used, he might have been in a position to demand that the price, effectively a platform from which to make his armed grab for Israel, be exacted in full."

"So Begin, you're saying, received information from Baron which was then passed on to the French Government," reasoned Kate, "and acting upon this information they instructed an agent to kill Ananda......"

"........ so as to thwart Mountbatten's attempt to consolidate Pridi's hold on Thailand," continued Gareth, "this to give them, the

French, a better chance of reasserting colonial rule in neighbouring Laos and Cambodia. If so, then with a loose word from Begin even greater opprobrium at the UN might have awaited....... and might still await, of course, even to this day."

"And also, now, in the present day councils of Europe, in Brussels, Stasbourg, and The Hague." For Jim this was fun. "Not forgetting NATO...... naughty girl that Diana. For *realpolitik* dictates that France be celebrated as our esteemed partner. One can see why our Secret Service has been concerned to sweep through the Palace!"

"And also why the same hitman who did the business in Bangkok should be re-hired now to tidy things in Cornwall," added Gareth, more soberly, "with a view to restricting the number in the know to a bare minimum."

"Precisely," interrupted Hugh Trembath firmly, "and no one's going to persuade me that the same *realpolitik* should not dictate our attitude. We give then the letters, they return their hostages and that's the end of it."

"Provided they hold to their proposed bargain," said Gareth. "If Jeremy's right with his hypothesis then could we not lean on this hidden hand to help ensure that its running dogs forgo the kind of savagery meted over at Tintagel? The French Embassy in London, Sir Edward, the British Embassy in Paris..... do you have a number or do you know some one who has."

"Embassies?" scoffed the former MP. "They'll be totally in the dark. This will be a deniable operation, as was the original assassination all those years ago."

"It's a pity Stephanie's not with us," said Gareth. "She would know someone who knew the right people. She spoke of that organisation which hunts down Japanese war criminals......"

"She did," joined Busbridge more optimistically, "and she mentioned Pierre Boulle's standing amongst these people, someone whose number *I've* got."

"Here?" asked the guardsman.

"At Jasmine Cottage. I can go back and try it, and were you to take me, Jeremy, then I'm sure he'd be very interested to hear what you've just told us. Is our 'Mr Big' really a French intelligence chief, a *Gallic Gustave*? We can't yet be sure, but Monsieur Boulle might be the man to identify any such figure, to tell him he's been rumbled, and that he might consequently be advised to ensure that those who bargain on his behalf don't renege on their deal."

"That's if he doesn't want a thousand times the stink that emerged from the *Rainbow Warrior* thing," added Kate.

"But Pierre would need time," warned Jim. "He'll ask us to leave this with him for an hour or so, probably suggesting that he might phone us back. Would that be OK Sir Edward, if I gave him your number here?"

"Fine by me, Mr Busbridge....... just mind how you drive Jeremy."

*

Helford

Stephanie emerged from *The Shipwright's*, fortified by a plate of its rich lasagne and full pint glass of its Draught Guiness. She would use that call box now, she decided, and accordingly set bridge-wards along the lane, only to make out a male figure moving stealthily towards her under the glow from the curtained windows of the cottages set in the bank above. He hadn't seen her yet, she was sure, for rather than concentrating ahead it was the estuary away to his right that took the man's attention. Not that this was was slowing him at all, indeed it was as if something out on the moonlit water was drawing him along.

If she moved to *her* right then he might pass without noticing her at all, but what could be so compelling out there she was wanting to know. She merely slowed and closer he came....... close enough now to be recognised. It was Tony Cross. She needn't seek the shadows.

"Tony?"

"Stephanie...... I thought I might see you."

"But you weren't looking for me."

"No, and I can't hang about. McBeamish went back to his Range Rover and from the back seat pulled out a rather sinister looking bag. Returning with it to Treath he's untied a small outboard powered boat at the waters edge, there I guess for the use of any who take the house, and set out past the sailing club jetty into the estuary......"

"......which he might be crossing, so as to fix something to the ferry. A listening device do you think?"

329

"Something explosive more like. I was losing sight of him over there, but if I can get to the ferry point......."

".......you ought, from there, to be able confirm your suspicions as to his target. In which case, Tony I'll not detain you. I'll see you back with Alan."

The diver hastened on, leaving Stephanie Wild to walk twenty precautionary metres beyond the phone box before doubling back to enter, and then dial.

"That would be officer Wild coming through on this number....... could you please confirm with this week's password."

"*KILKHAMPTON*."

"That's fine, and are you making a report or....."

"I have an enquiry," interrupted Stephanie. "I'm down on the Helford River, south bank, and wondering about shipping movement in Falmouth Bay and beyond."

"How much beyond?"

"To the Dodman and a further ten miles, to the Lizard plus twenty."

"A few seconds while I call that up on my screen.........here it comes now. Can be quite a busy little quadrant, but not tonight. What could be a couple of tankers or container vessels waiting to drop into Falmouth for repair, or just to fuel; a coaster, looking to be Par bound; and then there's the fishermen out from Mevagissey and St Mawes; and down here, closer to the shore......that would be the Cadgwith inshore guys I guess. Not an unusual picture."

"And radio traffic......nothing irregular or inexplicable?"

" 'Fraid not Stephanie, at least at first glance. It can be like Clapham Junction around there, you'll know, what with Goonhilly and Culdrose."

"Thanks, keep watching...... I might be getting back to you after midnight."

Alan, left to himself, had moved the other way, back down towards Treath House. But only so far, for he was wanting a closer look at that mobile home wherein Tsuji now had to be likewise alone. The interior was lit still, but with blinds shrouding the rear and side windows the windscreen perhaps offered better. And accordingly our surveillance specialist carefully edged to the front of the vehicle.

Behind the driver's seat hung a curtain, drawn, but only partially There was a gap, and through this a glimpse of rearward fittings, and amongst these if one had the line, a part profile of the chairbound, seemingly dormant occupant. Half a head was discernible, with half a face, the one shoulder, and the upper third of the attached limb. Not a lot, but even with chin down and eyelid too, sufficient to evince a full on menace. Could this fiend be dreaming, or was he merely thinking........back to Shanghai, back to Singapore, or even Bangkok...... or ahead, maybe, to his next sizzling pan of offal?

A decent sized rock from the fore shore could put an end to that grisly appetite right now, thought Alan, his one restraint being the possibility of triggering a vehicle alarm. Too much of a possibility........ as was the ruthless response that might then ensue. He could get away himself, he was confident of that, but the hostages would be placed too gravely at risk.

So he retreated. The moment passed, inaction prevailing over action. Would this be cause for regret? He hoped not.

*

Returning (over Goss Moor)

"Well he gave me a good hearing, Jim."

"Because yours is a good theory, Jeremy....... right down his street. There's another good novel for him in that. But you did stress our urgency."

"I did," confirmed the driver, "and he'll be straight away on to it, he said. while advising that we needn't rush back to Carwinion. It's going to take a lot of calls, he reckons."

"If this means he intends to be thorough then we can't complain."

"Yes, we just let him get on with it." Busbridge looked at his watch. "It's ten now, so for six hours at least we're best assuming no news to be good news."

"It's a shame we didn't have this Stephanie with us, what with her knowing the man too."

"No Stephanie, no Eamon, and not even so much as a note through the letterbox." Busbridge sighed in exasperation. "And why not, we must ask. Why no word?"

Jeremy drove on. He had no answer.

"And it would be good, too, to get some sort of word to Tony Cross," continued his passenger. "I tried again before we left, but still no reply."

*

Helford...... close against the sailing club

"Did you see Tony, Stephanie?" whispered Alan

"I did, on my way back."

"And you didn't think to accompany him?"

"He shouldn't be long. You make it sound like I've failed in a duty."

"You're a fellow watcher, a professional. No doubt you have a good reason for not doing so."

"No doubt I have," bridled Stephanie, reluctant as she was to concede to this man that she might be answerable to him. "I was keen to get back here, Alan ....good enough?"

Alan nodded. Her rebuke acceped, a parity was restored. If something had come of that call made to Morwenstow then probably it would have been shared........ but nothing had, so until *she* decided otherwise it could remain a matter between her and the Station.

Footsteps were heard. This was Tony.

"McBeamish is on his way," he said.

"So you picked him out over there," said Stephanie.

"Just about, in the moonlight, together with the object of his attentions."

"And this is the ferry," said Alan, "as we guessed."

"It is, and one has to be curious as to the nature of those attentions...... though I think we can guess again."

"The IRA being the IRA," agreed Stephanie. "So our options?"

332

"I go back to my inflatable......."

"You're not bringing that around," said Alan flatly.

"Go on," tutted Stephanie. "I'm listening."

"As I was saying...... I go back to my inflatable. I wait an hour then slowly bring it around to come up this estuary, over there, keeping close to the far bank. Once the ebb slackens I can row the last mile......no noise, no lights. I'll have tank, mask, wetsuit, and underwater torch."

"And then you'll do what?" asked Alan.

"Depends on what I find, but where one can assist in the defusing of a situation...."

"....without making the intervention at all obvious......"

"...one ought to be given every encouragement," said Stephanie.

"Good...... so if I can leave the pair of you to get better acquainted I shall be on my way. Once done, I'll move further upriver before crossing back into Frenchman's Creek."

*

While in Treath House.....

.... one by one the hostages were being loosed from the cord and the tape, each being granted sufficient time and freedom to use the bathroom, but no more. In turn, young then old, they moved quietly and as quickly as their joints allowed, knowing compliance to be essential to the comfort and safety of all. Non co-operation was a non-option as again, in turn, they were re-bound.

Until the ransom was secured they would be safe enough, supposed Chas, but what then? A smooth transaction was it to be, or a massacre....... of the good guys, of the bad guys, or of all?

Helen and he knew too much, that was his fear. The old Judge might not have uttered the key name, but there were those details, of the Royal photographer and his unexpected and untimely death........ the significance of which, even if as yet obscure to them, might suffice for their own death warrant.

*

333

Near Tsuji's van

"So with Trelissick having held a first mystery and then Ince a second, Tredethy is giving you a third."

"Except that we've not yet fathomed it, Stephanie." Frustration simmered beneath Alan's calm demeanour. "We need someone to get hold of things, like Jeremy did with his getting in to Carwinion, and then Eamon with his jetting across to Ireland. Where are they now? I ask."

"Perhaps they've wanted for your leadership," suggested the fellow professional. "Kate spoke of warnings from you.......but was that enough?"

"So many, that was the problem. Consider, for instance, the connection between Carroll and McBeamish. Last time this was useful, but this time......"

".......you're wary, Alan, and rightly so. I can confirm communication between them, and the latter turning up here, tonight, isn't down to co incidence. McBeamish has certainly had an input from Eamon, but our friend is unlikely to have guessed Tsuji to have been a joint benficiary. They'll have known about Chas going to London, and why. Denning as a next stop wouldn't have taken a lot of working out. Even you've managed that."

"Thank you Stephanie....... But when you say *they*. Do you mean those who've hired McBeamish and Tsuji?"

"I suppose I do, whoever *they* might be."

"You don't know?"

"One can't be sure, can one?" Stephanie challenged back.

"One can't," conceded Alan. "But the others," he persisted. "Were they shaping some kind of consensus?"

Stephanie thought.

"There was a difficulty in seeing any further than France," she eventually said. "On getting wind of Mountbatten's scheming, someone of that flag might have hired Tsuji to kill Ananda. The idea would have been to keep Bangkok under a vigorously anti red administration.

"As was achieved".

"This was is the theory," confirmed Stephanie.

"Which is as plausible as any, I'll admit."

"Kate reminded us of the recent ruthlessness of the French in New Zealand."

"Of course, that *Rainbow Warrior* thing," nodded Alan, "in the end a propaganda disaster."

"So they wouldn't want anything else coming out;" continued Stephanie. "It has to be contained......"

"......in Cornwall, if not eradicated. Mmm, I suppose Helford has to be nearer than Auckland."

"Do I sense scepticism?"

"Just an open mind, Stephanie.,... something to be cultivated in our line, as you well know."

"Even as time runs short?"

"All the more important, if the facts are to be accurately perceived. One has to guard against a range of possibilities. It's of course, but it's not our way to plump for just one to the exclusion of the others we might know......"

".......and even the others we might not."

"Exactly, and we must keep back now Stephanie. See, there's a door opening down at the house."

"And yes, it looks like McBeamish."

They kept low as he rejoined Tsuji, the pair again retreating to the sailing club, and to a usefully discarded dinghy cover from which they could fold for themselves a makeshift cot.......used by each in turn as the other continued the watch. But little moved, only the tide, inching down to its low water mark and the moment for Tony Cross, the amphibian of the small hours.

*

At Carwinion......

......a matching vigil was slipping by, the steady tic of Sir Edward's mantleshelf timepiece being no less remorseful a measure than the lap of estuary tide. Jeremy prescribed for himself early dose of shut-eye. Boulle's return call was likely to be later he'd told the others, suggesting as he'd done in the car to Busbridge that they needn't be overly dismayed at having to wait.

But if throughness was a prequisite for success, it wasn't to be counted a guarantee. The long shot might just as easily miss, and in the little time that could be left for a fresh approach he would need a freshened mind.

And at least partially refreshed it was, when stirring at 4am he found the father and grandfather entering the final stretch of what for them could only be a totally sleepless night. Busbridge, by then, was fast flagging, and Gareth and Kate already a-doze after stoically keeping this most curious of men company through the smallest hours.

All, though, were sharply tuned to that telephone and when, 50 minutes later, it did at last trill, around they did gather, daring hardly to breath let alone speak. From Jeremy, after confirmation of identity, it was then just a sporadic *'oui'* or *'non '* as the story from France came steadily through, drawing at the last an effusive *'merci, Monsieur Boulle, merci beaucoup'*, from the lecturer.

The receiver replaced, Jeremy turned then to his audience.

Baron

*

Helford

Where now was Tony Cross? The question that neither Alan or Stephanie dared voiced as each sensed the other's mounting concern. Had the diver's initiative proved fruitful, they wondered. While hardly a Buster Crabbe scenario it would be good to know that he was at least safe, and their own position un-compromised.

Not that anything was yet indicating otherwise, so maybe theirs was a natural desire, as professionals, to have things as much as possible under their control. And this was how Cross viewed the situation, having re-crossed as planned to tie his inflatable in Frenchman's Creek to then hike back to the village over the fields of the intervening spur. Having then crept towards Treath along the river shore as far as the trees below the carpark offered cover he now had as good a view of Tsuji's van as the others and, while lower, possibly an even a better angle on Treath House. He was placed also to reserve some freedom of action. It was his boy in there. With a personal stake in this business, he wasn't along just for the ride.

*

Carwinion

"So if there'd been anything to find out then he would have done so. Is this what we're to conclude?"

"No one could have tried harder, Gareth," answered James Busbridge. "Certainly not in the time we gave him. He wasn't going to say that Jeremy is wrong......."

"......just that I'm less likely to be right than we might previously supposed," shrugged the lecturer. "And we shouldn't therefore hope that what we've put to him can earn for the hostages any gentler handling."

"So are we ready now to give them what they want?" asked Hugh Trembath, desperation bringing to his enquiry the tone of a demand.

"I think we always have been," re assured Kate. "I've heard no one suggest otherwise."

"We're sorry," said Sir Edward. "It was a good try...... plausible certainly, and well meant. Now, though, it'll soon be light. We must think about getting ourselves down to *The Ferryboat*."

*

Daybreak (Helford)

For the watchers, peering through the early light, Tsuji's van might have been a long incubated egg....... laid in the age of the dinosaur perhaps, or in a Sigourney Weaver picture. Still initially, it begins then to rock on its suspension, a response to movement within, movement towards the rear door which clicks smoothly open as if willed by the dawn.

New life will it hatch? Far, far from it......wizened and chairbound, here is its antithesis. *In Arcadia et ego*, and a sylvan morning must brace itself for one of Father Time's grimmest apprentices. He is lowered and then followed out onto the dew by his Fenian factotum who, after securing the door, helps then to guide this malign motorised emaciation of a man towards Treath House.

Alan and Stephanie move too, to keep them in sight, at least until they reach the door. Tony Cross, noting their movement, will catch them up....... but not yet. He had been sizing the van, and here was his opportunity to make a closer inspection.

*

Across at Helford Passage.......

...... Hugh Trembath eases his Landrover against the front terrace of *The Ferryboat*. Next to him in the front passenger seat is Sir Edward. Gareth and Jim Busbridge, with their letters, travel in the rear. Jeremy, bringing Kate, is no more than half a minute behind. Being less familiar with the road, and perhaps less sure of his brakes, he negotiates the steep gradient down to the waterside pub with understandable care.

The ferry waits at its floating jetty, being readied by the ferryman for the first crossing of the day....... after which he can start counting off the last two dozen of the season. But he has twenty minutes yet. Any early customers must assemble on the beach while the boat's weary diesel is coaxed through what at his time of year is a customary stuttering start.

As yet though, unsurprisingly, there is only the one..... Hugh Trembath. He has been handed those vital letters, the 'letters of transit', and now anxiously paces the shore alone, casting sporadic glances across the water. He will have been spotted, he knows, if not from the ferry point then from Treath, but hidden to him his adversaries will stay, as will their preparations, until he hits that far bank. For a while it will be only he that is exposed as, from both sides, the concealed binoculars scan warily, but as yet vainly, for any departure from the proposed deal.

But preparations have been apparent to Stephanie and Alan, rejoined as they have been now by Tony Cross. Martin McBeamish has emerged alone from Treath House and climbed to the carpark and his waiting Range Rover. Now, as the ferry motors across, he starts the vehicle to carefully drive around to the ferry point, there to make the initial contact.......one to one it seems.

The ferry makes its passage. It touches land, and is tied. The sole passenger is now over, and he climbs to the access path above the jetty. He pauses momentarily for a brief look back at the northern bank, before shielding hedges to his left and to his right channel him village-wards to whoever and whatever might wait.

McBeamish meanwhile has turned and parked where lane peters to path. He climbs out and within eight strides finds himself facing the ransom bearer......and it is he who speaks first.

"Mr McBeamish........I've seen pictures of course, in papers and on news bulletins. Hugh Trembath, I am, son to Sir Edward and father of the girl you hold. I trust she is unharmed?"

"As you are unarmed, we hope." McBeamish steps forward and Trembath raises his arms to allow a body search. "Thank you Mr Trembath, of course you are. But as we continue you will do well to bear it in mind that I *am* carrying a gun. I assume you have brought that which was requested."

"I have what was demanded." Opening his waxed jacket Trembath reached right handed to an inside pocket, producing therefrom two envelopes. "I had anticipated, though, that there was to be an exchange. Are you likewise ready to pass the agreed consideration? I see no one."

"I don't have the hostages with me, not yet. I must put these documents to my associate. If they pass his scrutiny then I shall bring the four of them."

"And if not?"

"Then I should imagine he would be very, very disappointed."

"Allow me to come with you, then. If there has been a mistake then I must take the brunt."

"Stay here, Mr Trembath. If this is to be done smoothly then four passengers is all I'll have room for. The ferryman waits here for how long?"

"Another thirty minutes." Trembath looked ruefully at the letters in his hand, before passing them with an ill-concealed reluctance.

"Long enough, I would imagine." McBeamish pocketed the letters and turned. "I hope to be back within twenty."

Guessing that Mc Beamish would be returning to Tsuji with the ransom, with or without Trembath, Alan and Kate had moved closer once more to Treath House. If and how those hostages were to be freed was still unclear, and still there was no clue as to how the captors might effect their escape.

Tony had agreed to move up to the car park where, with the authority of a fellow parent, he could intercept any reckless attempt made by Trembath to follow McBeamish's Range Rover back to Treath. There were people here doing plenty on his behalf, he could be told, and care was due lest those efforts be wrecked.

Each passing minute, though, made any such intervention less likely. The lane stayed empty. Trembath, sensibly, was staying put........ as no doubt instructed, thought Cross. And this helped. for there was more movement now down to his right at Treath House.

The main door had opened, and a column was emerging onto the short approach path. McBeamish walked ahead, erect, watchful, leading the four cowed hostages; first, a wobbling Lady Denning supported by Chas, then her slightly steadier husband moving stiffly on the arm of Helen. Tsuji's two-man army followed, one half holding a weapon at the ready, the other at the rear, escorting the chairbound Colonel.

Alan and Stephanie, bush concealed, kept down and kept silent, the eyes of the former going to each captive in turn, searching without joy for any remnant of spirit.......while for the latter? Nothing mattered more than *The Butcher of Singapore.*

And she saw it in his demeanour. What he'd come for had been secured and the important escape, his, was now on....... but in which vehicle and by what route? She looked out onto the estuary, half expecting something fast and armed to come skimming in from the sea for an embarkation off the sailing club jetty, something launched from an off-lying ship, or submarine even. If this was to be the means then now, as McBeamish slowed by his Range Rover, was the moment. Nothing of this kind was to appear, though, as the vehicle doors were opened for the Dennings and Chas to be coaxed onto the rear seat, and then Helen in as the front passenger.

"He'll drive them around to the ferry," whispered Grigson "If I head up through the carpark then I should at least be across the ford before them."

"And I'm to keep watch here?"

"If you would Stephanie. But please," he added, briefly squeezing her hand as he slipped away, "no heroics."

So she stayed and stayed low as McBeamish, his consignment packaged, was now summoned across to the mobile home by Tsuji. Having had them ready the rear hoist the Colonel had then ordered his accomplices to seemingly designated stations in the cab, driver and 'shotgun', the task of loading and fastening him into the back being for some reason reserved for the Irishman.

And that reason........ might it be a snare? wondered Stephanie, for Tsuji could have a pistol and be placed to use it on McBeamish. She shuddered. Those henchman of his might then similarly dispose of those cooped in the Range Rover.......a chilling prospect which she was helpless to avert.

She focussed on Tsuji, in that chair, being slowly lifted, his hand now at the height of his acomplice's head. Was it going to draw a gun. Yes, here it was....... but not for immediate use. McBeamish had seen it, produced his own and climbed smartly into that vehicle himself. The pair were acting together, to a plan of which their targets, sitting side by side in the cab, were never to know. The silenced barrels spat almost in unison, as likewise lolled two now lifeless heads from two bullet shattered necks.

His gun pocketed, McBeamish skipped down from the van's rear and made smartly for his Range Rover. Key in hand he climbed behind the wheel, and now could be heard firing his vehicle to immediate and baffling life. What kind of plan would have him leaving Tsuji in such a position...... isolated and effectively immobilised?

He was off to the ferry, as Alan had anticipated. There was no better explanation. He would then return, but to what? That seaborne swoop, launched in from gunboat or submarine which would snatch them and their prize to safety? If, by dint of that ruthless culling of personnel, this seemed all the more likely then why might its arrival be so delayed? For of such an intervention there was still no sign. This was the puzzle; and it was also, she realised, an opportunity......a dream opportunity in fact. For here she stood, totally without constraint, placed and also equipped to demand answers from Mr Elusive himself, Colonel Manasobu Tsuji, self styled author of *Japan's Greatest Victory*

Her gun she knew to be fully loaded. His, so recently used, probably was not. She also held the advantage of surprise, something not to be squandered with too clumsy an approach to that rear door.

Briskly she stole forward, intent on that handle, hoping that it would give at the first left handed yank...... the pistol being ready in her right. And it did, to reveal her enemy, in his chair, in her sights. At the sight of her gun, levelled at his head, he glanced to his own........ betraying its position, shelved within reach but not sufficiently so as to now risk the slightest movement towards it. With a step up and two strides the woman was on to the thing and tossing it forward, over those corpses, deep into the well of the cab. Now she had her man, totally at her mercy.

"Whoever you're with you've come too late." He was calm. He was defiant. "What you want has been destroyed. Ask the Judge, ask any of them. You'll find the embers in the house, warm still, in the grate."

"What I want, Colonel Tsuji, is justice."

"On whose behalf, tell me."

"Tens of thousands of Chinese civilians, mudered raped, in Shanghai, in Singapore."

"And not the scores of thousands of German people fire bombed to death in Dresden, and the Japanese similarly incinerated at Hiroshima and Nagasaki? But I suppose there are killing sprees and there are killing sprees. The Allied bomber pilot who succeeds in his task and wins the war, he is a hero. The Japanese soldier who fails at his and loses, he is a criminal."

"So you mut be pardoned, you say, because war allows for an all-in contest......."

"....... and if it is fought to the death then people must die."

"But wars end, Colonel Tsuji, and yet afterwards the killing will sometimes continue. You were in Bangkok, were you not, in June 1946? Operating under the disguise of a monk? We know you killed the King, for why else would you be here?"

"I was a soldier still," claimed Tsuji. "No longer with the Japanese Imperial Army, true, but enlisted nonetheless....."

"......and '*having to follow orders*', is that not the line?"

"It was made plain to me that I either kill or be killed."

"Made plain to you by the French, that's our guess. They were wanting Bangkok more tightly policed. Too much weaponry was passing through the port, *en route* to Haiphong, *entrepot* for Ho's nationalist hordes. Discredit Pridi, see Pibul re-installed.......this was their answer."

"An interesting *rationale*."

"And correct?"

"Partly," said Tsuji, "but with a gun at my head I'll not disturb any of your assumptions. You wouldn't thank me, and nor would anyone else."

"In case they're on the way, eh? If so then I'll take this opportunity to introduce myself. My name is Stephanie Wild. My father, who died before I was born, was Colonel Cyril Wild. You might remember him from '42. He was a Major then."

"Major Wild......I think I do, at Singapore. Did he not assist General Percival in the formal surrender?"

"He did. In the photographs they each carry a flag. The General's is the Union Jack, my father's is the white."

"But at least he honoured us by an attempt to learn and use our language."

"A skill that was to help him survive more than three years of cruel imprisonment. I've been told that when liberated he'd achieved an impressive fluency, something that promised to stand him in good stead in his his subsequent work."

"But this was prevented?"

"By his death, as you well know Colonel Tsuji. His plane crashed, shortly after leaving Hong Kong for Singapore."

"And you want to blame me for that also?"

"Not directly, but I wouldn't put it past those with whom you enlisted, those whose concern then would have been to protect you, and whose concern now will be to protect themselves," Stephanie tilted her head towards the corpses in the front, "even at the cost of further deaths."

"Thugs, that pair."

"As were those blown up in the London pub......but not so that Mr George over at Tintagel. And thug or not, I'm not sure that anyone, even one with your taste for blood, can be deserving of the unholy desecration visited upon their bodies."

"*Unholy*....... by your western ways, perhaps, but do you not say that one man's poison will be another's meat? Singapore was not saved by breaking bread and sipping wine. It fell to effective leadership, which for me finds ritual expression in a hunger for flesh."

"Tales of which I find hard to stomach."

"But you somehow find them compatible with the doomed French attempt to subjugate Ho's Home Rule movement in Vietnam, which, while being a conflict about nationhood and just reward for labour, was also, don't forget, a Holy War. Roman Catholicism was big in Saigon, big and beleagured, meaning that the patriots and and the planters were joined too by Christ's crusaders. Tsuji shook his head dismissively. "And you would have it that I, a veritable Saladin, was on *their* payroll!"

"So I'm to think again?"

"Yes think again Miss Wild, and think further than Johnny Frenchman. Find a bigger player who competes in a far, far larger game, who plays to win, and who now, at long last, is looking to look like he might."

"Uncle Sam?"

"Our very....... "

".........with his Cold War, East against West. And he would take you on, one who famously devoured the liver of one of his sons?"

"*And* he killed your father, to keep me alive, for also destroyed in the doomed plane was a dossier that spoke of my possible involvement in the shooting of Ananda. It recommended that on capture I be closely questioned on the incident."

"And under interrogation you might have revealed that you'd already been captured by the Americans, and earned your release with an undertaking to do that task, the task deemed essential to the preservation of the Mahidol succession."

"As indeed it was and is preserved," confirmed Tsuji. "The contrived abdication in favour of Chula was pre empted......"

"....... because someone betrayed Mountbatten's scheming, a close aide with access to those vital photographs. So who? I ask."

"Forget Mountbatten's photographs, think photographer instead. He'd used more film in Lausanne than Mountbatten knew and had developed his own set of prints. Baron, he called himself, but he was really one Henry Nahum, a Jew. Realising their worth to the Americans he alerted the Jewish Agency who, in Washington, had by then infiltrated active Zionists into every significant adminstrative department. He's been dead now for a good few years, but no one was more effective in this role than a character who went by the name of Ulius Amoss. Washington was initially split on the issue of a Jewish homeland......."

"......... the cheap oil lobby tending to be Arabist."

"Exactly but there was another commodity that the White House and the State Department were coming to value even more."

"And this was?"

"Information........ and, in particular, information on supposed Marxist subversion."

"You say *supposed*," queried Stephanie. "Is this to imply that the threat was over hyped?"

"Certainly on the home front it was."

"You refer I suppose to that House Committee set to investigate *un American activity*........"

"........which even one such as Ronald Reagan was moved to warn, lest it might overplay its hand," confirmed Tsuji. "But my point is that well before '45 Mr Amoss and his team of fellow Jewish *provocateurs* were already looking forward to whipping up what was to become the McArthyite witch-hunt, knowing full well that this would inflate the value of the Zionist's warehoused information on Communist infiltration....... both at home and abroad."

"So working in Washington, these people set about deepening the distrust of Moscow, stimulating a hunger for information that became a pathological dependency, an addiction almost."

"And if David Ben Gurion's Jewish Agency could, through the likes of these pushers, feed and intensify this addiction....."

"....... then the Zionists had a means of weaning the once

sceptical white anglo-saxon protestant away from his previously over riding thirst for oil," reasoned Stephanie. "And this was what did for poor Ananda, you say."

"Baron betrayed Mountbatten's scheming to the Jewish Agency," explained Tsuji. "Their man, this Ulius Amoss let's say, he finds a buyer for their information in Washington. Washington pays with a pledge of diplomatic and material support for the Zionist project, then acts upon the information to shore up its own position in Thailand......."

".......and with the deed done the Jewish Agency is further empowered by its knowledge of US perfidy in Bangkok."

"The job was conceived of long before it was offerd to me," continued Tsuji.

"So that recruitment was when?"

"Towards the end of October '45, after having been captured by the Americans in Laos earlier that month. By then the unit assigned to the task had been shipped out to Japan so that they might finalise their plans under the awesome protection of General MacArthur. And necessary to these preparations, of course, was an awareness of the progress being made by Mountbatten in his scheming, paricularly as to his success or not in the grooming of Chula as a putative Rama. In this, that phtographer continued to be of use. I shot the King in June '46. I can confirm that from at least eight months before to easily two months after, he would have been in regular contact with my Japan based control."

"So after agreeing to this proposition, put to you in October '45........."

"........I was smuggled back into Bangkok at the turn of the year."

"Disguised, as you said, as a Buddhist monk."

"It was too easy. Security at the Palace was woeful. But for the work needed on others I might have done the job a lot sooner."

"And those others?" asked Stephanie

"Pibul the wartime collaborator, he had to be rehabilitated; and in England, as I said, there was Chula. The possibility of an abdication, for political rather than personal reasons, was being talked up by Mountbatten. Financial incentives were being mentioned. All this had to be countered."

"And it was."

"With equal stealth, Ms Wild. This is where Bira offers such a valuable account....."

346

"......in that journal of his."

"Yes, and as this went on the photographer was well placed to further observe and inform."

"Without attracting suspicion......? I guess that identities were masked with false names."

"And I've been told that he was able to utilise a personal postal service," revealed Tsuji, "courtesy of your Mr Profumo..... he whose later career as a Cabinet Minister was to end in disgrace."

"And this would have been while holding that army post that frequently took him to Japan."

"Out and back....... whatever his failings as a politician in the early 1960s we can say that seventeen years earlier he proved a very useful courier."

"And you, Colonel Tsuji, proved yourself an excellent assassin. But what happened to our excellent photographer? Does he still live, or did he know too much?"

"He's dead, but not because he knew too much. Finely rewarded careerwise, he was doing well...... until '56, the year of Suez. The Americans took exception to his suggestion that they might do more to make a success of the Anglo-French-Israel action against Egypt. Whatever he might have said, to them it sounded to much like a veiled threat....."

".......to go that step further, and start telling what he knew, about Bangkok."

"And with the Americans you simply don't do that, especially if you happen to be about to go into hospital for an operation......however minor."

"But ten years earlier, Colonel Tsuji, they used you to kill a reigning monarch, and he not even a declared enemy of theirs. Why go to lengths so extreme, and so cruel? What was of so much worth to them?"

"It was widely assumed *then* that the French would hold down Indo China, that Chiang would hold down China itself, and that even the Dutch could keep communism at bay in Indonesia......."

"...... as we British were to do in Malaya."

"Thailand, though, was different, largely because it had never been colonised. The withdrawal of my army of occupation had left a power vacuum that was at once both alarming and tempting."

"And Mountbatten was well placed to respond."

"Very well placed, with an army in Burma and more ships and

guns in Singapore, a Chula-Pridi combination was his bid for control over the sovereign land between."

"Which, in MacArthur's view, would have been too loose a control."

"Like the French, MacArthur preferred Pibul back, but this wasn't about policing just the one port......"

".......Bangkok...."

"......in the one country....."

"Thailand."

"No, for growing within the American military community was the realisation that Washington could yet find itself having to police the whole world, in which case it could be prudent to have a big stick to hand in every region thereof. Here in Cornwall they have an airforce base, just one of the many in this country and the many more throughout Europe."

"A proliferation with which Mountbatten has, on record, admitted himself to be less than comfortable."

"Exactly Miss Wild, so we must bear in mind that back in '46 MacArthur's people would have been concerned to reserve for themselves a free hand to establish a similar presence in Thailand, and from where they stood the prospect of an abdication by *both* Ananda and Bhumibol was forcing their hand."

"To take the trick they needed an intimidated King Bhumibol and grateful Chief Minister Pibul combination, such as was effectively secured by the murder of Ananda."

"You have it, Miss Wild. Move on twenty years to Robert Macnamara's Rolling Thunder bombing offensive against anything that did or did not move along the Ho Chi Minh trail. More missions took off from Thailand than from any other country."

"A flawed strategy as it turned out."

"But people weren't to know that," said Tsuji, "certainly not in '46, in a flattened Japan. Listen......"

A constant drone, deep and distant at first was growing louder. It was the sound of a motor, fast approaching. On the water was this, from the sea? Stephanie could see nothing on the estuary, not even the ferry.

"The US Cavalry I presume," said Stephanie, "coming in by gunboat?"

"By *gunship*, Miss Wild. The promised Chinook helicopter is here." Dust was blowing against the windows, clouding their view of whipping bush and branch all around. Now the down-draught was causing the van to rock, and gravel to kick up against its sides. "They'll be training guns on our doors," Tsuji was now having to shout, "with orders to fire at any who might emerge. Kill me, and when they open the doors they'll kill you too, for certain. Your one chance is to keep me alive and to bow, as I had to, to *force majeure*!"

"And McBeamish?" The Range Rover had just returned, with the driver now alone. He pulled up, leaving space for the lower rungs of a cable strung rope ladder to clatter to the ground.

"He'll be going up with them," answered Tsuji as three crewmen climbed down from the so loudly heard but still not seen hovering aircraft. Down also was lowered a dangle of chain, hawser, and bar……. a cradle, when assembled, sufficient in dimension and strength to lift and transport even so bulky a vehicle as Tsuji's van.

McBeamish scaled, as upwards inched the helicopter, feeling for the strain, the twin rotors roaring in triumph as with power in hand the van was ssmoothly lifted off of its tyres. Now the crew were on the ladder, and climbing still as their under slung load swung clear of the trees. Under twin jet thrust they would soar now for the clouds and the open sea, thought Stephanie, clinging for balance with her left hand to Tsuji's anchored chair whilst keeping her pistol to his head with her right. This machine could only have emerged from a cargo hold, to whence it surely had to return.

But as they moved out over the estuary, seawards the craft did not turn. Keeping low it instead wheeled up river, offering to Stephanie a through the windscreen glimpse of the ferry, well into its crossing now with those aboard transfixed by the spectacle above.

"Culdrose ahead," pointed Stephanie. "Climb any more and they'll be scrambling the whole squadron."

"We're expected, Miss Wild. Look out there, in the sky beyond the base, that's a USAF fixed wing transport. Right on time it'll have room for all in its fuselage……van too. It'll land on the main runway and taxi up for a rendezvous at this end of the field. In ten minutes we can be turned and ready, this time for a more comfortable take off."

"Tidy work," acknowledged Stephanie grudgingly. "For the lads above it'll be task done, getting this thing up from Treath and over the perimeter fence."

"Which leaves the finale promised to me by Mr Martin 'Bomber'

McBeamish. A nice touch, the distinguished Lord Denning sharing the same fate as the distinguished Lord Mountbatten. Just seconds now, I'd say, while the ferry at mid way is still in sight."

And above them, in the Chinook, McBeamish was counting those last seconds down, radio control in hand, finger on the switch .....five ....four ....three ....two.....one ....   NOW!

And from below came the crack of explosive, borne on a wave sufficient to momentarily jolt the gunship upwards, causing its motor to surge briefly as if, for that instant, lightened of its burden.

Leaning to a window, McBeamish checked down for his handiwork........the plume of smoke, the scatter of debris, of body, of limb. But of this there was nothing. Intact still, the ferry was sailing on, and no longer towards *The Ferryboat*. It was veering up river now, as if with hopeless, defiant pursuit it could boast impregnability.

Something had blown, but what?

Ulius Amoss
a shadowy presence.

Tony Cross who, in the early hours, had stripped the ferry of the explosive planted earlier by McBeamish knew exactly what. He hadn't anticipated the helicopter, and nor would he have known of Stephanie's ambition, now fulfilled, to introduce herself to Masanobu Tsuji. Had he, then his intervening dispositions he might well have modified. He could for instance have reconsidered that idea of taping some of the retrieved explosive behind one of the front wheels of the Colonel's mobile home.

This would merely immobilise the vehicle, he'd calculated, if not severing that wheel completely then at least wrecking the brake hydraulics and the steering linkage, his intention having been to arrest flight rather than jeopardise life.

But there is flight and there is *flight*, and in these unforseen circumstances a modest preventative initiative now threatened lethal consequences....... and not only for the bad guys.

The detonation *had* blown the wheel off, and also fractured the forward of the two cradling chain loops. The van had suddenly pitched forward through ninety degrees causing Stephanie to be thrown between the corpses in the front seat against the inside of the windscreen. One of the front doors, loosened by the blast, now swung open. Tsuji hung above her, strapped as he was in the fixed chair, and he was reaching for something.......reaching for the pistol she'd dropped and he'd spotted, almost within his grasp, if only he could stretch, as the van swung pendulum-wise by the one remaining weakening loop.

She had to move, but it she no longer had it in those not so young legs to get to her knees let alone climb to her feet. But there was water beneath still, so by instinct she squirmed head first for the open passenger side doorway, moving for the floor in the hope that the belted body on that side might shield her. Which it did, and this was as well, for Tsuji now had that gun in his hand, a hand that was straining between the seats........until, with a further jolt, the remaining sling snapped, leaving the helicopter to soar and the van to plummet.

Down it plunged, 80.....90.....100 feet to hit the river, and on down before a fast expiring buoyancy purchased a final bob to the surface. Quickly the vehicle there did fill, until with a slow roll it at last settled, just below Groyne Point, to a depth of twenty feet....... sufficient to drown *The Devil of Shanghai*......... but not the doughty daughter of Colonel Cyril Wild.

*

Kerrow Downs

"Alan bloody Grigson," gasped Carroll, "it's about time you turned up!" These his first words following a painful removal of the tape that had kept him gagged for well over twelve hours. He leant forward and away from the barn wall. With those cuffs off he could help untie his feet and, hopefully, at last stand. "And thank God you've got a key. I was starting think the bloody woman had thrown it away. You've spoken to her I presume. Is she around at the caravan?"

"She'll say more later. I left her down at the Trembath's where a grateful family was sorting for her a fresh set of clothes. Chas is with me, and his father. You might want to listen to the boy's version of events first as you get yourself cleaned up........useful practice for him before he attempts to explain things to his young lady up at St John."

"So more guns was it, to go with that which our Stephanie pulled on me?"

"More guns Eamon, and more explosive. What we can hope to be the last of it we've just found here, your van having been booby-trapped. We understand Mr McBeamish called yesterday evening, you might not have known that."

"He was expected." Carroll straightened from rubbing each calf in turn.

"But Stephanie got here first, which was as well for you," said Grigson. "Had she not then probably you would have been shot, as was the rest of the surplus manpower."

"But McBeamish is still alive."

"To the best of our knowledge, he is."

"And he wouldn't be coming back this way?"

"Very unlikely, Eamon. He'll be keeping low, and you would be advised to do the same. Allow us to destroy that van, and have it put around that his device claimed your life."

"Where then?"

"A good long holiday, then a fresh start in a different city.......maybe a different country, maybe a different identity."

"So easily said, Alan, by one such as yourself. Clearly, though, you've been impressed by Ms Wild's intervention on my behalf. How was this inspired, intuitively do you think, or........?"

"By enquiries she was able to make at Morwenstow, that's where she had a critical edge. While the rest of us could be no more than suspicious of the contact maintained between yourself and McBeamish, she became aware of a match between information fed out by yourself and coded messages arriving back into this area. If the full route which could have given the identity of those responsible for this relayed transmission remained obscure, not so the telling features that marked it for the attention of those whose dissection skills had been evident at *The Duke of Connaught* and Tintagel"

"So while heading up the IRA, McBeamish is also in the pay of some one else."

Grigson looked at his watch.

"We're due at Kate's in an hour, Eamon. Stephanie will be there to tell you all this herself, about an agency that has hired IRA before and no doubt will again."

"I never realised."

"Something she guessed. Had she thought otherwise then you would have been left to your fate."

"And this agency........obviously a big player."

"Truly big........which having used a Japanese war criminal once would appear to have had no scruple about attempting to do so again. And with some success, I must add, if we can believe that what they sought to have destroyed was. In the matter of the young King's death the prestige of a major power will remain undimmed, as will the prestige of two Monarchies."

"So, Mr Grigson, you can speak in terms of a success shared."

"When those to whom I answer express satisfaction then, professionally, yes."

"While personally?"

"Death is always a matter of personal regret. To be involved in mankind is to be diminished by any, be it of the good guy like Barry George, of the less good like Kellegher and Conlon, or even of the downright bad such as *The Devil of Shanghai* and his none too gentle care staff. It follows that one must be thankful when those who encounter mortal peril survive....... Lord and Lady Denning, Chas, Helen Trembath, plucky Stephanie Wild......and yes Eamon Carroll, even yourself!"

*

THE END

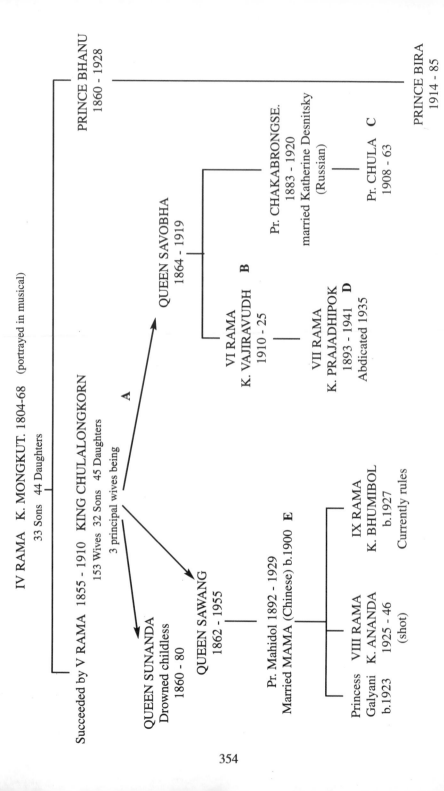

IV RAMA K. MONGKUT. 1804-68 (portrayed in musical)

33 Sons 44 Daughters

Succeeded by V RAMA 1855 - 1910 KING CHULALONGKORN

153 Wives 32 Sons 45 Daughters

3 principal wives being

A

QUEEN SAVOBHA
1864 - 1919

VI RAMA
K. VAJIRAVUDH **B**
1910 - 25

VII RAMA
K. PRAJADHIPOK **D**
1893 - 1941
Abdicated 1935

Pr. CHAKABRONGSE.
1883 - 1920
married Katherine Desnitsky
(Russian)

Pr. CHULA **C**
1908 - 63

QUEEN SUNANDA
Drowned childless
1860 - 80

QUEEN SAWANG
1862 - 1955

Pr. Mahidol 1892 - 1929
Married MAMA (Chinese) b.1900 **E**

Princess
Galyani
b.1923

VIII RAMA
K. ANANDA
1925 - 46
(shot)

IX RAMA
K. BHUMIBOL
b.1927
Currently rules

PRINCE BHANU
1860 - 1928

PRINCE BIRA
1914 - 85

Note on Thai Royal lineage

A.   As was his preogative the Vth Rama (K Chulalongkorn) directed that the succession should fall to the (male) issue of his 3rd principal wife (Q Savobha)

B.   Accordingly K Vajiravudh was made VIth Rama in 1910, and on dying with no male heir was succeeded as VIIth Rama by his brother Prajahipok in 1925, another brother (Pr Chakabrangse) having been disqualified on taking a Russian wife.

C.   Prince Chula was a son of this union.

D.   Objecting to a kerbing of his powers by *The Promoters of Political Change*, K. Prajahipok abdicated in 1935 to live out his life in exile (in Surrey).

E.   Wary of an empty throne attracting political mischief the *Promoters* deemed a reversion to the issue of Q. Sawang the most desirable course *despite* her son (Prince Mahidol) also having taken a foreign wife. If, with the defeat of the Japanese in 1945, the Mahidols had chosen to abdicate then, with this precedent overturned, Prince Chula's claim on the throne would have been as strong as anyone's.

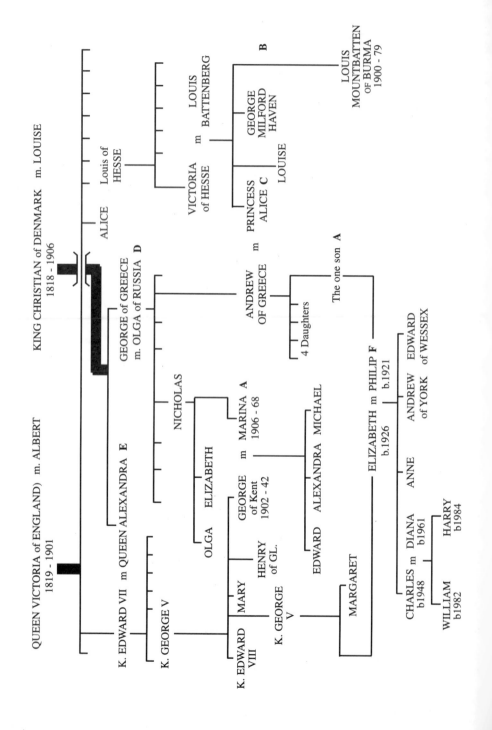

Note on the House of Windsor.

A   Both Marina and Philip were great grandchildren of King Christian of Denmark.

B   Louis Mountbatten and his siblings were (through their mother and grand mother) great grandchildren of Queen Victoria.

C   Louis' sister Alice married Prince Andrew of Greece. Their one son is Philip.

D   Philip and Marina shared George of Greece and Olga of Russia as grandparents.

E   George of Greece was a brother to Queen Alexandra, wife of King Edward VII, mother to George V, and therefore great grandmother of Elizabeth II.

F   If Philip was short of money in 1947, and displaced somewhat in terms of domicile, he was certainly not short on pedigree......something that might have rankled with Elizabeth's mother (a mere Bowes-Lyon) and grandmother (Mary of Teck).

Acknowledgements

I am frequently asked as to how much fact I include in my fiction. I will usually reply that if I go to a bookshop or library and browse the non-fiction shelves then I will often find amongst the histories, the biographies, and the memoirs, characters whose real life adventures no novelist (not even one so good as le Carre!) would ever dare invent....... as vividly exemplified by Mama Mahidol (1900-95), Tania Gaubert(1913-86), Prince Bira, and even the likes of Christine Keeler(1942 -), and Tsuji(1900-87?).

The ultra respectful Philip Ziegler (*Mountbatten*) might dodge Baron (unlike Sarah Bradford in *Elizabeth*), but even he can throw up tantalising glimpses of the likes of Peter Murphy(d1966) and Ulius Amoss(d1961).

The latter, with his shadowy role in American and Israeli intelligence, would not have been out of place in Norman Mailer's epic *Harlot's Ghost*, or in de Niro's recent film *The Good Shepherd*.

On the Thai monarchy, Bosco Books of Looe found me a second hand copy of William Stevenson's useful *The Revolutionary King* (Robinson), and whilst a year ago browsing the 'Political Studies' section in a Sydney bookshop I happened across *Kings, Countries and Constitutions; Thailand's political development1932-2000* (Routledge), an academic text, this, written by Kokbua Suwannathat-Pian.

His section on the mystery of Ananda's death includes mention of a letter written to the American State Department by a Thai officer named Major Arkadej, himself a son of the Regent who ruled whilst Ananda was at school in Switzerland.

Writing on the 16th September 1945 Arkadej expresses hostility towards Pridi and the liberals, considering them;

"Leftist and communist supporters." He goes on to state his preference for a form of *"Republic under American pattern and guidance rather than a puppet King with the English wielding the baton behind."*

He further alledges that;

"The English Free Thai organisation was formed to make an opportunity for the Siamese Royalists (who'd followed King Prajahidok into exile on his abdication in 1935) *to re-enter Thailand, sweep out the party in power, place their leader* (Pridi) *as Premier, revenge the*

wartime leaders and recover the Royalist property….. Included in this plan is the scheme to find means to let the present King Ananda Mahidol abdicate his throne and place Prince Chula Chakabrongse on the throne with the English influence and protection behind him."

Other books I hve found useful include

On Chula and Bira;
The Prince and I by Bira's first wife Princess Ceril (Veloce Publishing)……… a loving portrait.

On the British Monarchy;
War of the Windsors by Picknett, Prince, and Prior (Mainstream Publishing)………a provocative piece of sustained muckraking.

On the Brownings;
The biographies of *Daphne* by Margaret Forster (Arrow) and the now sadly deceased Judith Cook (Corgi)…… each sympathetic to Tommy(1896-1965).

On Lord Denning (1899-1992);
Lord Denning: a Life by Iris Freeman……. An excellent window into his times.

Tania's adventures and Tsuji's are well chronicled on the internet, as are the triumphs and the disasters met by Menachem Begin(1913-92), and Jack(1915-2006) and Valerie(1917-98) Profumo.

As part of their 1960 world tour King Bhumibol and his Queen came to England. Formally received and accorded full honour by Elizabeth and Philip, they were entertained at Coppins by Marina and children (Eddy of Kent, Alexandra, and Michael). While it might be well belived that Uncle Dickie made himself scarce, I like to think that Prince Chula of Tredethy joined the party as a welcomed guest.